NEVER SAY FOREVER

ONE NIGHT FOREVER

DONNA ALAM

Cover Design: LJ Designs
Image: Miguelanxo Fotografo
Editing: Editing 4 Indies

ALSO BY DONNA ALAM

The following are all standalone titles written in relating worlds. You never know where your favourite character might pop up!

No Ordinary Gentleman

ONE NIGHT FOREVER

Liar Liar

LOVE IN LONDON

To Have and Hate

(Not) The One

The Stand Out

PHILLIPS BROTHERS

In Like Flynn

Down Under

Rafferty's Rules

GREAT SCOTS

Easy

Hard

Hardly Easy Boxed Set

HOT SCOTS

One Hot Scot

One Wicked Scot

One Dirty Scot

Single Daddy Scot

Hot Scots Box Set

Surprise Package

AND MORE

Solider Boy

Playing His Games

Gentleman Player

“Behind every exquisite thing that existed, there was something tragic.”

~ Oscar Wilde

1

FEE

"Hello? Charles, can you hear me?"

The call connects, my friend's response an ominous crackle followed by some mostly distorted vowels sounds.

". . . re . . . ou . . . i . . ."

"Charles?" I pull the phone away from my ear to glance at the screen, desperately hoping we're still connected because I need help. I also have something very important that I need to tell him. "I could literally junk punch you right now."

Exactly that.

". . . ou . . . ee . . ."

"I'm stuck up the side of a mountain, lost. Which is bad enough, but Fred has a puncture, and guess what? There's no spare tyre!" I don't know why I'm bothering to tell him, considering he's the reason Fred, my little Fiat, doesn't have a spare. "This is the absolute last time I'm loaning you anything," I continue. *Okay, rant.* "Seriously, you won't get so much as a teaspoon from me, so you'd better start packing one with your lunch!"

". . .ma . . . vou . . . rie . . ."

"You promised, *promised me,* that you'd get the tyre fixed last week."

"Ai—"

The crackling halts, and I'm left looking down at the now-dead phone in my hand. With a strangled cry, I raise my eyes heavenward, but divine intervention isn't on the cards today. Instead, the grey clouds part, allowing the late afternoon sun to beam down happily. If I feel like crying, the least the sky could do is cry with me.

It doesn't, so I give in to frustration and kick the tyre instead.

"Fudge knuckles!"

But the action is more a glance than a blow, plus I use the sole of my shoe. Angry or not, I'm far too sensible to add a broken toe to my current woes. I fold my arms, then let them fall, carelessly dropping my dead phone through the open window. It bounces off my purse and tumbles to the floor, then I hear the sickening sound of the glass screen clipping something metal under the seat.

"Really?" I fume. I'm so done with today.

I really should've made sure Charles understood I was lost before I bitched about the missing spare tyre. I'm generally not so short-tempered, but a girl can take only so much, especially after driving around aimlessly for an hour on scarily unfamiliar roads, including some without barriers and potential sheer drops down a freakin' mountain! No wonder my nerves are fraught. And to add insult to injury, I'm lost up here because of him. He'd called a couple of hours ago, begging me to pick him up after he'd had an argument with his latest love interest.

"Because one swallow does not a boyfriend make, Charlie boy," I grumble angrily, angry with myself for this situation and angry with him for not replacing the spare.

And extra angry he'd sent me a text ten minutes ago to say he and Anton had made up and that he no longer needed rescuing.

"Urgh!" A wash of frustration floods my veins. I hate how this level of toxicity is poisoning my mood. So I close my eyes, take a deep breath, and try again.

"*Ommm.*" I push out the sound on a slow exhale, chasing away my critical thoughts as I try to bring a little peace to my mind, body, and soul. When I take a yoga class, *Om* is how we begin and end each of the classes; it is said to be the primordial sound, ancient and restorative. A sound that connects all living beings to nature and the universe.

I'd like to connect my hands to Charles's neck . . .

Channel more Zen. It's not like I have the greatest track record with dating either.

"Ommm."

When I open my eyes, I'm still in the middle of nowhere. Though I'm at least calm enough to realise it's a very beautiful sort of nowhere. Shielding my eyes, I gaze across a carpet of green hills and valleys, the road winding down like a smudge of white chalk as though all the way out to the Mediterranean Sea. As the crow flies, I'm less than thirty minutes away from both beach and city, but as I don't have wings, I know I can kiss my planned afternoon of beachfront bottomless pomegranate martinis goodbye.

There's only one thing I can do. I'll just have to rescue myself.

I angle my gaze up the sharp incline ahead, the mountainous terrain craggy and grey. Between me and the summit, an ancient-looking village full of ochre-coloured buildings seems to cling to the mountainside, the landscape between here and there dotted with black and white goats. While the road down would undoubtedly be easier, I didn't see a garage as I passed through. Meanwhile, I had spotted a sign for the same pointing up ahead. It's a strange place to have a garage, and maybe the workshop won't be open, but at least it'll have a phone.

Medieval-era villages have phones these days, right?

I sigh. Whichever way I go, it's going to take me forever to reach civilisation in these heels. Heels that, as I take a step backwards to pull open the car door, twist from the thin ankle strap and snap at the heel.

And there goes my Zen . . .

"What in the blueberry fuck muffins is my life right now!" My shoulders slump, and with a strangled sob, I drop my hands and head to the little Fiat's roof. If there ever was a time that God, the Universe, and the goddess that is Mother Nature would forgive a little profanity, surely it would be at the point of finding myself lost, stuck halfway up the mountain with a flat tyre and a dead phone while wearing a summer party dress and pretty yet broken spindly heels.

"Fuck, fuck, fuck nuggets!" I punctuate my profanity against Fred's baby blue roof with my curled fist before deciding this just isn't doing my feelings justice.

Feelings. So many feelings. And most of them murderous.

"Charles, you little buttmunch!" I jack-knife straight and begin to yell through Fred's open window as though Charles can hear me through my broken phone. "When I get my hands on you, I'm going to strangle you with your Gucci belt!"

In a better frame of mind, I might've judged the road to be quiet enough to have my little meltdown in private because it doesn't seem to be the kind of road that has a lot of hitchhiking prospects, even if I were a less cautious kind of girl. But I'm not really in the emotional headspace for thinking due to the large levels of angry I'm currently brewing. I stomp on the sandy rubble beneath my feet, wobbling heel and all, just a shopping cart and a quart of tequila away from crazy lady territory as I continue to yell.

"That's your *new* belt, Charlie boy, the one I secretly think is really, really ugly, and gayer than jizz on a handlebar moustache! Your patron saint"—*Cher*—"would excommunicate you for wearing that particular colour of snakeskin you rotten, selfish, pain in my—"

"Is it pink?"

"Pussy!" I whip around at the interruption, not quite able to stop my tirade. "Is what pink?" The word is immediately followed by my raised hand and the much more sensible, "Please don't answer that."

Despite my request, he does so anyway. And in English, because that's the kind of day I'm having. In the middle of the French countryside, would it have been too much to ask that an actual Frenchman would've thought to interrupt my mini-meltdown? A non-English-speaking Frenchman, preferably.

"The belt." His voice is deep and amused, his accent, I realise, American. Because of the way the sun is beginning to set behind him, I can't make out much more of him other than to say he's tall. "The other, a gentleman would never refer to," he adds.

I snort inelegantly. "Gentlemen? They died out with the dinosaurs, didn't they?" It's hard not to be bitter, not just about Charles but also my missed afternoon drinks. The very same drinks my friends put together to cheer me up after I was unceremoniously dumped last month. Though dumped isn't really the right way to describe the new man in your life disappearing like a puff of smoke. So you could say I'm completely off men at the minute, gay, straight, or motherfluffin' otherwise.

"I'll refrain from suggesting you've been hanging around with the wrong kind of men." The confident note in his tone makes it sound as though he's doing exactly that. Confident, deep, and a tiny bit amused as he takes a couple of steps closer. "Manners aren't a fashion statement," he adds, swiping up the wrench I'd flung down in frustration after realising the spare was gone. "A gentleman knows his actions say more about him than his words."

Ooh, an action man, my mind unhelpfully intones. *Probably a rich one, too.*

Because only the rich have this kind of confidence, I've found. I don't need to glance at the car behind him to know the man is wealthy. And while I'd ordinarily steer clear of rich men—because they tend to think very highly of themselves, on a largely groundless basis—I take a moment to remind myself that this stranger didn't have to stop for the crazy lady talking to herself by the side of the road.

Not many would.

But as I finish this little conversation in my head, any reply, retort, or response is robbed from my tongue as he steps closer. In a *made-for-TV moment*, the setting sun crests his head, briefly blessing him with a golden halo. Another step closer and the whole of him comes into focus . . .

And oh, my giddy aunt.

He is *lovely*.

Can you describe a man as lovely? Because if you can, this man in front of me is lovely personified, and that's saying something, considering we're standing in the South of France, the European home of the beautiful and the rich. I'm not entirely sure why the two go hand in hand, but they certainly seem to.

Maybe plastic surgery?

Not that this is a face that's ever met a surgeon's scalpel.

The shadow of late afternoon sun seems to underscore the sharpness of his cheekbones and strong jaw, accentuating lips that are full and finely sculpted. I hold up my hand to shield my eyes, the sun's lowering rays making it hard to discern the colour of his eyes, but not their delight, as my gaze travels the length and the breadth of him. And there really is quite a lot to look at; the broad shoulders, a solid chest, and a trim waist defined by a dark leather belt. A sudden breeze irons his pale shirt to the hard lines of his torso, revealing a strip of tanned and toned abs as it flutters and flicks up the hem. Shorts that were probably once a pair of jeans and a scuffed pair of deck shoes complete a very casual look. It isn't really a look that screams wealthy. More like gardener. Or yacht hand.

"Are you okay?"

I'll credit his response with a smile that's barely there. He slides a pair of sunglasses to his chest pocket with such studied nonchalance that I'm certain he's used to stunning women dumb with his looks. *That must be where the confidence comes from,* I think as my gaze slides to the car behind him. The convertible appears so old it ought not to have made it up this far.

I haven't answered, and I'm back to ogling him again.

"I've had better days." I keep my response low-key as I move my attention to the front passenger wheel, prodding it with my toe because there really is no reason to increase my appearance of idiocy. Not when he's probably already witnessed me hopping around like Rumpelstiltskin on speed.

"Looks like you had quite a blowout."

I glance up as he begins to fold back the sleeves of his shirt, his gaze following mine to the offending tyre. Pinching the fronts of his shorts, he squats down in front of me, the movement causing the hem of my short dress to flutter against my legs. I don't think I imagine how his gaze lingers there or how my stomach twists not unpleasantly.

"I can help you with this," he adds.

"I appreciate the offer, but you really can't."

"Sure, I can." His gaze lifts to mine.

Oh, my. His eyes are fathomless. Blue bordering on black. *Indigo?* Maybe it's not the colour that's so arresting but their intensity. One thing I am certain of is that I don't imagine the way his gaze rises, starting at my toes.

My whole body tingles under the weight of his scrutiny as, with a flick of his wrist, he releases the jack, bringing the wheel back to the ground.

Hell. I should've known the jack came *after* those lug nut things were loosened, but in my defence, the last tyre I changed was under the supervision of my dad the year I turned seventeen. I suppose the fact that the jack was lying loose should've set off alarm bells. Charles-sounding ones, probably.

I am, 'ow you say, sorree, mon cher. Wee-waa! Wee-waa!

He will be sorry when I get my hands on him.

Charles, you are dead to me.

For at least a week.

"That's a fierce-looking frown. Don't worry, we'll get you back on the road in no time."

"I didn't hear your car on the road." I make no attempt to push away the hair that blows across my cheeks as I glance at the convertible. I can't decide if it looks like it belongs in a museum or the scrap heap.

Every other car you seem to pass on the Riviera has a six-digit price tag. The lure of the lifestyles of the rich and famous is very real. Men out here seem to think a fancy sports car is a must when, in my experience, it often seems to be a classic case of overcompensating. Not for a lack of dick but of decency.

"Aren't old cars supposed to be noisy?" I ask, directing my gaze back his way.

"That isn't an old car." His teeth gleam before he turns back to his task. "It's a classic."

"Is that what we're calling rust buckets these days?"

At his chuckle, my mind suddenly quiets, but it's not his low tone that stops me in my tracks or the way he fits the wrench to the first of the nuts, giving it a powerful twist. Nope, it's the accompanying masculine grunt that short-circuits the wiring of my brain, sending it straight to the gutter.

The gutter would do, but the back seat would be better.

"Y-you're much better at this than me," I find myself stammering like a girly idiot as blood begins to fizz in my veins. And my lashes aren't fluttering because I have grit in my eyes. I'm not sure what's come over me because I'm not ordinarily so Penelope Pitstop. *You know, hay-ulp! Hay-ulp!* It could be the way he handles those nuts—I mean, the wrench—that makes me feel hot, or maybe it's the way his shirt stretches across his chest and shoulders. While these both are sights to behold, they pale in the titillation stakes when judged against this Grade A forearm porn show. Sculpted muscles and veins flex and stretch under skin that looks a little like warm caramel.

Work it, baby . . .

Oh, yeah.

Just like that!

My job and my studies have taught me that the body is an amazing machine, but I'm clearly not examining him as a mechanical specimen, or else how could I find the contours of his wrists appealing?

"Can you change a tyre?"

I find myself blinking down at the sound of his deep baritone, my cheeks beginning to sting as I find his gaze angled my way.

"I can't change that one." For some reason, I find I'm not quite ready to tell him he won't be able to either. I mean, if I can't have pomegranate martinis this afternoon, there should still be enjoyment, right?

"It's a pretty tight fit." He twists the wrench, exhaling the kind of tight grunt that makes my insides flutter.

"That's what she said." I turn my attention to the green valley, my words a quiet longing not meant to reach his ears. "And whoever *she* is, she's a lucky girl." Despite my intentions, as my gaze drops, I note the ghost of a smile hovering on his lips.

"So it's like that, is it?" he almost drawls. Something wicked shines in his eyes as they rise.

"Oh, haven't you heard that before?" I find myself blundering on. "It's how we say it in England." My accent suddenly very *jolly hockey sticks*, rather than my slightly modulated North London. In reality, the British version of 'that's what she said' is the much more confusing 'said the vicar to the actress', which I've never thought made much sense. Anyway, the stranger turns back to the matter at hand, though not fast enough to hide his continued amusement.

"Well, you jacked it pretty good," he murmurs.

I find myself snickering—how can I not?

Yeah, baby. I jacked it real good.

So. Much. Innuendo. And I don't even think he's doing it on purpose.

"Are you going to share?" He glances up from lashes that would make a camel jealous. "Or is that some other kind of inside English joke?"

"It's nothing." I hide my smile behind my fingertips, but the man isn't an idiot. That role in this interaction has already been filled.

"Sure." His amusement rings clear. "Then I guess the joke must be me."

To heck with it. What's the point of having such a gorgeous audience and keeping my titillation all to myself? I press my hand to the hood to steady myself and my wobbling heel before I sigh a little theatrically.

"You see, it's just, well, I've been trying to give up on innuendo, but you're making it so, *so* hard."

"That's what *he* said," he retorts with an enigmatic smile and a slow shake of his head. The kind that says he can't believe he's taking part in this ridiculousness. "Something tells me you're all kinds of trouble. The kind of trouble that doesn't stop at punctured tyres."

My insides instantly light up like a Christmas tree.

"Me?" I press my fingertips to my chest, camping up the theatrics. "I've never been an ounce of trouble my whole life!"

This is all so delicious. Moments ago, I was facing a trek uphill with nothing but my frustration for company, and now, I'm bantering with a stranger who is twice as delicious as any pomegranate martini. *And just as intoxicating, even just to look at!*

What's more, he seems to be enjoying this exchange as much as me.

"I guess I'll have to take your word for it," he drawls. "Even if I'm not buyin' it."

"I'll have you know that *I* am a paragon of virtue."

"Sure. I bet you don't ever curse, either."

"I absolutely do not," I reply in my most saintly tone.

"Is that right?"

While he's clearly happy to play along, I feel he requires further persuading. Or impressing. Or maybe he just needs to get off his knees and come and kiss me.

That's what would happen in the movies, right?

"I'm a good Catholic schoolgirl. Former schoolgirl, at least. No jailbait here." I laugh a little nervously. Ack! Could I be any more obvious? It's not as though I look like a schoolgirl, though he's obviously older than me. Maybe late twenties, early thirties? I wonder if he's a deckhand from one of the posh yachts down in the harbour, or maybe he's one of those sailor types who bounces around the world in his own little yacht. It would certainly account for his tan and those delicious creases around his eyes.

"Is that the new pope's way of getting down with the kids, using buttmunch as a new catechism?"

A man living an itinerant life on the open seas. How romant—

—ic.

My heart pounds once, loudly and belatedly.

"Did you just say buttmunch?"

"I guess you're right, it's not much of a curse, but I'm

not so sure where *fuck nuggets* comes to play on the scale." His eyes widen salaciously as he adds, "I can't see His Holiness muttering *that* at Mass."

"I'm sorry?" I reply, my mind still working around a delay. At least, that's what I think I say. So why, when the word hits the air, does it sound like I say *pussy*?

"Is this where I ask if it's pink again?"

I shake my head, a little like a horse shaking off flies. Surely, I did not just say *that* in front of this gorgeous man. Life is not that cruel. Maybe I banged my head on the steering wheel when the tyre blew, and I now have a problem with my hearing? Or maybe this is some kind of lucid accident-induced dream?

Lucid or lurid? I guess only time will tell.

"The holy trinity of buttmunch, fuck nuggets, and pussy. Did I get that right?" He looks so gorgeous when he's amused and trying not to show it.

"I . . ." Groan like I'm in pain because, in a funny kind of way, I am.

Mortification, I think it's called.

Maybe I can convince him I have amnesia?

Or a head injury-induced bout of Tourette's?

Or maybe I can just tell the truth.

"Okay, so I might swear a tiny bit," I eventually reply a little defensively as I hold my thumb and forefinger a smidge apart. "But I don't ordinarily curse like a sailor." Not fucking much, I don't. Truly. "But if you'd had the sort of day I've had"—*the sort of year I've had*—"you'd be cursing, too. Anyway," I add a touch accusingly, "I thought you said you were a gentleman."

"Do you see anyone else on their knees in front of you?"

His answer stops me in my tracks. No, it's not his

answer. It's the innately suggestive note in his tone. Before I have a chance to respond, the last lug nut loosens, and my rescuer pulls the tyre free. Laying it flat on the gravel, he stands and pulls a handkerchief free from the pocket of his pants. He begins to wipe the dark marks from his long fingers.

This is madness. I cannot *find his fingers attractive.*

"Y-you're definitely good at that," I find myself stuttering. "Very good."

He glances up from beneath the sweep of his dark lashes, and heat rises under my skin in the place of a well-deserved cringe. An endless moment passes between us when neither looks away. But the instant he does, I forgive him, feeling every inch of my skin tingle as he begins a slow perusal of my body. His attention caresses the flare of my hips, meandering along the length of my bared legs in a look that seems to say *you have no idea how good I am. How good I can be.* A look that causes a very particular kind of ache between my legs.

"Good at the car thing."

I mentally kick myself for trying to fill the silence, ridiculousness bettering nervousness as I continue to stare at his gorgeously large hands. Despite being covered in grease, road dust, and crud, I long to reach out and touch them. For them to touch me. And I don't care that he's looking at me like he has a front row seat to the thoughts running through my head because all I can think about is how I've never seen a nose as straight as his or a mouth as expressive. I wonder if he knows how much his mouth gives him away? This is a man who laughs a lot, I can tell. It's in the way his lips twitch at the corners when he's trying not to laugh and the fine lines at the sides of his mouth bracketing the full lushness between. But what his mouth doesn't tell me, doesn't even hint at, is what it would be like to kiss him. His lips look like they'd be soft, but his kiss? That remains a mystery. Would it be gentle and soft or strong and masterful, or even—

I force myself to stop. The man isn't going to kiss me just because he had the decency to stop and help a fellow motorist.

"Good with your hands, I mean," I find myself wittering. "As well as dirty—I mean your hands are dirty." *Gah! Shut up!*

"I don't mind getting a little dirty in the service of a beautiful woman. That's what you wanted to hear, right?"

"What?" Even as I ask, I'm replaying his answer in my head. He's suddenly so much closer, and not only is he lovely to look at but he smells lovely, too. Masculine and woodsy, undercut with a hint of spice. Anyway, he smells better than I ought to notice and after manual labour, too.

"You like to play word games." The timbre of his voice sends a wave of goosebumps across my skin, and a million fireworks explode as his hand finds the curve of my hip. "Teasing and innuendo."

"B-bantering, yes." Oh, my. It feels like forever since I was last touched by a man. *And it felt nothing like this.* I find myself backed up against the car. The space between our bodies is so tiny, he must be able to hear the frantic gallop of my heart.

"Games are fine, but I have this question that I can't get out of my head." His hand drifts up towards my hair, and I wonder if he can feel me trembling or if he senses how reckless I feel.

"What is it?"

"Do you really only curse when you're angry?"

"What else would make me . . .?" My words and

thoughts trail away as he anchors his hand at the nape of my neck.

"I stand by what I said. I'm not going to tell you that you've been hanging out with the wrong kind of man." His dark eyes linger on my lips before finding mine once more. "I'm going to show you instead."

2

FEE

The wrong kind of—

My mind snags on his phrasing and the way he'd said the same earlier, but only briefly. *Oh, so briefly*. Because his eyes are full of intent as I allow him to tilt my head to his satisfaction, my mind becoming as empty as Fred's trunk. As his lips slant over mine, I find myself sucking in a surprised little gasp at the shock of it. Not that he'd taken me by surprise with his kiss but rather the sheer intensity after just one touch of his lips.

I've been kissed before. Of course I have. But in the not quite twenty-five years on this planet, I've never been owned by another's mouth—never been held captive by fingers that tangle in my hair, holding me immobile as a tongue tests and teases—as *his* tongue tests and teases and tastes. His lips are so full and soft, and his attentions so thorough. I'd wondered what his kiss would feel like, but I hadn't imagined it might ruin any that follow.

My body begins to yield, shaping itself to his as the moment builds between us. I find myself twisting handfuls of his shirt at his back, anchoring myself to him as he steals my very breath. With one hand still in my hair, his other slips down to cup my bottom. Hard pressed to soft, his deep hum of approval resounds through to my core.

Dust kicks up around my ankles as a car suddenly whips by, the first to pass since I'd pulled over—since he'd stopped to help me. The driver's hand is a constant on the horn as it speeds past us, and we spring apart in shock like a couple of teenagers caught feeling each other up at a bus stop.

My head follows the rapid progress of a red-coloured Renault, my cheeks no doubt turning the same colour at the blur of lewd actions of its passengers.

My rescuer's hand makes a *V* at his chin, his forefinger idly swiping his bottom lip. "Fucking kids." His expression seems boyish almost. The bulge in his pants not so much.

I dip my gaze to the ground because my, oh my, that certainly seems like a handful . . . or a whatever-full, depending on where you're thinking of putting it.

Decisions, decisions, giggles the little devil on my shoulder who sounds suspiciously like Charles. And then I realise while thinking of the stranger's, *ahem*, *proportions*, he'd spoken, and I'd totally missed what he said.

"I'm so sorry. What was that?"

"So, once more for the cheap seats?"

"Even the nosebleed section would still get a good eyeful," I find myself murmuring, a certain something pulling at my attention again. "I don't know about cheap seats, but I'm having very cheap thoughts. Oh!" I clap my hands to my cheeks, snapping my gaze to his. "That was so inappropriate. And I'm so sorry. I really don't know what's come over me." His answer is a burst of laughter that's deep and free and really quite lovely. Encouraged, I turn my palms to the darkening sky and offer a small shrug. "I suppose they do say it pays to advertise."

"I'm going to take that as an encouragement."

"You can take it however you want." I shiver. Now that we're no longer wrapped around each other, I notice the night is drawing in, and the air is beginning to cool.

"Is that a promise?"

"That all depends on what you have in mind."

"How about I fix this, and you follow me to Saint Odile." He points to where the terracotta buildings cling to the side of the cliff face.

"The little village up there?"

"The little village up there," he agrees, "where you can make good on your promise."

"That's very forward of you," I reply a little saucily.

"There's a decent auberge up there. An inn," he adds, his soft smile tempering my own. "You could buy me a glass of wine." *First.* He doesn't say it, but it hangs in the air between us all the same.

Get to know each other first. Before. *Avant,* as the French say.

My gallant, my chevalier; his words are so sincere. But the way he looks at me is not so gentlemanly. More like he can't wait to get me naked. *The limb-flailing, sheet-twisting, scream-loud-enough-to-wake-the-goats-on-the-hills kind of naked.*

The exact kind of naked my bruised ego might appreciate.

"I have a confession to make." His brows rise but not before his gaze falls to my hand. Is he double-checking there's no trace of a ring? If at all possible, I think I like him a little more just for that. "I don't have one of those spare tyre thingies. Or even one of those little patching kits." I have an awful habit of scrunching up my nose when I'm uncomfortable, and I find myself doing so now, adding in a small shrug for awkward measure.

"And you let me take the tyre off, why?"

"In my defence," I reply quickly, "I did try to stop you. But do you know how hot it is watching a man do manual labour? Well, you probably don't," I consider, given my gaydar is completely silent. "But it is. Was. You were. I mean, the plumber who fixed my leaking tap last month was *not* a joy to watch, mainly because he exposed so much crack, I could've parked a quad bike in it."

"Okay . . ."

"Go ahead, laugh, but it's true. Not all men are created equal," I continue, digging a hole big enough for me, my mortification, and Fred the Fiat, apparently. "Not all men would've stopped to help me. But you did. And . . ." I pause to untangle my suddenly clumsy tongue, wondering if I should just pitch myself off the side of the cliff and be done with it. "I've had a really crappy day on top of a really crappy couple of months, and the truth is, I just enjoyed watching you too much to stop you."

"You enjoyed watching me take off the tyre?" he asks a little uncertainly.

"Yes. It's not a weird fetish or anything. Your muscles definitely helped."

"I guess . . . I admire your honesty." He looks like he wants to chuckle again.

"As much as you've admired my legs?"

Ha! Touché, am I right?

"You caught that, huh?" he says, making his way to the other side of the car. Opening the driver's door, he climbs in.

"What are you doing?" I deliver my question through

the passenger window, my fingers curled over the glass. Maybe I should buy a sign for the dash like they have on roller coasters—you need to be *this big* to drive this car, or in other words, somewhere under five foot five—because he looks like a giant sitting in the driver's seat, even sliding the seat all the way back. "This thing isn't going anywhere. You've already taken off the tyre, remember?"

"I remember. I'm taking your honesty and your legs for that drink." The engine turns over, and I pull back from the window when it becomes clear he's securing Fred. Windows up, car locked, he rounds the car placing both the keys and my tiny purse in my hand. "We'll drop off the keys at the village workshop," he murmurs, tilting my chin. "And maybe later, you can watch me take off something other than a tyre."

I die. Right there on the spot.

It seems like the drive to the village will be a short one, and absolutely preferable to a hobbling trek uphill. Especially as a fat raindrop suddenly splats against the windscreen, the first of a sudden deluge that sounds like a thousand hammering fingertips on the car's canvas soft top.

"Looks like we made it just in time," he says as he turns the key in the ignition. The car unexpectedly thrums throatily to life, more a roar than the rattle I'd expected.

The wipers at least have the decency to squeak.

"That glass of wine is definitely on me," I demur, ducking my head to stare at the downpour. Storm clouds gather higher up the mountain, dark grey staining the twilight's lighter shades. "This dress is dry clean only and would probably be more doll than woman sized by the time I traipsed up that hill."

"I don't see a problem with that." In the darkened car interior, his teeth are a flash of white. A sudden thrill washes through me. I know I shouldn't feel like this, but the anticipation of what's to come is almost killing me.

And what's to come is . . .

Me. I'm sure of it.

I'm sure my mother would have a fit if she could see me now, but the only stranger-danger risk I'm in is that I might explode from anticipation. Though I am my mother's daughter, aka cautious, so I take a moment to assess my current situation.

Have I been lulled into a false sense of security by his help or his easy manner?

No. I don't think so. I'm not getting serial killer vibes from him. Maybe because I'm sitting in the front passenger seat and not the trunk.

Or the boot, as we say at home.

Or *le coffre d'une voitre,* when in France.

I wonder if he speaks any French. It would be pretty hard to work in the region without the language. I also wonder if he feels as I do. Needy and reckless, almost like I'm operating a little outside of myself.

"Are you going to tell me your name?" The sound of his voice brings me back to the moment, my answer somewhat of a shock to even me.

"I might."

"Only might?" he answers, amused.

"Maybe we could just see how this evening goes."

"Interesting." The lights from a car going the opposite way sweep over his face, highlighting his expression before shadowing it again. I'm not sure if that look was amusement or determination. Maybe a mixture of both.

I bite my tongue to prevent a dozen questions from offering up every thought in my head. Maybe it's the darkness that makes the moment feel like a confessional. Everything is easier in the dark. Except maybe finding your bed without stubbing a toe or two. I glance furtively his way again, noticing how his wrist rests almost negligently on the top of the steering wheel, the tension pulling the tendons taut. My gaze wanders a little higher, snagging on a little more of that delicious forearm porn, my thighs clenching against the worn leather seat as a wave of nervous anticipation washes over me.

"You look so deep in thought." The words almost burst free from my lips. "It makes me wonder what you're thinking."

"Does it?" He glances my way with definite amusement this time. I think maybe that's all he'll offer when he adds, "I was wondering if you'd like to know my name."

Yes. Desperately. I want to know who he is and where he comes from and if he really got those crinkles at the corners of his eyes from squinting at the sun while on a yacht. But I'm also a little anxious, I think. I don't want to get into the conversation about how I'm supposed to be in a bar overlooking the azure blue of the Mediterranean, drinking overpriced cocktails while my friends encourage me to flirt with the eye candy there. I don't want to tell him how annoyed I am at Charles or how sick I am of my job or how my love life is the pits. Mostly, I don't want to admit to the fear that my life might never get any better than this. I've been messed around so much by men, and I desperately want this to be different. Defining. A moment when I stop letting life happen to me and instead make it happen.

"So you're like, an international girl of mystery."

"Hardly." I snort. Good thing he can't see what's going on in my head.

"Then you're unconventional."

I bite my tongue from making some quip about the Brits and their eccentricity, but I don't fit the stereotype. I'm not normally a creature of whimsy, and no one who knows me would describe me as quirky or bohemian or anything as interesting as that. But tonight, maybe I can be.

"Convention is overrated. You know what isn't overrated? Wine." I turn my attention back to the rain-pelted window, wondering if I'll need a glass or a bucket to carry me through my charade.

A few minutes later, the car drives through an ancient-looking arch heralding the entrance to a tiny town, the kind that was built when cars were horses and with neither the topography nor the inclination to accommodate the change. Well, save for a car park. As luck would have it, the garage is to the right of this, though in keeping with my luck today, it's already closed.

"What are we going to do now?"

"I happen to know the owner lives at the top of the village. He'll be in the *auberge*, the local inn, right about now."

"How convenient."

"I thought so."

"You must be a local," I return while thinking it's more likely he's holidayed here at one point. Maybe rented a *gite* or little house in the village.

"Something like that." He ducks his head, peering out

into the dark, wet night. "We'll need to make a run for it." He glances across at me as I begin to contort myself a little, reaching down to loosen the strap of my shoes.

"I already broke the heel," I explain. "I don't want to add breaking my neck into the bargain."

"I half expected you to want to stay in the car."

"Never promise a girl wine and expect her to cry off."

The little devil named Charles cackles from his position perched on my shoulder. *Wine and a chance to watch him take off more than a little tyre, cheri?*

"There." Ignoring his—my subconscious—insinuation, I drop my shoes into the footwell and reach for the door handle. "On three?"

Before I can begin to count down, he's out of the car and rounding to my side, though I meet him before he can reach my door, sliding the long strap of my purse over one arm and then my head.

"Ready?" Without waiting for an answer, he takes my hand and begins to jog across the parking lot then into the labyrinth of pink-cobblestoned streets.

Oh, Jesus. I'm not sure which burns more, my lungs or my calves, as I dash along beside him. On second examination, I decide it's my feet as they slap against the wet cobbles that shine slick in the moonlight.

The path opens out to the town square, the stuccoed *Hôtel de ville,* or local town hall—not to be confused with a provider of temporary accommodations—displays a very soggy *drapeau tricolore français,* or French tricolour, from its flagpole. In the centre of the square stands an ancient water feature, the kind that was, at one time in a very distant past, functional rather than decorative. We cross the lamp-lit square and turn left into a vaulted alleyway where two rows of narrow houses snake up ahead.

Despite the obvious aging of the buildings, the immaculately kept doors to these little houses have trailing bougainvillea and neatly trimmed greenery.

"I hope you know where you're going," I pant out, wondering if I should summon the energy to be suspicious of his answering nod. If he's in the habit of kidnapping women, his choice of lair leaves a lot to be desired. The people who live here must have the stamina of mountain goats, and this coming from a woman who runs Hiit, Barrecore, spinning, and all manner of torturous exercise classes for a living.

We turn a corner, the village's second most imposing building looming ahead. Stucco paintwork and sash windows framed by *niçoises* style louvered shutters, the hand-painted signage boasting:

La Belle Auberge
Hôtel. Restaurant. Salon de thé.

Thank the Lord! Though they can keep the *thé,* or tea. This girl needs a roof, a towel, and a bucket of wine, stat!

We burst into a tiny foyer, our laughter and exuberance filling the space.

"Man, the weather is ridiculous."

"So bad," I agree, slicking the rain from my bare arms with my hands. I shiver as I twist my hair over my shoulder, wringing it out over the fibrous doormat. A scarred wooden reception desk faces the doorway with an old-fashioned mail cubby hanging on the wall behind it, a half dozen or so old-fashioned keys occupying the brass hooks. My chilled skin registers the heat of an open flame and the stone fireplace at the far side of the room. A pair of leather wingback chairs stand like sentinels guarding the one other occupant of the room, a basset hound lying prone on the well-worn hearth rug.

"Someone paid attention to the weather forecast," I say, drawn like a moth to the proverbial flame. "Come and warm up." I throw the invitation over my shoulder as my companion presses the troublesome door closed, pivoting to face me.

I'm very suddenly no longer moving. Or cold, come to think of it. In fact, I'm very much the opposite, rain probably turning to steam on my skin. I suppose you could say I'm having a moment—a *TV adaptation Mr Darcy wet from the pond* kind of moment—as I stare at the way his pale shirt clings to his torso and all its deliciousness. *Pectorals, shoulders, and biceps, and so, so much more.* Droplets of water slap the terracotta floor as he slides his hand through his wet hair, the action painting his shirt to the ladder of his abdominals.

A ladder to the kind of heaven my fingers twitch to find.

"Are you okay?"

I swallow before mumbling something about being thirsty. Suddenly, very thirsty.

He doesn't answer. Not with words, at least, as his lips curve into a shamelessly wide smile. A smile that is the kind of perfect only enhanced by sharp bicuspids, canine teeth providing him with an air of wolfishness.

"How about you put those cheap thoughts on hold until I find the guy to take care of your car?"

"Should I come with you?" My offer is half-hearted, not only because my bum is now warming nicely by the fire but also because I keep making a fool of myself. There's every chance I might turn into my mother and insist he gets out of those wet things. Though not necessarily because I worry he might catch a chill.

"You should stay here." Stalking across the space, he comes to stand in front of me, his gaze heated as it dips. My eyes follow his to find he's not the only one suffering a wardrobe malfunction, the rain having rendered my dress almost transparent but for the camouflage of the floral pattern.

I fold my fingers under my elbows, which does nothing to hide the hardened points of my nipples. Regular old Fee would never have the nerve to be so audacious and would probably apologise for looking like something that the cat dragged in, even if the way he's looking at me makes me feel more like a queen than a bedraggled kitty.

"At least it didn't shrink."

"No, it did not," he answers, his tone suggesting it didn't need to.

"Do you think I should take it off?"

With an amused shake of his head, he meets my eyes. "I have no idea what to do with you."

"You don't even blush when you're lying." My voice sounds huskier, and the words? I have no idea where they're coming from.

"You're right," he says, those dark blue eyes never leaving my face. "I have all kinds of ideas for you."

"I like a creative man."

The huff of his soft chuckle blows across my cheek before he pulls away. "Don't go anywhere," he says, ducking under a low ceiling beam on the other side of the room.

"Never. You promised me wine, remember?"

With one last look of amusement, he disappears into the murky corridor beyond.

I don't know whether to giggle or squeal as bubbling

anticipation builds inside me like a bottle of fizz. Because neither would be cool, or even seemly, I crouch down and stroke the dog instead.

"Someone's getting lucky tonight," I whisper, rubbing one of his velvety ears. "Spoiler—it's me!"

"Mademoiselle?"

I pop upright, jack-in-the-box style, clapping my hands to my arms as though cold, hanging on to what little modesty I have in this dress.

"*Oh! Bonjour.* You startled me."

By her expression, she already knows she did. "I see you've made Claude's acquaintance."

I pause for a moment, my attention sliding to the beam my *acquaintance* just ducked under. His name is Claude? He so doesn't look like a . . . *aaah.* She means the dog.

"*Oui.*" Now that I've stopped patting him, Claude sits up, his baleful hound-dog eyes pleading for more. "He looks like a good dog."

"Well, he's good at being a dog," she answers with a sniff, bringing the sides of her cardigan closer across her ample chest. "And he has fleas." *Okay.* My hand retracts from his coat awkwardly. "Don't worry, they're not catching." She pats her steel grey hair. "And he isn't allowed upstairs into the rooms."

Rooms. That's right. This is an inn. With rooms.

And beds.

Not gutters.

Or cramped back seats.

My mind lingers, beginning to whir with scenarios and possibilities. He'll come back, and we'll drink wine. Flirt. Maybe retire to a rented room where we'll get to know each other a little better. *In the naked sense.* But maybe this could be on my terms, not his. Maybe this could be where Fee gets her groove back and makes all the moves. I'm tired of being told lies, pretty and otherwise. My luck has been so bad with men that when my last boyfriend turned into will-o'-the-wisp, I didn't even have it in me to cry. My love life is terrible, my job is going nowhere, and not to sound melodramatic, I feel like things might spiral out of my control.

Like before. Dark times from not too long ago.

Before I know it, my mouth is running ahead of my brain.

"Do you happen to have any free rooms this evening?"

"Of course." The woman inclines her head. "It is the end of the tourist season," she adds, probably for appearance's sake.

"Great." As I twist my purse from my hip, she makes her way to the reception desk, lifting the counter before taking her professional post.

"Are you visiting the Saint Odile?" she asks, flipping open the huge, old-fashioned registration book and swinging it around to face me.

"Sadly, no. My car broke down." I guess it's as good an explanation as any, I decide, as I pick up the plastic pen chained to a stand. I find myself prevaricating, the pen hovering over the columns.

Name. Address. Nationality. Passport number.

I know she'll need some proof of identity like a driver's license, passport, or similar.

Proof of who I am, at least in document terms.

I want this. Tonight. But this is not who I am. Is it?

"Perhaps your stay has something to do with the handsome young man in the bar?" I look up into the woman's very eloquent expression. "You arrive together, but perhaps you are not *to*gether."

"My car broke down," I find myself confessing. "He stopped to help me. I don't really know him." And I don't want to leave behind enough information to risk becoming his booty call.

"Ah." She drags her understanding out over several syllables.

"I'm sorry if that's shocking. It's just—"

"*Non*. You do not need to explain to me. Young people did not invent *la passion,* you know. *Ni le sexe*." *Or sex.*

"Of course." I shrug uncomfortably and go back to my pen hovering when the shadow of the opposite leaf begins to close over it.

"Give me your driver's license," she says hurriedly. "I will take a copy for security. I won't register you officially."

"Do . . . you accept cash?"

"Always," she answers with a smile.

Our transaction is no sooner complete when my companion, my gallant, returns. He holds a wine bottle in one hand, and a pair of wine glasses dangle from between the fingers of his other.

His smile is open as he brandishes the bottle in my direction. "Your car—"

"What kind of establishment do you think I am running?"

We both turn to a haughty voice behind the counter, my own stomach swooping to my bare toes.

"Not a piece of luggage between you and barely enough clothing to satisfy a church service!"

"*Je vous demande pardon?*" I beg your pardon? But it doesn't sound like he's begging her anything. To my ears, his delivery was a little more like *what the fuck*. But his

French is perfect as he launches into a volley of, "I'm not quite sure what—"

"A room booked, my goodness. Our best double, no less!" Her gaze sweeps him quite critically, up then down.

Oh, God. I should interject and tell the truth. Explain that the wanton hussy with the (now) frizzy hair just assumed he'd like to spend the night with her playing a game of hide *le saucisson.* Or I could lie and say I'd booked the room for myself, and the woman is just confused.

Before I have a chance to decide, the nutjob, sorry, the woman behind the counter bursts out into a raucous smoker's laugh. "Oh, my goodness. His face! I'm sorry, my dears," she says, once composed, "but I could not resist." She straightens the registration book, which makes me think she'd be a terrible spy.

He opens his mouth to answer, closing it again only to clear his throat. Then his brows dip, retracting rapidly when he notices the old-fashioned key gripped between my fingertips. I become aware that his mouth isn't the only expressive part of him as his eyes darken and his understanding becomes very, very apparent.

"Ah!" The woman cackles again. "Ah!" she says like this is the greatest of mysteries. "Go, go!" She makes a shooing motion with her hands. "Discover the delights of room number four!"

Wordlessly, I find myself turning and heading for the low-hanging beam on the opposite wall, utterly mortified at providing our host with so much entertainment.

"I was young once, too!" Her words follow us down the hallway as, with a wince, I realise neither of the rooms in this corridor are number four.

With any luck, our room will be so far away, it'll be morning before we reach it.

What the hell was I thinking?

His shoes echo behind me on the stairs.

What the hell is he *thinking?*

Well, I guess I'm about to find out because the door to room four is the first on this floor.

I fit the key to the lock and with a deep exhale, push on the door.

3

MONSIEUR CHEVALIER

"I'm sorry about downstairs." Without turning or switching on a light, she makes her way to the window, her body framed by the moonlight. The rain has subsided, a steady trickle against the windowpane replacing the earlier deluge.

"You have nothing to apologise for." I close the door softly behind me and follow her across the sparsely decorated room. Placing the glasses on the windowsill, I splash a little of the uncorked bottle into each as she stares down at the dark flowing liquid, almost as though mesmerised. She follows the motion as I raise the glass to her mouth. "I like a woman who knows her own mind."

Her eyes are dark and trusting over the rim as I tip a little past her lips.

Trust. Would she trust me if she knew what I was doing on this mountain? If she knew what I was running from? But you can't outrun the past, especially if that past isn't your own.

Her gaze lowers demurely as I take a sip from the same glass, and she turns back to the window, almost as though the action was too intimate. Can that be the case for the woman who boldly booked this room? I've been in enough anonymous hotel rooms before but never have the circumstances been like this. Never have I been turned on like this.

The glass *clinks* against the windowsill as I place it down, my free hand grazing her hip as I move behind her. The other I use to gather her hair to the side as I press a kiss to the silken skin of her neck, a tiny, jagged exhale seeming to push the tension from her body.

"Just so you know, I'm fine with taking direction." As her head rolls a little to the side in invitation, I slide my lips a little farther, my index finger drifting along the zipper running down the back of her dress.

"And with the power of suggestion," she whispers, her voice all husk and want.

"That wasn't a hint," I whisper. "More like a wish." Her skin smells of flowers and feels like petals as I continue to lavish her neck with slow, teasing kisses. "A wish upon a star," I continue, lifting her right hand and pressing it to the cool glass. Our joined fingers seem to almost touch a brilliant star in the night sky.

"Oh, you're good."

"So I've been told." Her rasping chuckle turns to a gasp as I graze my teeth over her neck. "Once or twice." My words are nothing but a low rumble of desire.

"Only once or twice?"

"Didn't anyone ever teach you quality over quantity?" I feel her tremble against me as my fingers sweep over her thigh to begin gathering the fabric of her short dress in slow increments. I may seem cool on the outside, able to make light of her words, but my heart thrashes against my ribs, and I burn with an overwhelming need to lose myself inside her.

I'd gone out for a drive to get away from the city, to try to clear my head of the past few weeks. I wasn't looking for company, but I couldn't leave her stranded on the side of the road, not even when it became clear she was standing there talking to herself. She looked cute, sure, but it's safe to say I hadn't the smallest expectation or intention of being beguiled. I haven't fucked in weeks, through a lack of interest more than opportunity. I hadn't gone looking and had stopped answering my phone. I wasn't interested.

But I am now.

Maybe the difference is in the situation rather than the girl. Maybe because she'd booked the room. *Booked the room and blew my mind.* Whatever the reason, I can't touch enough of her, can't feel enough of her as I press my hand a little heavier to hers before drawing it away. I snake my arm around her front, sliding it under the already heightened hem of her dress. Her reflection in the darkened window is heavy-lidded and soft-mouthed as I begin to trail my fingers along the thin ribbon of elastic on her underwear before pressing her between my hand and my cock.

"It also seems as though you can read minds." Her words are halting and stuttering as I cup her heat

"Beautiful, I can also take a hint." My utterance is part appreciation, part thanksgiving as my hand slips under the elastic to slide a finger between her already slick lips.

Her reaction is reflected back at me as clear as the pale lace of her underwear, her breathy sigh fogging the glass. Soft-eyed and wanton, she is slices of moonlight, dress, and underwear, slivers of soft satin skin as my hand bunches the dress at her hip, the other curled between her thighs.

"*More.*" My gut twists with need at her rasping demand and the way she rocks against me, desperate I take her there.

I give it to her, pressing two fingers deep inside her, curling them there.

"You're such a good girl." Her insides spasm around my fingers in response to the invasion and my words. "I can't wait to get my mouth on you, make you so shiny and slick." Her gasp is sharp and sweet, her surrender as satisfying as the skin of an apple yielding to the press of teeth. "You'd like that, wouldn't you?"

I grow rock fucking hard at the sound of her whimpering, "*Yes,*" as I slide the now wet fingers a little higher to circle the soft rise of her clit. Pet and circle, toy and tease. The sight and scent of her drive me to the brink as I paint the tight bundle of nerves with her own wetness until her breathing is rapid and her words are incoherent.

She bucks against my hand, the sensation altogether too much as her fingers splay against the breath-fogged window.

"*Oh, God. Yes!*" The meat of her palm strikes the glass, planting the seed of an idea.

"Are you trying to catch someone's attention?" I whisper, bringing my lips to her ear. "Would they look up and see you being fucked by anonymous hands?" In the window, my body is just a silhouette showcasing hers. "Would they stop and stare, wait to see your beautiful face as I make you come?"

I paint the picture for her as I paint her pleasure to her softly swollen clit. She keens, the extra layer of delight making her body arch and twist as she chases my feathering fingertips.

"You like the sound of that? Of being watched? Maybe I should've bent you over the hood of your car and fucked you there on the road."

Her free hand drifts up to wrap around my neck, pulling my mouth down to hers. "I might've let you," she whispers against my lips. "Just please don't stop."

I thought I was turned on before, but I guess I was wrong. The way she rocks into my touch, the sound of her need—it drives me fucking wild. I begin to regret starting this here, standing in the window, and wish I'd instead thrown her on the bed. Spread her out like a meal to feast on until nothing was left of her but sighs and bones. Yet I don't want to stop this as the tremble in her belly echoes the knot in mine. Because I want this—the knowledge of this. The ownership of her pleasure and the feel of her coming around my fingertips.

At least, to begin with.

My cock aches as I spread her open, making a *V* with my fingertips, exposing the ribbon of her flesh to the night air. I begin to flick and strum until the sounds of her pleasure ring through the air, holding her there, pressed against me, until she's twitching and spent. Her body reacts like a live wire at my final brush.

"Oh, God." Her voice is hoarse, and her shoulders heave as she collapses forward, her palms pressed to the windowsill like the experience was altogether too much.

"If we'd fucked on the side of the road," I murmur, bringing my mouth to her ear, relishing her shivers, "I wouldn't have experienced the pleasure of you booking this room. I liked that." The soft peal of her laughter vibrates through her body and into mine. Full circle, I start where we began, gathering her hair to the side to kiss her neck. "I liked that a whole lot."

"I aim to please." Her tone is a little amused, and her voice a little husky from her cries.

"I thought that was my line."

"Oh, believe me, you did," she says, her attention turning to the rain-slicked square once again. "The thought of someone watching me . . ." She frowns, maybe trying to convince herself that some things are better in fantasy than reality.

"The stars were your audience." A tremulous shiver runs through her as I trail the backs of my fingers down her bare arm. "Only they saw you shine. And they were envious."

"That's very sweet," she demurs, her attention returning to the stars beyond the glass. "Everything looks better by moonlight."

"You are beautiful. By daylight, moonlight, even in the heart of a storm."

"You really are a sweet talker." She throws the playful accusation over her shoulder.

"Ask me which I like best."

Her smile becomes a provocative lift of one brow. "How do you like me best?"

"I like it best when the storm is in you."

FEE

Such silken words as his hand drifts to my zipper, his intent clear. He's going to make me come again, though I doubt he knows his words have me halfway there by themselves. Who says flattery gets you nowhere? Well, whoever it was, they're wrong.

I have never had a man make me feel like this.

This beautiful.

This wanton.

This free.

I'm going to take this evening for what it is. A gift. An act of human love, no matter how temporary. I'm not so experienced in the realms of one-night stands, given this is my very first, but it doesn't feel as sordid or selfish or wrong as I thought it might. In fact, it feels almost like we have a kind of elemental connection.

Maybe I'm overreacting but what I do know is it feels like nothing I've ever experienced before.

A girl might lose her head to a man like this. I stretch like a cat at the soft susurrus of my zipper. *Maybe even a little of my heart.*

Along with the perception, my breath catches in my throat, yet the brush of his hands across my shoulders sweeps away the thoughts and my dress along with them. It flutters softly around my thighs, pooling around my feet. One strong arm bands my waist, his body like a cloak against mine. So much sensation. So much need.

"You're so very beautiful." My answer is a sigh as he presses a soft kiss to my spine, flicking the clasp of my bra loose. The straps slide down my arms, echoing the ripple through my insides.

How can you want something so much you physically ache?

A shiver of anticipation rolls down my spine as he slides the silky triangle of my underwear from my hips. Hands pressed to my shoulders, he coaxes me to turn.

"Let me look at you."

I tilt my chin even as I lean against the windowsill to help my unsteady knees, yet I find I feel a certain kind of deliciousness being naked before him, especially as he's still fully clothed. A kind of power play. As his gaze devours every inch of me, turning my nipples to hard points and deepening the ache between my legs, there's no doubt in my mind who has the upper hand.

Those dark eyes. The hard outline of him, like a gun ready to go off.

All mine.

Because of me.

I have the winning hand here.

I'm not sure if he reaches for me or I for him. All I know is I'm in his arms, and our mouths are all gasps, clashing teeth, and questing tongues. My fingers pluck at the back of his shirt, desperate in my pursuit to feel his heat. His skin.

Success. I smile against his mouth as my hands slide under the cotton, the reaction swallowed by his growl of approval as he brings our bodies closer by clasping handfuls of my butt.

"Fuck, this ass."

I whimper, and my knees physically weaken as he presses his teeth where my neck and shoulder meet. "Not a chance," I manage to reply, though that wasn't exactly his intention, judging by his deep chuckle.

"This ass looks as though it was honed by the hands of God."

I press my lips over his because this body was honed by hours in the gym and this is a truth he doesn't need to hear. If I'm honest with myself, I've spent too many hours in there lately. As my life had spiralled this month, I'd fallen into old patterns. Patterns of punishing exercise and extreme portion control.

Everyone has their coping mechanism the nefarious voice whispers from the back of my head. *At least your vice is healthy.*

Whether it is or isn't is a question for another day, all thoughts vanishing as hard presses soft, his erection a sudden and solid presence between my legs.

Maybe not *all* thoughts vanish.

Like those of getting him naked.

Of getting my eyes on him.

My mouth.

Just everything.

"You're so pretty." His eyes dilate like a drop of dark ink on a blank sheet of paper before he presses me back against the windowsill, framing my breasts with his hands. "So fucking perfect." His thumbs stroke the hardened points of my nipples when he bends to run his tongue across each in turn. The sight of him there does something to me, my lips parting with a sigh, his body an elegant arch before mine. But as his gaze crawls up my body, the sucking pull of his mouth sends a shower of sparks right through me, twisting my pleasure into something else entirely.

"Oh, my God." I press his head closer, the sensation drawing at my very centre.

"Not quite." His teeth flash white and wicked in the moonlight. "But I'll gladly take you to heaven."

"Big head," I whisper through my own smile.

"Beautiful, I'm big all over." As though I'd voiced any doubt, he lifts my hand to press it over his obvious erection. Emboldened, I give it a little squeeze, and he grunts, his body bowing into my hand, the sound a puff of air against my cheek.

"Seeing is believing." I run my palm over his hardness before tucking my fingers into his waistband, almost desperately plucking at his shirt.

"Do you want to see me put my mouth on you?" His hot whisper curls around my ear, exploding a little farther south. As he drops to his knees, I find I have a fistful of his shirt, and as he moves, I pull it up and over his head.

"That was some trick." The blade sharpness of his cheekbones is more pronounced by the moonlight. His eyes darker and a little more wicked, the look echoed in his smirking half-smile. His body is everything I thought it would be, everything his wet shirt hinted at. Hard angles and slopes, his every muscle is defined. A thrill courses through me as I trail my fingers over his shoulders, his expertly trained muscles tensing beneath his skin.

"I don't know," I demur as he places his hands on my thighs. I grip the windowsill at my back, my own muscles tautening at his touch. *At my anticipation.* "I think you must be the one with all the tricks. How would I be the only one naked?"

"Maybe because you're the one with the magic." His voice is rough as his big hands slip between my thighs, spreading them wider. He presses two long fingers deep inside me, and I cry out, my body arching against the windowpane. The cold glass adds a layer of sensation as his hot mouth engulfs my clit with a velvety groan.

Oh, Jesus! The man is good at this.

He reaches up to pinch my nipple, the light brush of his tongue its counterpoint, my body bucking wild against him.

"*Yes!*" I bring my hands to his thick hair, anchoring

myself, as his rough whispers praise and promise, his tongue and fingers just glorious. But this is just the appetiser, it would seem, as he spreads my legs wider and begins to truly devour me.

"Oh, God. I really can't—yes, like that. *Oh, yes! Yes!*"

"Give it to me," he commands, beginning to pressure and flick my clit over and over again. He growls, "Give it up, beautiful."

My senses are truly heightened. I'm aware of every brush of air against my skin, the sound of my rough breaths and the rasp in his. The cold glass at my back and the hot flick of his tongue, and how the taste of our mutual pleasure seems to permeate the air. I've never experienced a high like it as my insides quicken, a white-hot intensity bursting through me, detonating almost at his command.

"Give it to me, beautiful. Come for me. Come on my tongue."

Oh, God, and I do, my spine an impossible arc as every fibre of my being draws tight before it implodes like a supernova. A starburst of bright lights, oxytocin, and dopamine. Pleasure spiralling outwards in a wave of euphoria.

There is nothing . . . nothing but this utter bliss.

I come to, pardon the pun, collapsed against the sill, my heart thrashing against my ribcage and my thighs trembling as though I've just completed a hardcore spinning class.

"I heard that every time a beautiful woman curses, an angel loses its wings and falls from heaven."

"What?" I look down to where he kneels. My throat is dry, and I swallow, not really able to concentrate on his nonsensical words, not as his lips shine with my wetness, and his tongue gives the bottom one a leisurely swipe. *As though he'd like to taste me again.*

"Well, my paragon of virtue, I lost count of your curses around the point you said I was a 'pussy-eating motherfucking superstar'."

"What?" Is he speaking in tongues? And why do I sound like I've just run a marathon?

"You. Profanity. Angel snuff porn."

"You have a very pretty mouth." Even if I can barely make sense of what it's saying.

"A pretty mouth for making out with your pretty and delectable pussy."

Now *that* I understand. I bring my legs together as I replay his earlier words, wondering why my legs are still shaking.

I don't know. Maybe something to do with experiencing the best orgasm of my life?

"The best orgasm of your life?"

I ignore the fact that he somehow heard my thoughts along with the satisfied grin he's currently wearing.

"It seems a little misogynistic, don't you think?" I murmur, directing the conversation elsewhere. "That angels only fall out of the sky when women swear."

"Beautiful women," he corrects. Standing now, he cups my face as he brings his mouth to mine. It's a light, teasing kiss, one I taste myself in.

"Damn that original sin." I clear my throat, wondering why it feels so illicit. How I can be speaking when I feel so overwhelmed.

"I don't make the rules." His response echoes through his chest as he draws me into his arms. "But if there's sin, I'm there for it."

"You know, I was told angels lost their wings when—"

I clamp my lips together. He really doesn't need to hear that.

"When what?" He holds me away from him by the shoulders, one corner of his mouth quirked in a curious expression.

"When you do . . . something else."

"I'm intrigued." His words are a dark whisper in my ear as his hands drift down to cup my behind. An aftershock of pleasure washes through me as the fabric of his pants pleasantly chafes, my nipples drawing hard at the press of his warm skin. "Spill, beautiful."

"Just something else. Something naughty." My words hit the air in a rush. Who knew I was a sucker for flattery? Or else this is a case of a good orgasm being like truth serum. Whatever the case is, I'm so pleased it's too dark for him to see my embarrassment, and I raise my gaze to his, sending up a silent prayer that none of these thoughts have made it past my lips.

That would just be *trés* awkward.

"Come on, you know you're gonna have to tell me." His words are delivered in a low-sounding chuckle and an accompanying solid squeeze of my bum.

"Well." I sigh with resignation. "According to Sister Edith's pious, though not particularly informative, health education classes . . ." I wrap my hands around his neck and tip up on my toes to whisper the rest in his ear. And then almost pass out from the feel of his skin on mine. "Every time you touch yourself in sin, an angel loses its wings." I experience the vibration of his amusement down to the very marrow of my bones.

"The real estate market in heaven must be fantastic."

He groans a deep and masculine sound as daring gets the better of me, my tongue darting out to caress his ear.

"I think that's why it's called ringing the Devil's doorbell."

"Wanna see if he's home again?" He angles his head as though to slant his lips over mine.

"And make the little cherubs and angels cry?" I press my palm to his chest, keeping him in place even as a tantalising pulse begins to beat between my legs. Could I even withstand another orgasm like the last? It's a risk I'm willing to take.

"I'm pretty sure the angels, like the stars, are dirty voyeurs."

I squeak as his hands slide down, hooking under my thighs to lift me. He begins walking backward towards the bed, his hands still full of my bum.

"So you're saying they deserve to be made homeless?"

He pauses as though appearing to think before it becomes clear it's just for effect. "What I'm saying is, let's fuck."

Oh, I'm good with that. I'm so good with that as he drops me to the bottom of the bed that I begin to yank at his belt, remembering how desperate I was to see him. But with a rasping laugh, he raises my fumbling hands.

"Oh, is this where I get to watch you take something off other than a tyre?" I push my hands under my thighs to stop me from clapping them.

"I have a better idea." His gaze is all pupil and wicked plans as he brings my hand to his mouth, and I gasp as he flicks my forefinger up, sucking it into his mouth. "Let's scandalise the heavens," he murmurs, feeding the wet digit between my legs.

And then he straightens, and I do get my show as he begins to slowly unbuckle his belt. The action is almost hypnotic, and I find I'm holding my breath as he releases himself from his zipper. Judging by his amused expression, I think my eyeballs might have fallen out of my head, cartoon style. I only hope I didn't make the usual accompanying sound which, from memory, is the honk of a hooter.

I've never found dicks to be beautiful. Necessary sometimes, more so than the bigger dick they come attached to. But this is different because not only is he gorgeous but this is also a thing of beauty as he begins to jack himself.

The muscles of his right arm tense and bunch in the dim light, his hand moving in slow, deliberate strokes, twisting as he reaches the sensitive head.

"You're not joining in." Not a question, but maybe a pointed observation, but not even two amazing orgasms makes me feel that kind of brave. Besides, I don't think I'd be able to concentrate, not as I watch his abs tighten, not as I viscerally feel the rumble in his next breath. I suddenly want to hear him make that noise for me, because of me.

"I have a better idea," I whisper, reaching for him. His body bows forward as I wrap my hand around the thick length of him, and he releases *the* sexiest sound.

Low, guttural, and filled with need.

"I like this idea." He gasps as I explore his silky head, the heft, and length of him in my hands as I note his every reaction. The way his abs tauten under my fingertips, how his thighs tremble at the brush of my breath. The way his brows pull in as though suffering as I ghost my lips over him. Suffering in the best kind of way.

His body arches as I open my mouth, swallowing him, taking him to the back of my throat.

"So fucking good . . ." His words are a rumble of

appreciation as I draw my lips back along his length. I glance up as he pulls my hair to one side and watch how he enjoys the sight of me sucking and lapping, of how I work him from tip to root. *Or at least to where my hand grips him.* His tight breaths and dirty whispers drive me on, my mouth working him sloppily, my moans vibrating around his flesh and joining his own. It takes me a moment to realise his hand is tightening in my hair, pulling me from him, dragging me to his mouth as he delivers the most punishing of kisses.

"You wanted to make me come."

"Fair is only fair." My voice sounds hoarse, and I wonder if my eyes are as dark as his seem. "But I was just enjoying you."

"Move up the bed." He's all command and action as he toes off his shoes and his shorts as I scramble backwards, but not before taking a moment to appreciate the very European lack of socks.

There's nothing quite so off-putting as a man naked but for his socks.

"What are you smiling at?" He takes a condom from his wallet before spinning the latter to the nightstand. The former he sheaths himself with quite beautifully, though I expect a man like him completes everything with a little panache. He's probably had lots of practise because practise does make perfect . . . even if that realisation is less than—

Like a bubble popped, my thoughts are no more as my body registers the brush of him between my legs. Moonlight cuts across the room, casting us in shadow but for the stripe of light slicing his shoulders, which is where I find my hands as he grips the back of my thigh. Warm, silky, yet so hard, the press of his crown at my entrance makes me tremble. I gasp as he breaches me, anticipating haste and the size of him. *Maybe looking forward to it, too.* I wasn't expecting him to take his time, for him to hold me, grip my attention as well as my body as he fills me with a kind of slow exquisiteness, his dark eyes never once leaving mine.

I'd known somehow it would be good, but what I hadn't expected was intimacy.

"You feel so good." His voice sounds tight, his words morphing into a low moan as he lifts my leg higher, giving me more.

Everything narrows to where our bodies meet, to where he fills me so deliciously. He's so big and so hard, and when his body flexes against mine, my body reacts as though lashed by electricity.

"*Yes!* That's—" A compliment I don't complete as his mouth covers mine, inhaling my words.

"So good." His words, his velvety groan, ignite a pulsing wave deep within me. "*Jesus*," he whispers tightly. But then there are no more words as he begins to move. No words but sighs of praise as each drive and flex of his hips works me into a delirious kind of frenzy.

"Fuck, you are beautiful." Still inside me, he pulls back, his eyes devouring the whole of me, the sweep of his gaze a tangible thing. "Look at how you take me." His head dips to watch as he rewards us both with shallow jab of his hips, his body almost undulating above me. And it's perfect, every second of this torture, every brush of his breath, and every halting whispered compliment.

I cry out as he falls against me, driving himself to the hilt with a groan, his hands grasping mine. Fingers linked, he pins them to the bed as he begins to move, hard and fast. The feeling of being under him, being held in place by him, being at his mercy as he takes his pleasure. And as he gives—*oh, how he gives*—drives me to the insane notion of keeping him there forever. I wrap my legs around him, his thrusts now shallow and fast, our whispers urgent and staccato.

Pleasure spirals through me as I revel in the feel of him over me. It's almost as though I'm aware of every inch of our joined skins. And he watches me. Sees me. Enjoys the tilt of my body as it matches the rhythms of his. Our sighs layer, feminine over rough as his velvety whispers possess their own filthy kind of reverence as he tells me how tight I feel and how beautifully I take him.

A dark captivating ache begins to build as my body gives in to his masterful thrusts, everything ceasing to exist beyond this, beyond him, beyond how I feel and the ancient bed squeaking beneath us.

I could let him fuck me forever.

It's my last sentient thought as I reach the peak and fall over the edge into the blissful abyss.

"I can feel you," he rasps. "Sweet girl, I can feel you coming around my cock." With those last words of encouragement and one more driving thrust, his body follows the rhythms of my own.

My body mourns the loss of his almost immediately as he collapses onto his back, the motion making a veil of my hair. Moments pass when neither of us speaks. Whether we don't want to break the spell or we lack the energy, I'm not sure.

But eventually, I turn on my side to face him.

"You're a man of many, many talents." I sound like a heavy smoker as I slide my hand to the centre of his chest.

"Take it from me," he says with a grin, "I fuck better than I fix cars."

"You're spoiling the fantasy."

"Oh, yeah? What fantasy is that?"

"If I told you, it wouldn't be a fantasy," I answer with a saucy tap to his chest.

"Not for long, it wouldn't." Lifting my hand, he brings it to his lips. His eyes gleam dark, his look lingering, the kind of expression that turns my insides molten once again. A look that leads to a kiss, and a kiss that leads to other things.

Without complaint from me.

I don't even complain in the morning when I lift my arm to shield my eyes from the early morning sun and find that, despite being a fitness instructor by day, I lack nocturnal activity muscle tone. *Ow, that shizz hurts.* Why the heck do my triceps hurt? I twist a little to find myself stifling a groan. My whole body aches—I feel like I've spent the night doing ab crunches interspaced by squats. It's a pity someone couldn't figure out how to make a fitness class out of sex because it has to be the ultimate aerobic workout with a little endurance training thrown in. Or at least it is with him. I try not to look at the *him* in question.

Try and fail.

He's so lovely this morning, sleep rumpled and mussed. Sunkissed skin and messy hair.

He was a really excellent instructor.

The most gorgeous man I've ever . . . worked out with.

Who am I kidding?

Last night was the best sex of my life. And I really ought to leave before I decide I want to do it all over again.

Oops! Too late.

But I won't give in.

I press my lips together as I attempt to roll to my side,

desperate not to disturb the sleeping beauty lying on his stomach next to me. His other hand reaches out suddenly, fingers splaying across my ribs as though he knows what I'm about to do. I lift his hand gingerly and slide out from the bed. As stealthily as I've ever been, despite the muscle twinges and niggles, I slip back into my underwear and dress. My body aches to shower, I so need to pee, and I'm pretty sure I reek of sex, but righting any one of these risks waking him. I can't take that chance.

It had seemed so simple last night. But in the cold light of day, everything is different. Real.

I slide my purse from the dresser, startling at the sight of myself in the mirror. It hardly looks like me; my hair looks like an abandoned bird's nest, and my dress looks like a used floral hanky. I trace my fingers over a mark on my neck as something dark and delicious blooms deep inside. I close my eyes at a wash of sensory memory. I'd felt him everywhere, at my neck and between my legs, his entire presence enveloping.

The woman in the mirror is wantonly dark-eyed, her body begging for a repeat. I could creep back to bed. Kiss him awake. Make love by daylight . . .

Until my hand drifts from my neck, feathering over my collarbone.

I've gotten so thin.

God knows I've felt out of control, like a failure, like life was happening to me rather than I was part of it. Lately, I'd fallen into old habits of spending too long in the gym and not enough at the dinner table. Exerting control in the only way I could. It's a dangerous ethos and a knife-edge I've balanced on before. But no more. No more punishment under the guise of being in control. No more living on supplements and salads as a point of power. It all has to stop.

I don't have to be that person. I can be someone else. Didn't I prove that last night?

I find I have no shame. Nothing to regret. And why should I? I spent the night being worshipped like a goddess. And like a goddess, I will leave this room.

Or like Beyonce.

A bottle of wine lies on the nightstand, drops of red staining the snowy pillow on the floor, bed linen clinging precariously to the bed. And then there's him. Sculpted muscles lying under caramel skin. It would be so easy to peel back the corner of the sheet covering him and wrap my body around his to rouse him, kissing him back to consciousness. But that would lead us back to him meeting the real Fee. The Fee from before. Not the Fee I intend to be.

The door creaks as I open, but my sleeping beauty doesn't budge. I slip from the room like a thief. I don't remember the staircase being as noisy on the way up last night, and as I tiptoe through the empty reception, I almost collide bodily with an old lady bowed over a broom.

"Oh! Vous m'avez fait peur!" You startled me!

Her response is a *hmph* sound as she very pointedly looks me up then down, her lips pulled tight like the strings of a purse and the wrinkles in her forehead increasing tenfold due to the weight of her frown.

A burn begins in my chest, the weight of her derision turning my skin beet red. Before I stop. Take a moment. And remember my promise to myself.

I made a decision. The choice is mine, and I won't berate myself for living life as I see it. Think what you want, old lady. Call me loose. Immoral. A slut. I don't care because I know the truth of it. Last night, I was valued. Last night, I was Beyonce—I mean, a goddess!

The last man I slept with? I played by the rulebooks. We didn't kiss until the third date or sleep together until the sixth. We'd talked about our pasts, our families, took time to get to know each other, or at least I thought that's what we were doing. But when he disappeared, it turned out not one thing he'd said was true.

I might know nothing about the man still sleeping in that little bed upstairs, but I know enough. And he's restored my faith in men, first by stopping to help me and later by making me *feel.* Want and wanted. Desire and desired.

One man made me feel like a deity while the other left me feeling nothing but used.

So shove your judgment, little old lady. I refuse to feel bad.

I'm tired of playing by the rules.

"*Bonsoir, madame!*" My tone is sunshine personified—fake it until you make it, right?—as I make my way around five feet of attitude in a housecoat and a floral headscarf.

Outside, I can't stop myself from glancing up at the first floor, a tiny part of me hoping to see him standing there. For him to run after me, to declare his undying desire for me.

A girl can dream, I think, as I make my way barefoot along the cobblestones.

After all, dreams are simply hope.

4

FEE

FIVE YEARS LATER

"Are you sure he won't mind us staying here?"

"Absolutely." Rose shoots me a reassuring smile over her shoulder as the key turns, the locking mechanism connecting audibly over the stream of constant questions coming from my four-year-old daughter.

Is this our new house?

Does it have a pool?

How high up are we?

How far away is my new school?

"Trust me. He won't even know you're here."

"So long as that doesn't mean you haven't asked him," I add warily.

"Yes, because I totally just charmed the doorman into giving me the key."

"I'm pretty sure you could charm the birds from the trees if you'd half a mind," I mutter, adding then a little more audibly, "I'm just trying not to tempt fate." Because if trouble comes in threes, I'd been served two accommodation disasters already today. I'll do my best to avoid a third, thank you very much.

"You're not superstitious," Rose scoffs.

I don't immediately answer because my move to New York has hardly been auspicious so far. First, the street where I'd arranged an apartment lease was featured on last night's evening news as the sight of a gangland-style shoot-out. Then this morning, when I'd eventually persuaded Rose, my absolute best friend and my employer, that we should at least check out the apartment if for no other reason than I'd already paid a hefty holding fee, the place turned out to be a total flea pit.

Actually, even fleas would probably turn up their noses at living there.

Do fleas have noses? I'm not sure.

It had looked so perfect over the internet.

"All I'm saying is you won't find me walking under ladders or crossing the path of black cats." At least, not today.

Rose chuckles as the door falls open, but I'm not joking. She pulls the key from the latch and steps into the hallway, her heels audible on the gleaming parquet floor.

"For the record, of course I've asked." She sends me a sly glance over her shoulder. "I just meant this place is so large, he probably wouldn't notice you were here. But as he's very rarely in New York, the point is irrelevant." She turns to take Lulu's hand. "Come on. Let's go investigate your new home."

"This isn't our new home," I counter, stepping in after the pair as the scent of beeswax hits my nose. "It's just a temporary stopgap."

The sooner we find our own place, the better, because from the moment the cab pulled up to the building's fancy canopied entrance, I've been uneasy. I hate that I've made such a mess of this. I'm an adult with a child to care for.

I'm supposed to be able to sort out my problems on my own and have my own contingency plans. Contingency plans that don't include a friend of a friend allowing me to stay in their very fancy Fifth Avenue apartment. I mean, who even has those sorts of friends?

Well, obviously Rose. Meanwhile, I just count myself incredibly lucky to be her friend, a friendship that's nothing to do with connections or money.

"I know." Her sing-song answer drifts from deeper in the apartment, the hallway darkening as I close the front door after me. I follow their voices, noting the pristine floors, dust-free mid-century wooden furniture, and the neutral palette of soft furnishings. Surfaces gleam, and large potted palms thrive. This place doesn't look at all unoccupied, but it does look expensive.

I pause at the ceiling-height French doors that lead to the terrace overlooking the treetops of Central Park as a sense of trepidation washes over me. Why trepidation and not excitement? This should feel like a dream come true, given I've wanted to live in New York since I'd discovered reruns of *Friends* as a teenager. From *Friends* it was just a hop, skip, and a click of the TV remote before I devoured all six seasons of *Sex in the City*, leaving me imagining myself wandering through The Whitney in impossibly high heels and drinking my way through mimosa-filled brunches in achingly hip restaurants. My imaginings were very Carrie Bradshaw and a lot less—

"*Mum-eeee!*"

Yes, her.

Mummy.

Me, I mean.

Lulu appears by my side and tugs on my hand, her

blue eyes wide and glittering. "We are *so* high! The tops of the twees look like broccoli!"

"Yummy, because broccoli is your favourite, right?"

"No, it's yucky," she replies emphatically. "Tante Rose says the twees are in a huge, huge park."

"Auntie Rose said that, did she?"

"Yes, and that it even has a zoo! A zoo with amimals."

"Animals, sweetheart."

"That's what I said. And it has a castle and an island and boats and hundreds and hundreds of playparks!"

"How many?"

"At least one-hundred-and-eleventy-two!"

I smile at her upturned face as she practically trembles with enough excitement for the two of us. No one ever prepares you for the wonders of parenthood—how a child's delight can make your whole day. How love for a child can make you strive to be the best version of you. Well, when you're not a sleep-deprived, leaking, feeding machine, but those days are behind us.

"Yes, and horsies! And-and I want to go on the horsies—"

"Those were carousel horsies," Rose corrects, entering the room.

Lulu's head whips around and back, her smile infectious. "Yes, like a merry-row-round." I don't correct her and not just because she's cute. "Can we go there this afternoon? Can we? Please?"

I run my hand over her dark, silky waves, courtesy of her father's genes. *Genes being his sole contribution to parenthood.* I might not have imagined a four-year-old as part of my New York daydreams, but now that I have, I can't conceive of it being any other way. Lulu was a . . .

surprise. Unplanned. And the absolute best thing that's ever happened to me.

"Maybe tomorrow."

"But I want to go today."

And I want a unicorn that farts rainbows. No, on second thought, I want one that farts hundred-dollar bills, but you can't always get what you want.

"We have too much to do today, but I know a wonderful girl like you will help me with all those very important jobs, which will mean we'll then have all the time in the world to visit the park."

"Time today?"

"No, sweetie, time tomorrow." Her bright blue eyes narrow, and I know what's coming next. Because as well as gorgeous dark hair and brilliant baby blues, her father also blessed her with a quick temper and stubborn streak that is approximately one mile wide. As sure as my bum seems to be heading south, she didn't get her temper from me.

Lulu, or Eloise when I want her undivided attention, is what my mother describes as *bold*, which is just a polite way of saying she's a bit of a handful. This, according to Rose, means she'll be running the planet by the time she's thirty. Which is preferable to being holed up in a penitentiary. "Or maybe we won't have time until next week if you're not going to help."

"Bah! I'm only little. What do you 'spect me to do?" she retorts, her palms raised in the air.

"Lulu, honey, why don't you go and choose your bedroom?" Rose interjects, causing my four going on twenty-four-year-old felon, I mean daughter, to dash from the room.

"I'm taking d' biggest woom!" Seconds later, a crash

resounds somewhere out of sight. "Oops! Was an accident!"

"Ah, hell." I hurry after her, praying that accident wasn't some family heirloom because this place just reeks of money, and my daughter is the kind of child who would find something to fall over in an empty room.

What does an apartment like this cost? Ten million dollars? Twenty? More? Numbers I can only imagine, at any rate. While the apartment is beautiful, the building is something truly special. Genteelly gothic; is that even a thing? The wrought-iron canopy set the tone the minute we got out of the cab. A liveried doorman, a marble lobby, original crown mouldings up the wazoo, this place was probably designed more than a century ago. I think I might've even spied a gargoyle out on the terrace.

"Doesn't this place have a staff quarters or something? If it has, we'd be better off confining ourselves to them."

"What?" Rose says, coming up from behind as I turn the—thankfully—undamaged urn upright. *Undamaged and not filled with dear departed Uncle Algernon's ashes, praise be.* "Don't be ridiculous. He said for you to make yourself at home, not to clean the home."

"I'm certain it wasn't an invitation to wreck the place." One glance at the small bronze figurine sitting on the gleaming console table in front of a wall of windows, and I know this is a home that isn't used to visiting children. Then from the corner of my eye, tiny, pudgy fingers creep across the table. "Leave it be," I command, turning into my mother for a minute. It's not hard to read Lulu's intentions because she's become a little light-fingered recently. I've put it down to the anxiety of moving to a new house, school, and country; the changes must be hard to process at her age. Hell, they're pretty tough at my age, and they make me wonder why I'm doing this at all because yes, I'm drowning in a pool of my own guilt. Mummy guilt. The very worst kind! Not that you'll find me using this as an excuse to pocket a piece of *objet d'art* that looks suspiciously like a Henry Moore.

Unlike some (little) people.

"I was jus looking at it." Her little fingers unfurl from the figure, and she steps away with a pout.

"Of course you were," Rose replies in a soothing tone. "And it's totally fine just to look."

"Totally fine to look. Not so fine to pocket it," I find myself muttering as I watch Lulu skip away. "Remind me who *he* is again?" I turn to Rose, picking up our earlier conversation thread. "The guy who owns this place, I mean?"

"Carson Hayes is a family friend," she answers airily. "Carson Hayes III." She laughs a little as though party to some inside joke. All I can think is he sounds ancient and more than a little pompous. Who the heck refers to themselves as 'the third' anything? Which I'm assuming he does or why else would Rose have mentioned it? But I keep my thoughts to myself because Rose moves in some strange (see: rich) circles these days. Besides, the man was nice enough to let us stay here on very short notice, I purposely remind myself.

"Wouldn't it be better if we just extend our hotel stay for a few more days?"

"And get to and from the hotel to Lulu's school twice a day?"

"We might find an apartment before she starts school on Monday," I answer brightly.

"That is highly unlikely, and more like impossible."

"But it's just weird, isn't it? I don't even know him, and he's letting me stay here."

"I know you hate being anything less than self-sufficient, but just trust me on this. He's a genuinely nice guy. If I'd known your accommodation was going to fall through so spectacularly, I'd have introduced you to him when he was in town last. Actually, no," she amends, her expression firming. "If I'd have known the kinds of places you were looking at, I'd have passed the job onto a relocation consultant myself."

Which would've cost more money, and she's already shelling out so much on my behalf. Or at least, the foundation is.

"The apartment was terrible, but the neighbourhood wasn't bad," I counter half-heartedly.

"Wasn't bad?" she repeats, though not exactly in the same tone. "What, in particular, did you like about it? Was it the corpse-shaped chalk line on the sidewalk outside of the building, or the tweakers hanging on every other street corner, or the dealers on the ones between?"

"Someone's been watching too much *Law & Order*." Lord knows this move has had enough drama so far to fill a whole season of the show.

"And *someone* shouldn't be so hard on herself," she retorts.

"What's that supposed to mean?"

"Babe, you look like someone kicked your puppy. Finding somewhere to live within commuting distance of downtown Manhattan is why there are relocation consultants in the first place. I should've realised you needed help."

"I'm not your responsibility," I reply wearily.

"No, but you are my friend," she retorts before leaving the room to investigate Lulu's shouts of "*cool!*"

With one more glance at the million-dollar views, I follow my daughter's giggles . . . to the room she's currently in, jumping on a bed as big as a helicopter pad.

"Eloise Rose! You get your bum down off that bed."

"Haven't got my bum on it. Just my feets!" She giggles a little breathlessly, ignoring my instructions completely.

Swiping her up, I deposit her to the floor and bend forward until we're eye to eye.

"We do not bounce on beds," I state in a tone much calmer than I feel.

"Yes, we do," she says, one hand sliding to her non-existent hip. "Even growdups do it sometimes."

"When have you ever seen me jump on a bed? Especially a bed that doesn't belong to me?"

"Well, Mia, my friend at school, says her daddy and his girlfriend bounce on their bed *all* of the time. They bounce on it and bounce on it, and they keep the bedwoom door locked so she can't join in. And sometimes her mummy *and* her daddy do it together."

"Oh. Well." I ignore Rose's snigger from the vicinity of the doorway.

"I think that's what you do, Mummy." She gaze narrows to comically thin slits. "You just wait until I'm not home to bounce on the bed."

"Believe me, it has been a long time since I bounced on a bed with anybody."

"You bounce all by yourself because you are a meanie pants," she retorts with a frown and a stamp of her foot. "You just want to keep all the fun to yourself."

If motherhood has taught me anything, it's that parenting manuals suck. Nothing can prepare you for a four-year-old with an attitude and an answer for everything. No amount of reasoning or time-outs work for my child, so instead, we have this; one little hothead and one cool response. And a battle of wills fought pretty much every day.

"I'm the mummy that wants to hide all the fun?" I ask. Lulu nods. "Well, you're the little girl who won't be going near a park or a castle or a zoo or even a carousel horse any time soon. What do you think, Tante Rose?"

"I think you should leave me out of this. I also think this bedroom is too dark for you, Lu. All this dark blue. Why don't you go and check out the other bedrooms?"

Lulu's eyebrows retract as though to say *well, can I?* I nod my consent, and she stomps off, muttering under her breath. As I turn to watch her, she pauses at the doorway, her internal battle as clear as the cute button nose on her face. I know she hates getting into trouble, but she just can't seem to help herself.

"I'm sorry," she grates out without turning. But she isn't. At least, not yet. At this point, sorry is just a word for her. "You're not really a meanie pants."

"Apology accepted."

"Nope, you're more like a meanie knickers," Rose whispers as Lulu leaves, the thoroughly British word sounding strange on her tongue.

"Let's leave my knickers out of this."

"I have no idea what I'm going to do when Rocco reaches this stage." Rose shakes her head, her eyes following Lu down the hallway. But Rocco, her and her husband Remy's little boy, has the sweetest disposition of an eighteen-month-old I've ever encountered. Not that I know a lot of children of that age, but he's certainly more placid than Lulu was. *Ever.*

"I'm not so sure this is a stage. It seems more like a personality trait. She's like the girl with the curl. When she's good she's very very good, but when she's bad . . ."

"She's never horrid," replies Rose.

"Just horrid to parent sometimes."

"But you wouldn't have her any other way."

"That's true. And you're right, she's never really horrid though her attitude sucks *a-r-s-e* plenty." I was never big on swearing before, which is just as well considering.

"And that's why, my friend, wine was invented." Rose moves to the bedroom window, another room with a million-dollar view. "And you know she'll be curing cancer or running some million-dollar corporation before she's thirty."

"She's certainly single-minded enough." Hence my tiny fear of her using her powers for ill instead of good.

"And she's a smart one." Roses gaze slides my way. "I think she might be on to something with the bed bouncing business."

"Subtle, Rose. Very subtle. I'm impressed with that almost seamless segue into the topic of my sex life."

"What sex life?" She grins, and I just shake my head.

"As if I'd be bed bouncing with anyone while my child is at school," I mutter, adopting the euphemism.

"I think you might've forgotten how. You know what Charles's theory is." She sends me a meaningful look.

"Oh, please. Not that again. I do not wear glasses because,"—I lower my voice to a whisper—"I masturbate too much."

Along with my denial, a vivid snapshot of a previous life flickers to being in my head.

Wanna see if the Devil is home again? The ghost of his sultry whisper curling around my ear, and I know if I close my eyes, I'll imagine the press of his hard body and the way his eyes seemed to see right to the core of me. Sometimes, I think I can still hear his deep chuckle. Feel it echoing deep inside me.

"Everyone masturbates." Rose's amused tone yanks me back to the moment.

"Yet it isn't a documented cause for short-sightedness," I respond, shaking off the final wisp of him, a moment of madness that seems like a lifetime ago yet still has the power to almost sweep my knees out from under me.

"I didn't say it was a good theory," she counters.

"I'm short-sighted because it's in my genes. And my bum has disappeared because I had a baby. It's called life."

"Your ass is still fine—fine with a capital *F*—though I'm sure a little bed bouncing would only serve to improve it."

"Is that so?" I reply scornfully.

"Yep. Bed bouncing is good for the mind, body, and soul. You should know that, you being a health guru and all. Orgasms are like chicken soup when you're ill. Or popping a Xanax pill when you're blue."

"Since when have you taken to popping pills?"

"I hear they're good," she says with a shrug. "But I'll stick to wine and sex."

"How about you also stick to your day job and stop worrying about me and my sex life."

"Love life," she corrects.

"When I find someone I'd like to *bounce* long term, I'm sure it'll all come flooding back. I can't help that no one has ignited my interest lately."

"Lately as in five years," Rose replies pointedly. "Honestly, you're so out of practice, I worry you might fall off."

"What?" My answer is wavery with laughter, the vision of such a mishap popping up in my head. "I don't even know what to do with that."

"That's what she said," she says, laughing as I move to stand next to her. "And you know what his reply was?"

Ouch?

"No more innuendo," I warn as she opens her mouth.

"But you just set them up for me so perfectly." She shrugs and turns her gaze to the treetops beyond the window. "Well, at least the view is better here than the last place."

"Most employers would've left me to fend for myself," I say, slinging an arm around her shoulder as I join her. "Let alone take an interest in my bouncing habits."

"It's a good thing I'm your friend first and your employer after, right?" Her own arm feeds around my back, digging into my waist and making me squirm.

"Friends don't tickle friends!"

"No, but good friends look after one another."

"Oh, we're getting deep now, are we?"

"I'm being serious. You hate anyone doing anything to help like it's a sign of weakness or something. It's like you've chosen to forget all the help you've given me. Remember when you drove from Nice to Monaco because I missed my bus and couldn't speak enough French to get myself home? We were barely even friends at that point—we'd only just met!"

"I only drove across the border. It took, like, forty minutes."

"That's not the point. You'd only known me a few hours."

"But I couldn't have left you," I reply. "Not when we'd bonded over our parents' love of ridiculously traditional

Irish names." Róisín for her pronounced Row-sheen and Fiadh for me. *Fee-a*. "And I don't hate that you help—I'm grateful to you for everything you've done, and you've done way more for me than I have for you."

Because I'm no longer running myself ragged at the hotel gym catering to rich women with butt's as tight as their purse strings. *Mega hours for minimal pay*. These days I'm more likely to be found running yoga and meditation classes as part of my role working for Rose's foundation. And when I get back to France, I'll be doing so much more because I plan to open a wellness centre to help women learn to love with their bodies through counselling sessions and movement classes. The fact I struggle with this isn't ironic, I feel, so much as it is a testament to how much pressure women place on themselves. I know I'm doing the right thing for the right reasons and am so happy that Rose offered me financial backing and has already secured a site. Rose is more than a friend. More than family. *More like my guardian angel*. She'd given me a job, invested in my education, and found me a placement in Manhattan to help me achieve my dreams.

We amble out of the room by some unspoken agreement because, as all mothers know, a quiet child is dangerous, when she says, "Let me remind you that the foundation will also benefit from the experience you gain over the next twelve months, from both our staff and our clients. Meanwhile, you took personal responsibility for a hot mess you'd known only for a few hours."

"Anyone would do the same."

"Nope. Only a good person would. A good person like you. A good person like Carson Hayes."

"Carson Hayes the third," I repeat, drawing his name out as I draw my fingers along a console table.

"You've both been good to me." The same as always, Rose is determined to play down the influence she's had on my life. "And this is just me, your friend, helping you out by hooking you up with the sweet apartment of one of my other friends while the boss part of me gets a realtor on the case. Besides, this place is perfect. It's only a ten-minute walk from here to school and then another five to your new office."

"Don't forget you're also the friend who got my child into the same school as Angelina Jolie's kids, too. Did you know that her kids go to the Lycée?"

"Yeah?" She shrugs, unimpressed.

"And that the waiting list is huge—I checked before I saw the fee schedule because, ouch!" Despite my humorous delivery, my stomach twists uncomfortably. Lulu is my baby, and I want the best for her, but it's my job to provide for her, not Rose's. But there's no way I could pay for an apartment in Manhattan and the Lycée's fees myself. Not without a lotto win. "She's only in kindergarten. A year at a public school would've been okay."

"I know." She shrugs lightly. "But surely a French school will be better for Lulu. Familiar, at least. I'm allowed to look out for my goddaughter," she adds a little steely-eyed. "It's all part of my nefarious plan. A French-speaking school will be a reminder of all that's waiting for you. Which means less chance you'll fall in love with America and allow yourself to be poached by a US company." She taps her temple with her forefinger. "There's a method in my madness, girl."

"Positively Machiavellian," I utter dryly. "Of course I'll be back. France is our home."

"Good. So, you'll be coming back with a bilingual daughter."

"Well, I did leave with one," I reply, amused. "I know I sometimes threaten to take her back to the store I bought her from, but you get that's an empty threat, right?" An empty threat that Lulu pays absolutely no attention to anyway.

Rose just rolls her eyes.

"I would've just kept her French up at home." The lengths Rose has gone to to make our move a smooth one is a little embarrassing. And the one thing I was meant to take care of—finding somewhere to stay—and I cocked it up!

"Well, now you won't need to because she'll have friends and teachers who speak the language, so you can talk to her at home in that strange accent of yours."

"I'll have you know my people invented the language. You get that's why it's called English, right?"

"English-shminglish." But then something very particular glints in her gaze. "And maybe just maybe Lulu will find herself with hot single sports teacher—a hot single *French* sports teacher.

"I think four is a little young to be dating."

"And maybe," she continues, ignoring my sarcastic reply, "that hot sports teacher will have a love for trampolining . . . on beds."

"Surely, there's more chance of me meeting an American than a Frenchman. After all, we are in America."

"Except you've lived in France for years and never dated a Frenchman there. Not to my knowledge, anyway." That's because my dating days were pretty much over by the time Rose became my best friend. "And honey, take it from me, French men are far superior bed bouncers."

"Well, I've never dated an American—" It's not exactly a lie, even if my heart does a secret little jump at the knowledge that some American men excel at bed bouncing—"but I have actually dated a Frenchmen or two, and their bed bouncing skills weren't all that."

"You must've gotten a couple of duds. Besides, it's been so *long*."

"Yeah, yeah. I've probably forgotten how. But I've been busy with work and study and motherhood. You know, all that kind of shit."

"My ears heared a bad word!" Lulu calls from a room at the end of the hall.

"So long as your mouth doesn't repeat it," I call back.

"Go out on a date. Put on a dress and a little makeup. Let down your hair."

"Are you saying there's something wrong with the way that I dress?"

"You always look great. But you always wear activewear."

"Because activewear is my office wear." Or at least, it used to be. I suppose I'll have to dress a little bit more grown-up for working in Manhattan.

"But you wear it *all* of the time."

"It's also comfy," I offer with a shrug. I follow the line of her gaze to my footwear.

"Sneakers? Again?"

"Yeah, but they're leopard print," I reply a little defensively.

"I give up." If giving up means an exasperated shake of her head. "I guess if I had an ass like yours, I'd wear running tights all of the time, too."

"I love it when you lie to me about my long bum."

"Oh, hush up! Your ass isn't heading south."

"We both know motherhood has lengthened both my patience and my posterior."

"You carry on with your bad self. No, really, I love listening to that self-deprecating shtick."

"It's not schtick. It's my Britishness. I appreciate you, Rose." And because she's tenacious and thoughtful, a great friend and a fabulous person, I plant a smacker of a kiss against her cheek.

"Good. Then you can take me out to dinner and put it on your expense account."

"Feed you on the company dime?" I ask, turning to face her as I press a hand to my chest. "I'm sorry, but I'm not that type of girl."

"What the hell are you doing being my friend, then?"

5

FEE

"We'll stop there for tonight," I say quietly, folding the corner of the page and placing the battered paperback of *James and the Giant Peach* on the nightstand.

"Mummy, would you rather be Aunt Sponge or Aunt Spiker?"

I push up from the bed, preparing myself for tonight's game of *how many questions can I ask before mummy's head explodes*. "I think I'd rather be me." And boy, has it taken me a long time to get to this point. Almost thirty years, to be exact.

"Why?"

"Well, for starters, because I get to look after you and not James."

"Because boys are stinky," she says, her button nose delightfully scrunched.

"True story." And long may she think that way. "And I don't like peaches. The furry skin gives me the heebie-jeebies."

"Mummy? If you get dead, who will look after me?"

"I suppose it'll have to be mean old Aunt Spiker." As I

pull the duvet straight, refusing to entertain the possibility of not being here to look after my babe.

"Aunt Spiker is only in the book, silly!"

"Is she? Then I suppose you'd have to look after yourself. You can get a job, right? To pay the bills?"

"No! I'm only this many years old." Her hand shoots from under the covers, three fingers held high. "No, wait." I bite back a smile as Lulu uses her other hand to peel one more finger from her palm with the most exquisite look of concentration. "There. I'm this many now. Four!"

It's an easy mistake to make when you only turned four a couple of weeks ago. I have difficulty remembering how old I am, though I'm still blaming that on baby brain. I wonder if I'll still be able to use the excuse when *she's* thirty?

"Four years old," I repeat. "Definitely old enough to get a job. You could wash dishes. Stand on a stool so you can reach the sink."

"No!" The word is more giggle than anything else. "I *hate* washing dishes."

"Then I'd better take care not to die." I bend to press my lips to her head.

"Mummy? Why do we got to share a bed when this house has so, *so* many of them?"

"*Have* to share a bed," I correct, tucking the duvet around her little body.

"Persactly!" she replies, her palms raised to the ceiling. My child is a touch dramatic. "Why do we gots to?"

"Well, first, Goldilocks, there are only five beds besides this one and—"

"I'm not Goldilocks," she replies with a giggle. "My hair is brown, not gold like yours."

Gold is a definite improvement on yellow, which is

how she's described it in the past. But just as my hair isn't yellow, Lulu's isn't brown, and as I run my hand over her head, the silky strands gleam in the lamplight. Her hair is so much more than just brown.

"Your lovely locks are chestnuts and honey and toffee and all kinds of colours. Plus, really squeaky clean. Listen." I make a squeaky noise as I rub the ends, and her giggle deepens.

"My hair isn't squeaky or made from toffee!"

"It's the colour of toffee." I inhale deeply then add, "it smells as good as toffee, too. Better be careful. I might eat it in my sleep and then you'd have to go to school bald."

"I can't go to school bald! Where would I put my wibbons? You're silly, Mummy."

"Yes, very silly."

"And silly for choosing this bed." Her little finger prods the mattress at her side.

"What does it matter, Princess Toffeelocks? We could be living in a castle with a hundred beds—and you might try every one yet *still* end up crawling into my bed during the night." Lulu begins to squirm and cackle as I tickle her sides, though I stop when I recall I've been suckered into the game again.

"It's because my sleepy arms miss you," she answers, wrapping them around my neck. Oh, Lord. How could anyone resist such flattery? "But why do we sleep in *this* woom?" She throws her hand out in the direction of the drapes; drapes that conceal a window overlooking a brick wall. "I want to sleep in one where I can see the sunshine and the tweetops in the morning."

It's hard to ignore the twinge of guilt. Despite Rose's insistence that we make ourselves at home I'd moved our bags into the staff quarters, even if I can't 'persactly, I mean exactly, say why. It's not like staying in this room has prevented me from frisking Lulu every morning before we leave for school. And it's not like we don't watch TV in the room Rose called the den. And if we're not in the den, we're making use of the fabulous kitchen. But something prevented me from unpacking our bags in one of the other five much plusher bedrooms. It's almost like this is a stay in an expensive hotel that I anticipate being unable to settle the bill for, or that I'm expecting to be stuck in the kitchen washing dishes because I can't afford to pay for my meal.

Like I said, it makes no sense, but here we are.

"Eloise Rose, you know what Grandpa would say about you? You have champagne tastes but beer pockets." At least, that's what he used to say about me along with the advice that I should get myself a rich boyfriend, funnily enough.

"Beer is yucky. I jus like lemonade."

"Which you're not allowed."

"'Sept when Grandpa gives me some. I don't like this stinky bedwoom." She folds her arms across her chest, her bottom lip protruding with extreme sulkiness.

"We're not going to be here for long." Though we've already been here a little over two weeks. Two weeks and Lulu seems so settled, especially in school, which I suppose proves Rose was right about settling her into a French-speaking school, even one where she's rubbing shoulders with the children of celebrities. Thankfully, Lulu is more impressed by how many Jellybeans her peers can fit into their mouths at once than who their parents are.

"Welp, I don't like this room."

"It's well, not whelp. A whelp is a puppy." I realise my

mistake before the complete statement is out of my mouth.

"Oh! Can we have a puppy? Please?" She presses her hands together as though a little prayer might help.

"We've had this conversation. We can't have a puppy. Not yet. Not until you're older."

"But I am older, remember? I'm one more year older," she reminds me, holding out her forefinger.

"You need to be at least another four more years older. That's the deal." And I hope to God we'll be in a position to have a dog come then or that her priorities (read: obsession) change.

"Welp, that thucks big hairy ones." Brows drawn together, she crosses her arms over the duvet again.

"I beg your pardon?" For some reason my mother's voice comes out of my mouth, and not for the first time. "Where on God's green earth did you hear such words?" Sucks big hairy ones? She didn't hear that from me. At least I hope she didn't. I'm usually much more circumspect when she's around.

"I heared it at school. And it does suck—and so does this bedroom. It sucks great big hairy ones!"

"Shows what you know," I answer, choosing to redirect because Lulu is shrewd enough to slot this phrase away as one she knows I don't want her to use, only to pull it out again somewhere much more embarrassing. Like in front of her principal, or the hoity-toity old lady from the floor below; the one who never returns my greeting when she steps into the elevator, but just looks down her nose at both of us. "Because this room is closest to the kitchen and tomorrow is Saturday. You know what that means, don't you?'

"Pancakes!"

"Exactly. Pancakes for breakfast. And because our bedroom is nearest to the kitchen, we'll be eating those pancakes in record time."

Her little face scrunches up. "I thought you said we were eating them in the kitchen?"

"I just meant we're closer so we'll be eating them sooner."

"I'd still like to see the sunshine, though."

"Then maybe we can eat them on the terrace, but only if you go straight to sleep." I don't want my child to get used to living in the lap of luxury, but I'll feed her breakfast on the terrace overlooking Central Park? *Because that makes sense.* "It's time to go to sleep. Snuggle in and I'll be back to join you soon."

"After you've had your night-time wine?"

I pause, denial on the tip of my tongue. But what the hell, no one can judge me for my glass or two of mummy medicine at the end of a long and stressful week.

"Yes, I'll be coming to bed after I've had my glass of wine. Night, night, sweetheart."

"I like it better when you call me your little cream puff," she mutters, turning over to face the other way.

"*Bonne nuit, mon petit chou,*" I whisper, turning off the light as I leave the room.

I make my way into the kitchen, the *designer* kitchen that's all marble countertops and sleek cherrywood cabinets, and pull out my eight-dollar bottle of white from the huge Subzero fridge.

Happy Friday to me, I think as I splash a generous amount into a glass. And the fun doesn't stop here because as well as this goldfish bowl of wine, I'm also going to have a long, lingering bath. The kind that will turn my fingers and toes wrinkly. The height of decadence; a bath with candles and wine!

Oh, the things that excite me these days . . .

I hang around the kitchen long enough to be sure Lulu won't wander out from the bedroom with more questions, finding my glass of wine woefully empty by the time she finally falls asleep. How the first glass always disappears so quick seems to be one of life's many mysteries. I'm mildly disappointed I didn't buy two bottles earlier in the week as I take off my glasses and tuck my—our—jointly owned iPad under my arm and make my way deeper into my self-imposed forbidden territory. In other words, the apartment.

The maid's room suits our needs fine, I tell myself, and not for the first time. It's big enough for the queen bed and chest of drawers and nightstand it contains. There's a little tub chair and a small walk-in closet, currently housing our luggage. But when it comes to the bathroom, the description 'woefully inadequate' doesn't quite cover it. It's tiny and more like a broom cupboard than anything else. The floor-to-ceiling subway tiles were probably fitted the last time they were in fashion, though I'm not sure green was ever quite the thing, along with a toilet, basin and shower unit all in Pepto Bismal pink. Even if there was a bath, there's no way a girl could relax surrounded by those colours. By contrast, the bathroom in the master suite would rival the platinum suite at *L'Hôtel du Loup* back in Monaco. Dark and masculine, the L-shaped space just screams luxury with its double vanities and a shower big enough to party in. But the focal point is a freestanding bathtub so deep that, when filled, the water comes up to my chin. While there are other tubs in the apartment, four more to be exact, they aren't in bathrooms quite as lavish as the master with its marble surfaces and richly decadent black and gold. Also, none of the other tubs let me stretch out my legs without touching the edge.

It's like floating on a watery cloud.

I light a couple of candles that I'd picked up in a dollar store on my lunch break yesterday and flick the lights off as the tub begins to fill. And I'm sure Carson Hayes III won't mind if I use a little of his fancy looking bath soak.

"Bergamot and peppermint," I read aloud from the label. *It's probably good for arthritic joints,* I think as I twist off the cap and pour a decent amount to the running water. Bubbles begin to form almost immediately. "How decadent, Mr Hayes," I murmur to the empty room with more approval than reprove.

As strange as it is staying in the home of a man I've never met, I feel that by living here, I'm gaining a kind of understanding of him. Well, as much as any ordinary person can because rich people are their own species. I mean, who owns a place as gorgeous as this and doesn't live in it? Does he live somewhere even nicer? Is there even such a place? By Rose's reckoning, he has a wandering soul, which sounds like a romantic way of saying he doesn't have a proper job. Probably because he doesn't need one; one look at this apartment and I just know he's old money.

But Carson Hayes III is also a lot of other things. At least by my deductions. He is quite a bit older than me and a man of taste and culture. A man who derives joy in taking care of himself. And there's nothing wrong with that. His clothes are timeless yet understated; a peek in his closet reveals tailored suits, cashmere sweaters, and brogues in shades of neutral and monochrome.

He takes care of his body; works out. Maybe he runs.

Whatever his exercise of choice, he does it in expensive running shoes. There are several well used pairs in the hall closet. *Size 11, if you're interested.* And speaking of sizes . . . I believe he's blessed in bulge department. Or delusional. Anyway, he orders extra-large condoms and keeps a small stockpile in his bedroom closet. *Maybe he got them on special?*

But the man is urbane and sophisticated and a lover of fine things, from the staples in his kitchen cupboards to the high-end products in his bathroom.

Speaking of which . . .

I leave the bath running and take the short route to the dining room because I also seem to know he's the type of man who orders a bottle, never a glass, and insists on settling the bill. He's not so gauche that he'd suggest splitting it. One look at his drink's cabinet—scotch, cognac, vodka, gin, several bottles of each and all luxury brands—tells me that Mr Hayes is generous. Or else he has a drink problem.

The former, I'm pretty sure. Because if the definition of generosity isn't allowing strangers to stay in your home, I don't know what is. So I'm sure he won't mind if I help myself to a splash of his twenty-year-old Macallan.

Inhaling the earthy smokiness of the whisky, I amble back to the bathroom comfortable in the knowledge that Carson Hayes III doesn't sweat the small stuff. In fact, I bet he doesn't even make a peep when his bedroom partner inserts their digit up his derriere, judging by the toys he keeps.

I know, I know; my snooping had become a little invasive this week, but the man has a whole drawer dedicated to the pursuit of sexy times.

Which leads me to believe he's a man's man and

someone really comfortable in his own skin. And while I can't be absolutely sure, I think he might be gay. Maybe bi? But definitely sexually adventurous.

My final observation, as I wander through the small library, re-examining the spines on the shelves, is that he's at least fifty years old.

The Odyssey.

All Quiet on the Western Front.

Lettres à une Amie.

Inferno, Canto 26.

Cicero; The Life and Times.

These are all books about old men. Older men probably read books about old men, right? It stands to reason. The older they get, the easier they become annoyed by things outside of their spheres. Reading about their contemporaries (i.e. older men) probably provides some level of comfort to them.

Back in the bathroom, I place my glass on the conveniently placed quatrefoil table before taking one of the artfully rolled towels from under the open vanity. They're probably just for show, but oh well.

My phone *bings* with a text from the real estate agent Rose has put me in contact with and, as the bath continues to fill, I open the link and begin to flick through the list of potential apartments.

Too pricey.

Too swanky.

Too far away *and* too pricey.

Too no!

This mothertrucker must think I'm loaded. Maybe I should take Bethany, my new colleague, up on her offer of help. A native New Yorker's input might be useful. That is, a native New Yorker who hasn't been dazzled by Rose's company profile and the knowledge that she's married to one of France's wealthiest men.

Google has a lot to answer for, if you ask me.

The bath is almost ready, and the room is filled with steam and the bitter-rich scent of bergamot as I strip out of my clothes. I pile my hair on top of my head and step into the tub while the last inch of hot water continues to cascade from the tap.

"Ooh! OW! Hot! Annnd . . . " I slide lower letting the hot water lap almost around my ears. "Utter, utter bliss."

It's been a long day in an even longer week. Not that I don't like my job, but I've been shadowing Marta the dietician, and it's a steep learning curve.

Twisting the tap, I reach for my iPad, planning to catch up on what's going on in the world. I also reach for my glass, enjoying the way the whisky's smoky flavour rolls across my tongue. I read a few emails, catch up on news from home via the BBC news app, then idly flick through my social media. It isn't long before I'm served an advertisement for a new dating app.

And they say our phones don't listen to us. Or at least Rose maintains they don't. I'm not about to make myself a conspiracy theorist's tinfoil hat but if our phones are listening to us, they need to do a better job because those are some wasted dollars, serving ads for gay dating sites to me simply after I'd spent an afternoon with Charles?

You're all wasting your money, I think to myself, swiping past the image of a hot man advertising E-Volve, the dating company everyone seems to know about these days. I swipe back to the image, considering the model used in the ad. He is pretty hot. So pretty and so hot, in fact, that if I had a rub hub, I'd definitely add him to it.

A rub hub. A spank bank. A collection of images and

clips of attractive men to thoroughly objectify during my 'special alone time'. I snigger because if I had such a collection, I would sneakily label it on this iPad as my *to-do list*. Because it would be full of men I'd do.

Virtually, at least.

Because that's what my sex life is these days; virtual. Or rather, non-existent. And though it's that way by choice, I really don't know how any single parent could make time for dating and sex between waking and feeding and playtime, fitting a love life around work and study, school drop-offs, pick-ups, homework, ballet, swimming, and piano lessons and . . . and . . . the never-ending list that goes on. *And on*. Most single parents don't have the energy to brush their teeth at the end of the day, let alone prepare for a date.

I guess collating a collection of hot men for said rub hub would also be pointless because there's only one direction my mind travels to when I'm getting busy. With myself. And that's straight to Saint Odile and the man who gave me the hottest night of my existence. It's his face I see when I close my eyes and slip my hand between my legs. It's the weight of his body over mine that I imagine, and his husky tones I hear in my ear. No one else, real or imagined, does it for me.

It almost makes me wish I knew his name. That we'd conducted that night on a first-name basis, or that I'd snuck a look at his driving licence before sneaking out the door.

Or not. Because then my rub hub would be perving over his social media posts; analysing if the girl in his latest post is his friend or girlfriend.

After overthinking the matter for a few more minutes, it becomes clear I'm not in the mood to reminisce this evening. Instead, I soak, and I soak, topping up the hot water a few times until my skin is ridiculously prune-y and my scotch is but a drop in the bottom of the glass tumbler.

The combination of wine, whisky, and heat makes my limbs deliciously loose and my mind pleasantly carefree. I'm not drunk; not on one glass of wine and a nip of whisky. Okay, one *large* glass of wine and a decent pour of whisky, but I'm only a little squiffy. But it's not like it's a school night, and I am over eighteen. Plus, the front door is locked, and my child is sweetly sleeping. No one is about to stick a fork in the toaster, a teddy bear in the blender, or experience the sudden urge to become the next Picasso using a family-sized tub of bum cream as their medium. All is as it should be, so if mama wants to get a little . . . relaxed, this is totally a safe space.

Until I hear footsteps.

Not the pitter-patter of tiny bare feet but the heavy, manly kind of footsteps.

Footsteps with a direction and a purpose.

Footsteps coming this way.

Oh, shit!

The hairs on my arms stand pin straight despite the steam in room as I go from slightly sozzled to immediately panicked, sobering in more ways than one.

The water sloshes over the rim of the tub as I pull myself up quickly, my hands gripping the side of the tub. My heart misses a beat at the sound of a voice, and though I can't make out the words, it's definitely masculine. He also seems to be on the phone. Or talking to himself.

My fingers slide on the slippery surface of the tub as I try to climb out, and I end up half-submerged and spluttering. Then I realise this, whoever this is, is now in the master bedroom. My first fleeting thought is *intruder,* but he isn't exactly being quiet as the door to the bedroom closes. Closes definitely.

Okay, slams.

Shit! Oh, shit!

Do I get out?

Stay in?

Duck so low that I potentially drown?

Where is there a straw when you need one? This is all the turtle's fault. There's never a straw around when you want one!

I swallow over the lump in my throat before realising this isn't likely to be an intruder but a man returning to his home.

To his bedroom.

Possibly to his bathroom.

Please, Mr Hayes, don't need to pee!

I don't decide, my hand instinctively reaching for my towel as the door to the bathroom suddenly creaks open. Light floods the room, and I freeze with my boobs squashed to the side of tub and my arm outstretched. From the corner of my eye, a blur of black and white and tan crosses from one side of the bathroom to the other.

Black, white, and tan isn't a beagle. It's a man. A man with his phone pressed between his ear and his raised shoulder as he untucks his shirt from dark suit pants. He begins to unfasten his watch, then his cufflinks, dropping each to the vanity, barely sparing it a glance. Which is just as well because, mirror! A mirror I can just about see myself in. And oh, my Lord, Carson Hayes III isn't a fifty-year-old man. I find myself squinting in his direction, guessing he's somewhere around thirty-five. And with a profile that looks like it could've been carved from marble.

Unless . . .

Maybe Carson Hayes likes men around that age, and this is his boyfriend? If so, I approve of his taste. He obviously likes the whole Wall Street titan look on his men. And then I realise I'm getting a little off track as he dips out of sight, swallowed by the recessed shower, his voice echoing off the hard surfaces.

"This has fucked up my whole weekend." *American? Why do I find this surprising?* "I just got home." *So probably not a boyfriend of Carson Hayes but the man himself?* "The flight was redirected. Yeah, a total ball ache, in more ways than one." His deep chuckle reverberates through the space. "I'll be in the city for the weekend, at least."

The subsequent sound of cascading water muffles the rest of his words, which is just as well because, what the what what? The whole weekend?

It's awkward enough that he obviously doesn't remember he loaned out his home, but I *do not* need to be discovered naked in his bathtub, for crying out loud! I need to get out of here before—

Motherfluff!

He strides across the bathroom once more—the man will wear a hole in the tile at this rate—pausing halfway between the shower and door, still holding his phone. And also his shirt.

I wonder if Carson Hayes the first and second were ever as ripped as the third, because the 3.0 version has shoulders and biceps for days. Plus, he has an ass only a blind girl wouldn't notice. *Thick,* my mind unhelpfully supplies. And yes, I'm still squinting, but I'm pretty sure the eventual crow's feet will be worth it.

He undoes his belt onehanded, the fly of his pants next, and like a magician's tablecloth, his pants disappear.

The long line of his toned thigh is almost bronze in the light, and by the bulge in his black boxer briefs, he's buying the right-sized prophylactics.

"Yes, I'm aware." His voice brings my attention back to his conversation. And his frown.

I too am aware. Aware that I suddenly feel very hot. But please, as lovely to look at as you are, please, please *go away. Let me climb out of the bath and escape before you actually see me—see more of me than we'd both be comfortable with!*

As though hearing my plea, he grabs one of the nicely folded towels and walks back into his bedroom. But the water in the bath scarcely has time to swish with my movement before he's back again.

Those poor floor tiles—

Wait. The man is naked.

NAKED!

And in profile. And sorry Lord for taking your name in vain for the eleventy hundredth time today, but sweet baby Jesus, the man is put together well. So well put together I think he might've been at the front of the queue when penises were being handed out. Or maybe he was at the back and was given his allotted amount plus whatever was leftover that day. And let me tell you, that day there was *a lot* leftover.

Myopia be damned; I don't need to do the short-sighted squint to see that.

But no sudden movements, Fee, or the mega penis might move closer.

Just slide your hands back into the tub and wait until he's in the shower before you make your move.

And so I do, and when he disappears once more, the sound of the shower door opening and banging shut, and I waste no time in clambering up. Which, as it turns out, is a mistake as he appears in front of me, the big ole shower-faker, only this time, he's facing the mirror above the marble vanity, his eyes on his phone as he taps something out.

My heart bangs so hard against my chest I'm sure if I glanced down, it would look like it's trying to escape, cartoon style. But that has to be the least ridiculous aspect of my predicament as my hands grip the sides of the tub, my body crouched half in and half out of the water. But not even my position stops me from some major ogling.

The rear view is . . . sublime.

He is a honey-hued marble carving of Zeus come to life. Deltoids, lats, and obliques; I'm able to name a half dozen more muscles thanks to many hours of study for my degree. But I'm not looking at him as a clinical specimen, not the way my eyes devour. And while my examination probably happens over the course of seconds, the moment seems to be endless, my gaze sweeping over those firm globes one more time before climbing the strong line of his spine and over one broad shoulder . . . to where his gaze meets mine in the mirror.

Fudge knuckles.

Fucksicles.

Oh, fuck!

This is not good.

6

FEE

Oh man, those eyes.

Why do they dance with amusement and not shock?

Panic overcomes my questions as I reach blindly for my towel, knocking it from the table and out of reach instead. Shock hits first, quickly followed by its good friend horror, embarrassment bringing up the rear end while also causing me to drop back into the water. *With the kind of splash worthy of a breaching orca.* I swipe up the muslin cloth on the side of the tub that I'd used to wipe off my makeup with no attention to spare for the empty whisky tumbler I knock to the floor. I hurriedly slap the small square of fabric to my boobs, but even with my forearm securing it to my chest, it's hardly what I'd call full coverage.

"I find there's nothing quite like a hot bath to help you wind down."

"I beg your pardon?" My answer isn't quite immediate, but sounds so very *mummy-ish* as, in the mirror, his expression reveals nothing but a barely-there smirk.

"A hot bath and a few fingers." He turns and leans

back against the vanity. Folding his arms across his broad chest, taut muscles elongate and flex in the process. His obliques look like some form of body armour, honed and pointing to—

Focus, woman.

No—not on *that*!

Focus on the situation before your eyes fall out of your head from strain.

Wait. Did he just say . . .

"I'm sorry, but are you talking about masturbation or the scotch in this instance?" I'd like to glance at the glass, but I can't seem to move my gaze from his. Okay, so I'm lying. I'd like to drop my gaze to an entirely different place, but that wouldn't be helpful and only encourage more staring.

"We could pretend I meant scotch. To be polite."

And, oh, my Lord, the man has the kind of voice that could narrate whisky commercials and sell crates of the stuff. *Smooth. Manly. Tempting.* Maybe that's why his voice seems sort of familiar. Maybe I've heard his work.

"Are you in the habit of discussing masturbation with women you've just met?"

"You'd be surprised how often it comes up."

With the mention of up, my gaze, of course, goes down. Can a person get heatstroke from a steamy bathroom? Because I think that must be what's wrong with me.

What's wrong with me?!

"Please don't say anything else." I hurriedly cover my eyes with my hand. "This is a highly inappropriate conversation." One that I can't believe I'm taking part in. "And please cover yourself."

"That hardly seems fair when you aren't. Though some gifts aren't meant to be wrapped."

"I'm *not* a gift."

"Our definitions differ."

"This is ridiculous," I begin to splutter. "You shouldn't be here—you shouldn't look. A gentleman would excuse himself and leave the room."

"This is *my* bathroom. By my reckoning, you should be the one to leave." His silky-toned words are nothing but a ploy, given the way his gaze roams over me.

But leave?

Right now?

"Oh, I'm sure you'd just love that, wouldn't you?" I mutter, scanning the immediate vicinity for something that might help when his eyes follow mine to the fallen towel, correctly calculating that it's out of reach.

"Maybe you should give it a try to find out."

"What are you doing?" I squeak as he suddenly pushes off from the vanity, negligently pulling a towel from behind him before wrapping a towel around his hips.

"You want me to lose the towel," he taunts, his hand at the knot. "You're right. Lose the towel."

"No!" I'm not sure anything would be evened out, judging from the slight tenting to the downy fabric that I can't help but notice now.

Honestly, it's hard.

Hard not to look, I mean.

The other thing isn't. You know. *Hard*. But it's getting there.

While also getting closer as he saunters my way.

With a jolt of panic, I slide a little deeper into the water before my mind registers the lack of bubbles on the surface of the water at this point. I grab the natural sponge balanced on the corner of the tub, a sponge I'd purposely ignored up until this point because what kind of person uses someone else's sponge, a sponge that has rubbed goodness knows to what bodily bits and crevices? But need overrules everything else right now as I plunge the sponge into the bathwater, squeeze it, then press the water-heavy lump over my nether bits, strategically covering them—covering it?—with both the sponge and my hand.

With a quick glance at my coverings, I glance back up at him, another reprimand at the ready, when the words die on my tongue.

That taunting voice. It's familiar. I *have* heard it before.

Those eyes, those cheekbones, and that sharp bicuspid I just know I'll see when his lips curve into a spontaneous smile.

Oh, my God.

I'm familiar with these features because I *know* this man.

Can it really be him? Half a world and half a lifetime away, or so it feels.

My nameless lover. My mountain rescuer and my one and only ever one-night stand. It's not like I'd ever forget him, even if I'd never set eyes on him again after that night in a little hotel on the side of a mountain. Barefoot and my hair in disarray, I'd made my way back down to the garage. I'd put the ridiculous cost of the tow and a new tyre on my credit card, asked for directions back to Nice, and drove Fred out of the little village without once looking back. Physically, at least, because I've looked back on that night so many times in my memory.

As hot as he was from the other side of the bathroom, up close, he's so much more . . . everything. And exactly as

I remember him. That's not exactly true, I realise as he seats himself on the edge of the tub. His hair seems darker, and the creases around his eyes a little more pronounced. He seems sharper, larger if that's possible, and a lot more intimidating.

"It's impolite to stare," I murmur, dragging my gaze from his, not exactly sure which of us the reprimand was for.

"Fair's fair, beautiful. You had a real good look at me."

"I am not having this conversation." I angle an imperious gaze his way. Though, by his amused response, you can't channel imperious when you're lying like a prune floating in a puddle. "I'm certain this isn't how you're supposed to react finding a strange woman in your bathtub."

"No? Well, it's never happened before. Maybe I'm not sure how I'm supposed to behave."

"I think you do, but you're ignoring the instinct anyway. You might make an effort not to look so delighted," I mutter, my attention sliding away again, though not entirely from embarrassment. Because looking at him is like staring at a light for too long. *Dizzying.* "You're pretty much holding me hostage in your tub."

"You're unrestrained. Free to leave anytime." There's a certain note in his tone, something I can't quite put my finger on. Something a little thrilling, perhaps. I like it more than I should as I continue to quiver, not entirely unpleasantly, hiding behind a bit of cheesecloth and a sponge. As if the situation wasn't confusing enough or awkward enough, the sponge chooses this moment to float to the waterline with a watery *pop* and an accompanying bubble.

I'm not even going to bother denying *that,* even if farting from nerves is an actual thing, according to my dad. I might be nervous, but not to the point of flatulence as I fish the sponge closer with the tips of my fingers, trying to tactically float it now in such a way as to protect my modesty.

As if that boat hasn't already sailed.

This is so trippy. Past meeting present with the audacity to look as delicious as my memories, memories I'd told myself had to be rose-tinted. Sadly, I'm not sure he can be thinking the same. He obviously doesn't even remember me. Which is a good because now there's nothing to compare me against. It's been almost five years since any man has seen me naked—since this man has seen me naked—and I'm pretty sure it would've been at least five more before I was ready to change that. I'm in pretty good shape—I teach yoga, eat well, and exercise—but I haven't had the time or the focus to allow a man in my life, never mind letting them see me naked. And my body is very different from . . . does he not recognise me because I look so different or I was just one in a long line of anonymous women?

And then another thought hits.

Oh, God, this is Carson Hayes. The third version! I'm pretty much naked in front of Rose's friend! I take the opportunity to look at him, really look, not his broad shoulders or pecs, but as the sum of his well-put-together pieces. I can't believe it's the same man, yet he is.

All this time, so close yet . . .

Oh, hell. I've screwed Carson Hayes. How am I ever going to explain this to Rose?

"You're not takeout," he murmurs ponderously,

completely unruffled by my immediate frown. "Are you a birthday gift?"

"Is it your birthday?" It's probably not the question I should be asking, but it's the one that falls out of my mouth.

"I'm always open to receive gifts in advance."

"You can't gift people." At least, you ought not to be able to.

"Not even willing ones?"

"I'm—"

"Now, don't go and spoil it. Let me see. I recently read about a naked cleaning service in the city, but the question is, what exactly are you here to clean?" His finger dips into the water by my ankles, swirling it. We both watch the whirlpool-motion before his gaze rakes over me, heavy-lidded and hot, coming to rest on the muslin bra top. My body reacts viscerally, like a muscle memory it had forgotten it possessed. My insides twist pleasantly, an ache building between my legs. "Or would that be service?"

How is this my mountain rescuer? My chevalier? My five-year fantasy? He was sexy before, sexy in my memories, but never this brazen.

"You don't happen to have a twin brother, do you?" I find myself asking. A bolder, though equally sexy identical twin? No, not quite identical. His hair seems darker. And his nose isn't as straight.

"Is that your subtle way of telling me you're too much for one man to handle?"

My mouth works silently, unable to deny his assertion in any kind of coherent form. The way he's looking at me? I don't think he's teasing.

In the absence of words, I shake my head.

"Good. I don't generally like to share."

I really don't know how to take that as his eyes flick to the sponge, something devilish sparkling in those indigo depths. This is the same man, I'm sure. He must just have an alter ego I hadn't the pleasure of meeting before. And frighteningly, I'm not so sure I don't like this version of him.

"If you could just pass me my towel. Please?"

"If you could just tell me what it is you're doing in my tub."

"Isn't it obvious?" I slap the water with my hand, which only serves to draw his gaze back to my (somewhat) nakedness. "I'm taking a bath."

"What kind of intruder breaks in to take a bath?" His lips quirk in the corners, lush and full between. "One who likes being punished or one who doesn't like to bathe alone?"

I inhale a sharp breath as his long fingers grasp my ankle, heat and the shock of it shooting up my leg as he pulls me closer to him. My reaction is purely visceral. It's like my body remembers the whole of it.

The whole of him.

Flustered and fluttering, I press my makeshift top back in place with a shaky hand. I raise my chin, though whether against the swish of the water or as a show of opposition, I'm not really sure. In fact, I'm not really sure about anything right now. I just feel hot. Incredibly heated. I really ought to get out of this bath.

"I-I'm Fee." Elbows clamped to my ribs, I readjust the sponge again. "I'm a friend of Rose."

"Rose?" His hand withdraws from both my ankle and my bathwater as he sits a little straighter. "You're not here from Ardeo?"

I shake my head, and though I wonder what Ardeo is, I don't ask. "She said you knew I'd be here. In your apartment, I mean. Not in your bathtub." Because I'm not a present. Or takeout, especially if that means what I think it means.

His whole demeanour changes in that instant. I can't describe or explain it, but it's like a coolness washes over him.

"Ah." He looks at me now, not like an illicit treat but like someone he might meet in the street. "A pity."

He didn't really expect me to fall out of his bath into his bed, did he? Not like I needed much persuading the last time, though he doesn't seem to remember. But back then, I called the shots, I remind myself. We were both into it and each other, but I booked the hotel room.

"Well, I guess I'm pleased to meet you." He holds out his hand, and ridiculously, I find myself shaking it. *With my elbows still tucked in.*

There is politeness, and there's ludicrousness. Rich people *are* another species.

"Rose said you wouldn't be here," I say in a small voice.

"There was an issue with my plane," he answers, moving from the edge of the tub.

His plane? His private plane? He really isn't the man I thought he was. *On so many levels.*

"I'm sorry to say you'll have to put up with me for the weekend."

"I-I'll book a hotel and get out of your way." *You know, in case you decide to order takeout and offer to share.*

"No need," he says, bending to retrieve my towel. "I told Rose that you should make yourself at home." He picks up the whisky tumbler next, cupping it in his palm.

"There's just one thing." I'm not sure if he mindlessly or purposely taps two fingers against the glass. I don't think he means it suggestively, but my cheeks pink all the same

"Of course." My answer is automatic because he's doing me a favour. There are bound to be *things.* Remember to rinse the tub? Don't put your feet on the sofa? Try not to break the family heirlooms?

"I suppose I should ask if you want the good or the bad news first." As he speaks, he begins to step backwards, and the movement has nothing to do with manners and everything to do with teasing me. This I understand even if I don't understand very much else.

"The bad." As though drawn by his removal, I find myself sitting up, my bent knees and crossed ankles aiding my modesty. *Hopefully.* "It's always better to end on a high note."

"Well, Fee, the bad news is you seem to have chosen to make yourself at home in my bedroom. The good news is the bed is big enough for two, and I'm excellent at sharing."

My mouth falls open, but before I can formulate a response, he winks and steps out of sight.

7

CARSON

"Your pancakes taste better than Mummy's."

The little girl seated across the island pats her rosebud mouth with a napkin, the picture of sweetness.

"The secret's in the buttermilk," I answer, putting down my own plate.

"Buttermilk?" she utters, stretching it over three syllables, "That's not a real thing. Butter is butter, and milk is milk."

"And buttermilk is buttermilk."

"Hmm." Her expression twists as she runs her finger through the smear of maple syrup left on her plate. "Mummy only buys soya milk," she says with a sigh. "It's good for died-geshtun."

Oh, shit.

Maybe even literally.

"You're not allergic to dairy, are you?" She glances up blankly. "Does milk make you sick?" This time, she shakes her head. "You and Mommy aren't vegan, by any chance?" Another shake, thank God. The last thing I need are more fuckups after last night.

I'd had a couple more drinks than was usual on the flight and a couple more when it became apparent I wasn't going to be spending my weekend between the thighs of . . . a willing woman, whose name currently escapes me. Instead, I was going back to Manhattan, a little drunk and a lot horny, and without the expectation of discovering the X-rated version of Goldilocks in my bath.

Was Goldilocks even English? Somehow, her accent just added to the authenticity. *The familiarity?*

I thought—well who the fuck knows what I thought. In all honesty, I can't blame the liquor, but maybe I can blame my upbringing because I was taught never to question any gift. I also wasn't about to question the origin of such a gift, assuming one of the fuck heads at Ardeo had a hand in her delivery. Which makes the old adage about asses and assuming true. Goldilocks might've been looking for a bed, but she wasn't interested in getting into one with me.

It might not have seemed that way in the steam-filled room or even when she'd followed me from the bathroom to my bedroom. I'd turned to find her standing in the doorway, the downy towel covering her from chest to shin. My gaze had fallen over her curves anyway.

I almost made some quip about her not covering herself on my account when I'd noticed how she held the towel in a death-grip at her chest. She'd lifted her chin and announced imperiously that, for my information, she was excellent at sharing beds, too. More specifically, she'd be sharing a bed with her four-year-old daughter that night, '*so it was just as well I had hands because I was just going to have to bloody well entertain myself*'.

She'd stomped out without a backward glance, pretty

much leaving me with my dick in my hand. Figuratively, at least. Bad enough that I'd forgotten Rose's friend would be using the place, but I'd also forgotten she had a child.

Well, fuck.

I thought I'd read the signs pretty well in the bathroom. The way her eyes had darkened, the catch in her breath as I'd held her ankle, and the way her nipples puckered under their thin veil despite the heat in the room.

I guess her head won over her libido. For one of us, at least.

"This owange juice is yucky. It's got bits in it."

I glance up and find the little girl using the napkin to wipe her tongue.

"Yeah, bits of orange. It's called pulp, kid."

"Tastes like bum."

I set off laughing, biting back the inappropriate for the audience answer of I've come across a few peachy asses in my time, sometimes literally, but never savoured an orange juice-tasting one. "Those are the best bits," I answer instead.

"You are so wong," she counters seriously.

"I am, am I?"

"Yes. I jus don't have the time or the cwayons to 'esplain it to you," she answers with the kind of seriousness that sets me off laughing again.

Little Miss Lulu here had stumbled into the kitchen this morning while I was making coffee. Without removing the thumb stuck in her mouth, she'd mumbled something that sounded like '*Norman is hungry*'. Norman, I later found out, was the name of the stuffed bunny clutched under her arm. As I'd tried to work out what the hell I was supposed to do, she'd then pulled herself up onto a stool and announced that it was Saturday morning, and therefore, time for pancakes.

I, being the lady pleaser I am, acquiesced.

If I couldn't please the mother, the least I could do was please the daughter. Which is not the kind of statement I thought I'd ever make.

"I do like pancakes with bluebs."

"Pardon?" Pancakes with *what the fuck?*

As my mind plays catch-up, I let out a breath long and low. Bluebs. She said bluebs, which must be kid speak for blueberries. *Nothing to do with pubic hair.*

"That's what Mummy says all the time. I beg your pardon. I beg your pardon!" Her parody includes a scornful shake of her little dark head. It doesn't resemble the woman I'd found in my bath last night with big brown eyes, lithe limbs, and the ultimate blowjob mouth . . . which are thoughts inappropriate to be entertaining in the presence of a child. Especially as I realise she's still talking. She pretty much hasn't stopped since she'd turned up.

But she's a lot more fun than the run I had planned.

"She also says what the fluff *lots.* And when she's really annoyed, and she doesn't think I'm listening, she says *what the farrrk!*"

"What the fu—fluff is going on here?"

"Mummy!" Lulu scrambles down from the stool, throwing her arms around her mom's waist.

I stifle a smile. The pair may not look alike, but they are wearing matching nightwear. Unlike her daughter, sleep doesn't cling to the mother. In fact, she looks wide awake and more than a little unnerved and—

Holy fuck!

It wasn't Goldilocks she reminded me of. It was her—the girl from Saint Odile!

No way. I am not conversing with the succubus who haunts my dreams on a regular basis, the woman who I've been unable to dislodge from my head for the past few years. Another country, another lifetime, broken down on the side of the road at a time when it seemed like my world was falling apart. She isn't so much the one who got away as the one who disappeared after the most passionate night of my life.

Motherhood looks good on her. *She* looks good. And not at all like a sultry demon, her wild hair instead giving her the air of a lioness protecting her cub. And fuck me blind for noticing she's a little fuller now, fuller in all the fun places that count.

"Not fluff, Mummy." My attention is drawn to the little girl, devilment flashing in her blue eyes. Her blue eyes and dark hair against her mother's brown and blonde. "You know you want to say *what the farrrk!*"

I know I want to.

"Come here," the woman in pyjamas commands, ignoring both my rough interjection and her daughter's goading as she lifts her against her hip. "What have I told you about talking to strangers?" she asks in a stern tone.

"Strangers live outside." Lulu takes her mother's cheeks between her hands. "Not in the kitchen. Oh!" Her eyes suddenly widen, her head swinging my way. "Are you a house elf, Uncle Carson? Like Dobby? Was it you that washed my bre'fast plate yesterday?"

"You don't have an Uncle Carson," her mother hisses, her gaze warily sliding my way. "And I'm pretty sure elves aren't that big."

"Maybe the ones that eat their vegetables are exactly

this big." My biceps give a little flex, one Fee doesn't miss, even if she's quick to glance away.

"He isn't a house elf"— Fee's second glance seems to confirm I'm too big for the role—"and you haven't met him before, which makes him a stranger."

A stranger whose dick you happen to have sucked.

A stranger who's currently looking at a kid wondering just how old she is, mentally doing the math.

"But he can't be a stranger 'cause I knowed his name. He told me to call him Uncle Carson."

Her mother's gaze cuts to me so full of loathing it's as though she'd just overheard me ask Lulu if she'd like to earn some illicit candy. While I'm not ordinarily so Zen about being insulted in my own home, I'll make an exception in this instance. Mom wakes alone and finds her daughter hanging around with a strange man—I guess some would find me strange—but more to the point, a strange man who might be . . .

Could it be that I'm—

Fuck, I'll make an exception because I don't have the capacity for much else right now. Does she even recognise me herself? I take a good look at her and decide she does. The best offence is the good defence, right? And fuck knows she has an abundance of that. *Walls and walls of that shit.*

But what in the name of hell is going on?

"You don't know that man," she whispers fiercely. "You shouldn't be in here by yourself. Why didn't you wake me?"

"I tried, but you said 'five more minutes for fluffs sakes'." Lulu imitates a snuffling yawn. "Your five more minutes are always *so long,* and Norman's tummy was already talking to me."

"If I could just say something here." The mother's gaze cuts my way once more, still unimpressed, but thankfully, no longer revolted. "It was Fee, wasn't it?" To think Rose knew her all this time. "I *am* actually Uncle Carson. At least to Rocco."

"Really?" Funny how, with that kind of delivery, the word sounded more like 'bullshit'. "Rocco who?"

"You haven't forgotten who Rocco is already, Mummy!"

"Shush, Lu. I'm talking to the man." She may address her kid, but her gaze is all for me, even if it's not exactly flattering.

The man. Is that *the man from my past* or *the man from my past who . . .*

My gaze slides to the little girl again.

"Rocco is the son of Rose and Remy. Friends we have in common. Small world, right?" Her response? Nada. "They live in Monaco." Still nothing. Maybe she's trying to process the coincidence. Or maybe she's trying to work out how to tell me something I should've been told a few years ago. Except we never exchanged names, just a whole lot of heat and passion. The likes of which I'd never felt before or since.

You know what else we exchanged? Fluids. Maybe even a little of the accidental baby-making kind.

"The three Rs of the house Durrand? Imagine the confusion with their mail." At least she's trying to process this insanity with dignity. Meanwhile, I'm spouting garbage while trying to remember the failure statistics of condoms. "It's kind of ridiculous that they gave the kid the same initials."

"Ridiculously cute," she asserts, her words short and her diction sharp as she tightens her arms around her daughter as though I'm some sort of threat.

Is that another sign? Might I be—

Or maybe I was more of an ass last night than I thought.

I push my hand through my hair and sigh. "I'm really only Rocco's honorary uncle but close enough that his parents trust me enough to be in his company."

"I've never seen you before."

"No?" I quirk a brow, my tone calling her out. *I know you remember it. No one could forget a night like that.*

"I-I meant at their house. You weren't at their wedding," she adds quickly.

That's right because there's no way that night could be a one-way remembrance.

"You could say Remy and I were estranged at that point."

"You weren't at Rocco's first birthday, either."

"That's not—" *My style*, I was about to say. "That is, I wasn't in the country at that point. I try to spend as little time on the Riviera as I can," I answer truthfully.

"None of this alters the fact that you don't know Lulu. Or me, for that matter."

"True. I don't know you as well as I'd like." That might've sounded a little suggestive, judging by the widening of her eyes. "That goes for both of you." Damn. I'm not at all sure that was any better.

"And you," she adds firmly, tightening her grip on her daughter, "you should've stayed in the bedroom with me."

"But it's Saturday, and Uncle Carson said he'd make me pancakes."

"If I overstepped the mark, I'm sorry," I add soberly, not truly sure if I mean I'm sorry for feeding her daughter an illicit breakfast or for suggesting I feed the naked woman in my tub last night something else entirely. Maybe sorry for the way I looked at her, for the things I said. Sorry for the later imagined acts of depravity inspired by the sight of her in my tub. "Blame the angels," I find myself muttering.

I see now what I should be sorry for is not recognising her.

"I'm Grandpa's little angel, aren't I, Mummy?"

Fee doesn't answer, her eyes as wide as saucers, her gaze fixed on mine as her whispered words fall in a rush. "Don't. Please don't say anything else."

The things I want to say to her aren't meant for our little audience because the things I want to say to her would only lead to the things I want to do.

To her. With her. And then start all over again.

"Can we start again?" Fee nods quickly because we can't go back. "I was making coffee when the kid came in, and I saw no harm in making her breakfast." How the fuck can my voice sound so completely normal when inside my head is complete chaos?

"I'm not the kid," the little girl complains. "I'm Lulu. Kids belong to goats. Children belong to people. Norman belongs to me, and Norman needed pancakes because his tummy was noisy!"

"That's very true. I could hear it from all the way over here. Which, by the way, is where I've been since Lulu came into the kitchen. Her and Norman on the stool and me over here." I gesture to the granite countertop between us. *No physical contact, inappropriate or otherwise, has been made.*

"I'm not suggesting . . ." Her words trail off, her fair eyebrows drawing together before she begins again, her tone a touch more even. "I'm not suggesting anything. But

Lulu couldn't have known for certain that you were familiar with Rocco and his parents."

Stranger danger for real. I thought for a minute she was concerned the kid had been inadvertently introduced to a parent. Or vice versa.

I can't be.

No.

Can I?

"I, er, showed her photos." I slide my phone out from the pocket of my shorts, my thoughts pinging around like the contents of a pinball machine. "You're welcome to view the proof." I swipe open the first photo of Rocco I find. We're on Remy's yacht, and I'm holding Rocco on my shoulders, who looks to be fifty percent lifejacket and fifty percent grin. I find myself smiling down at my phone before I remember who's supposed to be looking at this, so I slide it across the countertop towards her.

She bumps Lulu higher on her hip, taking a step closer to pick it up.

"Feel free to scroll. But maybe not too far . . ." I add an *aw, shucks* grin because that might've been a little too much truth.

"I want my juice." The kid begins to wriggle, obviously too long and too heavy to be held there against her will.

Fee puts down both my phone and Lulu, who inadvertently pulls a number of her mom's shirt buttons loose.

"Lulu!" she exclaims. As she clutches the sides together in her fist, her eyes meet mine, her expression an adorable pink.

Just when I thought this day couldn't get any better.

8

CARSON

"Just stop," she whispers, her eyes pleadingly wide.

"Of all the mornings not to be wearing my contact lenses."

"What about last night?" she mutters scornfully as she turns from me to refasten her shirt. Which is a little like closing the gate after the horses have escaped the corral. *Such pretty horses, too.* "Were you wearing your lenses then?"

"Last night? No." It's an honest answer. The lie is in suggesting I don't possess perfect vision in the first place. "Can I get you a coffee?" I turn, which allows her a little privacy, though it's mostly just to hide my growing smile. Aged nine, nineteen, or ninety, a man is hardwired to appreciate breasts, and an unanticipated glimpse or flash is the highlight of any day.

"Thank you, but no." She helps Lulu onto her stool before sliding onto one herself. "Don't drink so fast, sweetie."

The kid puts down her glass, her next words muffled

and spoken into the neck of her own pyjama shirt. "Mummy has big boobies."

They're certainly a good handful and bigger than I remember. Though I have sense enough not to say so as I pull out the jug of freshly squeezed juice from the fridge, turning back to her stifled groan and pinked expression.

"They say discretion is certainly the better part of valour." I push the jug across the countertop, her eyes rising to mine.

"And picking your battles is certainly a large part of parenthood," she murmurs, misinterpreting my point.

Is this where I should ask her about the kid's father? Obliquely? Abruptly? Ask her if the little girl currently wiping pulp from her tongue is mine? I open my mouth as my mind continues to spin, finding myself asking instead, "Is Fee short for Fiona?"

"It's short for Fiadh."

"Fear?" I repeat, turning from pulling a glass from the cabinet.

"*Fee-a.*" Not fear, not even close to it. There's something almost lyrical about the way she says her own name.

I place the glass in front of her as she eyes the jug, probably wondering where the juice came from, given there was very little of anything in the fridge. But you can't have breakfast without OJ, as far as I'm concerned. If I'm cooking breakfast, I'm doing it properly. Besides, what's the point of paying a concierge service tens of thousands of dollars each year if they can't get a dozen California oranges to your door in under thirty minutes?

"My mummy's name is Irish," Lulu announces. "And my real name is French."

"Lulu isn't your real name?' I splash a little juice into

the glass when it becomes clear Fee isn't going to do it herself. "I guess that must make you a spy or some kind of secret agent."

"I'm not a spy. I'm Eloise!" she says, giggling. "Eloise Rose Abernathy."

"*Bonjour, Mademoiselle Eloise.*"

"*Bonjour, oncle Carson,*" she intones, and her French accent is flawless. Rose did say her friend was relocating from France. What a head fuck that she's been within my reach all these years.

"*Eloise est aussi un très joli prénom.*" I speak in French mainly to distract my overworked brain, telling her she has a very pretty name.

"*Carson est un nom très amusant,*" she replies. Apparently, Carson is a funny name.

"Your French is very good."

"Thank you. So is yours."

"Drink your orange juice," Fee prompts her child.

"*Maman ne parle pas français?*" Mommy doesn't speak French? As my gaze glides to her, Fee sends me a withering look .

"Of course she does, silly!" Lulu giggles.

Yes, I know that. I remember that. And now it looks like I don't. Damn.

"It's not polite to call people silly." Along with the reprimand, Fee lowers her lashes almost demurely as I consider it's probably also not polite to mention her mom is the hottest woman I've ever held in my arms. That she's haunted my dreams. That I've been chasing the same kind of high since that fateful night.

An image of that night suddenly flicks to life in my head. On all fours, her blonde hair twisted in my fist as I pressed biting kisses to her lips, her long exhalation ringing through the room as I'd ease myself into her. My cock throbs suddenly at the images filling my head. Something about her manner is so proper, so tightly wound, and so unlike the carefree woman who'd booked us a room.

And I want her still.

I wanted her last night, and I want her now. I've wanted her every night I've thought of her since Saint Odile, wanted her so much it sometimes hurt. Not that this means anything right this moment. I'm hardly going to get to bend her over the countertop with the kid in the room, even if she looks at me like she worries I will.

The kid . . . Lulu.

Her kid. *Mine?*

She has my colouring and maybe even a little of the Hayes *go fuck yourself* attitude.

"We're going to the zoo today," Lulu announces, her eyes shining with excitement. "Do you want to come, too?"

"Mr Hayes is far too busy to come to the zoo with us."

"It's just Hayes. Or Carson, if you like."

Ignoring me, she turns to her daughter. "The zoo will have to wait until this afternoon. We have to find a hotel first."

"But you said—"

She cuts the kid off with a quelling look. "I know what I said." Neither her tone nor her expression is sharp, but the warning is still there. "But *Mr Hayes* is home now, so we need to find somewhere else to stay."

"Why?" The kid frowns, her mutiny marked in the jut of her tiny chin. "This 'partment is huge."

"She's right. There really is no need for you to leave." And no way am I ready for them to leave. Reaching for my coffee, I take a leisurely sip. "Not for space and not on my account."

Lulu seems to take this as answer enough, transferring her attention to her fluffy bunny.

You're going nowhere.

Because I need to know more about you.

About this.

About everything.

"This was only ever meant to be temporary." She gives a tiny but dismissive shake of her head. "We've outstayed our welcome."

"You were a pretty welcome sight to come home to last night."

"I can't believe you said that," she mutters, taking a sip from her glass.

"I can't believe you're drinking a roofied orange juice."

She immediately pulls the glass away from her lips before sending a reproachful look. "That's not funny."

"Not even a little bit?"

"I can't . . ." She lowers her voice, speaking quickly now. "I never thought I'd see you again."

"It's crazy, right? Talk about seven degrees of separation."

"More like just one."

"Rose," I agree, nodding slowly. What a mindfuck. All this time she's been within reach.

"I-I don't want. I need you to keep what has happened—"

"Keep it a secret?" Her response is an eager nod. "Which part? That we've met? That we go way back? That we've seen each other's genitals. That we've f—"

"What's gentiles?"

"I'm not sure *Mr Hayes* knows, sweets. But if he had any, he'd be at risk of losing them this morning."

"Okay." I hold up my hand. Message received and no further action necessary. Topics of conversation and language are hereby moderated for so long as there's a minor in the room.

"I bet he knows what a kick in the gentiles can do." Fee purposely keeps her gaze from mine, but I, and my balls, get the point loud and clear.

"Yes, but what are they?"

Should I point her in the direction of a Ken doll? Do they even still make those?

"I meant to say gentle, honey. But I'll speak more carefully from now on."

"My name isn't honey." The little girl giggles. "I told you already. My name is Lulu. And I bet you don't know that my mummy's name means wild?"

"That I did not know." But I can believe it. I turn my consideration to Lulu because I can't look at her mother right now. Not without wanting to take her shoulders in my hands, though whether to kiss her or shake some goddam information from her, I'm not so sure. What I do know is the only wild thing about her this morning is her hair. The rest of her is solemn and determined to remain serious. Aloof.

"It's funny because she's not the wild one. *I am.*"

"I don't know. Something tells me your mommy can be pretty wild sometimes."

"No, she isn't. My granny calls me bold. She says I'm a bold girl and not like Mummy at all. Oh! S'cuse me." Lulu clambers down from her stool quite suddenly. "I gots visit the little girls' room," she yells over her shoulder, her feet rapidly pitter-pattering on the tiles as she leaves the room.

"The girl I met in Saint Odile was bold." My voice is lower than I intended it to be, smoother. Something warm licks at the pit of my belly as her cheeks turn rosy again. "She was wild. And like fire, she couldn't be controlled." Her eyes widen as I step closer, bracing my hands against the island countertop, my shoulders popping and my biceps flexing as I bring my gaze level with hers. "There's a little wildness in everyone, angel. I guess it just takes finding the right person to bring it out."

"I-I should keep an eye on Lulu," she says, as she begins to slide from her own stool, but not before I reach out and catch her wrist.

"I still see the wildness in you. I saw it shining in your eyes last night."

"I have a daughter to tend to." The muscles of her arm taut, she utters the words through gritted teeth.

"A daughter that's gone in the wrong direction for the nearest bathroom."

"No, she hasn't." When she pulls, I let go, but she doesn't leave the room. Rather, she stands just out of my reach. "We're staying in the room just on the other side of the kitchen."

"There isn't a room. . . the maid's room?" What the fuck?

"It's perfectly adequate," she replies, cutting off any question as her expression firms. She might not think she's wild, but she's seriously stubborn. What kind of guest chooses to stay in the maid's room when there are five other far superior rooms available? "It's very kind of you to allow us to stay here, but we'll be moving into a hotel today."

"I get it. It's kind of embarrassing to bump into an old flame, let alone find out you're staying in their home."

"We are *not* old flames," she mutters.

"No? I don't know about you, but that night undoubtedly burned itself onto my memory." Nights when it rains. Nights when it doesn't. Sometimes when the moon is just right. I remember it all.

How could I not have realised this was her?

"You don't know what you're saying."

"You might like to think that, just as you'd like to think you'll be staying somewhere else tonight."

"What is that supposed to mean?"

"Easy, angel. I just meant you'll have difficulty getting a room without a reservation. Not without paying big bucks, I mean."

"Don't call me angel."

"It's how I've remembered you. Though I might've gone with Cinderella after finding your shoes in my car the next morning." The only trace of her that morning but for the raw scratches on my back and the lingering trace of her perfume. "How have you remembered me?"

"Who says I have?" She raises her chin a fraction higher.

"Maybe you didn't need to. Maybe every time you look at Lulu you see me."

A thousand emotions flicker and fade across her face, none of them making much sense. Pain? Sadness? Resignation, I recognise.

"No." She shakes her head, the muscles of her neck moving with her deep swallow. "The answer is no. You're not Lulu's father."

"You know that for sure?" My words are firm but not hard, and my relief? Non-existent. *Which is fucking weird.*

"Yes. I am."

"And I'm supposed to take your word for it?"

"Why wouldn't you?" she asks, looking genuinely confused.

And I'm grasping *why?* Shouldn't I be ecstatic that the kid isn't mine? She's cute and has buckets of character, but a kid? For a man who's professed the intentions of never being tied down, I seem kind of disappointed. *Feel disappointed.*

"Because I take care of what's mine, angel. And if—"

"Please don't." Her whisper is frantic, her posture seeming to almost roll inwards. "She's not yours because, if she were, she'd be a month older than she is, okay?"

"You're sure about that? About the date, I mean."

"I'm hardly likely to forget who I've slept with. Or when, for that matter."

"So you keep a diary?" I'm immediately aware of the misplaced derision in my response. The jealousy in my sneer. How many women did I fuck in the month before our mind-blowing night? More than I care to remember, for sure. Possessiveness isn't my thing. Live and let fuck is my usual policy. So why do my insides twist? Why do I suddenly feel the need to claim them both as my own?

"Some of us don't need to keep a record," she retorts. "Not that it's any of your business, but there was you, and before you, I had a boyfriend."

"And after? Now?"

"Neither are any of your business."

"So Lulu's father was your boyfriend," I assert, my tone flat.

"Yes. You're off the hook. For fatherhood and for accommodation."

"What about Rose?"

"What about her?"

"Do you want to tell her about us, or should I?"

"There is no us." Her eyes turn flinty, her words sharp-edged.

"One night is still a history. One night that could've easily spilled into another if I hadn't scared you last night."

She barks out an incredulous laugh, her spine suddenly ramrod straight. "I wasn't scared. I mean, you must find naked girls in your bathtub all of the time." She suddenly grabs Lulu's plate and silverware, rounding the island, and heads for the sink. "Do you feel compelled to tell Rose about them?"

"This is different."

"Oh, I'll say. But, of course, your behaviour was totally reasonable, so if there's anyone at fault, it must be me for not falling into your bed, right?"

"That's not what I meant, and you know it. And for the record, I wouldn't have complained." Instead, I would've worshipped her from the tips of her toes up.

"That was perfectly clear," she answers with a small huff.

"You know, there was a lot clear about last night." I keep my tone even as I stand behind her, the water continuing to pour from the faucet. As I bring my lips to her ear, her shoulders lift, and she sucks in a hard breath, her fingers gripping the edge of the sink. Just a whisper of air separates our bodies as I whisper, "Despite your efforts and your little outfit." Lightly drawing the tip of my finger from her shoulder to her wrist, my next words are nothing but a low rumble of desire. "I might have apologised for my behaviour, but I can never be sorry for seeing what I did."

I'm not entirely sure what I'm doing here, but I know I want her. How many nights have I been unable to sleep because of her? Imagining my hands gliding over her body, remembering the taste of her kisses and the moonlight on her skin. Her cries as I'd made my home between her legs. I've often wondered if I got a second chance whether I'd ever come up for air again.

She turns to face me, and for a moment, I think she might tip up on her toes and kiss me as pleasure twists at my insides. But she hesitates. *Vacillates.* Before pulling away. *Emotionally and physically.*

"What's Ardeo?" she asks, her attention falling to the towel she winds in her hands.

"It's just a friend's company." It's an answer that isn't strictly true, but if I tell her the truth, there's every chance she'll go running for the hills. And I don't want that.

"A friend's company that delivers girls?" She arches a brow, and I find myself smiling. I turn off the running water. The things that Ardeo can deliver would probably blow her mind. "Are you laughing at me?" she asks haughtily. "Or do you find everything funny?"

I pull open the dishwasher by her hip, causing her to step back. After dropping the dishes onto the appropriate shelves, I face her while keeping my expression purposely blank.

"You know, you didn't exactly run screaming from the room."

"No, because you pretty much held me captive in your bathtub." Her voice wavers, but it isn't fear that causes her to take a step backwards or her eyes to shine as I take a predatory step after her. Another, and another, as she backs herself up against the pantry door. Toe to toe, I allow my gaze to fall over her. I'd like to show her what being held captive really means. To take her hands and press them above her head. To kiss her until her knees are weak and the only thing holding her up is the hand I press between her legs. I'd keep her on the edge for so long that she'd cry, then make her come so hard she'd swear she saw stars being born.

"That's not true, though, is it?" I brush the wildness of her hair from her face, run my hand over her shoulder, my other hand pressed into the wall by her head. "You didn't ask me to leave. Ask me not to look."

Jesus, I haven't enjoyed a breakfast like this in a long time, even if my usual appetite runs to the kind of breakfast in bed that doesn't come until I tell her to and certainly never involves orange juice. A breakfast in bed, yes, but with more body parts and a lot less talking

"I-I said a gentleman wouldn't look." Her dark gaze slides from mine. She knows the way she'd implied I was no gentleman in sultry, husky tones isn't the same as screaming bloody murder and yelling for me to get out.

"But it wasn't a gentleman you were interested in. It was me. I think it's still me." I settle my hand on her pyjama-clad hip as I angle my head. "You liked me looking at you, just like the girl in Saint Odile. You look at me as though you were about to—"

"This is madness. You're mad." She lifts her chin, her fiery gaze two narrow slits. But she's not fooling either of us. "You should wipe that smile off your face."

"Why don't you do it for me?" With your mouth. With your kiss.

"I insult you, and you smile?"

"I've been told I have a winning smile."

"I'm sure you don't need my compliments."

"But I'm open to them."

"Who are you?" Her eyes widen a touch as though no

one has ever sparred with her. Wanted her. As though no one has ever hung on to her every word.

"I'm Uncle Carson. Didn't you hear?"

"I wonder if Rose knows Uncle Carson sometimes *orders in* from time to time," she says, changing tack.

"Are you implying I look like the kind of man who needs to pay for sex, angel?"

"Let me go," she answers, but there's little conviction in her words.

"Tell me the truth. You like me looking at you . . . touching you."

She turns her head, exposing the elegant column of her neck as she presses her hands to my chest. "Stop playing with me."

"Who's playing?"

"Just stop. Please stop." Her fingers curl in the soft cotton at my next words.

"I've never forgotten you." As our eyes meet, her gaze is full of such longing that it almost knocks me off my feet. She tightens her grip, her soft sigh blowing against my cheek, our lips drawing closer as though magnetised. "I would've drunk your bathwater just to get a taste."

Her breath hitches and—

"Eww, that's disgusting!"

We spring apart, Fee's eyes wide with panic.

"Uncle Carson, didn't your mummy ever tell you that you can only play pretend in the bath? No drinking the water. It's not howgienic." Lulu's gaze turns suspicious as she plants one hand on her non-existent hip. "What were you two just doing?"

"Nothing," Fee answers quickly. "We weren't doing anything. Why? What were you doing?"

"I went to the bafroom." I don't fail to feel the weight

of Lulu's attention zoning in on me, even if I am currently looking at her over my shoulder. *No need to invite questions about why I have a tent pole in my pants.* "Were you trying to kiss my mummy?"

Yes, yes, I was. Item number one on my new wish list.

"My goodness, whatever makes you think that?" Not only does Fee's response sound a little manic, but so does her burst of forced laughter. "Carson was just telling me a secret." Her mother's manic smile doesn't appear to fool the kid. "Weren't you?" she demands, her gaze swinging to me.

"I'm not sure it was a secret." I don't bother to bite back a sly grin.

"Oh! Look at the time. Time to go to the park!" Still using the same overly bright tone, she skirts around me and my hard-on.

I grab a towel as I turn and notice the kid eyeballing me suspiciously.

"Come on, sweetie. I think we should go and get dressed." Taking her hand, she almost drags the kid from the room.

Damn. You can't blame a man for hoping things would've moved in the other direction.

9

FEE

"Mummy, I think New York is famazing."

"Famazing?" I call after her as she skips a couple of steps ahead.

"Yes. Fabulous *and* amazing," she says, throwing her arms wide. "Can Uncle Carson come with us next time?"

Uncle Carson. Only I would get myself into a situation like this. I had zero intention of being there when he woke this morning. I thought for sure I'd be out of the apartment before he even raised his head. And I would've been too, if I hadn't spent the night thinking about him and then slept through my bloody alarm. And now I can't help but replay his questions over and over again in my head, and the way he looked at Lu. Which wasn't exactly like he was ready to run for the hills.

A familiar pang of *what if* reverberates through me. Familiar because, five years ago, it was something I'd wished with all my heart to be true. I'd wanted so much for my baby to be the result of a night of white-hot passion and emotion and fun. Yes, because he was fun. I'd longed for her to be fathered by my teasing gallant, the man who looked at me as though I were a goddess rather than the man who implied I owed him a fuck after six dates and a couple of fancy dinners. Because while I might've implied that Lulu's father was an old boyfriend, I was stretching the truth. *Just like that man was only ever interested in stretching my knicker elastic.* I might have tried to persuade myself he was my boyfriend. He might even have played a part in that illusion, but when he disappeared overnight, it became quickly apparent the sentiment was far from reciprocated.

I didn't know I was already pregnant that night. I didn't find out until a couple of months later, and even that brought its own sense of shame. But I lived, and I thrived. *We thrived.* But what I don't understand is how my stomach still aches as I remember the disappointment when I discovered Lulu wasn't his.

Then this morning, after the whole hot-and-heavy deal where the only thing separating our bodies were my pyjamas and his (impressively tented) thin shorts, I'd practically shoved clothes at Lulu and hustled her out of the door without even making sure she'd brushed her teeth.

Which she hadn't, she later reported with delight.

Freaked out doesn't even come close to covering how I'd felt. I still can't quite believe that I allowed him to speak to me like that, never mind that I'd almost kissed him. This isn't me. This isn't how I operate. Ever. Kisses aren't trifles to be frittered away on men I barely know or men who make me feel so unlike myself I'm frightened.

In an effort to escape and ignore the riot of feelings rushing through me, we'd wandered the park most of the day. We visited the petting zoo, watched the boats on the lake, then ate lunch in a café overlooking Sheep Meadow.

While Lulu contented herself with french fries and ice cream, I would've ordinarily listened to her chatter, indulging in a little people watching. But instead, I searched hotel listings on my phone. As it turns out, as well as annoying and sexy—annoyingly sexy?—Carson Hayes was also right about the price of hotels over a weekend. *Mega bucks.* I couldn't in good conscience claim a night in a hotel on my expenses, and I couldn't personally afford to squander money on a point of pride.

Pride. Who am I kidding? It wasn't pride that kept me out of his apartment all day. More like fear. Not fear of the man or his advances, but fear I'd give in to them. To him. Fear I'd give in to the urges, to the parts of me he'd awakened with just the most glancing of touches and those smouldering looks. As he'd pressed his forearm against the cabinet near my head, my heart had beat wildly, the subtle scent of his cologne assaulting my senses and my memories. I'd balled my hands into fists to prevent me from grabbing his T-shirt, to prevent me from bringing him closer because his throat was almost in licking distance, and I was seriously considering it—considering it all. Forgetting that my daughter was just a few feet away, I was mesmerised by the presence of him and the blood thundering through my veins.

Despite my supposed straight talk, he had me at that very first teasing quirk of his sensual lips, turning me literally weak at the knees.

Weak at the knees is fine, I intone silently. *It's weak at the knicker elastic I need to be concerned about.*

I can't remember when a man last looked at me like he did. *Last night. This morning.* And I'm lying to myself again because it was him.

And how I'd wanted to be seen again.

I was mindless to anything but being consumed by him. At least, until Lulu had burst back into the room. Guilt had replaced need like a dousing of cold water over flames. She'd never seen me with a man before. I don't date—ever. And I promised her when she was just a wee bump that she would always be my number one priority. That we'd be okay on our own. I won't go back on that promise, and I'm not about to confuse her by kissing a strange man in his kitchen. *No matter how much I want to.*

But thank goodness she hasn't asked about us almost-kissing again.

Finding somewhere else to live is now my number one priority. I can't stay in his home for so many reasons. But for tonight, I'll have no choice.

One more night together without me jumping him.

I can do that.

If I lock myself in the bedroom and maybe barricade it for good measure.

It's late before we head home. I mean, back to Carson Hayes' apartment. We've surely explored the child-friendly delights of Central Park to the limits of one day. And though I'm sure Lulu would be content to run wild into the twilight, I'm also sure the place doesn't have the same vibe after dark.

"My feet are sore, and my tummy hurts," Lulu complains as we step under the fancy-pants marquee entrance to the equally swanky building.

"Well, your feet will be in bed soon."

"Good evening, miss, ma'am." An unfamiliar doorman inclines his head as he pulls the door open. I guess he must work the evening shift, and as we don't normally go out in the evening, I've never met him.

"Hello!" Lulu chirrups, her aches suddenly forgotten.

"Thank you for opening the door." I love how she remembers to thank the doorman every time. She may be a bit of a handful, but she's an unfailingly polite handful. She practically dances through before turning to face him. "My granny might be coming to visit soon. You shouldn't open the door for her," she adds in a whisper.

There's not much point in telling her we won't be living here then, especially in front of the doorman.

"But that's my job." The doorman smiles, all avuncular kindness and patience.

"No. Don't." Lulu's pigtails whip back and forth as she shakes her head. "I told her on the phone we live in a place where a man in a uniform opens the front door for us, and she asked us if we lived in a prison. And when I said no she said God gived her hands so she can open her own bloody doors."

"Okay, Lu, let's go!" I know, I'm kidding no one. She said what she said, and we all heard it, but sometimes, talking over your kids prevents more tales of poor parenting from falling out of their mouths. "I'm sure the nice man—"

"Martinez, ma'am."

"I'm sure Mr Martinez hasn't got time to listen to tales of"—my mad mother—"granny."

"I have all the time in the world for sweethearts like you." He smiles kindly down at her again, and she just beams back at him. And like all mothers, the smile of my own child brings a smile to my face. *Urgh! Just look at the three of us smiling like loons.*

"Well, let's go," I say, ushering her along the marble entrance in the direction of the elevators before she feeds him another gem.

"What a nice man, Mummy. Wasn't he a nice man?"

"Lovely." The doors open, and we step into the mirrored car. *God, I look a fright.* "You want to press the button?" I begin to flatten the escaped wisps from my ponytail before I catch myself.

I'm being ridiculous.

I'm not trying to look appealing for anyone in particular.

And those aren't butterflies swimming through my insides.

"Oowee! My tummy still hurts."

"I'm not surprised." I glance down. "You ate so much at dinner."

"But it was a big pizza," she replies as though this is an adequate explanation. "And you can't leave pizza. Not in New York. The man said so."

"The man"—known also as the waiter—"said he would put it in a box for you to bring home."

"I brought it home in my tummy instead!" She rubs over her T-shirt gleefully. "I like New York pizza, even if it's silly how they call it pie. Pie has meat and vegebables in. And gravy on top."

I listen, with at least half an ear, as Lulu chatters about the delights of New York pizza versus the pizza she ate in Rome and Granny's skate and sidney pie (also known as steak and kidney pie). As the elevator rises, my limbs begin to feel jittery with nerves though I force them to behave. I can act unruffled. Cool.

"Mummy, why are you pulling a duck face?"

Oh, no. She's right. I'm actually pouting at the mirror. For the love of God, have I regressed to my teenage years? I know it's been a while, but this is ridiculous.

"Now you look like you need a poo."

"Shush. This is my thinking face."

"Grandpa says some of his best ideas come to him when he's doing a poo."

"Please never repeat that again." Time to have a word with my dad.

The elevator *bings,* and the doors slide open. As we step out, I'm sure I've left my stomach on the ground floor. After I unlock the door, we slip our shoes off, hang up coats, and Lulu is still chattering. Honestly, this child would talk a glass eye to sleep. She'd talk underwater!

Pizza, pizza. Something about her teacher at school. Being sneezed on by the goat at the petting zoo. I guess I must be making the right kinds of responses as we make our way deeper into the apartment before she veers off to visit the little girls' room.

I just need to remember not to put myself within kissing distance of him, I think as I carry on towards the kitchen.

The kitchen. The room that I've been trying not to think about.

The room he made me quiver and want in.

The room I almost raised my lips to his in.

The room I find him leaning against the countertop, no longer dressed in running clothes but dark jeans and a fine knit sweater that clings to the delicious parts of him. Well, some of them. *As far as he's concerned, his bounty knows no bounds when it comes to scrumptiousness.* A glass of something deep and red dangles negligently from one hand, and the thought crosses my mind that he looks as handsome as the devil himself. *And twice as sinful.*

"You wear glasses."

At Carson's almost delighted assertion, I find myself touching my black frames, suddenly regretting ignoring Charles's suggestion that I dress like a sexy librarian when I wear them. *Glasses are très hot,* he'd intoned when I'd gotten my first prescription shortly after Lulu was born before going on to say he preferred his librarian with a penis. But I own neither the proper attire nor the penis for either of those fantasies, not that it stops me from glancing down at my skinny jeans and running shoes as though to check.

"And you're wearing another tight top," I say, looking up again to run my gaze over him. Again. *Ack!* "I suppose you're going to tell me you have trouble buying clothes that fit."

"Nope." He pops the *P*, refusing to be goaded. "But someone wise once told me it pays to advertise."

Oh, God. I said that, didn't I? And he remembers! Forgive me if I give a little swoon. Internally, at least.

"You've been out a while."

My attention snaps back to his, the sound of his deep voice reverberating through my insides. I hate myself for the effect he has on me, the lack of control I feel at just the most fleeting of looks. No one in the history of me has ever made me feel like he does, clothed or unclothed.

As a result of this frustration, my answer sounds extra snarky in response. "I didn't realise I had a curfew, *dad*."

"Come on in and tell Daddy what you've been up to all day."

A pulse of longing ripples through my insides because the way he's looking at me isn't paternal. Not one bit.

"Does that ever work for you?" You know, that whole deep, rumbly and all kinds of suggestive and sexy? Because, oh my, it's working for me. I've never been into age play, and calling anyone daddy at this stage of my life seemed ridiculous not two minutes ago. Now it just seems ridiculously tempting. Where can a girl find a pair of knee socks in a hurry?

"What do you think?"

I think *spank me, Daddy, I've been a bad, bad girl. Or at least, you make me want to be.*

"I don't pretend to know or want to know what you think." Well, it's partly true.

"Are you going to come into the kitchen or hover on the threshold all evening?" he goads, adding another of his range of smiles, which I'm beginning to remember, almost possess a language of their own.

He turns to the cabinet behind him, pulling out another glass.

"That all depends. Are you going to try to kiss me again?"

He inclines his head as he answers, "Lady's choice."

"The lady chooses *not*." My reply is definitive, even if it lacks veracity, but as he sets both glasses on the kitchen island, pouring a little wine into the empty one, I find myself pulling up a stool in front of him.

He had me at wine. No, that's not true. He had me at Saint Odile, and my life hasn't quite been the same since.

"You're sure you wouldn't prefer to sit on my knee?" Why does he have to smell so good? The scent of his cologne and the hint of soap cling to his skin. Maybe I should sit somewhere farther away.

Like Canada.

"I'm fine where I am, thank you."

"I called Rose," he murmurs, scissoring his fingers at the bottom of the glass and sliding it towards me.

"What?" The glass doesn't even make it to my mouth. "Why would you do that?"

"Not for whatever reason you're telling yourself."

"Carson." I swallow over the sound of his name, over the realisation that it's the first time I've ever used it. "I want. No, I need you to keep what happened between us . . . between us."

"Are we talking about last night or five years ago?"

"All of it." I swallow again but in fear this time. I've built myself such a carefully constructed narrative. Girl meets boy. Boy woos girl before dumping her. Girl finds herself pregnant and vows to love her child enough for two. This is what my friends know of me. This is what they believe. I can't allow them to find out now that I also hooked up with a stranger in a fit of pique, let alone that the stranger turned out to be my best friend's friend. I'm not ashamed of that night, but I also don't want to revisit it. Okay, that's not exactly true because since the man before me whipped off his shirt in the bathroom Friday night, I've been unable to think of much else. Along with how much I need to resist.

I promised myself at Lulu's birth that if my child can flourish without a father, I could do the same without a man. And I want so much to prove to Rose that the reason I'm in New York for the next twelve months hasn't changed. That I'll give it my all while I'm here. That my focus, outside of my child, will be all for my job. Rose has created such a wonderful legacy with her inheritance. She's dedicated it and much of her life to the care and advancement of women, and I include myself in that. I could've trained anywhere in the world, stayed in France, yet she knew I had a childish yearning to experience life in New York, and that's how I find myself here.

I won't have her believe I'm not giving this opportunity my all.

I owe her more than that. I owe my child, too. But most of all, I owe myself.

"Believe me." His voice brings me back from my

mental morass. "I'm not about to discuss any of that with Rose." He picks up his glass, studying the play of light against the dark wine. "But the truth is, if she finds out I've been here, she's more likely to ask questions. And if she found out you left suddenly, she might even jump to conclusions. And by the way, I did mean what I told her before you arrived. You're welcome to stay as long as you need. The place sits empty most of the year anyway."

"But you're here now," I answer quietly.

"About that." He pauses, his countenance turning suddenly serious. "I have something I wanted to discuss with you."

10

CARSON

Fuck. *Fuck!*

I swallow back the words balanced on the end of my tongue, a proposition, a moment of madness. I was about to offer her the apartment for as long as she has need of it, that I could be gone in the morning, leaving her to her life.

Or that I could stay.

Stay here. With her. For tonight. For tomorrow. For as long as it takes to explore this thing between us. This thing that twists my gut, filling my head with impossibilities. I know she feels it. I saw it in the kitchen and felt it in the rise of her chest against mine. I could stay until we're both sated. Stay until we're no longer greedy for more. Stay until she finds out how I live my life, how wrong I'd be for her and the girl. Stay until she hates me like I deserve.

"Carson?"

I come back from my dream world with a bump, not a bang; the ways she says my name tells me it's not the first time but a repeat. I force my hands into my pockets to hide how they've curled into fists, the phantom of her ponytail almost real between my fingertips.

"I'll be gone by morning, and the place will be all yours again." That's the way it has to be. So I don't hate myself and she doesn't hate me.

"What? No, I can't do that."

"For as long as you need," I continue, cutting off further protestations. "And I'm sorry about last night. If I'd realised who you were, I wouldn't have teased you." *No, if I'd realised who you were, I wouldn't have teased at all. I'd have taken. And you would've given because I know I read the signals right.*

"Apology accepted," she replies evenly. "Though I suppose it begs the question exactly who you thought I was or where I came from." Her cheeks immediately turn a delicious pink, almost as though she can't believe what she just said.

I bite back the sly grin. Does she really think she can hide behind her wine glass?

"You really want to know? Curiosity killed the cat, so they say." And this is a little kitty I'd like to kill by orgasm overload, even if my second thought isn't as compelling. If I tell her, her cause of death would more likely be shock.

"You're right," she answers just quickly enough. "I really don't need to know."

"That's probably sensible." Maybe sensibility is something I should learn. "Where's that accent from, anyway?" That's it, do the right thing. Move the topic away from where your cock leads.

"England." Like I hadn't worked that part out already.

"London, right?" I tap my finger against my mouth as though thinking. This time she nods, though she gives nothing else away. "What part?"

"North." The look she sends my way is almost withering. "North London."

"Hackney? Haringey? Should I keep guessing? It's not like I plan on stalking."

"Camden," she replies eventually and with a roll of her eyes. "Stalk away. In London, I mean. I haven't lived there since I was eighteen."

"So I should stalk you in France?"

"By all means," she mutters. "Given I'm not there, either."

"Are you going to tell me a little about yourself?" A little more than the tidbits Rose fed me, hopefully. I still can't believe she's been so close to me all this time.

"Would you like me to fill out a tenancy application?"

"How about we just get to know each other a little better," I reply, ignoring her tone. Give me a little more personal stuff. So you like a daddy play? Don't deny it. I saw your eyes widen, little girl. "So, Camden. Home of the lock and the market. But I think I detect a little something else in that accent, too." A soft lilt of something almost lyrical. "Is it Scots?"

"My granny is Irish," Lulu suddenly supplies from behind her mom as she hopscotches into the room, reminding me of two things. One, my sister used to love to play hopscotch, and two, I need to keep my budding obsession in check for more reasons than one.

Family. I wonder if I can still count them as that, considering they no longer acknowledge me. Fuck them.

"Ah, that must be it." I raise my wine to my mouth as her gaze follows it there. A little English, a little Irish, a lot hot, and so fucking delicious to fluster.

Have I always had a thing for women in glasses? I don't recall thinking them crazy hot before. But there's just something very proper about the vibe a woman in glasses gives off. Maybe something that suggests virtue. And the opposite of virtue is always vice. It's a good path to travel, let me tell you.

"I was borned in France," Lulu announces, repressing my amorous zeal. "But I'm not *really* French."

"So that makes you Frenglish, right?"

"No, I'm just Lulu. How many times do I gots to tell you?" She giggles as her mother releases a tiny breath, almost as though relieved the exchange stopped there. "Uncle Carson, will you make me pancakes in the morning again?"

"Eloise Rose, stop being so forward!"

"I'm not forward," she retorts. "I'm bold."

"Hey, Lu. If I promise to make you breakfast, will you give me a few minutes to talk to Mommy?"

"Oh, no, you don't." Turning, Fee grabs the kid, planting her on the stool next to her. "Sit here and play quietly on my phone." Sliding her phone from the back pocket of her jeans, she hands it to her small hands.

"Can I buy a new game?" Lulu raises her eyes along with her question, the picture of wide-eyed innocence.

"Don't push your luck," her mother retorts.

"Is she intended as an audience or a human shield?" I slide an amused glance the kid's way, who is now engrossed in the screen. Fee's answer, when I look back, is a narrow-eyed stare. "You should've just said you find me irresistible. That you can't trust yourself to be around me."

"Funny," she says, sounding anything but amused. "I thought you wanted to talk. Not annoy."

Well, I'm having fun. I try to temper my enjoyment as I place my glass down and lean against the island counter.

"I realise I wasn't meant to be here," I say, my tone turning serious. "I apologise for turning up unannounced."

"What you should apologise for is your behaviour, not for turning up in your own home."

"Well, that would be an insincere apology."

"A normal person would at least try to look sorry."

"Normal is overrated," I answer with a shrug. "But I told Rose the place would be empty, that you could stay as long as you needed. I'm sure she'd realise this was a genuine mistake on my part, but beyond that, I do wonder what you'll tell her."

I generally don't care for what people think, but I'd like to hang on to Rose's good opinion. God knows it took me long enough to prove I was genuine in my interest in her foundation. Would Fee tell her about last night? About our history?

"I'm not about to mention any of this to Rose," she mutters adamantly. "But this is your home, not mine. It isn't appropriate for us to stay here, especially not after, well, you know."

"What isn't appropriate? A friend of a friend staying over?"

"We're not staying over, though, are we? We've been living here for over two weeks already. But you were right about the price of hotels," she adds, obviously discomforted. "But we'll be out of your hair as soon as we can."

"Our past doesn't have to change things. This could work out for both of us."

The look she sends me is so cold it'd freeze the balls off a snowman.

"Get your head out of the gutter, angel. I just meant you need a place to stay, and I don't exactly like leaving this place empty. It's true," I add as she looks unconvinced. "You've looked after the place. And saved me from worrying about my plants."

"Yes, because you're the sort of man who worries for his Ficus," she answers witheringly. Besides, I know for a fact you have someone watering them already. Someone comes in when I've been at work to vacuum and dust, too."

"You got a house elf like Dobby," Lulu pipes up. "An elf who washed my bre'fast plate."

I set off laughing. I'm not sure the old family housekeeper would appreciate being referred to as an elf, even if she has shrunken and wrinkled over the years.

"You know, you'd be surprised to discover the things I worry about."

"You mean things other than the state of the Dow?" Fee's retort is sickly sweet, but I'm so much more than just a rich asshole. If she'd allow herself, I think she'd realise that . . . I'm a rich, *horny* asshole.

"Sure, the Dow. The glass ceiling. Food security. Deforestation. Global health standards." Not to mention Rose, her family, and her foundation. The guys at Ardeo. Annie, the old housekeeper who I can't persuade to retire and who is capable of more loyalty in her arthritic dusting hand than the rest of my family combined. "And I worry if anyone is talking to my plants when they water them."

"I can talk to your plants," Lulu pipes up.

"You could? That would be helpful."

"But you got to pay me."

"Lulu!"

"No, that sounds fair," I answer, biting back a grin at her mother's horrified expression. "And what would an enterprising girl like you charge for this kind of service?"

Lulu's eyes narrow as she contemplates her answer. "Five dollars, I fink."

"Five whole dollars?" I repeat. The little girl nods solemnly. "I guess that sounds reasonable."

"Terrible, more like," Fee exclaims. "Not to mention a little mercenary."

"Not when she's underselling herself." This I deliver by speaking behind my hand. "I pay the current service a whole lot more."

"I meant five dollars for each plant," Lulu amends cheerfully.

"Eloise Rose, don't be greedy!"

"Mummy, shush." The kid mirrors my actions, holding her hand to her chin, not quite covering her mouth but rather speaking over it. "He can afford it. He has ten shiny watches in a special drawer in his wardrobe, remember?" She cheerfully holds both hands up in the air, fingers splayed.

"Oh, Lord." Her mother's shoulders sag in a moment of parental mortification. "I sometimes wonder where I got you from."

"From your tummy!" she announces gleefully. "Or Amazon!"

"We do *not* go snooping around people's homes. You know that."

"I know *you* did."

"I certainly did not."

"You certeidly did."

"She doesn't know what she's talking about," Fee says before her head whips back to the kid as her little voice pipes up again.

"Er, 'scuse me, Mummy, but I sawed you looking at his shoes."

"At my shoes?" If I sound thoroughly entertained, it's because I am. "Do you have a shoe fetish?" I ask, resting my chin on my fist. "Or are you one of those people who thinks the size of one thing relates to another?" I can't remember when I was last so entertained in my own home.

"I don't know what you're talking about," she says quickly, averting her gaze.

"Oh, I think you do. And you and I both know that in my case you've already found the old adage to be true. Big feet, big—"

"Arse," she mutters between clenched teeth.

"How come you get to say arse?" Lulu's sweet face is suddenly mutinous.

"Young lady, there had better still be ten shiny watches when Carson goes to that drawer."

Carson is an improvement on Mr Hayes, but maybe not as interesting as *Daddy*.

"I was jus' looking," Lulu mutters as her attention returns to the phone.

"Five dollars per plant, per week, wasn't it, kid?" Her expression clears almost immediately, and she begins to nod. "It's a deal."

"We got to shake on it." Her small hand thrusts out above the counter, my own engulfing it.

"Do I need to worry about her slipping my watch from my wrist at this point?"

Fee shrugs. "At this point in time, she hasn't honed that particular skill set. But I'm afraid she does like to borrow, as she calls it, but it's a habit that relates mostly to things left lying around at eye level. I generally frisk her before we leave the house."

"Good to know." I bite back a grin. "Especially as you're staying."

"I didn't agree to that."

"A deal is a deal, right, Lu? You don't want me to sue your child for breach of contract."

"Is beach of contrapt very bad?" Lulu's expression turns ponderous, and though Fee gives a sharp shake of her head, the little girl's attention wanders almost immediately.

"You really are like a dog with a bone," she mutters. *And every dog has its day, angel.* "But I just don't get why you would open your home to strangers."

"Because a stranger is just a friend you don't know yet," pipes up Lulu, who, it seems, has already perfected the art of pretending not to listen.

"Exactly. If *Sesame Street* can't be the voice of reason, who else is qualified?"

"Actually, that's W.B. Yeats. He's an Irish poet." The latter she adds a little self-consciously, as though divulging some part of herself she'd prefer to keep private.

"You're sure those aren't Big Bird's words?"

At last, she smiles. It was hard-won but worth it. "'*Come away, O human child. To the waters and the wild with a faery, hand in hand, for the world's more full of weeping than you can understand.*'" Her head jerks up, and she blinks, her eyes a shade of gold I'm pretty sure they weren't a moment ago.

The hairs on the back of my neck stand like pins, my body simultaneously hot and cold at the same time—my insides fiery and molten, a chill coating my skin. What the fuck was that? Maybe it wasn't Goldilocks I found in my bath last night. Maybe it was queen of the faeries.

"Sorry." She shakes her head, rapidly reaching for her

wine. "That's one of his. Yeats, not Big Bird's, I mean." Another smile, this one a little sadder. Is it bad that I'm counting?

"It's beautiful." Just like the woman in front of me. "Even if I still think your poet's been stealing from *Sesame Street*."

"It's one of Lu's favourites," she says, smoothing her daughter's hair, as dark as hers is light.

"I can see why. Maybe you'll read it all to me sometime."

"Like a bedtime story," echoes Lu.

"I'm not sure about stories, but it is time for our bed."

What I wouldn't give for that kind of invitation from her.

"What? You're not going to abandon me at nine thirty on a Saturday night, are you, roomie?"

"I'm sure you don't need us for company." Her words are delivered through a derisory chuckle as she slides her phone from her protesting daughter's hand.

"I'd certainly like your company. Both of you. You'd like to stay up late and watch a movie with me and your mom, wouldn't you, Lulu?"

I might not be a parent, but even I know that was a dick move.

"Can we watch Poppy's movie?" The kid angles her head like an inquisitive terrier.

"Sure, Lu. That's my favourite," I answer as her mother groans.

Whatever it is, if it gets me a couple more hours with Fee, I'm in.

And on some level, probably a masochist.

"And there has to be popcorn," the kid says, clearly feeling a sense of her own power in the exchange.

"I thought you had a tummy ache." Fee places her hands on the kid's shoulders, steering her towards the door.

"'S gone," Lulu protests, wriggling out from under her hold. "I wanna watch a movie with Uncle Car. It's the weekend, remember?"

"Want to watch a movie," Fee amends, frowning as I interject,

"Yeah, Mom, it's the weekend. Don't go spoiling the vibe."

"We'll see if you're still wearing that smirk in an hour," she says, throwing down the gauntlet before turning back to the kid. "Fine. But you need to get dressed for bed first."

"Deal-ee-o!"

"Does that go for me, too?"

Her frowning gaze flicks my way, scanning me from the head down. "No. You better stay fully clothed."

I don't know about clothes, but I'm still wearing the same smile as the pair leave the kitchen. One of them to slip into something more comfortable, the other probably to frown a little more. I do a quick reconnaissance of the cabinets on the hunt for popcorn. Finding a microwave pack, I stick it in the machine for the allocated time, then open another bottle of Chateau Margaux, topping up our glasses with the open bottle. Then I make my way to the den to cue up Lulu's movie of choice when she bounds into the room.

"I want to sit next to Uncle Car!"

"Don't climb over the back of the sofa!" Fee rebukes, following her in. "Honestly, anyone would think you're half monkey."

Rolling off the seat cushion to stand at my knees, the little girl pops her hand on one hip. "Sweet or salty?"

I like to think I'm a little of both, but I guess that isn't an appropriate answer. "Can't you smell the butter?"

She nods her approval and sits to my left. "Mummy, you sit next to me and make me the ham in a people sandwich!"

A people sandwich sounds like the kind of weekend I was looking forward to before my plane broke down. But if there's going to be a P.G. people sandwich . . .

"I think your mommy should sit next to me. How else is she going to reach the popcorn?"

Fee tries and fails to suppress a superior grin as she takes a seat on the other side of Lulu, her eyes meeting mine over her child's dark head. "Good try."

"Your loss," I reply. "I happen to know having the meat in the middle makes for a better people sandwich experience."

Her eyes widen, but it's not all shock. Not given the way they darken.

"Uncle Car, you're not listening."

Thank fuck for the popcorn bowl on my lap right now.

"Sorry, sweetie. What was that?"

"I said Mummy and me have matching pyjamas. Look!" She plucks at the button on her pink striped shirt, but the pair aren't wearing exactly the same pyjamas because Lulu's finish at her ankles and Fee's hit only mid-thigh.

"That's, ah, super cute." I swallow, my voice suddenly husky as my gaze sweeps those toned and tanned legs just out of reach, toned and tan, skin like silk. Legs I still remember being wrapped around my head. My cock tightens as I recall the firmness of her calf in my palm and the way it tightened when I'd pressed my teeth to her inner thigh. The feel of her ass in my hands and the way that her thighs shook as I made her come.

"Mummy said we look like a pair of crimimals from Candyland." It's certainly criminal how much I want her mom right now. "She didn't want to wear them," she adds with a shake of her head. Her story checks out, judging by Fee's expression. "But we always wear the same jim-jammies at the weekend."

"Maybe your mommy is right." I drag my eyes from those fucking legs to her face. "Maybe she shouldn't be wearing them at all."

"You're impossible." Somehow, her tone is less defiant as our eyes meet, and she reads my intentions. She makes me impossibly hard, and I think she knows that.

"Bring on the trolls!" the little girl growls, her voice oddly gruff for someone so small and sweet.

"The what?"

I'm the recipient of another superior glance as Fee says, "You'll see."

We settle down to the movie, the kind which makes me wonder if the producer double-dropped acid to make this asinine shit, but before we're thirty minutes in, I can feel the warm little bundle pressed up against my arm growing heavier and heavier. Then her chin tips to her chest, her head beginning to nod with each inhalation.

"I guess that's why they call it the land of nod." Fee shuffles to the edge of the couch, her smile for her child serene. "I'm surprised she made it this long. She should be exhausted after all that running around Central Park."

"You were there all day?" Her head bobs. "You guys must've had fun."

"What was less fun was ringing around half a dozen hotels," she murmurs.

"I did try to warn you."

She looks up sharply. "Do try not to sound so smug."

"Why, when I was right?"

"When you're right, you shouldn't gloat," she replies a little pert. "It isn't very flattering."

"And counting others' sins doesn't make you a saint."

"I think I must be at least a little bit saintly to be having this conversation with you."

"True." I bring my glass to my lips. "I do wonder what you think my sins are."

"Many and plentiful," she replies, the corners of her mouth twitching with a smile.

"Come on, you can be a little more specific than that. I'd give my left nut to know what it is you're thinking."

"Just the left one?" She cocks one provocative brow.

"I guess that all depends."

She doesn't sigh, and she doesn't shake her head, but she may as well have. "Don't you ever get tired? Don't you ever want to turn it off?"

"This is all on you, angel."

"I'm not sure how," she retorts.

"Because fantasy thrives within an air of mystery."

Her cheeks begin to pink, and I am a sucker for that look on her, but as her feet touch the floor, she signals a definitive change in the tone of our foreplay.

Sorry, *conversation.*

"I suppose I'd better get sleeping beauty to bed."

"I can take her."

"No, I've got this," she says, threading one arm across her daughter's back and the other under her knees. "Come on, princess."

"*Princesse,*" the little girl answers, seemingly still asleep and in French.

"*Oof!* You're getting heavier by the day."

"You're coming back to finish your wine, right?"

The most perfect pair of legs ever to wear a pair of pink pyjama shorts halts at the door to the den. She doesn't turn but offers me a hint of her profile as she says, "I don't think that would be a very good idea."

"I can't finish this on my own." A lie. "And I don't want to waste this vintage. Don't you know I opened it just to impress you?" About this wine, I give no fucks. What I want is that bundle of pink and gorgeous and blonde to come back here and spend a little time with me because I've become a masochist, and if I can't spend a little time with her *beneath* me, I'll settle for sitting with her side by side. *Making her blush a little more.*

"Okay." Her shoulders move with her reluctant acquiesce. "But just for the wine. It would be a shame to waste something that tastes so nice."

"My sentiments exactly," I answer, my gaze sweeping over her again.

I get rid of the popcorn and top up her barely touched glass, and when she re-enters the room, I'm back on the couch and the music playing in the background is the exact kind you'd expect to hear from speakers picked up from Bang & Olufsen.

More bang. Less Olufsen.

"That's not exactly subtle." She inclines her head in the direction of Marvin Gaye's dulcet tones coming from the speaker system. She bends to grab her glass from the coffee table, but it does nothing to hide her amusement at calling me out.

"Subtlety is overrated," I murmur as she takes a seat on the other side of the sectional. And way out of reach. "So, what now?" Hooking my arm over the back of the couch, I bring my knee up onto the seat as I turn to face her. "Wanna make out?"

"I, ah-hem. No."

"Liar."

The flash of her smile is brief and sweet, and I can't take my eyes off her legs as she brings them up onto the cushion, curling them a little. Lithe and toned and still wearing a summer tan. I wonder where her tan ends. Is she a bikini kind of girl? It would be a shame if she's not. So, string or highcut? Boy shorts or thong? So many questions, but I can't regret that five years ago we didn't keep the lights on. Because in the moonlight, she glowed like an angel yet burned like sin.

"I'm going to finish my wine, then turn in."

Turn in to the maid's room. What the hell is that all about?

"Come on, live a little. It's barely ten."

"Lulu isn't the only one who walked her feet off today. Seriously, I'm shagged. Shagged tired," she adds the quick qualifier. "That *wasn't* an invitation."

"As I recall, when you issue invitations, they're pretty clear." The way her cheeks suddenly glow makes me want to find out where her blushes run to.

"So that's what you want to go with? Conversation about that night? When you don't know me. You don't know what I do for a living. I could be a complete psycho!"

"You'd have to be a little bit crazy to be Rose's friend. Who, by the way, told me what you do for a living." If I recall, she wants to make women's lives better. Little does she know we have that in common, though our methods might be very different. "And no. I don't need you to fill out a rental application."

"You mean you don't want to know if I have any criminal convictions?" she asks saucily.

"Only if they're interesting ones," I reply with a grin.

"Funnily enough, I am currently contemplating murder." She sends me a narrowed glance more playful than serious.

"With mitigating circumstances, you'd probably swing manslaughter."

"I could have terrible hobbies." She glances around the room almost exasperated. "Messy, destructive ones that could obliterate your home. I could own a pack of vicious dogs."

"But you don't. So whatever will we talk about now?"

"Fine. Okay. I can see where this is heading, so let's get it over with." She shrugs, a jerky motion, then takes a large mouthful of her wine. "Though five years is little late for a dissection. There should be a statute of limitations for these things," she mutters, setting the glass down.

"You want to talk about it? That night?" *Not* where I thought this conversation was going, but I'm game. "Are we comparing notes? Telling dirty stories? Because I really enjoyed that thing you did—"

"I don't need a blow-by-blow critique—"

"Nice choice of words." I lean forward and pick up her neglected wine glass, passing it to her. She looks like she might need it. "And in the right region, at least."

My God, the way her eyes had shone in the moonlight. The feel of her soft hands electrifying the coarse hairs on my thighs. The way she'd watched my expression as she'd taken me to the back of her throat.

"I-it's not often you have sex with someone you know nothing about," she continues, ignoring my goading. Outwardly at least. But, man, that blush gets me right in the crotch. "I suppose there's bound to be curiosity. Things you've wondered about over the years. And you're smiling again. So I guess it's just me who wondered."

"I would *love* to talk about it." Almost as much as I'd love a repeat. "As for thought about it? You might even say constantly."

"Flattery. That is to say, I don't believe you. And we are not talking about sex." Her eyes dart away, and I watch as she takes a sip from her glass.

"Good, right?"

"If you mean the wine, yes. It's delicious."

"The wine is good. The sex? The sex was outstanding."

"And we're still not talking about it, but I don't mind discussing what got us there."

"A broken-down car, as I recall. Attraction. A flirty glance. A little innuendo." Or a lot.

She shakes her head with indulgence this time, but she's thought about it, all right. The way we met. That night. She's thought about me.

"I meant what you were doing up there that day."

"I was escaping," I answer simply and with more truth than I'd usually care for. "My grandfather died the day before, and I guess I needed to get away." It's not the whole truth, but it's all I'm saying.

"I'm so sorry." And she looks it. Looks like she means it, which is more than I probably deserve and definitely more than he deserves.

"No need." What I thought was love turned out to be control. What I thought was business acumen turned out to be a rotten soul. He was a man whose solitary intent was that his business, his name, be carried on long after he'd departed the world. He deserves no one's sorrow and definitely not that of a woman.

"Is that how you were lost?"

Lost. She could say that, for a while at least.

"Were you lost?"

"Answering a question with a question." She waves the glass in front of me as though she has my number. "There's no shame in admitting it. Men get lost. I know this for a fact." Her eyes are meltingly seductive, and I don't think she even knows. She makes me want to spill all of my thoughts and bare my soul, which would be the wrong thing to do. No need to send her running for the hills. "You can admit it, you know," she adds a little mischievously.

"I know men get lost." Men lose their way plenty often. And sometimes, like right now, they get lost in a woman's gaze. How come I've never noticed the thin line of gold that gilds her dark eyes?

"I wasn't irresponsible enough to set off without a spare tyre, just so you know." I'm beginning to understand she's exactly the opposite of irresponsible but find my lips twisting themselves into a teasing quirk anyway. "It's true! I'd loaned Fred, my little car, to my friend, who then had a puncture but forgot to tell me he hadn't replaced the spare."

"And you still call him a friend?" And why do I detest the idea of another man having access to her?

"Well, he's not the most reliable," she demurs, twisting a loose thread from a button on her pyjamas.

When she refuses to hold my gaze, I find my gut clenching, a sudden risen thought manifesting itself into actual words. "Is this friend Lulu's father?"

She sets off laughing like it's the funniest thing she's ever heard. "Her dad? I think that's the funniest thing I've ever heard! He is the least reliable person I know, but even as I'm saying this, it strikes me that he's still more reliable than Lulu's actual father."

There's a lot to dissect in that, not that I have the opportunity as she carries on.

"And of course, you're wondering about Lu's dad. Most people do," she adds with no little chagrin. "Why isn't he around? What is he to us? But the answer is very simple. He wasn't interested."

"Then he's a fool." And a fuck head.

"Yep, his loss," she says with an imperious sniff. "It's all a very short story that ended in a breakup that left me feeling very, very bad about myself. Shortly afterwards, I met you on the side of a hill, and I snatched back a little bit of happiness." She shrugs lightly, her attention sliding away as a tiny frown mars her brow. "Obviously, I didn't know I was pregnant at the time."

I imagine her all alone with a swollen belly, and it hits me right in the feels that Lulu could've been mine. That I might've been that fuck head. That she had no way of finding me.

"Well, you're raising a great kid," I find myself saying, pushing away the uncomfortable thoughts.

"Well, I like to think so. And I'm sure you're now able to say so, content in the position of finding out you're not responsible for her in any way."

"If she were mine, I wouldn't have ignored my responsibility."

"He didn't exactly ignore it," she mutters under her breath before coming back to herself and changing the subject, if not deftly then decidedly. "As for that afternoon, not only was I without a spare because of said friend, but it was his fault I was lost, too. One minute, he needed a lift, and the next, he decided he didn't need rescuing."

"You must be a very, very understanding friend."

"Or an idiot." She reaches for her wine. "Anyway, I was cursing him to high heavens when you caught me. It was *not* my finest moment," she says with a rueful grin.

"It was the highlight of my day." Highlight of my month. My fucking decade.

"Don't." She groans, hiding her face in her hand.

"It's true. You were so cute in your tiny dress and your crazy, wheeling arms."

"I've never been more embarrassed."

"And I've never been more turned on."

"By the crazy lady?" She looks unconvinced. Pink and unconvinced as she takes a sip of her wine. "Do you have a bit of a fetish, Mr Hayes?"

"You know, I'm not sure if I like it best when you call me Mr Hayes or Daddy."

"Stop." The edict isn't issued playfully, not that it stops me when I've found my stride.

"What? We're only getting to know each other better. But coming back from the bar to find you'd booked a room." I shake my head slowly as though, years later, I still can't believe my luck. *Can't believe my luck that she's here.*

"Like you didn't plan it that way all along."

"I swear I didn't," I reply with a chuckle. "I'm not saying I mightn't have thought about it."

"But you knew there was a hotel up there." Turning to face me, she curls her legs farther up onto the couch, unconsciously mirroring me as I bring my wine to my lips. "It's not the kind of place easily found."

"If you recall, I said there was an *auberge*." An inn. "I didn't mention any hotel."

"You were obviously wary of scaring me off," she says, her tone a little prim.

"You've got it all worked out, haven't you?"

"Not really. I'm just guessing."

"But you've thought about it." This she neither confirms nor denies as her gaze flicks to a loose thread on her pyjama shorts. *And those fucking legs.*

"Well, it's not exactly a regular occurrence, having sex with someone whose name you don't know." She looks up from the thread when I don't answer, but there's no way either of us is ready to go down that road.

"I'm familiar with the area. The region." My diversion seems to work, so I spill a little more. "My mother's family was from Saint Odile. When I was a kid, we used to spend summers on the *Cotê* and go up into the mountains when it got too hot."

"That sounds idyllic."

"It was until she passed." Passed seems like such an inadequate description for such a terrible way to die. *Snatched. Snuffed out. Robbed in the prime of her life.*

"How awful." Her hand briefly presses my arm, her expression so sorrowful on my behalf. "How old were you, if you don't mind me asking?"

"It was a long time ago." Though the images are printed indelibly on the insides of my eyelids. I can still see the clouds of dust billowing through the streets, people appearing like zombies from beneath it. I wasn't in the States when it happened. Like most of the world, I watched with disbelief, glued to a screen with tears streaming down my face. All that's left now are memories. And her name on a memorial. One of almost three thousand souls taken in the name of hate.

But I can't bring myself to tell her any of that.

"She left me a little real estate up there. I didn't know it at the time, but that was where I was heading that day." A tiny house in the hills, a place away from the madness.

Sometimes, I find myself there, and other times, I go there to escape.

"You have a house in the village, and you didn't take me there instead?" The lightness in her tone brings me back to the moment. Back to her. "Or was that the next step in your nefarious plan. Maybe that's why you didn't tell me about the hotel."

"Do I need to remind you who booked the room?"

She tries to hide her embarrassment behind the glass but not before delivering her retort. "Do I need to remind you who kissed the pants off whom by the side of the road?"

"I think you might need to." I pick up the bottle and top up my glass before moving to do the same with hers. "Because I'm pretty sure I had shorts on when we got to the inn, and I know you were wearing panties . . . mainly because I remember peeling you out of them."

"You rotten—oh!" Fee grabs the throw pillow from the seat between us intending to hit me with it but before she does, the rim of her glass and the bottle collide. "Oh, no!" Cupping her hand now against the side of the glass, she attempts to stem the spill, her gaze darting to the sage-coloured linen beneath. "Quick, do something."

Maybe later, I'll look back and tell myself it was the wine that brought a flush to her cheeks. Or maybe I'll blame my actions on her for being so fucking irresistible or on the scent of her perfume for invading my senses. But I can't think of any of that now as I lean closer, not working on instinct but rather need. Her dark eyes flare like embers even as I do just as she'd asked—I do something to stop the spill—and take her hand into mine to lick.

I lick a line up her palm. Lick the pads of her

fingertips. Feel the sharp hitch of her breath in my own chest even as she bites down on her bottom lip to contain the sound. Her hand doesn't move from mine, and she doesn't protest as I take her glass, placing it down on the coffee table. She doesn't speak, doesn't move, not for a beat, but I don't think she's stunned. Not as I turn back and she launches herself at me.

Finally. I think rather than speak this relief as our mouths meet in a clash of lips and teeth and tongues. Her hands sliding into my hair, anchoring me there, like there's the possibility I might prefer to be somewhere else. Fuck that noise as I grip the back of her thighs and pull her to straddle me.

"We shouldn't." Her words are a hot whisper feathering my lips even as her grip tightens on my hair. A rasping moan rumbles from the back of my throat, sounding more beast than man as she unwittingly toys with my pleasure-pain responses, our mouths fused together in an endless kiss.

She tastes exactly as I remember. Of wine and sweetness, of want, and heat and fucking bliss as she presses her body against me, close yet not nearly close enough.

"I want you so fucking much." Since she walked into the kitchen at breakfast. Since I found her floating in my bath. Since she crept out of the hotel room five years ago.

But I can't tell her any of that as she drops down on my cock and rocks.

I lose the power of fucking speech.

"But this is so wrong," she whispers, her tongue swiping across the seam of my lips. "Complicated." But how complicated can it be when I don't have the power to process thought? Not as she kisses me like she means to fuck me because this isn't a woman at war with herself. This is a woman whose body is in command.

"Fuck wrong, angel." Because nothing that feels this good could ever be wrong. Fuck the consequences. And for a man who prides himself on his control . . . "Just fuck me."

I feel her smile against my mouth as I let her lead, my mouth at her mercy, her hot centre brushing against me. Her fists full of my hair, she jerks my head back, the sensation somehow hardwired from my scalp to my cock. I ache as she presses kisses along my jawline, then curse as she reaches my ear and her teeth close over the fleshy lobe.

"*Yeah. Just like that.*"

"You like that." Her words are a tantalising breath in my ear, despite their hesitancy, but there is nothing tentative in her movements as she rocks over me. "God, you feel so hard."

I swallow over my need, over my desire to flip her under me because if this is the way she wants me, I'm hers for the taking.

"It's all you. All for you."

"I made you hard." She undulates over me, her smile audible as she presses her lips to my neck.

"Fuck, yeah, you did. The way you feel. Your scent. Your beautiful mouth and the way you kiss me. And the taunting heat of your sweet pussy." Her kisses become hotter, wetter almost immediately, and I growl as she scrapes her teeth against my carotid artery. She's building a pyre on which we'll both burn.

"What are you doing to me?" she whispers, the heat of her burning through my jeans.

"Not as much as I want to." I slide my hands up the

legs of her shorts because we're not close enough. I need her under me—crave the touch of her skin. And maybe she feels the same as her fingers rake down my chest. I jerk at the unexpected sensation, bucking up into her, my cock as hard as an iron rod. "I can't wait to get my mouth on you. Can't wait to hear you scream."

As though in answer, she presses her mouth to mine as she begins to pluck at the hem of my sweater. All thoughts of right and wrong, of complexities and repercussions come secondary to the burgeoning weight of our need as we scramble to pull it over my head.

At fucking last.

I groan as her warm hands find my chest, struggling to pull my cuff free from where it's caught on my watch, so it takes me a moment to realise she's studying me. Her dark eyes follow the flex of my lats, the tightening of my abs as I fight my way loose.

But the way she looks at me . . . it would inspire a man to many a misdeed.

"I need you," I growl, finally pulling free and in doing so almost toppling her from my knee.

"Oh!"

"You're going nowhere," I growl as I band my arms around her back to pull her against me.

"That was close." She slides her arms around my neck, her chest rising and falling with tight little breaths.

"Not close enough. I need to feel you, angel. Let me have you."

We are a flurry of motion. Her hands on my belt and mine on her shirt. Lacking the patience to play nice with the buttons, I pull it over her head to reveal *not* what I expected. A pink T-shirt? Promptly pulling at the hem, I whip it up and over her head . . . to find a tight, white undershirt.

My eyes lift, hers dancing with merriment, her bottom lip rolled inward as though to prevent a giggle.

"Is there a problem with the thermostat in your room?" I find myself asking. Three layers and counting? "What's next? A chastity belt?"

She gives a quick shake of her head, her shrug just as fast. "Maybe. Sort of? I suppose these were insurance policies against you seeing . . ." Her fingers retract from my zipper to grasp the hem of her undershirt, pulling it up and over her head.

"You wore extra layers of clothing to—"

"Hide this."

"*Fuck*." My curse is drawn out over endless syllables, unprepared for the sight in front of me. Extra layers of clothing to fuck indeed. "You're a cruel, cruel woman," I rasp. Sliding my hands around her ribs, I skim them upwards to frame her breasts. Breasts barely encased by what looks like a balconette bra made of sheer lilac cobwebs. I've seen her naked before, and yes, I was blessed with an inadvertent flash this morning, but this is different. This is gorgeous. And this is all for me.

"My eyes are up here."

"And lovely eyes they are too, but I'm a little busy greeting my old friends here."

"Really?" Her giggle draws off as I run my thumbs over the rosy pebbles of her nipples.

"Yes, really." My whisper sounds rough, but this, this is such a sensation overload. The heat of her pussy over me, the silk of her skin. The fucking sight of her. I'd thought her body perfect before, but she's grown into her perfection. There's an abundance about her that wasn't there before. I slide my hands along the gentle flare of her hips, cup her soft, full breasts as I lower my mouth to her nipples.

"Please . . ." The hunger in that word causes my gaze to rise from my exploration, my gaze meeting hers. Dark and hungry eyes, their gilding of gold lustrous with desire. A gaze a man could drown in. "Please, Carson, just touch me." Her words are little more than a tremulous breath.

Her hunger and pleas make me harder than ever, my name on her lips like a benediction I don't deserve. But it's not in my nature to give in at a first request. I like my lovers a little desperate and a little unhinged before I give in.

"Tell me," I whisper, following the ruffle of her bra with my finger, trailing it over the swell of her breast. "When you chose your underwear this morning, were you thinking of me?"

"Don't tease."

"Oh, sweet girl, you have no idea." Her eyes flame at my words, and she whimpers audibly, pushing herself into my hands. But I keep here there as I use both thumbs and forefingers to tease her nipples into hard peaks. "Tell me."

"Y-yes." The word stutters from her lips, her spine arching as she presses herself into my hands.

"Thinking about me seeing you? Touching you?" My head dips, and I trace the rise and fall of her flesh with my tongue.

"*Yes. Oh, God, yes.* I thought about your big hands on me. The sucking marks you left on my body, but I didn't mean for you to see."

"You weren't going to let me see you? Let me do this?" Curling my fingers into each of the cups, I watch as her breasts spill free. What a sight she is, pink-cheeked, dark-eyed, her mouth open softly and pouting. I take her nipple between my lips, relishing the tenor of her sigh as she wraps her hand around my head.

"Oh, that's . . . that is so good."

I growl my agreement against her skin. I love that she's into this, love that she's so fucking responsive. When I eventually move my head, her lavished nipples are taut, wet, and shining in the lamplight.

"Goddam, I want to fuck these." Make them shine with other fluids.

Her laughter is sudden and free, and I note with gratification she didn't disagree. Slotting the idea to another time, I slip my hand around her, unclipping her bra as the other tugs the ribbon tie of her pyjama pants.

"Please don't tell me you've anything else on under these because I need this pussy on my face."

"You're dirtier than I remember."

"Get naked, and let me refresh your memory."

"Mummeee!"

We halt—hands frozen awkwardly in clothing, eyes wide and ears peeled. At least until Lulu's next sorrowful wail when we become a flurry of motion. "I got popcorn coming out of my n-n-nose!"

It's a cry that doesn't announce her appearance but comes from the hallway. Fee almost vaults from my legs, stumbles, then bangs her toe on the edge of the coffee table.

"Ouch! Ouch." She hops around almost comically. "Holy fluff!"

"Almost." It was almost heavenly.

"What?" Her brow puckers, and as she swings around to face me, her hair coming loose from her silken ponytail.

"M-m-mummeee!"

"I'm coming, sweetie. My top. Where's my top?" she whisper-hisses, whipping her bra from the couch before deciding against it as necessary.

"Here." I hold out her undershirt, and she whips it from my hands, stabbing her arms through the holes.

"Can I help?" I scan the space behind the back of the sectional for my sweater when her derisory laughter brings me up short.

If she has any buttons left on her pyjama shirt, she doesn't bother to fasten them before she begins to hobble away. And her answer to my offer of help? Words thrown over her shoulder.

"I think you've done quite enough."

11

FEE

I lie awake most of the night, barely daring to breathe, let alone sleep.

After rubbing Lulu's back while she cried and vomited, cleaning her up, stripping the sheets, and soothing her to sleep, there really wasn't any point going into the den to see if Carson had waited. It was far too late by then.

So the reason the dirty bed linen is stuffed behind the bathroom door rather than in the washing machine in the laundry room is . . .?

Shut up, brain.

I wasn't going out there because I shouldn't have been drinking wine with him in the first place, okay? And that's why, when he'd knocked softly on the bedroom door to check if we were both okay, I'd tightened my grip on my child and pretended to be asleep.

Sweet girl. The endearment was like a flicked switch, turning the feminist in me to goo. His dark whisper made my insides glow, and I wanted so much to be good for him. Because surely, good little girls get their just rewards.

Especially when they're sitting on him.

Be strong, I remind myself. You're a woman. A mother. Not anyone's good or sweet girl.

"Because kisses aren't trifles." Trifles to be frittered away on a man who has no plans of being Lu's father and my forever.

"Ooh, Mummy. Don't talk about trifle when my hummy still turts."

"What?" At least she didn't pick up on kisses. "Your tummy still hurts?"

"Why are you whipsering?"

"Because . . . it's early, and maybe Carson is still asleep."

"Uncle Carson promised to make me pancakes with bluebs this morning."

"Did he?" Now *that* is a breakfast I'm not partaking in. Maybe I can persuade her to go to a café for crepes instead, and we can sneak out again. "You shouldn't eat pancakes. Not after you were so ill. How about—"

"It doesn't matter 'cause he's not here." Lu throws her arms around her chest, her brow pulling down low.

"Not here?" I repeat, pushing up onto my elbows. "How do you know?"

"'Cause his bed is tidy, and he isn't in it."

"You shouldn't be snooping in Uncle Carson's bedroom." *Who knows who or what you might find when you do?* A horror-filled thought suddenly hits me then, but for Lulu's tummy troubles, it might've been *me* she found in there this morning.

After everything I've done to protect her.

After everything I've done to normalise her life without a father.

Cradling her chin in my hand to guarantee her

attention, I bring my eyes level with hers. "His room is off-limits, Lulu." And so is he, even if I seemed to be temporarily deaf and blind to those facts last night.

Worse than that, I took the lead.

Oh, God. What have I done?

I rode his lap like a pony at a county fair!

What must he think of me?

That I'm the world's biggest cock tease.

And that is some cock to tea—nope, not going down that road.

How will I face him after this?

Maybe I'll need to fake my death?.

I am the worst person in existence, and not just because I flaked on him without a word of explanation. But because I blamed it all on him.

You've already done quite enough. When that was all on me.

"Can you let go of my face now?"

"Sorry, sweets. Urgh!" Pulling my pillow from behind, I press it to my face in an attempt to muffle my mortification. *I* was at fault last night. *I* took the lead.

"Is your tummy ouchie, too?" Lulu tugs at the edge of the pillow, her sweet face filled with concern.

"As a matter of fact, it is." Swirly and sickly and cramping with anxiety. But there's nothing else for it. I'll just have to pull on a pair of big girl knickers (not the kind that have a demi bra to match) and next time I see him, I'll apologise.

I'll reassure him, *it's not you, it's me.*

Even if it is *actually* him, because the last man I rubbed myself against like a cat in heat was, in fact, him. For five years, I've managed to behave with perfect decorum. I've become practically revirginized! Yet a couple of nights under the same roof as Carson Hayes, and I've become a rampant strumpet.

I need to tell him that I'm not the same person I was before and that I wasn't even that person back then. I've always been responsible and played by the rules. That my behaviour last night, and the night so long ago . . . is all on him. Because I've never felt the attraction, the strength of feeling that I have for him.

My secret lover. The night I've told no one about.

Oh, my fudge knuckles. I press my hands to my burning cheeks. I'm so embarrassed that I'll have to have this conversation with him that I could almost go and live under a bridge instead.

"Mummy? Is the chest Uncle Carson keeps at the bottom of his bed for his toys?"

Yes. Some very particular toys.

"No. It's full of bedlinens." His toys are in a drawer in his closet.

I know. I should practise what I preach on the prying front, but in my defence, I only looked once.

Once was more than enough.

"How do *you* know that? It's locked."

Because the key was on the dresser.

Okay, the top drawer of the dresser.

Under some socks. That is, the key to his toy stash. I'm not at all sure what's in the blanket box. Honestly, after the toys, I didn't dare look.

"Because it's called a blanket chest," I say, using my *because I said so* tone.

The man obviously has a very active and varied love life judging by the array of toys in there. The thought is quickly followed by another, a one much less welcome. What happens if he brings someone home while we're here? My stomach twists like a rusty chain as the thoughts continue, sudden and unwelcome with images accompanying them. Carson. A woman in his bed. Faceless. Nameless. Not me.

"I promise I wasn't looking at the watches again." My daughter's voice brings me back from a place of dread. A voice that says she was doing exactly what she promises she wasn't. "But Norman's tummy was talking," she says, brandishing her tatty rabbit. "He wanted Uncle Car to make pancakes."

"Well, if he's not here, he can't make them." And if he's not here, he won't be tying anyone to his bed who isn't me. At least, not this morning.

But he might've left last night for that exact purpose.

Or similar.

I hate my brain right now. Whether he left last night to tie up a hundred women should be no concern of mine. At least, that's what I try to tell myself as I push the mass of dark waves from Lulu's face. "He probably had to leave on business."

The kind of business we started on the couch last night.

The kind of business that left him as hard as a pole and without an outlet.

"Or maybe he's out running!" Yes, that could be it. He definitely takes care of himself. I've seen the evidence. Plus, all those running shoes in his closet, and yesterday morning he'd looked dressed for exercise. Shorts and compression tights and one of those T-shirts meant to wick away sweat that, in his case, were more like an advertisement for those delicious broad shoulders, chest, and abs.

But as an explanation, this sounds much more appealing, even if it means I'll still have to face him soon because vertical exercise alone is better than finding him doing the horizontal kind with someone else.

"I don't think he's running, Mummy. I think he's not here, and he's not going to make me pancakes even though he pwomised." Mutiny sits in the jut of her chin.

"It's too early for tantrums," I say with a groan.

"I'm just cross!" She wraps her arms around her chest —the four-year-old version of folding them. "Because I'm distapointed."

"Disappointment is a fact of life." Especially where men are concerned. "You'd better get used to it." *I wouldn't be surprised if he's thinking the same about me this morning.*

"When I get big, I'm going to make pancakes for breakfast every day."

"But for now, I guess you'll just have to do with weekend pancakes made by yours truly."

"Who's Yorls Trudy?"

"Never mind," I say with a sigh. I wonder if I should book her a hearing test?

There's an envelope on the kitchen countertop when we finally make our way there.

An envelope addressed to Lulu.

"For me!" She whips it from under my fingertips, ripping it open though it isn't sealed. "It's a pretty parrot!" she exclaims as she pulls out a correspondence card illustrated with what looks like a macaw in the top right-hand corner. I didn't think people still used correspondence cards and find myself smiling at the whimsy in this one. "And dollars! Lots of them. Five and five is ten, and one more five is fifteen . . ." She bends to pick them up as they flutter to the floor.

"Aren't you going to read the card?" I ask, wondering what the letter might mean and if there's a message in there for me. *Like I deserve one . . .*

"After I've counted my money. I'm rich!"

"All you need to do now is keep the plants alive." At least until we move out. Soon. Very soon. Because we can't stay here, not now.

"Dear Lulu," she begins to recite, running her finger under the masculine script, which turns from a spikey cursive to print after just a couple of words. "Please find en . . . enclosed. You read it, please." She thrusts it into my hand. "His handwriting is too messy."

"Dear Lulu," I begin, "I hope you're feeling much better this morning." My heart gives a little pinch. How can someone so . . . provoking be so sweet? "Please find enclosed the sum agreed upon for the position of plant whisperer for the next two months." From pinch to plummet, my heart hits my heels. He's not here, and he's not coming back anytime soon. It's a fact that makes me feel a little tearful, apparently.

And so it should. I ought to be ashamed. I've driven the man out of his house! He obviously can't bear to set eyes on me.

I scan the rest, intending to give her the highlights, relieved there's no sign of anything resembling 'please tell your mom from me to drop dead'. But the fact that there's not one word in it intended for me makes me feel wretched.

It's only what I deserve.

"Can you not read his writing either?"

"Oh. Sorry." My gaze is still on the letter, though

unseeing, I begin to read again. "Well, it seems the plants in this apartment like to know how the Yankees are doing."

"What's a Yankee?"

"It's a baseball team. You know, the sport with teams and a bat and a ball. It's very popular here."

"What else does it say?"

"His plants also like to know what the weather is like outside and enjoy being read to occasionally." I consider keeping the rest from her but say it anyway. "Mr Hayes says—"

"Uncle Carson."

Split the difference? The hot man I almost humped last night.

"—he says he's sure they'd appreciate hearing some Yeats."

Is this my punishment? I don't get the opportunity to explain or apologise, but I do get to read Yeats to a couple of parlour palms? Lulu might like me to read Yeats to her occasionally, especially his tales of fairies. What little girl doesn't adore the sort of creature who leaves gifts for the kind-hearted and teases the surly?

Hmm. Maybe Carson Hayes is a fairy.

An outsized one?

There are few four-year-olds equipped to read the works of W.B. Yeats themselves, but maybe he didn't know that, not being a parent himself. Whatever the case, it looks like, for the foreseeable future, I'll be reading W.B. Yeats to a bit of greenery under the supervision of a four-year-old dictator. Sorry, *manager.*

"Hmm." Lulu's expression turns thoughtful as she taps her finger against her cheek. "I can't read that good.

Maybe we can find some on YouTube, and they can listen from my iPad instead?"

"That's a really good idea."

"A good idea that deserves pancakes for breakfast?"

Rose is right. This kid will probably end up ruling the world.

12

FEE

"Get a wriggle on, Lulu. We're going to be late." My heels hammer against the marble foyer, and I'm already regretting that I didn't slip on a pair of flats. "I know it's called the *school run*," I throw over my shoulder, "but that doesn't mean we have to dash in at the last minute every day."

"I can't be fast on Mondays. Also, my feets don't have wheels," she retorts as she continues to dawdle.

"Good morning, ma'am." Mr Martinez, the night doorman—porter?—is still on duty, and he beats me to the door.

"Morning." I pull my skirt a little from where it's bunched at my thighs. "I think wheels ought to be included on the four-year-old model, at least between the hours of seven and nine in the morning." I turn back to my daughter as she idles along, her tiny pink backpack strapped to her back as she watches dust motes swirling idly in a shaft of sunlight almost in a state of wonder.

How could anyone be angry with something so darling?

Frustrated? Now that's another story.

"I'm sorry?" His voice brings me back from my ruminations, and I give my head a quick shake.

"Kids have two speeds Monday through Friday. Stop and slow."

"So true," I reply with a chuckle. "Do you have children?"

"Two girls. My eldest, Sophia, is a senior. She's looking for a babysitting job if you don't mind me mentioning it."

"No, I don't mind at all."

"It's just, you don't seem to have a nanny or anything, and she has experience—lots of little cousins—and references, too."

Nanny. Pah! We don't even belong here, Mr. Martinez.

Not that I'm going to confide any of that in him.

"I don't really go out much in the evenings," I answer with a tiny shrug. Even as I do, it strikes me as a good plan to have someone lined up as an emergency backup. I'll be moving soon, fingers crossed, but there can be no harm in asking to meet the girl.

"Miss Eloise goes to the French school, right? Sophia's high school is nearby. You know, if you ever need her to . . ."

"Help with the school run? Actually, that's a really good idea." Especially as I'd been offered a spot to run an early morning yoga class at the clinic last week. I wonder if I can tell them I've changed my mind.

"Ed," he prompts. "And if you find you ever need her in the evenings, she could come in with me. And we live close by, so getting home is no problem."

While I don't think my conscience could cope with sending a teenager out into the streets of Manhattan at night, the idea of having someone else to rely on is becoming more and more appealing. "Maybe I could meet her?" I say as Lulu reaches the door. Finally!

"Sure. Anytime." He beams widely back at me, which makes me wonder if I'm doing him a favour rather than the other way around.

"*Allons-y, ma chérie!*" Oops. I forgot I'm not refer to Lu as *darling* outdoors. It's bad for a four-year-old's street cred or something. "Come on!"

"One other thing, ma'am? We need to enter the apartment today for maintenance work."

"Oh. Does Mr Hayes know?" My stomach flips as his name passes my lips.

"Er, yeah." The man tugs on his ear, suddenly shifting from foot to foot. "We received his instruction this morning."

I bite back the urge to ask if he knows where he called from, my mind returning to the weekend and the complete mess I've made of things.

"Ma'am?"

My frown retracts as I move on to the things I can control as I do a quick mental scan of how the place looks. No knickers left on the floor and no bras hooked around the backs of chairs. *Or stuffed down the back of sofas.* "That's fine. Do you need the key?"

"No, ma'am." Now he's smiling at me as though I've said something cute. "It's all taken care of. You have a good day now."

"Bye, Ed!" Lulu skips out onto the sidewalk, and I grab her hand. "I thought we were in a hurry," she asks, looking back at me. "You talk too much."

Pushing aside the awkwardness of being lodger to a man you've shagged, I really will miss the convenience of living in Carson's apartment when we move out. It's just a ten-minute walk to Lulu's school, and a few minutes more to reach the clinic. I can't say how relieved I am not to have to deal with the subway every morning, or the train as the network seems to be referred to here. But I expect we'll have to get used to it at some point, sadly.

"Morning, Fee." Lizzie, the receptionist, or front desk executive as she prefers, shoots me a beaming smile as I bustle in through the clinic's front door. "It's a lovely morning, isn't it?"

"Gorgeous," I agree, sliding my cardigan from one shoulder. It's not terribly warm, but hurrying like a mofo can make a girl feel a little flushed. "Any news on my paperwork?"

"Sorry." She gives an apologetic shrug. "I'll chase them up again today." Until my qualifications are accredited, I can't sit in on any of the sessions, which is really what I'm here in New York for. I want to hone my counselling skills, learn more about client reactions to Compassion-Focussed Therapy, and even see if hypnotherapy is for me, not as a client, but maybe I could look into adding it to my skill set. But for now, I'm basically hanging around the office of this upscale (even for Manhattan) women's wellness centre, which is mostly a weight management clinic. Not that I'm not enjoying myself. For starters, the team members are a little bit loopy. *My kind of people.*

"Oh. Do you think it would be okay if I left this on the reception desk?" I pull out a collection tin that Lulu brought home from school. "My daughter's school is having a charity drive for the homeless."

"I'm not sure." She stares at the tin covered in Lulu's

artistry—the yellows, reds, and blues not at all in keeping with the clinic's tastefully beige reception. "I'll have to ask Ethan."

"It's meant to be filled with spare change from home, but as there's only her and me at home, I thought popping it here might raise a little money." I find myself shrugging, picking it up again. "If you don't think he'll want it on the desk, I suppose I can just take it into the office."

"Sure." She nods happily, seeming much relieved. "I think that might be better."

No making the rich clients feel uncomfortable in the clinic, Fee.

Or in the swanky 5th Avenue apartment building. Poor Mr Martinez. My request made him feel uncomfortable, even if he did stick a couple of dollars in the slot.

"Wotcha, love!" Bethany, one of the junior psychologists, calls from across the office as I bustle in, her greeting more Dick Van Dyke in *Mary Poppins* than anything remotely authentic.

"Morning, Bethany."

"How was that?" she asks eagerly, pushing her dark bob behind her ears. "Am I going to pass for a real Londoner next summer?"

"Sure, you'll blend." Marta, my favourite dietician on staff, sniggers. "Talk like that, and the locals will warm to you in no time. That or throw you into the Thames."

"I ain't bovvered." Beth sniffs, which only reinforces her impersonation of the movie chimney sweep, then gives an affected shrug.

"Where on earth are you getting all this from?" I throw the question over my shoulder as I make my way over to the desk I've been designated, plonk down in it then slide my purse into the drawer.

"I went down an internet rabbit hole last night."

"You're supposed to be studying for your doctorate." Marta sends her a disapproving look over the top of her laptop.

"I'll get there," Beth replies with an airy wave. In the short while I've worked here, I've learned that despite being both in their late twenties, Marta has worked her butt off to get where she is while Bethany comes from money and has a pretty blasé attitude about work. But despite the office banter, they're both passionate about helping people lead happier, healthier lives. Except for Bethany's (recent) ex-husband, who can "suck donkey dick" before either of them would lift a finger to benefit him.

This is the kind of place that should have one of those signs that reads: *you don't have to be crazy to work here, but it helps!*

I find I fit right in.

"At least you're not the last one in this morning." Beth turns her attention back to me, her finger waggling side to side in the air between us. "No trip to the 'bucks for *you* as punishment."

And this is why I'll never be late, not if I can help it. I don't have the money to waste in Starbucks on chai lattes, skinny muffins, and fruit salads for the whole office, or even the three of us. Besides, we all know that position falls to Ethan every day. That is, whenever he finally deigns to join us. As owner—part owner?—of the clinic, as well as also being a sports psychologist by discipline, he can well afford it.

"I thought we were supporting the little café on the corner now, not the mega conglomerate?" Marta quirks a brow as she sits back in her chair.

"Ah, but that was before Fee saw rats on the sidewalk." Beth sounds as though she wants to laugh, but it's true—I thought they were terriers at first.

"This is New York." Marta pulls a pen from her flame-red messy bun, pointing it in my direction. "Of course you saw rats. Quit kvetching."

"I'm sorry," I murmur primly. "Just because I don't fancy sharing my bagel with the cast of *Ratatouille*. But by all means"—I press my hand to my forehead then begin to shake—"you enjoy your leptospirosis latte." I'm in the middle of miming a lepto-induced seizure when the boss walks in.

"I think we should all have what Fee is having," Ethan announces with a grin. "Though dropping acid at work is usually frowned upon."

"It was supposed to be leptospirosis," I say in a small voice that goes unheard at Beth's dramatic announcement.

"Oh, my God. I think I love you." She prises her and Marta's coffees from the cardboard coffee carrier in his hand. "This is *just* what the doctor ordered."

"Maybe it will be if you ever get your doctorate." Marta gives a tiny yet disapproving shake of her head as she accepts her coffee.

"For you." Ethan places the carrier on my desk, passing over my usual matcha latte with a flourish. "What's in one of those, anyway?" He leans nonchalantly against my desk, his broad thigh pressed against the edge.

"Japanese green tea leaf," I answer without much conviction.

"What's this?" he asks, picking up Lulu's tin.

"It's for a fundraising drive my daughter's school is running. It's for the homeless."

"Cool." He places it down again . . . without putting any money in.

I really didn't know how to take Ethan. I mean, he seems nice and is always laughing, though we have very little interaction professionally. Surely the fact that he buys us coffee every morning shows he's generous. *Doesn't it?*

"I brought it in for donations," I say, giving the tin a shake.

"Good idea." He turns away, deliberately obtuse or just a bit imperceptive, I don't know.

For the love of God, do I have to hit you over the head with it? No, I suppose you'll just drop a few rungs in my estimations.

"So, what's your excuse for being late today, Ethan?" Beth peels the lid from her cup, blowing a little suggestively on the froth. "Was it Amber? Kelly? Amelie, maybe?"

If he's supposed to be the boss, why does he let the staff tease him like this?

"You know he only likes one taste," Marta says, joining in. "Those girls were so last month."

"You make me sound like a bad man." He turns to Marta with an exaggerated pout.

Tight fisted.

"So it's them, not you?" Marta's tone turns arch. Maybe I'm not the only one who has a low opinion of him. As well as tight-fisted, he's the biggest flirt I've ever met. Maybe with the exception of Carson Hayes, perhaps. I'd like to think Carson is more discriminate, even if, in reality, I have no idea who he's flirting with right now. My stomach swoops unhappily, and I push the thought to the back of my mind.

"You know what they say. Classy women don't have one-night stands," Beth interjects with a tinkling laugh. "They have auditions. Maybe Ethan just isn't getting the callbacks."

"Do you hear what they're saying about me?" He turns to face me again, and I resist the urge to shake the donation tin again.

You should hear what they say about you when you're not here, I think but have the sense not to say. He's still the boss, and I'm here as a favour, so there's no way I'll join in with their teasing.

"Ladies." He turns a little dramatically to the other members of his audience. "You're hurting my heart."

"Or we would if you had one." Strolling over to him, Beth pats her palm in the centre of his chest. "Hollow, see? Just like the tinman."

"I bring you breakfast," he says, lifting her hand and pressing his lips to her knuckles, "and you give me abuse."

"And that's the way you like it."

"So you've heard, huh?" He winks, then lowers her hand, grabs his beverage of choice from my desk, then leaves the room. "I gotta class in twenty. You girls have fun."

"Oh, my God." Beth exhales a rush of air as she collapses dramatically into the chair on the opposite side of my desk. "I really need to get laid. Every day that passes, I get closer to sleeping with him."

"Really? Sorry, I didn't mean to squeak." I try not to pull a face as I add, "I mean, he's good looking—"

"In that obvious, older guy way." Beth takes a mouthful of her coffee, seeming to scald her tongue. "That is, if you like Botox and a perma-tan."

"You could do worse. The man has money," Marta

suggests.

"Ew, no. Besides, his parents own this place, not him. He's like the eternal playboy or something."

"But it'll all come to him." Marta angles her head, sending a superior glance my way.

"What are you looking at me for?"

"Men and money," Marta repeats. "She already has money, and I already have a man."

"Oh, what, so by the process of elimination, it has to be me?"

"You're forgetting she lives in a 5th Avenue apartment." Beth hooks a thumb my way. "With endless views of the park."

"Yeah, but it's not mine."

"Then why not you." Marta shrugs before moving her attention back to her laptop.

"I thought you and the guy with the apartment were a thing." Beth's voice pulls my attention, and I shake my head.

"I'm more like the lodger." She looks back blankly. "A roomie?" I try, the word coming to me courtesy of American sitcoms. I decide it's probably best that I don't explain that Lulu and I live there without the presence of our so-called landlord. I don't want her to turn up on the doorstep after finding herself unexpectedly in the neighbourhood.

"Is he good-looking?"

"Does it matter?"

"Who'd want to give up a view of the park?" She stands from her chair, triumph settling around her shoulders like a cloak. "And you're more than roomies, I can tell. I'm sensing a little sexual tension around that cute mouth of yours."

I force my mouth to relax, my lips pursed like a cat's bum. Tension yes, but sexual?

More like sexual frustration, for me at least.

"It's not like that." I drop my gaze to the contents of my cup because it's not like anything. I need to face the facts. Just because we had sex years ago and then we almost had a repeat on the sofa doesn't mean Carson is interested in me. I mean, he might've been interested in the moment, like any man. But now?

He can't be because his very actions point to the opposite.

Besides, he owes me nothing.

Which is pretty much what he's delivered.

No note.

No text.

No phone call.

Nothing to suggest he'll return at any point.

Which is just as well, I tell myself again and again, because it saves me from the embarrassment of apologising. From locking myself in my bedroom. From pointing out that heavy petting on the couch—hell, any surface—can't happen again.

"Are you sexin' without the serious?"

Beth's questioning tone captures my attention. "Sorry, what?"

"You and him, are you friends with benefits?"

We're not even friends.

"Since when has my sex life become a topic for discussion?"

"At least you have one." She waggles her eyebrows comically. "Did you not just hear me say I'm this close to having sex with my older yet slightly creepy boss?" She holds her thumb and forefinger an inch apart.

"You won't do it," Marta mutters without lifting her head. "You can't even swallow a raisin. You'll never survive an old penis."

I chuckle, though press my hand to my mouth.

"Shows what you know." Beth hooks her arm over the back of the chair to slide Marta an expressive look. "You know, I haven't had sex for so long that I actually moaned when my massage therapist laid his hands on me during my appointment last week. Moaned! Like I was enjoying it way too much." My chuckle turns to a snorting laugh. "Go ahead, yuck it up, but I'm serious. My dry spell is beginning to resemble the damn Sahara."

My laughter morphs to something that sounds much less pleasant as I begin to fire up my computer. "I bet your dry spell hasn't lasted five years."

Oh, hell. The words fall from my mouth without a thought, the office immediately falling deathly silent. Beth freezes, and Marta's keyboard tapping halts. Even the traffic outside seems to stop.

With a groan, I plant my head on my desk. "Please, please, *please* forget I ever said that."

"What the hell?" I'm not sure if it's shock or awe I can hear in Beth's voice. "You're gorgeous. Young. Single. Totally hot!" With each word, she ticks off the points against her fingers, sounding a little more hysterical on my behalf. "You lived in France, the home of *l'amour!* French kissing, French letters—French men!"

"I have a child," I answer with a tight shrug.

"So do over half the childbearing-aged women in the US! If you can't find a man, what chance do I have?"

"I'm not looking for a man." I keep my gaze resolutely on my screen, my fingers hovering over the keys. *I already found*—scratch that thought. Five years without a spark of interest in anyone until now. How can that even be? "What I need is an apartment," I say, forcing my mind from the topic of Carson Hayes.

"Girl, you need both. But I can only help you with an apartment."

"I was actually going to ask if you knew a decent realtor." Not one determined to waste Rose's money.

"I can probably do better than that. My sister has a place over on 107th Street, between Amsterdam and Broadway she's looking to let."

"Why didn't you say so," Marta gripes.

"I didn't think she was serious," she throws over her shoulder before turning back to me. "Why would anyone want to leave a view of the park?"

"Because it's just a stopgap." I wave away her question. "But your sister's place?"

"It could be kinda perfect. She's moving in with her boyfriend but doesn't want a long-term lease or move all of her belongings. You know, just in case."

"Of course." I find myself nodding, my insides a strange mixture of excitement and dread.

"I'll call her now." She stands and makes her way over to her own desk. "See when's good for you to have a look around."

"Great! Beth, I don't know what to say, except thank you. I *so* appreciate your help."

"No problem." Phone in hand, she angles her gaze my way. I can't exactly make out her expression as she adds, "One good turn deserves another, though, right?"

"Of course," I reply without thinking. I have to do this. I have to move on. I can't carry on living where I am. Because I can't get Carson Hayes out of my head.

13

CARSON

Glasses chink, the hum of conversations and laughter mingling with the sultry sounds of a band playing somewhere. I pause on the threshold of the ballroom as I cast my gaze around the room, gowns of a dozen colours and a hundred more hues make the ballroom looks like a meadow filled with summer blooms. And penguins, oddly enough, courtesy of the usual dress code for these kinds of events. *Black tie.* Though tonight I've shaken things up a little myself by wearing a white dinner jacket over black everything else. It's quite a dapper look, or so my tailor tells me.

My heart sinks, and I ask myself once more what I'm doing here. There are so many more pleasant places to be. Like in my apartment making myself at home between a certain woman's legs. But the reason I'm currently standing in The Drake Hotel in Chicago and not in my apartment in Manhattan is the same as always. Penance. The sins of the father might not be visited upon his descendants, yet I'm compelled to atone for my grandfather's misdeeds.

"Why, Carson Hayes, don't you look almost edible tonight."

Penance, I silently remind myself as I fix a smile on my face and turn to take my admirer's hands. "Only almost?"

"No one likes a man who fishes for compliments, dear."

"Yet here you are."

"Incorrigible man." She swats me with her tiny purse, something barely big enough for a compact, let alone a wallet. But I know she's good for a sizeable donation.

"You're looking particularly lovely tonight, Miss Carter." If lovely is a testament to the art of her surgeon's skills. What is it with some women's desire for eternal youth? Don't they understand that there is beauty in every stage of a woman's life?

But we must all play our parts, and my part is to squeeze donations from tight purses, especially from cattle heiresses with nothing but boy toys and diamonds to spend it on.

"It's Adrienne," she purrs. "You must call me Adrienne. As I've told you that so many times before. You know, Carson, I've a mind to make a *very* generous donation tonight."

"And I'm sure the good patrons would be delighted to hear it."

I exchanged a night with an angel for this.

No. I removed myself from the temptation of an angel because she deserves better than me. *You've already done quite enough.* She's right because I want her with a force that can't be good for either of us.

"It was a particular kind of donation I was thinking about. A very large contribution. Why don't you come sit with me?" Her mouth a small moue, she walks her fingers up my lapel. "Maybe we could sneak out. Go somewhere quiet and talk for a while."

It's a talent that she can make *talk* sound so tawdry.

"I'm sorry, Adrienne. You know I can't do that." Covering her fingers with my own, I lift them away. "If you want to discuss a donation to the foundation outside of tonight's event, you know where to find me."

"I have your assistant's details. And I don't want to discuss it with him."

"Tucker is my business partner, not my assistant. He takes care of the details." For Ardeo.

"While you take care of business?" She quirks a brow, her tone jaunty. "Or so I've heard."

"Some things are better experienced than alluded to second-hand. I'm sure you'll appreciate that. Now, if you'll excuse me, I see someone trying to catch my attention."

"Tell 'em to get in line." Her drawling assertion follows me, and I'm pretty sure I can feel her eyes glued to my ass. I fully expect she'll have made that call before the end of the night and for there to be a bidding war for our New York evening. *Which will aid Rose's foundation*, I remind myself.

A nod here, a handshake there, my mind turns to the matter at hand before my head is turned by a familiar laugh.

"*Remy? Merde, mais qu'est-ce que tu fais ici?*" What the hell are you doing here?

"We've come to help you squeeze a few purses." His hand claps my shoulder as he makes a grab for my hand.

"Rose didn't mention you'd be attending." My head swings around, expecting her to be but a few paces away. "Where is she?" Because where one half of the pair is, the other is usually somewhere close.

"Lusting after my wife still, I see." He grins widely. He loves to bust my balls about the one time I hit on Rose. She's pretty, and I'm male, but that was about the extent of my attraction. Actually, it was also about getting under his skin. But that's all behind us now. His attention slides to the usual third of the Remy/Rose party; Everett, the head of their security team. "Maybe I should've broken more than his nose when I had the chance. What do you think, Rhett?"

"If it'd been up to me," Everett replies, "I should've let you run him over in the Range Rover." He smirks. "If I remember, you were all for it back then. And quit talking in French. We're in an English-speaking country."

"We only speak French to protect you from Carson's terrible jokes."

But we all know this isn't true. Everett, or Rhett, understands the language perfectly. He just happens to butcher it when he opens his mouth.

"So, where is she?" I ask again. Tonight is one of Rose's benefit balls for the international charitable foundation she chairs. While she doesn't attend all fundraisers, she and Remy are almost inseparable.

"Rose is at home with Rocco." His expression firms. "He came down with a virus a few hours before we were due to depart."

"Is he okay?"

"Yes, it's just a cold, but his ears are sore, poor little man. We were worried the pressure in the plane would make it worse. But Rose was adamant we should still attend."

"She doesn't like to break a promise, does she? But how come I had no idea you were all planning on being here?"

"Because Rose planned it that way," he says with a small grin. "She wanted to fly to New York and surprise Fee."

"But none of us wanted to spend hours trapped with a screaming snot machine." Rhett's words, almost muttered into his glass, earn him a flash of angry green eyes from Remy.

"Or maybe his parents didn't want to put him through further suffering."

Rhett snorts. "Since when have you become an expert on parenting? Oh, that's right. Since you spent five minutes with Fee's kid?"

"How is that going?" Remy asks, his penetrating regard now on me.

"Going?" I answer blandly. "I'm not sure what you mean."

"She's staying in your apartment, so Rose tells me."

"Yes, but as you can see, without me in it."

"Except you forgot she was staying at your place." This from Rhett with a sneer. "And turned up unexpected, right?"

"I see my mistake has been the topic of conversation. I fucked up. Forgot she was there. And if you ask Fee, I'm sure she'll tell you I was just as surprised to see her there as she was me." *Hopefully*. I add a small rueful smile as a little embellishment to my tale while doing my best to ignore the sudden tightening in my crotch. She was so pink and blonde and deliciously discomforted. And, of course, naked.

"Arrive at night, did you?" There's a certain note in Rhett's tone. A note I don't particularly care for.

"Not that it's any of your business, but yes."

"Sort of like, *who's sleeping in my bed?*" he intones in a voice deeper than his own.

"What the fuck is he talking about?" I ask, catching Remy's gaze.

"Yes, what is it you're trying to say, Rhett?"

"That he probably went sniffing around to see which bed she was in," he retorts, levelling his attention on me. "Like a bear sniffing for fucking honey."

"And the honey is . . . your business, is she?" *Is that what's eating at his crotch tonight? Does he want a taste, or has he had one?* My mind trips seamlessly to Lulu and her parentage. *Both he and Lu have dark hair.*

A fist twists my intestines, though I force the implication away.

Remy and I didn't start on the best of terms back when he was determined to snatch up the European construction arm of what was then my grandfather's company. Our dealings were . . . fractious. Aggressive. But that was before I realised who my grandfather was.

If I'd known, I might've helped wield the axe.

Though Remy and I have buried that particular hatchet, with the help of Rose, I can't say the same for his shadow. But I don't give a fuck for Everett's opinion, and I don't care what he thinks of me. He's the hired muscle, not a friend. All I need is for him to keep a civil tongue in his head. Or barely civil, as is usually the way with him. It may sound strange, but I've always liked him more for it. I fucking abhor people who are impressed with wealth, people who fawn and kowtow as though money makes a person special.

Dark hair and similar colour eyes.

Could it be? Really?

"Maybe Fee is my business." My words pitch steely

and low, and I step into him when he answers my aggression with a little of his own.

"After five minutes?" Toe to toe, we're evenly matched. We're both former military, and we both know how to fight.

"What if I make her my business," I growl. "Her and the kid. Because if you can't take care of your own fucking business, maybe someone else should."

Everett smiles, all malice and teeth, his gaze roaming over me with contempt. "Fee's a smart girl. She knows better than to trust some rich twat who'll just fuck her before fucking her over."

"You think I would put her in that position?"

"I've heard about you and positions. And places. And prices," he mutters only for my ears.

"Boys, boys," Remy interjects with an amused chuckle. "As entertaining as watching this display of testosterone is, we're beginning to draw attention for more than our very handsome and striking appearances."

"He fucking started it," I growl, wondering exactly how much Everett knows. And how.

"Do you want me to say I'm putting an end to it? Just take your pissing contest elsewhere. This is a benefit to raise funds to aid the cause of stamping out violence against women, not creating it between a couple of dogs sniffing over a woman."

Is that what this is? It's not Lulu? Everett has a thing for Fee?

"When he tells me what business she is of his, I might just do that."

I register the weight of Remy's hand on my shoulder before I register his words. "Fee is family. Mine and Rose's, and yes, even Everett's. Understand Fee and Eloise are alone in a strange country and, as our family, we are all concerned with both their well-being."

"As I told Rose, they're both welcome to stay in my home." My attention swings back to Rhett. "And they do so alone."

"Of course. And we can trust Fee to make her own choices," Remy says, turning to Rhett. "As she has in the past."

"She knocked you back, didn't she?" I try not to crow, though not very hard. And he knows it. *Too bad, asswipe. If you haven't sealed the deal in the South of France, you're not doing it on my turf.*

"Fiadh doesn't date," Remy interjects. "Ever."

"What's that supposed to mean?" I find myself asking, turning back to him.

"Just that. She hasn't been in a relationship since before Lulu was born."

"She turns them down." Rhett's tone is venomous. "Won't even go out for a coffee with a bloke."

"I'm sure you can't know the workings of her life that closely." I could crow a little more at this point, but I won't. Because what happened between us on the sofa was hotter and sweeter than any coffee. And more addictive.

"But we do. She and Rose are as close as sisters. She works for the foundation, and she lives on the grounds of the family compound. Some family you choose. *Tu le comprends, je pense.* You understand that, I think."

Yes, I understand perfectly. From cocksure to cold in an instant. I know what happened on the sofa can't happen again. I'd be crossing boundaries. Risking the ruin of friendships because this is a woman not with baggage but one with guards. And why? Has she been hurt before? How fucking bad?

The noises of the room come back to my ears in a whoosh, and I grasp I've missed what Remy said.

"Sorry, what was that?"

"I said we should circulate," he repeats as Rhett returns his empty champagne glass to a passing server's tray.

"In your case," the asshole says as he turns back, "he means charm some women out of their wallets."

"For a good cause," Remy adds, sending his security detail a puzzled look as Rhett adds,

"Their wallets, remember. Not their underwear."

I return my glass too, but not before grabbing another. "Sounds like someone might be a little jealous. Do you need help getting laid, Everett?"

"I don't need your fucking help."

"You're sure about that?"

So, we circulate. I flatter, kiss a few ladies' hands, dole out a few compliments, and dance a few dances. I spend thirty minutes in the role of the auctioneer and garner a few laughs, brush off a couple of advances, and flatter those who assert 'if only they were a few years younger'. And I'm just about to leave, as usual, before dinner is served, when I find Everett blocking my path on the way out.

"What now?" I almost groan.

"I have a question for you." He appears to be the picture of ease with his shoulders pressed back against the wall and his hands stuck in his pockets. For once, not even his tone of voice betrays him. "Are you running a prostitution ring?"

I bark out a laugh, stunned and entertained. But I'm also wary. Very wary. "Why would you even ask that?"

"It was a yes or no question," he says, pushing away from the wall.

"No. The answer is no. What the fuck do you take me for?"

"Honestly? I've no idea. I know you're former military. Marines, wasn't it?" He pauses, his shoulders suddenly filling the narrow hall when I neither correct him nor bite. "Come the fuck on. I know you were a Navy SEAL, even if I don't understand why."

"You're not the only one confused." Pulling my cuffs straight, I proceed to examine the fingernails of my right hand as though scrutinising a rough spot. Why does he care? And more to the point, where the fuck is he getting his information from?

"Rich boys like you don't end up at the pointy end of the stick, not unless there's something wrong in there." He taps his forefinger angrily to his temple.

And unbalanced people run prostitution rings? What the fuck?

"Do you want to tell me why *you* signed up? Why you ended up doing three tours of some fleapit of a country as a flat head?" Everett's gaze flares. I can't be the only crazy one here, and I'm not the only one who's done a little digging. Everett is a former member of Her Majesty's Special Air Service. *The SAS.*

"For the same reason lads of fifteen lied about their age and ended up on the front lines a hundred years ago."

"For King and country," I answer with a dismissive snort.

"From lack of choices."

"My reasons are my own," I counter angrily.

"For pimping out your men as high-class escorts?"

"You've got some fucking balls," I growl, stepping into

him. “You know nothing about my business dealings, and you know nothing about me.”

“If this is about to blow up in the foundation’s face—”

“I would never do anything to risk Rose’s reputation. Or her work.”

“Given how your grandfather—”

“What is it they say about throwing stones in glass houses?” I retort, jabbing an angry finger his way. Then it dawns on me; Everett isn’t trying to goad me into a reaction as payback for whatever he thinks is going on with Fee. “You’re worried about Remy. About his family’s past.” A past linked inextricably with my own and with Rose’s. Like some unholy trinity.

“I don’t like secrets.”

“That is unfortunate, considering who you work for.” I like Remy, but the man makes me look like an open book.

“I’m paid to keep his secrets.”

“Which, in turn, will keep mine.”

The man glowers at my answer. “Unless you’re doing something stupid. Something to risk it all coming out.”

“Which I’m not.”

“You’re a loose cannon, Hayes. And you make no fucking sense,” he spits, his contemptible gaze roaming over me. “But I’ll get to the bottom of this, and when I do, you’ll wish you’d just fucking told me.”

“You think I’m just some playboy messing with people’s lives? Well, fuck you. I enlisted because my mother was one of those poor unfortunates stuck in the North Tower on 9/11. I enlisted because I was a stupid kid who wanted to make sure that no one, no one person, one family, one city, one fucking country, would lose a loved one because of terrorism.”

It fixed nothing, achieved nothing, except pissing off

my father for throwing away my education. *My station. My life*. He could barely bring himself to look at me, worried that the loss of my mother had made me a zealot.

But I wasn't. I was just an asshole kid. A couple of days into my first tour of Afghanistan and I was swiftly abused of my lofty ideals. But then my father died, still not understanding, and I went to work for my grandfather. And that was where I discovered that terror comes in many forms.

"That's . . . surprising," he answers soberly.

"Try fucking senseless." Stepping back, I glance down and straighten my cuffs, though my insides are still boiling with rage.

"And the other thing?"

I feed my hand into the inside pocket of my jacket, pulling out a card. "Let me save you the trouble of digging. Call this number and meet with Tucker. He'll tell you what you want to know."

"Tucker?" He's still frowning as he lifts his gaze.

"That would be one of my prostitutes. You know, if I'm the pimp."

I walk out without looking back.

14

FEE

Pulling my phone from my pocket, I answer on the third ring, just as we're coming in through the door on a grey Tuesday afternoon in September. Despite it being autumn, sorry, *fall,* the air outside feels heavy, but maybe that's because I'm still not used to the bustle of people and traffic. It's hard to believe I've been here more than a month already and harder still to think I'll ever get used to the array of smells—good and bad—the crush of people and the rumble of the subway under my shoes.

"Hey, you," I answer with a smile. Tucking the phone between my shoulder and my ear as I pull off my jacket.

"Hey yourself!" Rose's greeting is as exuberant as my own, which makes my smile all the wider. Knowing she misses me as much as I miss her is the next best thing to a warm hug.

Lu's shoe suddenly flies through the air, narrowly missing a mirror.

"That's not how we take our shoes off, Lulu," I warn, pulling the phone away from my ear.

"*Sorr-ee,*" she sing-songs back. "Who's on the phone?"

"Tante Rose."

"I want to speak to her." Lulu makes starfish grabby hands, her smile taking up half her face.

"Shoes and bag first."

"Aw!"

"Did I call at a bad time?" Rose's voice echoes down the line and across continents.

"No, your timing is perfect. We've just this minute gotten home."

"Home?" Her delivery of that one word is laden with a dozen things and most of them teasing.

"Well, it's home for now, at least. But I have news on that front. We've found somewhere to live!"

"Well, that's great. Did the realtor help?"

He helped annoy me, I suppose, by showing me nothing but ridiculously priced apartments and those too far away.

"No, actually one of the girls at work has offered me her sister's apartment. She's moving in with her boyfriend, and apparently, it's quite a volatile relationship so she doesn't want to let the place long term.

"That sounds a little less than great. What happens if they split up?"

"Well, nothing for the first three months because I'll sign a lease for at least that long. And by then, I'll have been in Manhattan for almost six months."

"Halfway to coming back to France. How does that feel?"

"Ask me in three months." I laugh. "I feel like I've just gotten here."

"Yeah, I guess. So, have you seen this apartment?"

"Yep. I picked Lulu up after school yesterday, and we

went to view it. It's pretty much perfect. It's furnished so cutely and is practically ready to move in to."

"I guess that's great." I don't dwell on her lack of enthusiasm as Lulu trudges into the kitchen.

"I think it's poo-poo," she mutters.

So it isn't quite 5th Avenue, but it's more than adequate for our needs.

"Would you like to talk to Tante Rose now?" I ask, sending her a quelling look.

"Yes, please."

I pass over my phone, and Lulu begins to fill her godmother in with the details of her New York experience.

School is good.

She likes her teacher.

Her new best friend is called Zara.

Does she know New York has spouts where steam comes out of all the time like an old-fashioned train?

The new apartment is small, but it's nice. (Lulu's turn to send me a look this time as though to say *is that fib big enough for you?)* She doesn't look forward to travelling by subway to school, and it's going to take *so* long to get there (she's right on that front, but what can I do?), and she doesn't know how she's going to talk to Uncle Carson's plants when she's living somewhere else and—

"My turn!" I say quickly, intercepting the call before she says anything else incriminating. "Say goodbye now."

As I reach for the phone, Lulu spins until her back is facing me, raising her shoulder to make it difficult for me to grab my phone.

"Yes, I did say Uncle Carson. Same as Rocco calls him. He showed me photos, and he made me pancakes for bre'fast and paid me lots of dollars to talk to his plants while he's on holiday. And do you want to know a secret, Tante Rose? I saw him try to kiss Mommy in the kitchen."

"Thank you!" This time, I snatch the phone out of her hand. "Isn't it amazing how fast Lu's accent has changed?" I witter, my heart beating a million times a minute as I bring it to my ear.

"*Uncle* Carson tried to kiss you, huh?"

"And he made me a princess—" I cut off Lulu the loudmouth's shout by clapping my hand across her mouth. "There was no kissing," I say definitively, shooting Lu a narrow-eyed *don't-you-dare* glance. Over my fingers, she glares back.

"He called and said you guys had met, but he failed to mention any lip-locking."

"Because there wasn't any. You know what kids are like," I declare a little half-heartedly. "Go and get yourself a glass, Lu." I send my daughter another frown just for good measure as I yank open the fridge. "He was here for, like, two minutes. And that was weeks ago." Eighteen days but who's counting. Not me. Even if his absence has been surprisingly harder to adjust to than the crush of people on the streets or the rumble of the subway underfoot. "I mean, why would I kiss him? It's just ludicrous!"

"I can think of one or two reasons." Rose's words are wavery with laughter. "Maybe even five years' worth of them."

"Ha, so funny," I reply in a withering tone. "So funny it's not actually funny at all."

"Even if kissing Carson sounds like a title to an awesome country song?"

"It sounds more like one of Taylor Swift's numbers. And you know her songs and me are never ever ever heard in the same room together."

"I'm taking a cookie." Lulu glowers, her hand already in the jar as though daring me to argue. If a cookie is the price of her silence, she's welcome to it.

"Biscuits. They're called biscuits," I call after her, asserting my authority when and where I can.

"When in Rome," Rose interjects.

"Yes, and when in New York, a biscuit is a cookie," I find myself mumbling as I watch Lulu ignore the glass of milk in favour of the den and mindless kids' TV.

More hush money spoils I'm not going to argue over right now. Not with an audience.

"But what does New York make Fee?"

Right now, a little jittery. "New York still makes me a dull girl, I'm afraid," I reply instead.

"There's nothing dull about you, even if your love life could do with a little sparkle. Speaking of, what did you think of kissing Carson?

"I did not kiss him." I wonder how many times I'll get to repeat that before the big man upstairs smites me good and proper as punishment.

"What did you think of him?"

"I don't think of him at all!" Except all of the time, and in a lot of those thoughts, he's wearing that naughty smile of his and very few clothes.

"That's not what I asked." It's Rose's turn to sing-song now, it seems.

"What I meant to say was he wasn't here long enough for me to form any kind of opinion."

"I find that hard to believe."

"I don't know why." Especially when I'm doing my best to convince you right now.

"You remember Amber, my friend?" she asks out of nowhere. "She's married to the Australian."

"Yes, the couple with the vineyard and twins." Plus a baby, I seem to recall.

"That's her. Well, she made me eat this spread called Vegemite when I visited."

"The stuff like Marmite?" I ask, wondering where she's going with this.

"You mean there are two versions of that travesty of taste?"

"Marmite is definitely an acquired taste."

"Well, she told me it tasted like chocolate. It did not. But what I'm trying to say, in a very roundabout way is Carson, like Vegemite, is what you might call an acquired taste."

Or is he a taste I seem to have acquired? "No idea what you're talking about," I say instead.

"He's not the kind of man a girl would have no opinion of."

"I have eyes in my head," I retort. "I did realise he's good-looking."

"That's not what I mean. You don't have to protect my feelings. I know his manner can be cold. Superior, even. It goes with the territory of his background being all stuffy wasp and urgh!"

But his mother was French . . . Luckily, I manage to keep that tidbit to myself along with my next thought. *Carson Hayes is so not stuck up. Maybe he should be strung up for disappearing off the face of the earth but—*

"I guess what I'm trying to say is his bark is worse than his bite," Rose says, her words interrupting my ruminations.

I swallow back the assertion balanced on the tip of my tongue because this is a version of the man I can't contemplate. Being on the end of his bite is nothing short of delicious. But his bark? It's hard to imagine he'd manage to remain serious long enough to be in a snit. Unless she means he goes around taunting everyone in his path, which would surely be exhausting.

"I don't know what to tell you, Rose. Other than I didn't get that version of him. He was friendly." How much so, I'll never tell. "Hospitable, even."

"Oh. Well, I guess that's good." But she sounds unconvinced.

"Besides, he was barely here twelve hours," I hedge, swirling my finger over a whorl in the marble counter. "How does a person get to know another in that amount of time?"

"I can think of a couple of ways," she says, using that annoying sing-song tone again.

"You would." And I nearly did. Pressing my hands to my stinging cheeks, I wonder how I can extricate myself from this conversation. "You know, I'm really unhappy about not paying any rent. I ought to, even just as a show of thanks."

A diversion!

"Give it up, girl." We've already had this conversation. "It's how you got along with Carson that I want to talk about."

A short-lived diversion.

"I've been too busy to even wash my hair, never mind give thought to the arrival of your friend. I'd forgotten he'd been here at all what with work and settling in, finding an apartment—"

"And talking to his plants." Deadpan doesn't even touch on her tone.

"That's Lulu's job, not mine."

"Yeah, because you're too busy kissing him." I know

she's not being serious and that she's only teasing, but that doesn't stop me from being flustered.

"You know how wild her imagination is. Plus, she's suddenly going through a hardcore Disney phase. She's obsessed with Prince Charming and the whole 'true love's first kiss' nonsense."

Someone throw me a shovel because it seems I'm digging a hole for myself. But I'm not lying this time, at least, because since we walked back into the apartment last Monday to find the maid's room had been cordoned off like a crime scene and an envelope with Lulu's name embossed on the front. Or rather, Princess Eloise Rose. The contents of the envelope proved to be an invitation to view a room on the other side of the apartment, a room fit for a princess. I'd barely gotten to the end of the message when she'd taken off like a rocket, her squeal of delight echoing through the place.

I found myself standing on the threshold of a room that, in the space of eight hours, had been completely transformed. I won't pretend to know why a man we barely know took it upon himself to arrange a complete redecoration of one of the bedrooms of his home, or even hazard how much it cost. Because it's truly beautiful. Decorated in hues of lilacs and blues—no gaudy pink for this room—a gold coronet sits above an antique-style bed with swathes of gauzy fabric falling from it. The whole room has a French feel to it, from the chandelier that sparkles like diamonds to the walls panelled to look like Versailles. It's beautiful, and Lulu loves it so very much. And I've no idea how I'm going to make it up to her when I take it away.

"I hope you told my homegirl she has to wait until she's older to find her one true love?"

I find myself wondering if it's the princess's bedroom or that she saw Carson almost kiss me that's made her a little romance obsessed. Though perhaps being pressed against the kitchen cabinet isn't everyone's idea of romance.

Unless you've been enlightened.

"Thirty," I answer eventually. "I told her she has to be thirty before she's allowed to date."

"Did you tell her she might have to kiss a lot of frogs before finding her Prince?"

"Some of us never get past the frog stage."

"Don't tell her that." I can't quite make out if her tone is sad or disappointed. Maybe a little of both.

"But the point I was trying to make is that Lulu isn't looking for her Prince Charming. It's me she seems desperate to set up." I pause and take a mouthful of Lulu's abandoned milk as I contemplate telling her about what happened at school yesterday. Why the hell not? "So yesterday, I went to pick Lu up from school to find her holding one of the teacher's hands. A male teacher, that is." Mr Farrow. "She introduced us, and before I knew it, she started to relay my life story to him, pretty much selling my good points to him like a mini madam in a brothel." Rose sets off laughing, and I can't help but join her. "God, it was mortifying!"

"I think it's kinda cute, better still if the teacher was cute, too."

"Yes, well, it was cute when she told him how lovely I am and how I make a very tasty sandwich and that I sometimes even cut them into little triangles. But it was less than cute when she informed him I have very big boobs and that my bottom isn't really getting saggy like I think it is."

"Oh my, that kid is hilarious!"

"She's a bloody nightmare more like."

"But was he cute? This teacher, I mean?"

"Not bad, I suppose. Not that it matters." It also doesn't matter that he gave me his number because I'm not going to do anything with it.

"Not even when it's obvious Lulu likes him?"

"That's . . ." Very sticky ground especially as, on the way home, she told me she thought Mr Farrow wasn't as handsome as Carson. "That's not the point."

"Then what is? Listen to the kid!"

"Look, if I did what Lulu wanted, we'd be living in a pink tepee in the middle of Central Park, not brushing our hair or washing our faces and living on cake and custard. So the answer is no, I'm not going to go out with him. If for no other reason than he didn't ask."

"Lu had better get on to that, then."

"Don't give her any ideas." I chuckle.

But Rose falls quiet, and when she next speaks, she does so carefully.

"Do you think she might be trying to fill a void? In her own way, I mean."

"She doesn't need a father." My heart pinches a little at the suggestion. She has men in her life; my dad, Charles (sort of) Remy and even Everett.

"I wasn't talking about a void in her life. I was talking about yours."

"If you're suggesting that Lulu thinks I need a daddy more than she does—"

"What?" That one word sounds positively gleeful. "A daddy, Fee?"

"I mean, a man. I've got a daddy, I mean, a dad."

"Sure you did," she asserts rather gloatingly.

"And in other news," I utter with a forced brightness and a deep hope that I can turn the conversation from whatever this is, "my paperwork should be through next week, so I can begin to sit in on consultations with clients. Not that I haven't enjoyed sitting in with Marta, the dietician's clients. And I know I'm not qualified to say so, but I'd bet my last five bucks in my wallet that most of them suffer from some level of orthorexia."

"That's great."

"It's not really." And I would know, orthorexia and I being old acquaintances. "Any obsession, even one focussed on healthy eating, can be damaging. But what is so very interesting is how different women's attitudes to food are between the States and France."

"Sounds like you're learning a lot, but are there any dating prospects in your office?"

"I thought we'd already established I wasn't in the market."

"I think you said, last time we had this conversation, that you were open to the suggestion, should the right man come along." I make a noncommittal noise because that's not how I remember the conversation going. "Is it just me, or is it odd that your opinion should alter after a visit from a certain someone?"

"What?" I reply, playing deliberately dumb.

"Have you any idea where he's gone?"

"Oh, we're talking about Carson again," I say as though displeased. "No idea, sorry." I only know he's left me feeling oddly out of sorts. And not just because Lulu hasn't left her own bed since she moved into the princess suite, something I, her mother, haven't been able to manage in four years. I'm not even upset that somehow, oh so mysteriously, my own clothes and belongings had been moved to the bedroom next to his, the bedroom that is the meat in the sandwich between Carson and Lulu's rooms. My clothes had been steamed and hung neatly in the adjoining closet, my shoes cleaned and polished, sweaters, jeans, and my ever-present workout wear were folded on shelves smelling of magnolia. Even my underwear had received the white-glove treatment, as though it were La Perla and not Marks and Spencer's.

How could I be annoyed? He was trying to do something nice for us, though the reason he did escapes me. And the reason I feel so jittery and hollow has nothing to do with bedroom relocations and everything to do with him not being around, I fear.

"He didn't upset you, did he?"

"How do you mean?"

"Just like Vegemite, he can leave a bad taste in your mouth. He can appear, well, damned rude."

"He wasn't—" He was a little vulgar, but no more than I liked. "He just wasn't at all what I expected," I find myself admitting instead.

"You mean drop-dead sexy? Hella hot?"

"Those are all your descriptions, not mine." Even if they both fit.

"Ah, then you must mean available."

"I suppose a man like him is the kind of available that's like a short-term loan."

Like one-night short term.

"What?" The word is tremulous with laughter.

"You know, I thought he'd be older," I say, hoping to divert her.

"He is. Older, sophisticated, and rich. He's like lady catnip, don't you think?"

"You are so transparent, Rose Durrand."

"I am?" And she's still laughing.

"This was all a cunning ploy, wasn't it? 'Stay in my gorgeous friend's empty apartment,'" I intone in a ridiculous rendition of her accent. "'He won't be home.' Was this your plan all along? To get me to shack up with the winner of virile bachelor of the year for a bit of casual bed bouncing—"

"Whoa, whoa, whoa! Virile bachelor of the year? Say what you mean, honey! Don't hold back on my account!"

"Try not to sound so amused."

"I can't help it. I haven't heard you pay a man a compliment since . . . since. Well, forever."

"Rubbish. I often tell Charles I like his outfit. And I compliment him on his haircut when he comes back from the barber every Friday, even if I do think the barber mostly just waves his scissors over his head." Because who needs a haircut every week?

"Complimenting your gay bff doesn't count."

"I'm sure Charles would disagree," I reply, sounding miffed.

"But you're right. Carson's hot. And *all* man."

"Thanks for mentioning it."

"My bad." Her voice wavers with ill-concealed laughter. "I didn't think it was relevant. You were looking for somewhere to live, not someone to share a bed with. I didn't know he would show up."

"Uh-huh. Couldn't have worked out better if you'd planned it, right?"

"But I didn't plan it," she happily protests. "Besides, the man is like, celibate or something."

My response? A snort. If that man is celibate . . . if that man is celibate, well, not only would it be a travesty, but what was he doing rolling around on the sofa with me?

And he certainly stirred up a whole lot of feelings in me, feelings I'm not used to, and feelings I'd managed perfectly well on my own up until he turned up. *With the help of my imagination and my hand.* Sadly, that no longer seems to be the case. I don't need a supplement or a herb to help because my issue isn't a low libido. It's exactly the opposite. Only, the Devil never seems to be home when I ring his doorbell lately . . .

"Okay, maybe not celibate," she amends, "but he doesn't date in the conventional sense."

"How can a person date unconventionally?"

"Does it matter?"

Yes, because if she thinks he's celibate, that means he's keeping secrets, doesn't it? I'm not so silly to think I'm the kind of woman who'd bring a man like him out of a sexual hiatus, and maybe this is why my denials shoot from my mouth like bullets.

"You brought the topic up, not me. Who said it mattered? Not me."

"Did he flirt with you?"

I could ask her what her definition of flirting is, but it would only lead to more questions. I'm pretty sure she'd have a whole lot to say if she knew the way he'd introduced himself in the bathroom. *As in unrepentantly naked and sinfully smirky.* Or the way he behaved in the kitchen, his dominant stance, and his soft, taunting words, the thoughts of which still make me tingle. I can't tell her about our heavy petting session and how, if Lulu hadn't woken, the outcome of that night might've been very, very different. Most of all, I can't tell her how much I miss him, which is ridiculous but true. I miss his taunting and teasing and his smart-alec retorts, and how his eyes dance with humour one minute and darken wickedly the next.

He was so good with Lu. Making her breakfast, enduring the *Troll* movie, and then making her a space fit for a princess. He's been so kind that it literally brings tears to my eyes when I think about it.

"No, he didn't flirt with me." At least, not in the traditional sense. "But he was provoking." I'm not lying because Carson Hayes is equal parts arousing and annoying.

"So he *was* rude to you," she murmurs unhappily.

"No, that's not it."

"Then I'm confused."

"Oh, come on! The man would lick himself if he could." Again, I'm not lying.

"I'm sure he'd never need to." Her words are heavy with meaning, and of course I bite.

"What's that supposed to mean?" Even as my brain lags behind, my body seems to understand as my stomach draws itself into an uncomfortable knot.

"Because of the line of women following him with their tongues hanging out." As she sets off chuckling, that knot sinks like a stone to my feet.

"Just my luck. I'm living in the home of a manwhore." A tart with a heart.

Am I being wilfully blind and pining after a man who probably hasn't given me a second thought since walking out of the door?

"I never said he was a manwhore. I mean, the man has to be having sex or else that would just be a colossal waste," she adds quickly. "You should see him work one of the foundation's benefits. Women from nineteen to ninety-five literally swoon as he walks past, tittering and fanning themselves with their big old cheque books. They just can't wait to jot down huge numbers to personally hand their donations over to him."

"So he's a manwhore for a cause."

"Not the way you make it sound. He's just kind of irresistible to women."

"And your point is?"

"I haven't really got one, but I will say while I have seen many a woman cast out her lure, I've yet to see him give even the tiniest of nibbles." *Carson nibbles are pretty special, le sigh.* "He turns up to our galas dateless, and he leaves alone, which just makes the ladies wild."

"I really don't know why you're telling me all this," I answer dispassionately.

"I'm painting the picture for you," she protests. "He's, like, unobtainable. Which just makes them all the more eager to get their hands on him."

"Have you thought that maybe he really isn't interested in women but doesn't want you to know?"

"You mean gay?" She laughs like this is the funniest thing ever, not at all picking up on the spite in my tone.

I'd almost wish him gay rather than share him with Rose's rich friends and hobnobbing buddies, the thought of which turns my stomach. But I know that as well as hella sexy, he's also one hundred percent straight. Not that it stops me from saying, "Just because you think it'd be a waste—"

"He hit on me once." She halts abruptly, and I think, for a moment, that's all she'll say as a fist grips my intestines, twisting them until they hurt.

If the thought of Carson bedding a bevy of anonymous women made me queasy, the thought of him pining for my friend makes me feel physically ill.

"But Lulu said Rocco calls him Uncle Carson." How does she not see how weird this is?

"It happened a long time ago," she replies airily. "I doubt he was even serious. But we're all friends these days, and he's a great help to the foundation. Even if he does still complain about his crooked nose. You know, after Remy busted it."

"He doesn't have a crooked nose."

Her tone is softer now, teasing put to one side. "You'd have to be blind not to notice how good-looking he is."

"He is, as you say, very easy on the eyes," I mutter begrudgingly.

"But don't let that façade fool you. Whether he runs hot or cold, or his behaviour seems confusing, he's a good man. A good *human*. And I swear this isn't some kind of setup. I might not know what his deal is with relationships, but I do know that when he takes you into his heart, and maybe also into his home, he'll be there for you in whatever capacity you need. You just need to decide if you'll let him."

15

FEE

These tiles are much kinder to my complexion, even if I still look like poo.

After a largely sleepless night, I consider myself in the vanity mirror, my reflection no longer tinged with a Wicked Witch of the West hue of my former bathroom. But there's no escaping the fact that I still look like crapola.

Damn my lack of sleep and damn Carson Hayes! Why couldn't he have been a portly fifty-year-old with a taste for twentysomething men? It would've made his flying visit so much easier to reflect on because it wouldn't be scrambling my brain, plus I wouldn't have been forced to lie to my best friend.

Okay, so *forced* might be an overstatement, but I couldn't have told her the truth. She probably wouldn't have believed me anyway. Not because I'm no socialite or a supermodel with legs up to my armpits, but because in the five years I've known her, I've shown little interest in dating. When I was younger, sure. As a young girl living 'her best life' in the South of France, I'd allowed myself to be dazzled by good-looking men, rich men, caught up in the party lifestyle. But all that was before I'd been burned. Dumped. Passed over. Before I'd been hurt.

I can't tell her about his visit now, the same as I can never tell her about meeting Carson the very first time. Not now, not after I kept our little interlude to myself all these years. And I certainly couldn't have told her back then, not without making myself look like a total ho.

Hey, Rose, I'm pregnant by my ex, but the bumhole has disappeared. And by the way, I also had sex with some random man I met up a mountain. Sorry to get all Jerry Springer on you and your perfect life.

It's all just so complicated, I think as I squeeze a little toothpaste on my brush. Even more so now that my libido has suddenly awakened after a long snooze. No matter. Carson Hayes is the last man I can turn to for help with that. Not when the pair are friends. There's no way I'd ever risk my own friendship with Rose . . .

And then once upon a time, he wanted her

I turn on the tap, watching as the water sputters for a moment as a whisper of last night's dream rises before me. *Carson dark-eyed and serious as he presses Rose up against the kitchen cabinets.*

Urgh. Don't think about that right now. Just brush your bloody teeth.

But how can I not think about it when I woke to a sense of loss and a swell of jealousy in my breast rising like a tsunami? I know it's ridiculous because Rose and Remy are the most loving couple I know—they can barely keep their hands to themselves! And Rose wouldn't cheat. Not in a million years. I know she doesn't have a thing for Carson, but maybe it's the other way around.

Maybe she's the one who got away.

Maybe he loves her, and that's why she's never seen him on a date.

Maybe, in his eyes, no one else can live up to her?

Believe me, I'm not about to tell Rose.

He'd said that after the incident in the tub—and I'd felt nothing but relief. But now I'm left wondering if he's secretly in love with my best friend.

"I have a grande soy macchiato and a hibiscus tea for badass boss bitch!"

I cringe as the barista calls out the order, but then remember I'm in New York and that no one bats an eyelash at people talking themselves up. Try that on the Starbucks on Camden High Street, and you'd definitely get a few funny looks.

"Oh, that's us!" Bethany's attention jumps from her phone, and she makes her way to the collection point. Alone. Because I don't want to be confused with a twat. Not that I think Beth is, but I can't think of anything that would make me feel more self-conscious (read: twatish) than referring to myself as a badass boss anything.

"Here you go." She passes my drink into my hands. "Shall we drink these on the way back to the office?"

"Sounds like a plan because if we take a seat, I'll be doing more than eyeing those muffins."

We step out into the crisp fall afternoon, the sounds and the smells still an overload to my senses. Pastries from the bakery next door and gasoline fumes. Hot dogs from the cart on the corner, the whiff of refuse from the next. I always thought of London as a city of extremes but nowhere seems as extreme as Manhattan with its trash bag piled pavements on one block and gleaming glass facades like the next. Madison Avenue with its upscale stores—Zimmerman, Celine, Dior—the kinds of places I wouldn't dream of stepping in, and not just because of a lack of ready cash because there's also my light-fingered Lu to think about. I don't want to get deported for harbouring a tiny felon.

"Do you know," Bethany begins, "that there's a garden in England that's dedicated entirely to poisonous plants? Like, the deadliest flora and fauna in the world."

"I'm surprised it's allowed." We pause at the crosswalk waiting for the sign to change.

"It's in the walled grounds of some castle up in the north. Near Scotland, I think. But I'm definitely going to visit it."

"That's a long way from London, you know. Relatively. I mean, I know the UK is tiny compared to the US, but Scotland isn't exactly a bus ride away." The sign changes, and we begin to walk again. "Well, it is. And it isn't. I suppose it depends on how you want to get there."

"That explanation was as clear as mud." She gives an indulgent shake of her head.

"And you plan on visiting this garden next year?"

"Yep. It might even be number one on the list of things I want to see when I'm over there."

"England has so much more to offer than plants that can kill a person, Beth."

"I know." A smile tugs at her lips, the gleam in her eyes a little fervent. "But I need to see if they have a gift shop."

"Don't tell me who you want to murder. I'd prefer not to be an accessory."

"When I only have one ex-husband?" Peeling off the lid of her cup, she raises it to her lips. "You must be excited about moving into your own place. Another week or two, I think Ally said."

"Yes, she did." Although, Ally, Beth's sister, also my new landlord, seems to be dragging her feet. "She says she wants to get the place painted beforehand. Which is lovely but unnecessary."

"What can I say? Ally is type A, plus a little OCD, plus a few other things no medication will ever help.'

"I must say she doesn't seem very excited about moving in with her boyfriend." More stressed. Which makes me feel slightly worried when I choose to think about it because I really do have to move out of Carson's place. That's Carson, the man in love with Rose. I push away the thought, still not entirely convinced it's true. But something is keeping him away. *I don't know. Maybe it's just work.*

"Our parents aren't exactly impressed, either."

"They don't like him?"

"They think he's not good enough, that he doesn't treat her like she deserves. That he doesn't earn enough. You know what parents are like."

"Not really. I think my parents would be happy to give me away at this point. They'd probably even chuck in a bit of cash to seal the deal. Unwed mothers aren't really the done thing in our family," I say with a short shrug.

"Do you have siblings?"

I nod, then wince as I scald my lips on the tea. "A younger brother. The apple of their eye. Well, apart from Lulu, that is." I'm probably painting a much blacker picture than the reality. My parents love me, and they dote on Lu. They'd just prefer for me to settle down. Preferably in a house on the same street as them. Which is never happening. I mean, I love them, but I can love them better from a distance, I think.

"I'll bet little Lulu charms everyone."

"When inclined." And when she isn't, heaven help us all.

"I'm so happy you're pleased with the apartment." She hooks her hand through the crook of my arm, giving it a little squeeze.

"Oh, I am. And I'm so grateful for your help."

"I can't think why I didn't mention it weeks ago. I guess I just thought you wouldn't really want to move out of a 5th Avenue apartment. I mean, who would want to leave an address like that?"

"It was only ever meant to be temporary." I angle my gaze away. Whatever Carson's deal is, I can't afford to lose my heart, or my knickers, to someone like him.

Especially if he's still pining for Rose.

"You didn't . . . you know, *do* the guy who owns it? And that's why—"

"No!" My steps slow as I pull my arm from hers. "Why would you even ask that?"

Incredulous much?

Also, methinks the lady doth protest a little too vigorously to sound convincing.

"Maybe because I'm having a dry spell?" She holds her hand up, palms to the sky as she shrugs, though she doesn't appear at all uncomfortable. "It's like that point in a diet where everything sounds tasty."

"Well, I didn't." I begin to move again, charging on ahead as I tell myself I'm not lying. Technically, at least. Beth trots behind me for a couple of steps before her hand slides through my arm again.

"Sorry."

"It's okay." My words seem stiff though I don't mean them to be. I'm just not comfortable lying. *Bloody Catholic guilt.* I'm still a big old liar pants. I might not have had sex with him recently, but I do have carnal knowledge of the man.

Perfectly wonderful, sensual carnal knowledge. Urgh!

"Isn't that the most gorgeous thing?"

It takes me a moment to realise we're looking in the window of a boutique as my thoughts linger elsewhere. No, actually, it's a lingerie store. "Oh, yes. It's lovely," I answer, intuiting she's lusting over a nightdress, a delicate gauzy thing that's so transparent the silver mannequin beneath is completely visible. Tipping my wrist, I glance down at my watch. "Do you want to go in and have a mooch? A look, I mean?"

"A girl would only wear that to bed if she had a man to help her out of it."

"I don't think that has to be true, does it?"

"You're telling me you'd wear that for bed on a regular old Tuesday night?"

"Well, no. Not me." I shake my head. "But that's because I'm more a shorts and T-shirt kind of girl." Fluffy socks, too. My nightwear is strictly PG, and some of it is even available in kiddie sizes. Not that any of this seemed to bother Carson. Rose said he can be uncivil, and that made no sense to me. Though in hindsight, he did stare at my pyjama-clad legs a little uncivilly. And the way his cock felt under me was downright rude.

"What are you smiling at?" Beth's sly tone brings me back to the moment.

"I was just thinking." About him. Again. A sure-fire way to torture myself.

"It's been a while since I've come close to having a

man peel me out of anything unless I count my ex trying to skin me out of fifty percent of my apartment." Her shoulders rise and fall with a deep sigh as she stares longingly at the nightie.

"Come on, let's go in. You never know when you might find yourself in the position to wow Mr Right." I pull on the door, a dainty peel of a bell announcing our intentions.

"Mr *Right Now* would do," she mutters as she follows me in.

I don't remember the last time I went shopping, or even shopping with another woman. You know, just for fun. My clothing buys have been mostly online since becoming a mother, or else lone lightning raids between other commitments, and very occasionally, shopping *a deux* with Lu. Which is about as fun as a case of tonsillitis as well as leaving me suffering the same symptoms. *Sore ears and throat along with a splitting headache.*

But I'm reminded that shopping with another woman can be fun, and after lots of banter back and forth, even more giggles, and a little encouragement from the sales assistant, I find myself leaving the store with one or two purchases of my own.

"I'm not sure I'll ever wear these knickers." Back on the sidewalk outside, I peer into the bag filled with froufrou underwear and crinkling silver tissue as I wonder if this statement is the same as when I wore my sexiest and barely-there bra, telling myself that Carson would never see it. *And he did.* "How can anyone justify paying so much for what is essentially a couple of triangles of ribbon?"

"That is such a cute word."

"What, ribbon?"

"No, knickers. It makes me think of the kind of undergarments that came down to a lady's knees. Once upon a time, maybe."

"Once upon a time now, because it seems to me these are exactly the kind of knickers just begging to be pulled down."

"If you get lucky."

"Well, I'm lucky I got them on sale, at least."

Her arm tightens on mine as she gives a little laugh. "You should've picked up that cute little bullet vibe, too."

"We're not having this conversation." I'm glad it's chilly out. It gives me something to blame for my red cheeks. Inside the shop and in front of the sales assistants, there was no such reprieve. *Oh my God, it's so cute. Look, it has a dozen settings labelled from* mmm *to* toe-curling, *and it's pink!*

What she doesn't know is I fully intend on going back to buy it. *Alone.* Because something needs to give . . . *it to me?*

"Ah, you're probably right." Her voice takes on a curious tone. "A girl should never buy a cheap vibrator. Believe me, and I should know." She pauses, but I don't think it'll last very long. "Want to know how I know?"

Called it.

"Is this going to be one of those stories that will make me want to cover my ears and sing really, really loud?"

"It's not a kinky story. More a cautionary tale."

"I'm dreading it already, but come on, we'd better get a move on. We're supposed to be back at the office already."

"Relax. Ethan's not likely to complain. Not when he thinks he's so close to getting his hands on all of this." She flutters her hand over her body as she does what I think is supposed to be a sexy wiggle. "So anyway. The tale of the cheap vibe goes a little like this. Me and the ex, we were recently over, and I was crying myself into a bottle of wine or two that night when, in my infinite wisdom, I decided an orgasm might improve my mood."

"Maybe someone should suggest that on a greeting card," I say with a snicker. "A finger bang a day keeps the blues away!"

Ignoring my faux shudder, she carries on. "The shithead felt threatened by sex toys while we were together, so after the split, I'd bought myself a cheap rabbit, and well, I got down and dirty and put it to good use." Beth slides me a look that seems to say you know how it goes. But there's no way I'm touching that. "Well, I had a good old time and cranked a few out."

"Don't!" I grab her arm to stop her from making the accompanying gesture.

"Do you want to hear the end of this story or not?"

"Does it matter?"

"No," she answers with a shrug. "Because I'm telling it anyway."

Just as I thought.

"So, I fell asleep mid-coitus."

"I'm not sure it's considered coitus if the penis is made from plastic."

"Okay, so I fell asleep on the job—banging my battery-operated boyfriend!"

"Keep your voice down!" I say, purposely ignoring the *tsk-ing* senior citizen passing in the other direction, the wheels of her shopping cart almost running over my toes.

"When I'm getting to the dramatic and painful ending?" Before my mind can run with that, Beth adds, "Because I woke up to the thing still buzzing and glued to my thigh. The cheap piece of shit had overheated and burned me!"

"Oh, Jesus. I bet that's scarred you for life," I say, wincing, feeling a phantom flash of that pain.

"Literally. I have a scar on the inside of my right thigh in the exact shape of an eight-inch penis."

"Oh, no!" I roll my lips inwards, my shoulders already starting to shake.

"Yuck it up, my friend. And then imagine trying to explain that to a new OB-GYN."

We giggle almost all the way back to the clinic, conversations bouncing from one topic to the next. But as we reach the clinic entrance, the way she says my name causes me to pause.

"What is it?" I turn to face her, my fingers retracting from the door handle.

"I have a favour to ask you." Her eyes dart away, and she looks suddenly uncomfortable. "I have this . . . party to go to, and I really don't want to go alone."

"Oh. You want me to go with you?" If I sound surprised, it's because I am. I know we get along, and we've had fun working out of the same office, but she's much closer to Marta than she is me. They've been friends longer for a start.

"Would you? Come, I mean? I hate going to parties by myself."

"Let me know what date."

"Really?"

"I don't see why not." I've had fun this afternoon, and she did help me find somewhere to live. I was going to buy her a houseplant or some chocolates and a bottle of wine to say thanks, but I can do this. "I mean, if I can get a babysitter. Just text me the details." There must be a reason she doesn't want Marta to know or else we wouldn't be standing out in the chilly air having this conversation. "I'll see what I can do."

"You're amazing!" I'm suddenly enveloped in a Chanel-scented hug.

"Okay!" I find myself laughing. Laughter that's very short-lived as my brain belatedly recognises something tense in her body language. "What is it you're not telling me?"

"You're putting those therapist skills to use already, I see." Making a fist, she play punches my arm. "Great observation, there, but—"

"But nothing," I mutter firmly. "Spit it out."

"It's a kind of a singles party."

"A kind of what?"

"A very elite singles party. Please don't say no—I desperately need someone to come with me."

"Yeah, well, it's not going to be me," I reply with an unhappy chuckle. And now I know why she hasn't asked Marta.

"Please. There's no one else I can ask. All my friends are either married or dating or—"

"Joining a nunnery?" The prospect is almost preferable.

"Come on, Fee. It'll be fun!"

"You know, I can't tell if it's the drugs you're taking or the drugs you should be taking that made you think I'd be up for this."

"But you're nice. *So* nice. And you're single, too. And I did help you find an apartment."

"So that's it? Blackmail." A box of chocolates and a plant would've been *so* much easier.

"No, not at all. Just say you'll think about it at least."

Beth presses her hands together in supplication, her pleas bordering on desperate. "Think of it as an anthropological kind of outing. Meet the New York singles in their natural habitat. You don't have to get involved if you don't want to. Just be my wing woman, that's all."

"This is going to cost me so much more than a potted fern, I can tell."

"What was that?"

I shake my head as I turn back to the door. "Just text me the details."

"Thank you! I'm so pleased you didn't say no!"

Yet.

16

CARSON

I stare at the half-open package on my desk, the torn wrapping heralding the unexpected arrival of something that seems to be called *The Ripstarter.*

"Jesus." Turning back the cardboard to read the address, I note how the ink has run thanks to the rain, though I can still make out how it's addressed to *Kinky Carson Hayes III.* I shake my head as a reluctant grin begins to creep across my face.

These fuckers . . .

Oh, man. I feel a phantom pinch as I lift out the contents, dropping the box to the floor.

Where the hell do they get this sort of shit? And who the hell could take this . . . this thing. I find myself musing, unsure what else to think. Whether it's *ribbed for his or her pleasure,* how does one refer to a huge chain of black rubber anal beads? The kind of anal beads that look solid enough to moor a yacht.

I drop them on the desk with a heavy *thunk.*

"Bunch of comedians," I mutter, snatching up my phone, scrolling to the names of the usual suspects and coming across Tucker's name first. I punch the icon next to his name, and as the line connects and begins to ring, I mentally tally the number of sex toys the assholes—sometimes referred to as my friends—have mailed my way.

The first to arrive a year or so ago was purported to be an oral sex night light. It looked like a cross between a spelunker's headlamp and a telephony headset and, according to the packaging, was called the *Going Down Right Night Light*. As ingenious as the creators may think themselves, I can't honestly review the product as it has languished in a chest at the bottom of my bed. Seriously, if you can't feel your way around a woman's pussy, you don't deserve to be between her legs.

As the chest began to fill, these "gifts" overflowed to a drawer in my closet. If they keep this up, by the end of the year, I'll have enough product to open the kind of store that would make a sexual deviant blush. There are at least a dozen flavoured condoms, including a particularly rancid-sounding bacon flavour pack with the unique tagline of *bacon flavour for both your lover and your pork sword's pleasure*. Other highlights include a pink pigtail attached to a tiny butt plug and another, not so petite, attached to a foot-long rainbow-coloured unicorn's tail. Not long after this turned up, a leather riding crop arrived in a package originally addressed to me, but with my name crossed out and replaced with the moniker *For the My Little Pony Lover*. I can only imagine what the guy from the post room thinks of me.

The call connects a split second later, and Tucker's voicemail greeting resounds.

This is Tucker. You know what to do.

"Tucker, Tucker. You nasty fucker. You shouldn't have.

And I mean that. You really shouldn't have." I cut the call, knowing he won't be able to resist returning it.

"Mr Hayes?" I look up as the feminine voice continues. "I think there must be a mistake with this invoice."

"Come in or get out. Don't hover at the doorway, Emmie."

"It's Aimee," she replies, not at all hesitantly but with a hard roll of her eyes. She knows I know her name but indulges my ridiculousness, though neither of us will admit to it. I'd have to be some kind of idiot not to remember after she's been working for me for almost five years, even if I have spent less than six months based out of this office. She sends me enough signed emails for her name to have stuck.

Emails. So many emails.

Sometimes I even answer them.

Well, I guess I answer enough to keep my grandfather's legacy afloat. The truth is, I don't give a fuck about his company, and I was happy to begin running his "global brand" into the ground after his death. But that was before I'd considered his workforce.

I take a moment to look at Aimee. Really look. Shiny dark hair, big brown eyes, pale skin; she looks much younger than her years, which I guess to be somewhere in the region of twenty-six, twenty-seven. I also remember the day I found out my grandfather had a type beyond the long line of women he paraded at public events and family dinners. Women I'd thought were just arm candy because surely the old bastard was so old and so ill it defied all logic that he could get it up.

The women who clung to his arm in public were a fraction of his age and fawning. Always attractive and often blonde, he had a knack for finding the kind of woman who'd give her right breast implant to marry him. Or maybe they had the knack of finding him, who knows. None of them seemed smart enough to realise the most they could expect from him was for their bills to be paid, and only for as long as he had use of them. A fact he was surprisingly sanguine about. He used to laugh as he said it was hard to tell who was screwing who.

But that was the public face of Carson Hayes the elder, a man so blinded by his own sense of importance that he not only gave his son his name but also insisted his firstborn grandson carried it, too.

I remember how I used to look up to him. Now, there's only revulsion. I hope he's rolling over in his grave at what his name has become.

While the public face of the man was brash, it turned out his private life and his private indulgences were much, much worse. I might not have been privy to the full facts until the end, but the man was a predator, plain and simple. Yes, he liked his women young, but behind closed doors, he also liked them vulnerable.

As Aimee clears her throat pointedly, I look. It's obvious how she got a job straight out of a Bronx high school in what was once the most prestigious building in midtown Manhattan. My grandfather probably had her in his sights, adding *poor* and *pretty* to the labels he liked. But I like to think she'd have nailed him in the nuts because Aimee Morales is nobody's fool.

I'm sure it looked like kindness or altruism or maybe madness when she was the only person on the executive floor who kept her job after he died. Once I'd cleared out the sycophants, that is, which seemed okay with the board at the time.

The board. Those poor bastards didn't know whether

they were coming or going considering dear old Grandaddy left me the controlling share. I find myself smiling as I recall my short reign of havoc. Until I remember Aimee's presence and note the quizzical look she's giving me.

But the fact Aimee still works for me has a little to do with my expectations of her at that time, which isn't a compliment, I expect, to either of us. She was so far down in the pecking order, I thought in promoting her to my executive assistant, her inexperience would only help me ruin things. *Ruin up his legacy.* It's probably weird that a part of me takes pride in the fact that she's a hell of a lot more competent than I gave her credit for. Competent. Ambitious. Even a little bit scary to some.

Fucking over Hayes Industries was the original plan, selling it off piecemeal until the company was nothing but dust. That was pure and unadulterated hate, brought on by finding out what kind of man he truly was. But it didn't take me long to realise that the cost of my rage wasn't rained down on only my name. Other people were suffering, Hayes employees. Thousands of livelihoods worldwide. His workforce was now my workforce. Men and women with families to feed and bills to pay are those without the kind of independent wealth that can make an asshole out of a man.

Yeah, I'll admit I was an asshole about inheriting. But I swallowed it all down and took my revenge elsewhere because I'm not a fucking ogre. I'm just the man who happens to have ogre-sized anal beads that his assistant is eyeing on his desk.

"Is there a problem, Emmie?"

Her eyes dart to mine before returning to the ripstarter. "I, er, no. That is . . ."

"I know it looks like something that might tow a boat, but I'm not thinking about buying a yacht." *Been there, done that, bought the self-indulgent T-shirt.* "They're actually anal beads, if you're wondering." Her expression suffuses with pink as I pick them up by the end, relegating the unholy rosary to the deepest drawer of my desk. "They came in the mail." I sigh. "Maybe a joke?"

"Yes, right. Okay. I see." So many affirmatives, though she doesn't look at all convinced.

"Or maybe someone's idea of telling me I'm a colossal asshole." The colour in her cheeks suddenly fades. "You didn't happen to send them, did you?" Narrowing my eyes, I point finger guns her way.

"I wouldn't even know where to buy such a thing."

"You don't surf the dark web in your spare time?"

"No more than you hang around dingy sex shops. Besides, if I was going to send you an insult, I would want to be sure you knew it was from me. And I wouldn't be addressing it to kinky nobody."

I've always found there's something about sex toys that feel a little . . . prescribed. Pedestrian. If you've got an imagination, you should use it. Same goes for fingers and a tongue. There is nothing sexy about pulling out a bright pink piece of plastic. Or worse still, the kind of pink that's flesh-toned. Actually, why are most sex toys so strange?

"You'd probably send me a chocolate dick to choke on, right?"

"I'm not that generous."

"All right." With a sigh, I hold out my hand for the paperwork. "Give it to me."

She cocks a brow as she drops the folder to the desk, springing back as though it's contaminated.

"As far as I know, anal isn't catching."

"It's *his* desk that I'm avoiding. Why can't you get new furniture?"

"Superstitious, Emmie?"

"No, but my *abuela* is tired of bringing me holy water to douse it with. I'm gonna start charging you on my expenses for sage I use to smudge the office, too."

"You're sure your God would agree with you flirting with pagan rituals?"

"I like to cover all bases," she says, pressing her forefinger to the middle of her glasses to raise the frames. "Besides, me and God? We have an understanding."

Since when has Aimee worn glasses? And why did I find that whole movement hot?

"You're staring. Why are you staring?"

I shake my head and drop my gaze. There isn't a thing wrong, yet a million things feel off. I don't have a hard-on for Aimee. And glasses aren't my kink. I just can't shake Fee and her fucking glasses from my head.

I have feelings for the woman, feelings that should've driven me from the country already. Yet I'm still here, sitting in an office mere minutes from where she lays her head.

Pushing away the narrative, the fact that I'm still in the city because she is, I grab the folder. Balancing it on my palm, I flick it open to an invoice from Atelier Interiors. I decide their marketing must be shitty, given the company name, even if their prices are premium, I see as I reach the final page and the balance. But their work comes highly recommended, and that's all I was interested in. *Even if the plan, the why, made no fucking sense.*

"Looks fine," I say, helicoptering the folder back across the desk. "Why isn't it with the accounts department already?" I'd insisted they finish the refurb of

Lulu's new room in under six hours. *While there was no one around to stop them.* The least I can do is pay them on time.

Lulu's room, I find myself thinking with a huff. What the fuck was I thinking? That some families are chosen, as Remy said himself. And by that, I can consider Remy and Rose's family as my own. *Because my family sure as shit aren't interested.*

So I was bound to feel a sense of responsibility. Besides, who wouldn't be charmed by that little rogue?

Refitting her bedroom was nothing to do with guilt.

Or because I desperately want her mother.

Because that can't happen again, I remind myself. *I'm not the right man for her.*

Maybe I should give Rose a call just to check in. See if Remy mentioned anything about the Chicago fundraiser or if Fee has checked in. Fuck it, I can't do any of that.

"Accounts flagged it and sent it to me." Aimee reaches for the folder. "I thought you should see it."

"And now I have. I don't see an issue."

"But the work is for the refit of a child's bedroom."

"And your point is . . . ?"

"You don't have any children."

"That you know of."

"What?"

"I said that I know of." The chair creaks as I lean back, steepling my fingers under my chin. "Do you think the fruit of my loins would be the Devil's spawn?"

"I should think you'd have trouble getting a woman to give you children," she mutters, slipping the folder under her arm.

"I think we both know I don't have a problem attracting women."

"Keeping them around, though? I bet that's a problem."

"But it only takes once. At least, that's what science says."

"You know what else science says?" she asks, backing away from the desk. "Finding the right woman might make your whole week. But anal beads the size of tennis balls make your *hole weak.*"

Laugher breaks free from the depths of my chest. "Why Aimee, I didn't know you cared about my hole . . . being."

"I beg your pardon?" She turns as she reaches the door, her nose scrunched.

"Never beg, Emmie. Not unless you're into that kind of thing."

"I am truly traumatised. And I'm going home. Early."

"Get a cab," I call as the door slams closed. "Put it on expenses." Because the train will be packed.

After she leaves, I stare at my laptop for an indeterminable time, unable to concentrate on anything as the rain begins to fall harder, now hammering against the windows.

I call up my emails, but the one I'm waiting for isn't there.

I realise I'm drumming my fingers against my desk, so I push back my chair with a little too much violence and begin to pace.

I hate this fucking office. The Aubusson carpet and library shelves. The drinks cabinet. *Well, maybe not that.* The fucking Edwardian desk that's so large it makes me think that the old bastard must've had a tiny dick.

I could have it remodelled. Burn the old, bring in the

new. Cleanse the place, like Aimee said. But somehow, I feel like in doing that, he wins.

And he will never win.

I stalk over to the window and slide my hands into the pockets of my pants as I stare at the streets below. The pathways are slick with rain as the weather washes the city clean.

She deserves better than me, I think as the rain lashes against the glass.

But what do I deserve?

Tomorrow, I guess. An Ardeo night, when I won't be cleansed but bathed in sin for the first time in weeks.

The thought comes to me like an epiphany. I haven't had sex since before I found Fee in my bathroom, so that must be it. That's why I'm fucking obsessed!

Saturday night will put an end to that. I'll fuck, and I'll move on. Leave her to her life. Stop my thoughts from bending to the image of her in my bed, her hair spread out like angel wings across my pillow, her eyes dark, and her arousal sweet and sticky against my lips.

One night and one brief interlude, and my body still remembers it all.

Remembers her.

I'm a fucking lost cause.

As my phone begins to buzz against the desk, I stalk across the office and snatch it up.

"Hi, I have a missed call from this number," a somewhat familiar voice purrs in a terrible parody of a woman's voice. "I'm ringing from Ardeo. A place where all your dreams come true."

"I don't remember my dreams being made of anal beads."

Laughter rings down the line. "Don't knock 'em until

you've tried 'em," the voice asserts, much more masculine now.

"Try them? I couldn't even if I wanted to because I'm pretty sure my sphincter turned in on itself in panic."

"I always said you were full of shit."

"Full of shit and making you a fortune."

"There's no denying that."

His response makes me smile. It's strange how something that started out as a one-off thing, a way to cheer up my brothers in arms, is now an entity all of its own. I'm gladdened to have helped them. *Emotionally. Financially*. The platoon and beyond.

"How are we looking for tomorrow night?" I ask, dropping into my seat.

"Things are looking good. Security has swept the place to protect the good senators and the other paranoid folk. Numbers are up on the Nice party, and we already have more interest in next month's gathering in Berlin."

"Gathering." I find myself grinning. "I never had you down as the euphemistic type."

"Okay, so business in the fuck fest industry catering to the rich and powerful is awesome. How does that appeal to your analytical sensibilities? Or even *anal*ytical." Tucker snorts, entertained by his own puny pun. "And speaking of assholes, *he* applied again. Offered to triple the membership fee."

"Fuck him." I retort, my jaw already clenching.

"That's pretty much what I said in my email. Only in more professional terms. Do you wanna know what the bids on your little sideline are up to?"

"Sure, but no names."

"It's all in the anticipation, right?" I stifle a sigh. Maybe it just used to be. "As of an hour ago, it's at a hundred and fifty G's." He blows out a whistling breath. "Well, I gotta go."

"People to do, things to see?"

"You know it."

The call ends without either of us saying goodbye, and my phone buzzes immediately, this time with a text.

TUCKER: Addison says the list is in. He's emailing it to you now.

Encrypted, of course.

ME: Copy that.

TUCKER: Hey, how much lube do you need to do anal?

ME: I'm sensing a punchline. Because a man in this business has tried it all.

TUCKER: You need a butt load

I find myself shaking my head. Tucker always was the joker of our trio, even when things turned bad. Reaching out, I fire up my laptop again, and sure enough, the invite list is available. Given that Ardeo was my creation, and I was our link to the so-called upper echelons and their depravities, and therefore, their purse strings, I still like to keep an eye on the invite list.

It's handy to know who you have in your pocket.

Senator. Judge. Legislator. Philanthropist. Hedge-fund manager. Hollywood actor. Film producer and his starlet wife. Billionaire pastor with a congregation he uses as his bank balance.

Alden. Brown. Garcia. Jones. Marudas. Mickleburgh. Sanchez. White. Yalden. Yuen . . . the list of names goes on.

I make a mental note of first-time attendees, people to keep an eye on, and people of note. Just as I'm about to close the document, I double back as something snags my attention. I scroll back to the beginning of the document.

Surname: *Abernathy.*

First name: *Fiadh.*

My mind must be playing tricks on me. Fiadh is an uncommon name. I've certainly never heard it until this month.

Irish, she said.

It can't seriously be her. This has to be a coincidence.

She's living in my place, rent-free. She's here for an internship, for fuck's sake. Where would she get the money, even for a one-night invitation, which is what she's signed up to as friend of a current member. *A recent current member.*

The more I think about the likelihood of this being the same Fiadh, the less likely it seems. But as a gnawing sensation continues to worry my gut, I decide to take the easier path of the two available to me as I pick up my phone again. In less time than it takes to consider the implications, I've opened the link to the file under the name and I'm calling Rose.

Abernathy, Fiadh. Guest of Bethany Aaron.

Still doesn't ring a bell, though Bethany Aaron has only been a member for a couple of weeks.

"Where in the world is Carson Hayes?" Rose's voice is warm and filled with genuine delight. And her greeting? Just a game we play.

"Wouldn't you like to know," I answer with the same sincerity. I like Remy, but I know, like me, he's always up to no good. *Money to make. Empires to crush.* But Rose is pure goodness, wrapped in unadulterated sass. I respect the husband. Like and admire the wife. Dote on the kid. Love the fuck out of the whole family.

"I'm gonna guess you're still in the States, given you were in Chicago a few days ago."

"Rose, you disappoint me. Didn't you once berate me for flying from Rome to Tahiti for a twelve-hour thing?"

"I think it was the *thing* I objected to, not your carbon footprint."

"Why do you always assume it's sex?" Even if she's not entirely wrong. An Ardeo weekend in Tahiti meant it was business *and* pleasure, even if I couldn't stay for both purposes.

"Call it a sixth sense. I was about to say I'm sorry I couldn't be there that night, but now I don't think I will."

"Aw, Rose. That's almost an admission that you miss me."

"Rocco misses you. And I'll admit to having insider information to your whereabouts because I spoke to Aimee," she playfully snipes.

"My secretary?" I find myself frowning.

"She's you're executive assistant, dumb ass. Without her, your organisation would fall apart."

"And you spoke to her why?"

"Carson, I speak to her all of the time," she retorts, exasperated. "You're pretty hard to pin down."

"That's not true," I reply silkily. "I just need the right incentive. And a promise that I'll have access to the handcuff keys."

"Nice, Carson. I do so love our conversations when they turn smutty. But I didn't call Aimee about you. I called because she's getting married and I wanted to ask her about her gift registry."

"Since when is she getting married?"

"Since she's been dating the same guy from the age of fifteen. Do you not listen to anything anyone says?"

"Quarter after two," I answer, just to hear her growl.

"I swear, you are a lost cause."

"But the love of a good woman is all I need to fix me, right?"

"I've given up on that score," she replies a touch caustically. "You'd better buy Aimee an amazing gift, all the shit she puts up with from you."

"As if I'd do anything else." I find myself smiling as I think of the "gift" in the deep drawer of my desk when Tucker's less than sage advice drifts through my head.

The couple who plays together, stays together.

It's probably bullshit.

It's definitely bullshit, considering where the advice came from. Or rather who.

"But that's not all you called to say, was it? Spit it out. To what do I owe this honour of a call?"

"Can't I call my friend for no reason?"

"You can, but you usually don't. Check-ins are more my remit." Hence her greeting. *Where in the world is Carson Hayes.* But thank fuck, we're back on track, even if my lead-in is weak.

"There seems to have been some confusion with the mail, and I was hoping you could tell me Fee's last name."

"That's weird, but it also reminds me, I had the funniest conversation with Lulu."

"About plants?"

"No, about you kissing her mother," she says utterly deadpan.

"That is weird. And something I think I would've remembered." And do. Almost constantly. The way her chest rose and fell with her breath. The warm press of her lips. The way she'd fed her hands into my hair as though to anchor me there as she took her pleasure.

"So very strange," she continues, this time with an air

of inconsequence. "You say you haven't kissed her, and she says she's sure you don't swing that way."

Oh, angel, you kind of overshot there.

"Which makes me feel like I'm living somewhere between denial city and crazy town, because—"

"Rose," I bite out, my reflection grim in the darkening windows, my scowl is reflected back at me. Crazy town, it is, if I'm gay, and she's partying at Ardeo. *She fucking wishes.* "Are you going to tell me the woman's last name?"

"Sometimes, you can be such an ass. I told her that too because it was only a matter of time before she found out herself. She's not like me, Car. She's softer. Gentle. So you'd better be nice to her."

"I've been exceedingly nice to her." If only she knew. I've tried being nice, and that didn't work. And if she's at Ardeo, all bets are off, nice or otherwise.

"Want to elaborate on that tone?"

"Rose," I growl for a second time.

"It's Abernathy, asshole. Fee Abernathy. And if you have her mail, you'd better get it to her soon because she's found somewhere to live."

I set that information to the side—where she resides is a matter for consideration beyond tonight.

"One more thing—"

"Promise you'll be nice first," Rose demands, cutting me off.

"I'm always nice, aren't I?" I slightly condescend.

"No," she answers baldly. "But what do you want?"

"I'm just curious. Remy told me she doesn't ever date. Why is that?"

"Are you interested in her, Carson?" There's a lot more encouragement in her tone than I'd credit her husband for.

"Rose." For fuck's sake. Being married to her must drive Remy crazy sometimes.

"Fine. But if you are, you should know she won't be interested in casual. She's hanging out for the one. But that doesn't mean—"

I don't hear the rest as I stare at her name on my laptop screen, the knowledge that she'll be there tomorrow reacting inside me like a tiny explosion of delight.

Delight that's short lived. A delight that becomes a shower of shrapnel, sharp and painful, bleeding thoughts and sentiments and bitterness.

Good. Nice. Kind. Honey hair and wildfire eyes.

Soft, gentle, and a liar, it seems.

But hardest to take is that she'd choose to fuck a stranger over me.

17

FEE

You look done up to the nines, I almost hear my mother say.

More like the tens.

"Oh, Mommy. You look so pretty!"

"It's just a dress, Lu." My answer wavers with a laughter that feels unfamiliar. Sort of girly and young, which is pretty much how I feel right now. When was the last time I wore my hair in anything but a ponytail? I can't even remember.

Sophia, Mr Martinez, I mean, *Ed's* daughter jumps up from the sofa in the den-like a soldier standing to attention. "You look beautiful, Miss Fee."

"Just Fee, unless you want me to feel ninety-two." Which, incidentally, is almost the same number of dollars I paid for this dress. *Picked out from the sales rack in Bloomingdales lunchtime yesterday.* I slide my hand down the grey-coloured silk, comfortable in the knowledge that no one but me will know there's a hole in the hem while wondering for at least the tenth time tonight what kind of singles night is black tie.

The executive kind, silly. The echo of Beth's disparaging voice resounds through my head.

"No, ma'am. I mean, Fee." Sophia blushes, and I make a flapping motion with my hand, insisting she sit back down. *We don't stand on ceremony here. We don't even belong in this kind of place!*

"Miss Fee sounds like Nanny McPhee!" Lulu sprays a mouthful of popcorn in my direction. "But you'd have to grow a wart here," she says, tapping her nose. "And I would have to be very, very naughty for you to get one of those."

"I'm not sure that's how warts work." Because if that were the case, I'd be as warty as a toad.

"In *Nanny McPhee*, it does. And you would need to wear your glasses, not your contact lemses, but some really ugly ones." As though I need the visual, she screws up her little face, making circles around her eyes using her forefinger and thumb.

Maybe she watches too much TV? I told myself I wouldn't be one of those mothers who plonk their kids in front of a screen, but sometimes a person needs a little quiet and—

"What time are you going out?" Lulu drops her hands to her side, angling her head like a terrier as she delivers her anvil-sized hint.

"Who braided your hair?"

"Sophia did."

"She let you brush it?" I almost squeak, my attention swinging to the teen.

"Because Sophia didn't make my head go like this," she barks, miming a little headbanging. "Do you know your dress has a hole in the back?"

"Er, yes. It's supposed to look like this." Expensive and

sophisticated and kind of sexy. Honestly? I don't even look like me. "Good job with the hair, Soph." She either has the magic touch, or those braids are the result of her not being in a hurry. The latter I decide, consoling myself. "But are you sure you're okay to stay late?"

The teen nods eagerly. "My dad is on shift until six a.m."

"Oh, I won't be that late." Or early, as the case may be. "I'll be back by eleven, definitely."

"That's okay, too, because my cousin said he can pick me up. I just need to give him a little notice. He drives an Uber on the weekends," she adds by way of explanation.

"Oh. Okay." Also, damn and blast. "Well, it sounds like we've got all bases covered." Unfortunately. "So, erm, my cell number is on the fridge."

"And pre-programmed into my phone, just in case." She nods decisively. "I have your friend's number, too. Just for emergencies. And don't forget, my dad is just downstairs."

"Right." No escape for me, then.

"Lulu's bedtime is nine—"

"And I'll be a good girl and go straight to sleep," my daughter adds with wide innocent eyes and a perfect disregard for the truth. "Because if I'm naughty, Sophia won't look after me after school anymore, and we won't be able to have any more girls' nights like tonight."

"Seems like you've thought this through." Again, unfortunately. "But she'll probably wake up at some point," I throw in as a last attempt at putting the girl off.

"No, I won't!" protests my little traitor.

"And she can be crabby." Hooking my thumb at my child, I pull a face. "See? Maybe we should just order pizza and watch a movie. I'm a girl, too."

"You're not a girl. You're a mommy," Lu mutters in a voice a little like Regan in *The Exorcist*. "You gotta go out, okay?"

"Okay, okay!"

"We'll be fine, Miss—we'll be fine, Fee. And you know, you look much too pretty to be staying home."

As my phone *bings* with Beth's text—**in the car downstairs**—I feel like I want to smile and cry at the same time, and I'm not at all sure why.

Lu, bless her traitorous little cotton socks, takes my hands and walks me to the door as though it's my first day at school. She presses a kiss to my cheek, practically propelling me out into the hall.

"Have fun, Mommy. See you later. Much later."

The door slams shut, and that is the end of that, it seems.

My already pinching heels echo as I cross the marble foyer, and Ed opens the door to a blast of chilly night air. He smiles and inclines his head, and I murmur my thanks, choking back the ridiculous desire to blurt out that I need thermals, not nipple covers for this dress.

Nipple covers. Now, there is an item I thought I would never need again. *Tiny pasties to pop over your nipples when going braless.* The sales assistant in Bloomingdales had suggested I pick up a packet to wear with this dress. I only hope they're a little more reliable than they were five years ago because I'd more often than not find them tucked into my waistband by the end of the night.

That's the covers, not my nipples.

My gaze slides to the right, ignoring the shiny grey Maybach purring at the kerbside. But as the driver rounds the vehicle and opens the rear passenger door, a familiar head pops out.

"Evenin' guv'ner. You lookin' for a roide?"

"I was looking for a cab," I mutter, sliding into the buttery leather before the door closes with an expensive-sounding *thunk*.

"I said I'd pick you up." Pulling out a silver compact from her purse, Beth examines her lipstick, her tone a touch arch.

"I thought *you'd* be in a cab, or maybe a deluxe Uberlux or something." Despite how it looks in the movies, few people in the city travel by cab.

My eyes catch those of the driver. Was that a smirk or derision? I can't make it out. I mean, I have my contact lenses in, but he still seems so far away.

Big fancy Maybach = wealthy.

"I spent the day at my parents'." She snaps her compact shut. "They offered me their car."

"My dad offered me a car once," I reply. "It was a Fiat Punto that had been around the block a few times. And it needed a new engine block."

"You're so funny," she says with a chuckle.

"Tea on the lawn this afternoon, was it?" I pull a prim face and mime drinking from a fancy cup complete with saucer, a smile tugging at my lips. "And a jolly game of croquet?"

"No. We're more like bocci people. But only in the summertime. You know, at our vacation home in the Hamptons."

"Okay, fancy knickers. I get the point." Her parents are loaded. Minted! But I bet they're nowhere near as entertaining as my olds.

"I do have on fancy knickers. Oh, wait. No, I don't." Her smile gleams wickedly as she slides her hand over her hip.

"Don't even," I warn. "Where are we off to, anyway?"

"Not far away."

And she's right because it isn't long before we're pulling up at a fancy apartment block.

"We could've walked." It's only a slight exaggeration. I wouldn't have gotten very far in these heels.

The car door is opened, and I slide out, almost literally. This might be the fanciest dress I've owned in a long while, but boy, is it slippery.

"Good evening. Welcome to Ardeo."

A woman stands in front of us in a black sheath dress. Blonde hair pulled into a sleek bun, and her makeup is understated. She looks like the hostess of a fancy restaurant. *Or a Stepford wife, the New York version, maybe.* I notice the leather-covered tablet in her hand and decide she must be the former. But that isn't a restaurant standing behind her; it's a residential building. And the hulk of a man guarding the entrance looks like security.

"May I take your names?" She smiles benignly, raising the tablet to check us in as Beth supplies her with the information. My spidey senses begin to tingle, along with my nipples in this dress. It's from the cold air, I think, rather than a sense of foreboding as she reaches into the open folder, sliding two different colour ribbons from the open leaf.

Maybe this is a singles event that supports a cause, rather than a profit?

I know my social life is non-existent, but it hasn't been *that* long since I was last out socially with other adults. I don't remember ribbons being a signifier of anything other than for charity fundraising. While I'm a great believer in paying it forward and doing what you can for those in need, the possibility of swimming in a sea of singles makes me feel about as relaxed as I would swimming with sharks.

It all feels so so weird; the ribbons, the exchange. The security guard escorting us to the elevator, an elevator programmed to one destination.

The penthouse suite.

"Why am I sweating like a dieter in a bakery?" A rose gold version of me makes chicken arms in the mirror as the doors slide closed.

"Horses sweat, Fee. Men perspire. Ladies glow."

"Well, I'm glowing like a glassblower's backside."

"Maybe you're excited." Beth's reply sounds hopeful, though her expression is less so. In fact, she looks like she's swallowed something distasteful.

"So, what's with the ribbons?"

She glances down at her hand. "Oh, I almost forgot. Here." She turns as though to pin the white ribbon to the soft silk of my dress.

"Don't put it there." Before she can poke the fabric, I move out of her reach. "I'll just stick it to the front of my clutch."

I'm already reaching for it when she snatches her hand back.

"You want this to be visible." There's something a little off about her smile as she wraps her own gold-coloured ribbon around her neck. "I know I will."

"Why is yours gold and mine white?" I stare at the jauntily tied bow she ties off to the side.

"Gold is for open."

"Open for . . . chatting? For love? For finding out what the washing machine does with all those odd socks?"

"Let's go with experiences."

"What about the white?" I look down at the ribbon between her fingertips.

"A spectator, I guess."

"What kind of singles event encourages spectators? Isn't it by definition a participant sport?" Maybe that's where the ribbons come in, whispers a ridiculous voice in my head. Ribbons for participation like a school sports day.

But how?

Beth doesn't answer as the elevators slide open to a low-lit marble foyer. A sleek baby grand piano sits in one corner and dark velvet chairs are arranged artistically around low tables giving the space the air of a luxury hotel. But it isn't a hotel because there's no reception desk or concierge. Besides, what sense would there be in putting the entrance to a hotel at the very top?

"I thought tonight would've been held in a restaurant," I whisper as a low hum of voices and sultry jazz drifts in from a room beyond.

"I didn't say so," she answers blandly as she passes over her satin jacket to a woman dressed identically to the one downstairs. Oddly, she then passes over her phone.

"You did say this was a private event, I suppose."

"Yes, very."

Beth and the coat check attendant exchange a look before the latter asks, "May I take your wrap?"

It isn't really a wrap, but a soft scarf repurposed as such, but I didn't have a coat to go with this dress. Plus, I judged correctly that pasties wouldn't be enough to keep me warm. I unravel it, passing it to the attendant. Suddenly, I feel a little exposed as I begin to fuss with the neckline, making sure the girls are covered.

I don't want to give the wrong impression.

"If I could just take your cell phone, too."

"Sorry?" I look up, fingers still wrapped around one of the thin straps.

"Your cell," the attendant repeats. "I'm afraid there are no electronic devices permitted beyond this point."

"But I need my phone." My grip tightens on my tiny clutch. "I've left my child with a babysitter for the first time tonight. Can't I just put it on silent?"

The woman just shakes her head, though smiles kindly.

"We can't go in unless you leave it." Beth's whisper is a little harsh.

"I need to be contactable. I'm sorry, Beth, but this isn't negotiable for me."

"I'm afraid rules are rules," the attendant murmurs softly.

"And I completely understand. My friend will just have to go in without me."

"I can't go in on my own," she protests, reaching out to clutch my arm. But I'm already shaking my head because there's something fishy about this whole thing.

What kind of singles event forbids electronic devices?

"How about I hold on to it for you?" Both our attentions swing to the woman. "If it rings or there's a text, someone will come and find you. Mothers do have their priorities," she adds before I can protest. "But they also deserve to let down their hair once in a while."

"Exactly! That's exactly it," Beth echoes, her relief coming from a place of self-serving rather than anything else. I feel like I'm discovering all kinds of things about her, like how she's more a *Charles* kind of friend, whose friendship I often think of in dog terms. That's not to say Charles possesses the boundless levels of love a dog does, but rather, he'll forget about you the minute you walk out the door. He's definitely not the *Rose* gold standard.

I watch in fascination as Beth slides a fifty from her purse, pressing it to the other woman's hand. "That would be wonderful, wouldn't it, Fee? She'll just be at the bar," she adds, slipping her arm through mine.

"I won't move from there." I'm not sure if the strongly-worded retort is for the attendant or my so-called friend. "The main bar." Just in case there's more than one. "And you're looking for a call from Sophia. This is ridiculous," I mutter, tugging my arm from Beth's as she propels us forward. What is all this extra bullshizzle? Fifty-dollar tips and ribbons and phones. "You've got some explaining to do."

"At the bar, I promise."

"I'm going to need alcohol for this explanation?"

Beth shrugs.

This does not seem good.

18

CARSON

The person you asked about has arrived, sir.

I read the text, slip my phone into the inside pocket of my jacket, and try to relax my jaw before my molars disintegrate.

"You're a grim-faced bastard this evening." Tucker joins me on the mezzanine, pressing a glass into my hand. "You got a toothache or something?"

"Or something," I grate out.

"Well, lighten the fuck up."

"And this is your prescription, is it?" I tilt the glass, the light hitting the single malt, reminding me of Fee's guileless eyes and the golden ring around her iris.

Guileless or a good actress?

Tucker raises his own glass, the contents water not vodka. "Only madness lies in the bottom of a glass," he replies with a small quirk of his mouth. He, of all people, would know that.

"Maybe I'm just tiring of all this." I gesture to the floor below this stylish three-floor residence that's costing a fortune to rent for the weekend, and the sea who've paid to be here. The rich and influential. All here to fuck without fear of opinions, judgment, or consequences.

"Not after the bidding war I just had on my hands. A bidding war I had to cancel."

"Flattery?"

"Hell, yeah!" he asserts, warming to his theme. "We should make it part of the business. Not an altruistic side gig. Extend the—"

My angry gaze cuts to his.

"Fine." He sighs heavily. "So we'll just leave it as it is." Both our attentions turn to the floor below once again when he begins to speak again. "Maybe you should look at them like I do." He gestures to the revellers below. "Like they're dollars in the bank." Then he takes a swallow from his drink, his expression turning pensive. "But maybe that doesn't work for you. Maybe money doesn't turn the rich on."

"Like him, you mean?" I retort, pointing out the tech billionaire below who tried to talk down the price of membership last year on account of his wife being, in his words, *fuck hot*. Being rich turns him on, so much so he doesn't like to part with his money. The other thing that turns him on is watching his wife be fucked by other men. The more, the better, as I recall. Which is convenient given she gets off on that, too.

"Okay, so maybe you should just pick another analogy for them. Like walking orifices."

Some of them are a little more than that on nights like these. Regardless, I find I have no interest in but one attendee.

"Just . . . stop talking." I'm not interested in conversation, or money, or indiscriminate fucking. I'm interested in finding her. In discovering if she's here for anonymous fucking when she wouldn't have sex with me—on the couch, the floor, my bed, hell, up against a wall. Wherever she may have preferred, I'd likely already imagined having her there already.

Sweet, lovely Fee. The girl all her friends want to protect.

She's holding out for the one? If only they knew.

Maybe I was too close a call. Maybe she couldn't risk letting her secret out. And maybe I'm a fucking fool for still wanting her, but I do.

"So you don't want to talk about your bad mood or the auction. What about the non-qual asshole you asked me to meet before tonight?" Around his glass, Tucker points his finger and thumb gun style at the people below and what is unmistakably Everett's head of thick, dark hair.

"So he came."

"Maybe he couldn't resist my pitch," Tucker says with a smirk.

"He might not be a frogman, but I hear he was special forces for the Brits."

"Candy ass," he asserts with a derisory sniff. "You know there's only hootin', lootin' and parachutin'."

Tucker is always a little high on Ardeo nights.

"Hooyah, motherfucker," I mutter ironically. "Where'd you meet him?"

"FiDi," he replies. "At a diner. We had breakfast."

"I hope you persuaded him to have oatmeal. He looks like he could do with the fibre."

"I could say the same about you. You know those anal beads might help you with—"

"Fuck, enough already!"

"Ha. You smiled." He moves closer, examining my face. "And look, it didn't crack."

"Asshole. Just tell me how the conversation went."

"He signed the NDA—"

Not that it will stop him from telling Remy, if he decides he needs to know. But would Remy tell Rose? My money says not. Our lives and lies are tangled, and though we never speak of it, we both know the knots are there.

"—then I just told him the truth. How Ardeo started as a means to help your Navy brothers. How when we came back from that shithole, things weren't the same. How we weren't the same. Divorces. Cheating girlfriends, people around us who didn't understand why we weren't who we used to be. How they couldn't understand. But he got it."

"He would." Active combat can only be understood by those who've lived it.

"He also said it didn't explain a thing. So then I told him how, in the beginning, Addison was this close," he holds his thumb and forefinger an inch apart in front of his face, "to blowing his goddamn brains out when Laurie left him. I said, you took him to therapy. And when that didn't work, you held a fuckin' birthday party for him when it wasn't even his birthday."

"You still griping about that?" I wasn't sure if Addison would make his next birthday. There was little for any of us to celebrate around that time. But men rarely need an event to enjoy pussy.

"My birthday was next, Car. If anyone should've been taking three women to bed, it should've been me."

"I can't believe we're still having this conversation. It worked, didn't it?"

"If marrying a hooker is what you call success."

"She was a stripper, not a hooker. And he didn't marry her." One man's meat is another man's poison, so they say.

Tucker sniffs and leans his elbows against the

balustrade. "So your friend down there? I told him how Ardeo was born out of the sex fogged air, post fuck fest in the a.m."

"So basically, you told the man we had an orgy to cheer up a buddy."

"The kind that Bacchus would've killed to get an invite to." He shoots me a sly grin.

"It was a good party," I agree.

"And then I told him how I had an epiphany—"

"How *you* had an epiphany? That's not how I remember it."

"That my epiphany was with your contacts, money, and reputation, plus my business acumen, we could really build something running a very particular kind of party for the rich fucks, and the famous fucks, of this world you inhabit. Charge those rich to fucks to get their rocks off with anonymity."

Ardeo nights are, I suppose, their *fuck you* to the world for people who live their lives in the public eye, their every moved scrutinised. On nights like these, for the membership price and their signature on a watertight NDA, they can explore every kink imaginable, and they can do it with an audience. Or they can watch. Whatever their preference is. One thing's for sure; you'll never read of their exploits on Page Six.

"You know it."

"I do." I've heard him tell this story before. "If you build it, they will come."

"Even squirt, some of them."

"You really are fucking crass."

"I'm also so very fuckin' happy in my work."

And that right there is the reason I don't regret a thing. That I've been able to help the men in my company move on with their lives is the reason I'm standing here. From Tucker and Addison as co-owners to the guys who work in supplies and security. We're not all here just to get our dicks wet.

"Well, hello sweet darlin'." Tucker wiggles his fingers in a wave to someone below. "Your guy will see it all for himself tonight." His gaze lifts to mine. "I told him if it wasn't for you, I wouldn't be living the life I do. Hell, none of us would."

I slide him a look of disgust. I hate it when he tries to sell me of all people on this. It was a business plan, plain and simple, just not the kind you could ever take to a bank. Not that we needed funds then or now, and the business has paid for itself a hundred times over. Why wouldn't it? Sex sells. Privacy with it, whether a resort weekend, a night in a manor house in London, a chateau in France, or from a superyacht in the Maldives. Rich people pay us to cater to their proclivities. But it's not about them. It's about helping the men I fought alongside find their place once more in the world.

And then later, it became about benefitting Rose's foundation kind of poetically.

"How'd he take it?" I eventually ask.

"He seemed stunned at first, then he started asking about you."

"And you told him what?"

"That I think you're a little crazy. That I'm a little jealous. That we all are."

"Un-fucking-believable," I mutter.

"That's what he said. Along with; how can a little dick be worth that much? You know what I told him?"

"Less of the little."

"Yeah. Built like a tripod, I told him. But I left the finer details to you."

I sigh then turn to him. "What?"

"I was thinking you might like to tell me why you cancelled your involvement tonight."

"If I'd wanted to explain myself I would have already."

"Who's the HVT?" *High Value Target.*

"Isn't that usually me."

"Not tonight, it isn't." He flicks his hand negligently over the balustrade, indicating our partygoers. Filthy rich, and just plain filthy. While I'll lie to myself and lie to my friends, is she down there looking for *the one*? And would that be the one whose dick she'll choke on or the one who'll fuck her asshole in front of all these fine, upstanding people tonight? "Who caught your eye down there?"

"You know, Tucker, usually when someone's pulling my dick, they have better tits than yours."

"Not tonight, they don't. Riddle me this, asshole. How can you be so good at keeping secrets and be such a terrible fuckin' liar?"

I don't even spare him a glance.

"If you grip that railing any tighter, it *will* bend, and we won't get our quarter mill security deposit returned."

Straightening, I slide my hand into the pocket of my pants. "I don't know what you're talking about."

"And I know you look like someone stole your puppy."

"I'm not sad," I mutter, refusing to look at him.

"I never said you were. You look more vengeful. Who's the lucky girl?"

She doesn't date. Everett's assertion pounds in my brain, blood pumping through my veins hot enough to scald.

Is this why?

Is this her kink? Her thing?

Maybe 'the one' is just a line she fed Rose.

Maybe she's living her life like me. Secrets. No strings. And if that's the case, why doesn't it make me happy? Happy that I could have her once more, right here, right now.

Because you wouldn't be the only one with access, and you don't want to share.

No, not her.

My hand tightens on my glass as I contemplate how only a small portion of members avail themselves to private rooms, the majority of our members getting off more on the public nature of the illicit, even more so than the fucking.

"Remember when we came back from our last tour, and I found out Kasey was foolin' around with someone else?"

This catches my attention. This discussion, this thing, this time in history—the reason Ardeo is business divided into equal shares. A business with departments, and accounts, and a legal jargon to hide behind.

This something we no longer talk about.

"I recognise that look you're wearing. I saw it in the bathroom mirror, even as I pushed the gun into my mouth."

He was wretched, heartbroken, and vengeful. Just a shell of a man.

But which of these does he see in me?

And as though hearing my question, he answers it for me. "You look like you want to play, Hayes. And not nicely."

"Maybe. Maybe not," I murmur as I raise my glass to my lips, my gaze sweeping the floor below once more. The reckless and the revellers. Those waiting to fuck and be fucked.

"Well, I'll leave you to your brooding. I gotta hit the head."

And then I see her. A lamb among the wolves.

As my eyes devour the sight of her, I know who I'll be eating tonight.

19

FEE

"A freaking sex party!"

Why in the blueberry fluff muffin would anyone bring me along to something like this? I mean, me of all people?

"Keep your voice down," Beth hisses back, her eyes sliding to a gathering which, at first glance, looks like an upscale cocktail party. An upscale cocktail party we're not entering as she pulls me into a corner. "That's not what this is."

I scan the room again. It all looks so normal. Pretty dresses and men in tuxedos, a mixture of ages and looks. But the one thing they all have in common is how relaxed they all look. Confident in their own skins.

I shake my head as though shaking off flies. At the end of the day,

"People have sex here." I stab my finger in the direction of the open door. "They pay a membership fee to shag each other. A party plus sex equals a sex party."

"Shag?" She arches a brow. "This is a very elite event. An adult lifestyle event."

"Oh, excuse me," I reply as though mistaken. "But I think you'll find that's still a mothertrucking orgy."

"It is not an orgy. Tonight is much more classy than that. The connections you might make here—"

"Connections? How can you even say that with a straight face?" Hand on my hip, I lean in a little closer, conscious of being overheard though a lot more freaked out. "I'm not interested in the kind of connections where people have paid for the chance to have sex with strangers."

"It's not just about sex," she argues. "It's about meeting likeminded people, about exploration—"

"It's about connections," I repeat, refraining from making the accompanying childish hand gesture. *A rounded fist, a finger, and a lot of poking.* "I get it."

"The people here tonight are the kinds of people you want to get to know. You can make professional connections, social ones, and romantic ones."

Because nothing says romance like an orgy.

"Okay, so what? They'll chat, have a drink, maybe stuff their faces with a few vol-au-vent? Schmooze and have a jolly good time, but at some point in the night, people will begin to whip their kits off and get it on. In a place that is clearly not a hotel. So that means they probably have sex in front of everyone. Probably with everyone!"

"You don't have to have sex. That's what the white ribbon is for."

I glance down at the ribbon crushed in my hand. Quickly shoving my clutch under my arm, I wrap it around the strap of my dress in the biggest, most noticeable bow I can.

"Jesus, Mary, and Joseph." I find myself muttering very much in the vein of my mother hearing bad news.

"Come on, it's not all that bad." Beth reaches out, touching my arm.

"It's not all that good, either. Come meet the New York singles in their natural habitat, you said. Think of it as an anthropological expedition. Be my wing woman!"

"And all of that is still true."

"You're telling me that all these people are single? That there's not a married or cohabiting couple among them?"

"Of course there will be. Ardeo is inclusive, single women and men, and also couples. And everyone here has been highly vetted." Beth raises her chin defensively.

"Swingers." The word sort of sneaks past my lips.

"I paid a lot of money to get here tonight—to get *you* here tonight—I really thought you might find it fun."

"A cervical smear would be higher on my list of pleasant pastimes."

"But your dry spell—"

"Is my business."

And this is the moment she begins to take me seriously, her fingers beginning to pluck at her bottom lip. "Oh, God, Fee, you can't mention this to anyone."

"As if I would." As if anyone who knows me would believe me. I can barely believe it myself.

"I mean it, you've signed a watertight and quite aggressive NDA. Or at least I signed it on your behalf." From serious to sheepish, I can't believe this woman!

"Are you having some kind of mental breakdown?" I thought the Riviera rich were crazy with their European *bon vivant*, pleasure-seeking attitudes. But this? Ribbons and NDAs and confiscated phones, not to mention sex with strangers, in motherfluffin' public! Sort of.

"I thought you'd be cool about it—I thought you'd thank me!"

"Did you not think to question why I haven't had sex in five years?"

"You haven't got a disease or anything, have you?" Her gaze roams over me a little anxiously.

"Of course I haven't," I grate out. "I meant I haven't had sex out of choice, not out of lack of opportunity. Even so, I know it doesn't have to be like this."

"But this is the start of my sexual renaissance," she retorts defensively.

"You got divorced." I take both of her hands in mine, and though she tries to resist, I'm much stronger than I look. *Carrying a toddler almost constantly for three years will do that to a girl.* "Of course, you're having a fucking reawakening, but it doesn't have to be anonymous sex."

"I don't think I've ever heard you curse before," she replies a little startled.

"That, I'm sure, will be the first fuck of many tonight." I frown as she giggles, pressing her hand to her mouth. "I don't mean like that."

"Look, I'm sorry I wasn't honest with you. But I was desperate. Since my divorce, I've tried all the usual; E-Harmony, Tinder, E-Volve, and I just keep making a mess of things."

"They're men, how hard can it be?"

"You know, I don't see a line of them outside of your door. Oh, I forgot. You had your door welded shut *five years ago*."

"Say it a bit louder, why don't you. I'm sure there were a couple of people in the West Village who didn't quite hear."

"Sorry," she adds, her posture suddenly changing as

her shoulders slump. I notice how her eyes glisten in the low light, so I decide against suggesting she go back to basics. Like downing a few drinks before shaking her butt on the dance floor of any nightclub in any town or city. I know I've been out of the game a while, but that's how it used to be done. "But if you go, I can't stay either."

"Jesus, stop with the sad puppy eyes! We're here." I shrug. "I haven't been struck by a lightning bolt from the heavens." Yet. "But I have provisos."

"Oh, thank you, Fee." She reaches out to hug me when I hold up a forestalling hand.

"I'll stay for exactly one hour." Even as I say it, I can't believe I'm not hightailing it out of this place, screaming. "For one hour I'm your wing woman, but within that hour, if your hands disappear into someone's boxer shorts, I'm off. Do you hear?" That would just make for an even more awkward Monday morning. "Also, I'm not moving from the bar, so you'd better get this renaissance of yours kicked off *tout de suite.*"

"I will, definitely. Let's go get a drink."

I'm going to need a veritable bucket of the hard stuff.

"Oh, God, I feel so nervous." At the large bar overlooking the Park, Beth fusses with her hair in the window's reflection.

"You feel nervous," I mutter, shooting her a grim look. "At least you've known all along what you were getting into."

"Please don't make me feel any worse than I already do." She keeps her eyes resolutely on the window behind the bar, refusing to look at me. "I'm sorry. Really, I am. I know you don't want to be here, but—"

"Of course I don't want to be here—" Lowering my

voice, I draw closer. "I'll be buggered if the first time I have sex after five years is at an or—an adult lifestyle party."

Beth's expression turns a little crafty "You're wearing the wrong-coloured ribbon for *that*."

"What? No! Not buggered in the bum sense. I'm just not doing it." My hand cuts through the air with finality. "Any of it."

"Message received, loud and clear," she says, bumping her shoulder against mine. "But thank you for staying to hold my hand. You know, the last time I was at a bar by myself was the night I met my ex-husband."

"Did you meet him at a party like this?" Party. Urgh!

"No, some dive bar," she answers with a small smile, her attention turning inward almost. "He was cute, and I was young. Or dumb. Not that it matters. He sidled up to me and said, 'Can I buy you a drink or do you just want me to give you the money?'"

"That's a weird chat-up line."

"I thought it was endearing. And that he was handsome certainly helped. But as it turned out, he only had ten dollars in his pocket and couldn't pay for my cocktail. So I paid, and he took the drink, and then three years later, he tried to take everything else I had." Her gaze rises, coming back to the moment. "He took my money and my self-esteem. He made me forget who I am. So I'm not going to apologise for being here tonight, but I am sorry I brought you along without telling you the whole deal. I thought you'd be surprised but that you'd be happy. I guess I fooled myself about that, too."

"I get it." Even if I still don't understand.

"I need this, Fee."

"Like a B-list actress needs a sex tape scandal?"

She smiles sadly. "I couldn't do it by myself."

"I think you mean you're tired of doing it by yourself."

"That, too." Her next smile is a small hopeful sort of thing.

"Okay." My reply is more beleaguered sigh than agreement, despite our mini pun-fest. "I said I'd stay, didn't I?"

"I just don't want you to be angry." She throws her arms around my shoulders, pulling me in for a hug

"You're ruining your chances," I mutter, fighting her off. "People will think you swing the other way."

"Oh, I don't think that will be a problem," she replies, her gaze sliding to the window again . . . and the reflections of the men watching us in it. *Oh, bloody hell.* "In fact." She turns to face me, resting her forearm against the bar, her fingers reaching up to slide a lock of hair behind my ear. "I think it might work in our favour."

"Your favour," I grate out through gritted teeth. Because as well as not being buggered, I'm not playing lesbian for the night.

"A dietician, you say?"

I nod even though that's not at all what I said I did for a living, then take a sip from my second glass of vino, if for no other reason than to prevent me from speaking . . . and telling him to piss *right* off. Because he didn't really ask what I did for a living. The arsehole doesn't seem interested in anything but my white ribbon and the challenge it seems to represent. His friend, meanwhile, is wooing Bethany.

Wooing? Enticing? Well, whatever the sex party equivalent is. But she's playing with her hair and acting all coy, so I think she's into him. And for that reason alone, I'll stay. At least until my hour is up or they slink off to a dark corner.

"You know, I like to watch, too."

"Excuse me?"

"Your ribbon." He reaches out as though to finger it when I jerk out of reach, jarring my back against the bar behind me. *Not on your nelly, mate. No fingering the ribbon. Or the girl.* "You like to watch," he asserts. "As an experienced attendee, I happen to know if you like to watch, you'll also enjoy participating." His oddly over-groomed eyebrows waggle over the edge of his glass as he raises it. Eyebrows aside, he's not bad looking, I suppose. The tux probably helps. But these are just observations because I have zero interest in being here for any longer than necessary.

"Like I said, it's my first time here. I'm taking it slowly."

"First times can be special." *I'm not sure he could've made that sound any seedier if he'd tried.* "I could be your guide."

Urgh. Hold my drink while I vomit in the potted palm over there.

I lean back inconspicuously to see how Beth and her (sex party) beau are getting along. The conversation seems so normal, the bits I can hear of it. In fact, it all looks so ordinary. Well, as ordinary as any posh party. People drinking and chatting in groups and couples. The men look so dapper in their dinner jackets, women gorgeous in designer wear. The only odd thing about the whole scene are the ribbons. Everyone wears a ribbon. Some more than one.

And I have so many questions about the colour coding for later.

Maybe this is how the rich run their sex parties. Maybe they chat and get to know each other before "retiring" elsewhere to the dirty deed. Because there's nothing scandalous or titillating going on here . . . until my attention snags on the sight of a gorgeous Amazonian redhead wearing a cream-coloured gauzy dress and nothing else. And if that isn't strange enough, she's leading a much older man through the throng by his tie.

That is . . . an odd pairing. And that body has spent a lot of hours on a reformer in a Pilates class. *Hers, not his.*

"What do you say?"

"Pardon?" My attention snaps back. *Oh God, please go away.*

"I see you looking at the pastor and his friend over there. Maybe we could join them. I'll look after you. I'm kind of popular at these events."

Along with chlamydia, I'd bet.

"I'll, erm, think about it." For exactly three seconds while I have another gulp of wine. Ah, that's good, even if the company is vomit-inducing.

"I'm sure you'll be familiar with the saying you are what you eat. You know, in your profession."

Something tells me we're not talking about macros; carbs, protein, and fats. Or even the importance of micronutrients; vitamins and minerals, and the like.

"I'm familiar," I answer carefully, steeling myself for the punchline.

"Well, let me put this to you. I must've eaten a fucking legend."

"Ha-ha. You're so funny." Funny strange. You know what else is funny strange? The sensation of your nipple covers dislodging themselves from your skin.

Peeeel and pop!

"And I must've eaten some donkey dick in a previous life if you know what I mean."

Or maybe some donkey brain, except that would be insulting to donkeys. And yes, please direct your salacious wink my way. It just makes me want you. And no, that wasn't an excited shimmy. That was me wiggling my nipple covers down my dress.

"Oh, is that Emma Stone?"

"What? Where?" I point over his shoulder and, as he turns, wiggle those little nipple cover feckers the rest of the way down my body, kicking one behind me before stamping my foot over the other.

"What was that?" he asks, turning back and glancing down.

"Spider." I smile a little manically, sure that losing your nipple covers is tantamount to whipping off your undies at one of these things. Please, *please* don't let anyone turn the thermostat down because my nipples are liable to announce their presence. "Sorry, you were saying?"

"I have a big cock. Wanna ride it?"

"Hmm. Not at the moment, thanks."

And just like that, we've reached the end of our little *tête-à-tête*. Mainly because I've reached the limits of my patience.

"Has anyone ever told you that you have the communication skills of a house alarm?" And just in case he doesn't get it, I bleat loudly. Twice. "*Waa! Waa!*"And yes, the noise does draw a bit of attention, which isn't what I'd aimed for. But the arse steps back, which was my aim, allowing me to squeeze past, albeit a little awkwardly, given I've a pastie stuck to the sole of my shoe.

As I hobble away, I glance down at my watch, relieved

I'd thought to wear it, given I don't have my phone. Twenty more minutes until my hour is up. Maybe I'll just check in with the coat check, then maybe powder my nose . . . which will also subtract a few more minutes out of what remains of my promised hour. I can literally feel relief trickling through my bones as I make my way through the throng on my way out.

Except I'm not really sure this is the way out.

I pause and push up onto my tiptoes. *I can see the bar by the window and the amazing view beyond, so that should mean the coat check is the—*

I spin around as hands land on my ass.

"Don't do that," I say to no one in particular, as my cheeks begin to pink. *Both sets of them.* I return to pushing through the crowd, thinking no matter where you are, there's always someone trying to push the en-envelope!

Oh, my! There are people in the corner touching each other—people getting jiggy with it! And one or two getting jiggy with themselves as they watch.

So much for tame.

My goodness! That's a bit of an eyeful!

I spin away, my hand pressed to my lips in the attempt to prevent a building giggle. I haven't felt so embarrassed since I uncovered my dad's outdated porn stash as a teen. There is no way I could have sex while people watch. Not without sniggering. I just couldn't—

JesusfuckingChrist! That looked like Everett, Remy's head of security!

Like a whirling dervish, I spin in the other direction, moving as fast as my heels allow. If that is him, and he sees me, at least I won't ever have to explain myself to him because I'd just die of embarrassment.

But it can't have been him. It's just my brain playing

tricks on me, frightening myself that I'll somehow be outed for being a deviant when I'm really just very, very normal.

Just like I thought Beth was.

I drain the rest of my glass, my eyes unseeing as my brain scrambles to unpick my mess of thoughts. Unseeing, not for long, at the sounds of a feminine laugh, I take in the almost tableau in front of me. I'm on the threshold of a corner room, two walls almost entirely glass. It seems like a dining room of sorts; a round wooden table with four chairs, two of them already occupied by men. Dinner jackets discarded, shirts open at the neck, the pair seem to be playing cards when a brunette steps between the pair, serving them drinks in lowball crystal glasses.

Oh. Not serving them but helping herself to the contents.

And oh, my, she is beautiful. The men are handsome too, and the trio either unaware of my presence, or else they don't care. And while I've no idea what keeps me in this spot, I continue to stand there as my heart pounds so hard it echoes elsewhere.

As the woman bends to place the second glass down, the man runs his hand up the back of her leg. My breath catches along with hers, her hand tightening on his shoulder and creasing the snowy white fabric of his shirt. They kiss. He touches. A stroke, a caress. Her black dress riding higher and higher as he trails his hands up her legs.

She laughs softly, licks her lips, then whispers something meant for only his ears. I know I should move. Move away. Not intrude. But as both men stand, I find I'm rooted to the spot, breathless with anticipation. My heart thunders and my core *aches*, and I wish that Carson was here right now. Because I wouldn't be watching, I'd be giving. Giving myself over to him. Giving myself over to the thrill, just like the woman in front of me.

One kisses her mouth and the other the nape of her neck, two pairs of hands roaming everywhere. She sighs. She whispers. Arches between them, her body pliant, her knees growing weak. Or maybe those are my knees threatening to buckle as I reach out a shaking hand, steadying myself against the wall.

Four hands lift her dress from the hem, the brush of the fabric a caress I can almost feel. The sound of it dropping to the floor echoes deeply inside me.

An arm wraps her waist, fingers slipping down her stomach and into her underwear. From the front, lips and fingers tease her breasts until she begins to moan and writhe, the press of two hard bodies the only things keeping her upright.

But not for long.

"*Yes!*" Her eyes are dark, and her excitement is palpable, her cry ringing through the room as she's spun from one to the other for a passionate kiss before she's pressed down to the table between them.

Her body convulses, her hands reaching out, her whispers of encouragement too far away to hear. Belts *clink,* a *whoosh* of leather sounds as they're pulled from the loops. But I'm not watching them. I'm watching her, fingers grasping, and her body wracked by shallow, excited breaths as she's kissed and licked, as her breasts spill from their lacy cups as the other manhandles and mauls her underwear. Four hands make the scene all the more torrid, all the more exciting as I stand, stock-still, blood rushing through my veins with a mixture of excitement and shame.

Pants are opened, cocks freed, her mouth not the only

part of her greedy to be filled, her thighs opening in invitation.

She begs.

She cries out.

I suck in a sharp breath feeling like I've gone too long without. Too long without a breath. Too long without sex as I stand here, imagining myself in this scene. Picturing Carson staring down at me with such possession from his position between my spread knees.

Could I do it? Place me in this position, with one man, with two? Satisfy this sweet, sticky need snaking through me?

Cries turn to moans. *Because it's hard to shout when your mouth is full.*

She looks . . . delirious. Blissed.

I force myself to turn away as the men swap their positions.

This should turn my stomach, this sordid scene, yet it doesn't. This voyeur feels nothing but envy and desire. The heady fusion of fear and thrill.

My reactions aren't at all in keeping with how a good person—a mother—should feel as I turn and stumble from the room, pressing my back to the cool of the wall, the only thing about the moment that feels solid or real.

I tell myself I need to pause to catch my breath. To try to make sense of why I watched, why I stood there, my insides pulsing emptily. And not because I need to press my thighs together in lieu of the overwhelming desire to slide my hand between my legs.

Two heart beats later, I swear I feel a change in the air: something not quite tangible yet something so real that a frisson of anticipation sweeps across my skin.

I lift my gaze, and hope sings inside me because

Carson Hayes is stalking towards me. I don't take a moment to process how or why or anything logical because all I can think is the man looks lethal in a tuxedo. His dark eyes spear me to the spot as he secures the button of his jacket like it's a declaration of war.

I lick my lips as he draws closer because I don't know what to say. Because I want to feel his mouth against mine. My insides are plump with the thought of it, my skin almost seeming not to fit any more.

He comes to a halt in front of me, and though I find I can't lift my gaze, I still devour the sight of him. The dark fabric coating his strong thighs, the pleat knife sharp. My gaze wanders up the broad expanse of him, halting in the vicinity of his chin as I scan my mind for something to say.

Fancy meeting you here.

I can explain . . . Some of it, at least.

Just, please . . . touch me.

I inhale, really not sure what I'm about to say when he beats me to it.

"Don't," he commands in a tone not at all like the Carson I'm familiar with. The man who is quick to smile and always ready to tease. "Not here." His large hand appears before me as the devil whispers, "Come with me."

I place my hand in his, finding there isn't anywhere I wouldn't follow him right now.

20

FEE

My hand still held fast in his as I struggle to keep up with his long strides, aware of the people we're passing. Their expressions are a mixture of enquiry and calculation. Jealousy, even.

"Where are we going?" As my heart continues to beat so hard it rings in my ears as arousal and alarm commingle into a heady internal stew.

"Somewhere we can talk. Without distraction."

That wasn't the answer I was expecting. I push aside the implication because no, I can't talk about what I'm doing here. Not after what I've just witnessed. If he'd caught me just ten minutes before, my conscience would be clear, and my knickers wouldn't be sticking to—

Ten minutes.

"No, stop." In a hallway now, I pull on his hand, pull with the full weight of my body. "I don't have my phone. I was only meant to be here for an hour."

As his feet come to a halt, I almost bounce into him, into his broad back.

"What did you hope to achieve in an hour?"

"Not whatever it is you're thinking." My retort is delivered to the back of his head, my uncomfortable heels bringing my height a little closer to his. As I try to pull my hand from his, his grip just tightens. "Lulu is with a babysitter, and I already had a mini heart attack when I found out I had to leave my phone at the entrance."

He turns to me then, his eyes an angry shade of midnight. "You didn't read the instructions?"

"What instructions?"

"The member's area of the website."

"I must've missed that bit," I snap back, my voice rising in intensity if not volume because he's not at all endearing himself to me currently.

"Which parts did you read?" He tugs on my hand, and I stumble into him, my free hand finding its way to the firm expanse of his chest. My clutch drops to the floor, and I find myself flattening my palm against his shirt, wondering if his heart is beating as hard as mine as I inhale a lungful of his scent. Why does he always smell so good? That damned cologne of his with the underlying scent of whisky and mint.

"So you didn't read the rules and regulations. The expectations." His deep baritone vibrates under my hand. "Maybe you stopped at the sales pitch when you were sold a sexually liberated paradise?" The backs of his fingers trail down my face, his words low and seductive. "Exclusive and hedonistic. A utopia for fucking."

"What about you?" My words sound even, despite how I feel, despite how I'm back to staring at his sternum. "Maybe I should ask what parts *you* paid particular attention to."

"I wrote the rules, beautiful. The reason you're wearing a white ribbon is because of me."

"I." Clap my mouth closed, then try again. "I don't know what you're talking about." Because he didn't choose it for me, Beth did. Surely, he doesn't mean he and Beth contrived to get me here. As my sluggish brain struggles to process all this, his fingers stroke the sensitive dip behind my ear. It doesn't help my cognitive skills, and I find myself biting back a moan as his lips follow suit. A press of his lips, the touch of his tongue, and I'm melting against him, my fingers twisted in his lapels.

"They said you didn't *date*." His sultry whisper winds its way through me as his hands clasp my hips. "Maybe they don't know you prefer to watch than participate."

Something hot bursts inside my chest at his accusation, thick shame and need trickling down to my belly as my mind works over his words. The significance of a white ribbon; it all now makes sickening sense. People don't pay to come to a night like this to watch; this isn't a spectator sport.

Unless that's your thing.

Unless that's your kink.

I can't even deny it because he saw me there, watched me as I watched. As I wondered what it would feel like to be *her*.

I blow out a tremulous breath. Mortified doesn't quite cover how I feel, but it's there, swimming in the morass as my skin burns under the weight of his fingertips and nuzzling lips. I'm pretty certain I no longer have cheekbones; embarrassment having scorched them clean away. There are other parts of me burning too, and not in an entirely unpleasant way.

I give a tiny shake of my head because, yes, I watched. How could I not? She looked so free. So in the moment. There wasn't a thought for afterwards, for awkwardness and consequences. I wanted to *be* her, yet I ached for him. For Carson to be the one to take me. To make me forget everything but him.

You should be careful who you ache for.

"Please don't," I manage to murmur, stepping away from the heat of him, glad my mouth still belongs to me even if my tongue feels about three foot wide.

"You don't want me to kiss you? To touch you?"

"I'm not here for the reasons you think."

"Yet here you are. Still." His deep baritone makes me wet when his assumption should make me incredulous. But when my gaze lifts to meet his, he steals any retort I might have with a kiss. No, not a kiss. An invasion. A thought-stealing, will-bending raid. His lips drive mine apart, his hands tangling in my hair as he feeds me his tongue as he would his cock. I am a willing captive but no spectator. *I won't come quietly.* Not as my body moulds itself to the hard planes of his as though I could be absorbed by him.

I moan a protest as his fingers curl around my shoulders, pushing me back against a solid surface. *The wall?* No, a door. But I don't complain as his body follows, his eyes raking over me like a feudal lord. I lift my arms, greedy for him when, lightning-quick, he presses them against the cool wood, circling my wrists with one of his hands.

"There's no one here, angel. No one to watch you fall apart." His gaze is positively electric as his thumb skims the shape of my breast, my nipple standing to attention under the thin fabric. "Not even the stars this time." He pinches, and my body jerks, the door handle rattling uncomfortably at the small of my back.

"I don't need an audience. I just need you."

The door opens suddenly, and the only thing stopping me from stumbling backwards is his strong arm wrapping my waist. In a motion that seems almost choreographed, he swipes up my clutch and takes my hand almost twirling me behind him. And then we're moving again, down a darkened service hallway and out through a second door, this time to an outside space. A loggia, vaulted and a little gothic, it seems much too atmospheric for such a modern building. My heels click against the sandstone flagstones as we pass an outdoor fireplace, seating and green potted palms before another door swishes open, and we're inside again.

The room we're in is huge, one wall almost completely glass with the trifecta view of river, park, and the city at night. While I can't ignore that this is a bedroom, the immediate space is meant for other more civilised things. A pale sofa, a glass table, and a pair of designer Barcelona chairs. The other side of the room is dominated by the biggest bed I've ever seen; a modern take on a four-poster, golden framed. Dozens of pillows cover the thing with cream-coloured gauzy fabric falling from all sides. This kind of room would be a perfect feature in a design magazine, though not one titled Orgy Pads of the Rich and Famous.

The door *clicks* closed behind me, though I don't turn. But I feel him, oh God, do I feel the heat coming off him in burning waves.

"My phone." I almost fall on it as I spot it on the glass table, grasping it to swipe the screen. *No missed calls.* I breathe a sigh of relief. "How did it get here?"

"I arranged it." Footsteps resound, a switch *snaps,* and a low light suffuses the room. "I knew you wouldn't want to be without it."

Carson Hayes isn't the kind of man who'd ignore a fundraising tin.

I turn, finding him leaning indolently against a credenza. Legs crossed at the ankle, the singular button of his jacket undone, his hands sunk into the pockets of his pants.

It's strange how the only truthful part of this performance is his gaze, a gaze that feels like the brush of caressing fingertips.

"Do you want to know why I turned on the light?" His question catches me off guard. "Because I sense this is you stepping out of your life for one night."

"That might be true." I dip my head as a wave of melancholy washes over me. One night is all I can allow myself.

There are too many uncertainties; what Rose means to him, what this night means to him. I can't be involved with a man who's at home at a party like this—a man who might be in charge of a night like this. I could ask him to explain, but I don't want to take the risk. I just want him to kiss me again and make me forget everything.

I fought my attraction to him for long enough.

I startle a little as he pushes off the credenza, my heart surely beating out of my chest as he closes the space between us.

"The light," he repeats, one finger carelessly flicking over his shoulder. "As much I enjoyed the aesthetic in France, moonlight won't work for me tonight." He captures my chin between his thumb and forefinger, forcing my gaze to his. "Because I don't intend on missing one thing."

"You might regret that." The truth is out of my mouth before I can temper it. "I'm not that girl I was back then."

Physically, emotionally, not that I could explain the differences to him.

"You are so much more."

I am . . . more. Larger. Certainly less waif-like. Fuller in the hips and breasts as well as flatter in the rear end. The fact is, it doesn't matter how hard you work to get back the pre-pregnancy you, you're never the same. Having a child leaves you forever changed, physically and emotionally. But then I realise Carson isn't looking at my body. He's looking into my eyes, looking at *me.* And something tells me, as he presses his palm to the base of my spine, he sees more than I'd ordinarily be comfortable with.

"Wait." I tilt my head as his mouth begins to descend. "What you said out there. I'm not single because I prefer watching others . . ."

"Fuck?" The way his lips form the hard fricative makes my knees weak. "But you did enjoy. Watching."

"Yes." My tongue darts out to lick my parched lips, my voice a little stronger now, a little less ashamed, because he of all people should understand. Maybe? "Yes, I did."

"Then I was right on that score." He angles his head, but I move back once more. I suddenly understand why Rose has never seen him with a woman. He isn't celibate. He might well be the complete opposite.

"You were also right about tonight. This can only happen once." My voice sounds stronger than I currently feel, but this is something we both need to hear.

"One more for old times' sake?" The gleam in his eye is a little frightening though I find myself nodding. "Then we'd better make it good."

Good enough to last a lifetime, I tell myself.

He doesn't try to kiss me again as his hand glides across my shoulder, taking with it the thin strap of my dress and exposing my breast. I bite back a gasp as his knuckle skates down it in a shiver-inducing caress.

"So beautiful," he whispers, capturing the tip of my nipple between his fingers. His gaze measures the weight of my reaction as he pulls. I whimper, and suddenly his mouth covers the tight bud. A swirl of tongue, a taut suck as his hand slides up my back, hooking under the remaining strap. My stomach roils with anticipation as much as dread as it slides from my shoulders, the silk of my dress snagging on my hips. Fear that he'll see me naked, yes, but also fear that I want this too much. That tonight won't be enough. But the noise in my head is drowned out by the man in front of me, his gaze liquifying my bones, his arms wrapping me like ivy and slipping the dress from my hips until I'm standing in the silvery pool of it.

"I thought I'd found Goldilocks in my bathtub that night, but you look more like the queen of the fairies stepping from a pool of moonlight."

"You don't have to flatter me. I'm already naked." Naked but for a scrap of lace and my heels.

"You really don't see yourself at all."

The button of his jacket slides across my bare back as he turns me, pressing back against his chest so hard that I can feel every muscle flex. We begin to move backwards but not towards the bed. Instead, we seem to be now standing *in* a closet. A huge and stylish closet with paintwork the colour of clotted cream, crystal chandeliers, and mirrored cabinetry that reflects endless images of a woman enveloped by a man.

"You don't have something to tell me, do you?" Anticipation fizzes inside me, my pussy contracting, my abs drawing tight. Despite the tangle of sensations, a lightness colours my question. "Because I've heard of coming out of the closet but not going back in."

His expression reflects mild amusement, yet his answer seems to be in the way he shrugs out of his jacket and the way he loosens his tie, all the while watching me, his dark eyes meltingly sexy. Without speaking a word, he begins to free my hair from its pins. Waves I don't ordinarily possess cascade across my shoulders, the sight of it seeming to do something to him. My eyes roll closed as he slides my hair over my shoulder, cool air and warm breath caressing my skin.

"Open your eyes." His lips are tender at my neck, the rioting fire rushing through my insides quite the opposite. "Let me show you how exquisite you are."

The woman in the mirror is languid-eyed, her mouth softly open and almost expectant. She looks like the kind of woman who knows what she needs. A woman who knows she belongs entirely to him. And he's so large behind me, his shoulders strong and square as his body frames mine in the mirror, making me feel dainty. Pale skin against sombre black as his arm curls around me, two long fingers coming to rest against my bottom lip.

"If you were mine, I'd kiss you all of the time." His grip on my hair ignites a million fires across my skin. "You would never doubt yourself for a moment because you wouldn't have time. You'd be too busy kissing me."

Wet fingers drift across my collarbone and down between my breasts as he watches my every tremble, my every held breath. The woman in the mirror is her own audience. Her cheeks flushed, her eyes dark, her golden hair slips from her shoulders as she tilts her chin with the imperiousness of a queen.

"If you were mine, you wouldn't long to be held

between two men." His large hand cups my breasts as he twists my mouth to his. "Because I'd make sure the only man you'd ever want is me."

And I ache, I tremble, and I burn as he ghosts his lips over mine. And how I want. Want what isn't good for me. Want what might change everything.

And then he kisses me. *Oh, God, does he kiss me.*

"You're shaking." His velvety words are just a breath against my lips.

"It's been a while," I whisper, even as I tilt my head, giving him access to more of my skin.

"You're not nervous. You're shaking because you want this, because you want to be mine."

I could disagree. But then I'd be lying.

Pulling me backwards, he lowers me to a velvet armchair with cabriole legs and padded arms. Arms which he suddenly grabs, setting it—and me—in the middle of the room. In a flash, he's in front of me, dropping to one knee. His fingers hook the string of my underwear, and I tilt my pelvis, the scrap of fabric tickling my legs.

"Very pretty," he murmurs, balling them into his pocket.

"Also very expensive." I reach out and stroke the silken strip of his bow tie, thinking how he looks like a gift half unwrapped. "So I'd like them back."

"I wasn't talking about your panties." He smirks as he cups the back of my ankle, sliding off my shoe. One shoe, then the other; he moves them to the side, his hand sliding under my knee.

"What are you doing?" My body stiffens, yet I still allow him to lift my leg over the arm of the chair.

"Relax, beautiful. I just want you to watch."

"Sounds . . ." Uncomfortable. And disconcerting. My gaze dips as heat floods my cheeks, yet as I notice the hard outline of him in his pants, I suddenly don't feel quite the same.

"Don't worry," he replies with a wink, "it only seems kinky the first time."

I suddenly get a glimpse of the Carson I haven't seen this evening; a teasing smile, those laughter lines bracketing the lushness of his lips. The Carson who is the bane of my existence, or at least the one I tell myself is. But the glimpse is fleeting as he pushes a finger inside me. I'm so wet. We both hear it, and both feel the evidence of it. And we both watch as he brings his thumb over my clit. Tension melts from my body. Then in one fluid movement, he stands, and I'm back to staring at the outline of his cock again.

He reaches for his fly, long fingers opening his belt before flicking the button open. He loosens three shirt buttons before abandoning the effort and pulling it over his head. As he surrenders it to the floor, a frisson of delight rolls from my head to my toes.

"Do you think about that night?"

I consider lying, though decide we both deserve better, answering with a quiet, "Yes."

"I think about how long it's been since I was inside you. How I've longed for it since." Before I can suggest right now, right here, works for me, he's behind me again, his hands tipping my gaze to the mirror.

"Look at yourself." I glance at the woman in the mirror, her hair wild and her eyes dark. "Did you really think I wouldn't crave your taste again?" My insides pulse emptily as he palms the bulge in his pants. I'm wet with impatience, and his cock is hard with anticipation. "Look at what you've done to me. If you were mine, I'd bury myself in your pussy and never come out."

His body snakes around mine as he sinks to his knees in front, his body bowing as his mouth meets my flesh in a kiss. I try to absorb the sensation, the soft press of his lips as my eyes flutter closed, my hands gripping his thick hair as though to keep him there.

Just *there.*

His touch is everything. Everything I remember, and everything I've missed.

"You're not watching," he draws back just enough to say, his expression not completely serious.

"Stop talking," I think I say. It's hard to tell as his tongue leisurely swipes my clit, and my body arches from the chair.

"The lesson is to look at yourself." His gaze flicks up my body, his dark look inciting. "I want you to see what I see. Why it takes all of my willpower not to kiss you whenever I'm near you."

A thrill washes through me. Can he really feel like this?

"I think you'll find *that* is my job." He reaches up, his thumb freeing my bottom lip from my teeth. And then his head bows as he returns to his task. Or not quite as I squirm at the teasing bite he presses to my thigh. "Still not watching." His tongue soothes the tiny sting, though he doesn't lift his gaze. Instead, he reaches down to grab my ankle, hooking my other leg over the arm of the chair, pressing a velvety groan into the very centre of me.

Oh, God. How can I be expected to watch myself in the mirror, to concentrate on anything but this bliss? His tongue swipes, and I think I might levitate, just a little, my hands rising to the back of the chair, my taut sigh a lament. A lament for what could have been in the kitchen or on the sofa. What could've been so many times if we'd only exchanged names five years ago. Five years yet I remember the way he'd loved my body as if it were only yesterday.

His mouth is sublime, his tongue driving me to the brink of ecstasy, the slick sounds of our coupling echoing through the space.

"Please." My hands grip the back of the chair as I cry out and catch a glimpse of myself. My head thrown back, my eyes are wide, my mouth a rictus of pleasure, the man between my legs a supplicant drawn from my filthiest imaginings.

The sight of us. The way he works me and . . .

"Oh, God. I think . . ." Already, my insides begin to pulse and twist.

"Not yet." His low possessive growl vibrates against my flesh, desire radiating through me in pulsing waves. But it's been so long, I'm not really sure it's up to me. Orgasms by my own hand aren't exactly spontaneous.

More practised. Less free.

But as his hands slide between my butt and the chair, he begins to slow, changing the pace. Deft flicks and teasing swipes. "You can't come yet. Not until you tell me what you see."

"I see me. Please." I find myself whimpering as I writhe. "Please touch me harder, Carson."

"You're so beautiful when you beg." His lashes cast dark shadows against his cheeks as he continues to tease. *A circle. A pet.* I chant my need, and his hand slips up my body, his fingers coming to rest around my neck.

"Oh, God, yes!"

A spike of almost violent pleasure wracks my body.

Why does this feel so right? Look so good? I can't concentrate on anything but the feeling between my legs, my eyes now glued to our reflection. The muscles in his back flex as he moves, his dark head stark against my skin. Between his dirty compliments and his sucking and licking, I can barely remember my own name. But I know the sight of us, our reflection, I'll remember it forever. Replay it again and again.

"That's right, sweet girl," he rasps, voice thick, "take what you need. Beg, plead. Ride my face fucking wild."

"Please." My throat is hoarse as I twist under him, my need spiralling. "Please make me come."

He draws my hips up, engulfing that tight bundle of nerves with his lips as he licks, swirls, and sucks, repeating the teasing torture again and again. He overwhelms me with such passion until I'm not sure where I end, and he begins.

"Such a good girl," he growls, buried between my legs.

And I must be, because this is like Christmas and Easter and my birthday all at once as I'm tipped over the edge, a glitter bomb in my veins as I push myself into his face, devoured and consumed, and coming so hard that my orgasm is surely like a grenade with a pulled pin as I rise to meet it. Rise to meet his tongue.

A party bomb.

A bomb for one.

"Oh!" I press my hands to his head. Carson's last leisurely swipe of tongue was just . . . "Too much."

As he pulls back his mouth, chin glistening with my wetness, his smile is part ruthlessness, part self-satisfaction. "I'm not sure there is such a thing. Not where you're concerned."

He stands and hooks his strong arms under my thighs,

my own rising to slide around his neck like the most natural thing in the world.

"That was some coming out," I whisper as he carries me into the bedroom, laying me almost reverently on the bed.

"There's no going back now." I'm not sure if his reply is in response to my joke or something deeper, but I don't ponder it long because his pants are surrendered next, but not before a condom is retrieved from his wallet. Black boxer briefs follow, then the bed dipping under his knee. He moves closer, thumbs skimming my hipbones, kisses delivered to my body until our mouths meet. It's a kiss that's neither frantic nor frenzied, but slow, like we have all the time in the world. A kiss that perfectly conveys desire without the need for words.

The way his fingers stroke makes me feel treasured and his lips are pure praise, and his breath trembles against my neck as I reach down between our bodies, my fingers stroking his silken head. He's so hot and so hard as I take him in my grip.

"I won't last," his deep voice rasps, even as he pushes into my hand, prompting me to squeeze. "*Fuck.* Yes, harder like that."

"I want to taste you again." I've dreamed of it so many times. The noises he made as he'd chased his climax and the power I'd felt when he did.

His answer is *the* most masculine groan, his body suddenly pliant as I work my way under him. In our need to lick and be touched, Carson pushes up to his knees, proud and erect, the ruddy hardness of him jutting between us like an accusation.

He seems more marble than flesh in the low light, yet his skin is pure heat.

He shudders as I take him in my hand.

Groans as I press a kiss to his crown.

Curses as I slide him into the heat of my mouth.

Pleads for divine intervention as I begin to move.

"That feels so good." The need in his husky reply heats my blood, and as he gathers my hair to the side to watch, I commit his languid expression to memory. "You look so beautiful like this." As I moan my approval around him, he flexes instinctively forward, pleasure twisting through me like a vine. His hand tightens on my hair as he strains against the urge to give in. My mouth and tongue embrace his slick length, desperate to give him a taste of his own delicious medicine.

"I need you." He pulls me back, my mouth coming off his length with a wet *pop.* Grabbing the abandoned condom, he rises above me, tearing it open with his teeth before sheathing himself and pressing me back against the mattress. "Take me inside," he demands, swiping his crown through my wetness. "Take me inside your body."

My body offers him no resistance as he drives forward, sliding himself to the hilt.

"Stop." My response is more breath than word, but he can't mistake my intentions as I slide my legs around him. *Don't move. Don't go. Just let me feel you.*

"Are you okay?" His forearms at either side of my head, his expression is fierce, though the way he smooths the unruly mess of my hair is the opposite.

"I-I told you it's been a while." It's the truth and also a lie. I don't need him to stop. I just want this moment to never end. His wide shoulders block out the light and shadow the scruff on his cheek. I want to catalogue every sigh and every held breath while savouring the feel of him seated so deeply inside me.

"I can take it slow." He presses his lips to my forehead, and I realise I'm a little disappointed that he didn't ask me exactly how long. "You just feel so fucking good."

I arch into him, his body responding in turn, undulating above me like a wave.

"I forgot what it felt like." I find myself whispering my admission.

"Good, right?" His words sound pained, the muscle in his bicep trembling next to my head.

So good. So right.

"You feel like heaven. So wet and so tight. You feel like you were built for me. Tell me you feel the same way."

I don't dare open my mouth. I can't trust what it might say, what it might reveal as utterly owned as I feel. Then my butt is in his hands as he lifts me in a change of depth and pace. Our carnal cries hit the air simultaneously.

"Tell me," he demands, surging into my body like it's something he owns. "Let me in."

"It feels like I belong." Sheets twisted in my fists, I'm like a cat stretching in the sunshine as I push back into him, my pelvic bones bruising as I grind against him harder still. I grate out his name, *yes, yes, yes!* "I-it feels like I'm yours."

"Mine!" My insides ignite, quicken at this one guttural word. At his ownership.

His hoarse groan vibrates against my neck, and I begin to thrash as he pushes deeper. It seems impossible he could have any more to give—that I could take any more of him. Though I will. I'll take it all, and I'll welcome it.

"If I was built for you, then you were built for me."

He ploughs into me with a curse, my pleasure so deep, I cry out a helpless, hungered sound. A sound that he swallows as we kiss and hold, press and grind almost as though we're one being.

"This is why I haven't since—this is why. I was waiting for you. Only you."

"*Fuck!*" His arms shake as he delivers long urgent strokes, reaching for my hands. Our fingers linked, he pins them to the mattress next to my head as he says my name over and over again.

Fiadh.

A half breath, a gasp, the wave of pleasure too strong to resist. My orgasm goes from smouldering to a white-hot burning flame. I'm coming hard, so hard, exploding in a burst of blinding heat and ecstasy, the whole world falling away as I come utterly undone.

Above me, Carson's arms shake, his body surging with one last thrust. "You are mine, Fiadh. This body and your wild heart. You were made for me." His face contorts in ecstasy as he finally comes.

21

CARSON

"You have the most perfect mouth," I whisper, tracing the contours of her beautiful face with the pad of my thumb.

These aren't words I'd ever thought I'd hear myself say at an Ardeo night. They're more truthful and honest, and certainly a different kind of spontaneous to *your mouth looks so good around my cock*. Because while that might be true, it's not enough to describe how I feel about the woman lying next to me, her body curling towards mine like a flower following the sun. Hands curled under her chin, she reflects back my happiness, though her smile is almost serene.

I expect I look a little fuck drunk myself. Drunk on her. Drunk on love?

I push the thoughts away. *Baby steps*, I tell myself as I consider the only thing missing at this moment is that I lack the soul of a poet because Fee is the kind of woman who deserves to have sonnets written about her. Not the kind of shit that compares her to a summer's day, despite her summery hair. Maybe these sonnets could compare her to the stars.

"Do you know," she begins quite suddenly, "that your tongue, an elephant's trunk, and the tentacle of an octopus all have something in common?"

Complex and a little off the wall.

"Carson, what are you doing?" She begins to giggle and squirm as I throw the sheet over my head and begin to work my way down her body. "Stop that!"

"I can take a hint," I answer, loving the feel of her small hand under my chin. But it had to be a hint. At least, there was only one direction my brain went after *tongue, trunk*, and *tentacle. You know, tentacle as in cocktopus.*

"That wasn't a hint," she protests, her cheeks taking on that perfect pink hue again. For the record, I'd discovered that her blushes run to her chest, not that she isn't deliciously pink in other places. Nipples the colour of cherry blossoms, the hue between her legs coloured more like the flesh of a cherry. *And just as delicious.*

"That's a pity."

"A pity is something you should have for my body." She leans down, pressing a smiling kiss to my lips. "I've had more orgasms tonight than I've had hot dinners."

"You must be positively starved," I almost growl, pushing myself up and over her. Tangled in the sheet as she is, we're not quite skin to skin, not that it stops the heat of her driving me wild. "But you were saying something about my tongue being like an elephant's trunk, I believe." With that, I rock into the centre of her, then lick the column of her neck. *I'm the whole package, baby. Tongue, trunk, and cocktopus.*

Man, I'm pleased I didn't say that out loud.

"*Oh, yes!*"

"Is that yeah, more trunk?" I surge into her once again. "Or . . ."

"*J-just yes.*"

"Tell me more about this tongue business," I rasp, pressing my lips to her neck.

"Th-they both work the same way. A bundle of muscles operating without the support of bones."

Sounds like I feel.

"*Bones.*" The word is just a rumble against her lips as I thrust my *bone*r against her.

"M-muscle tissue is mostly water." Her hands reach for my shoulders as her thighs widen. "They contract, osmotic pressure causing the whole thing to expand elsewhere."

"Osmosis," I draw the word out like it's the sexiest concept ever as I begin to undulate against her, rock fucking hard and full of plans for where I'd like to expand. "I feel so educated." Right now. How we got here from elephants, I've no idea, but I don't care either. In fact, words? Thoughts? What the fuck are they?

"If your tongue was the same size as an elephant's trunk." A gasp. "I-it could uproot trees."

"Can you make do with one that can tie a knot in a cherry stalk?"

"It can?" She pushes against my shoulders a touch, and I try not to smirk at her eager question. "I mean, you can?"

"That's not even its best trick." The flare of her eyes reflects her understanding almost immediately.

"Yes," she asserts on a gasp, her body arching against me. "M-making me come."

I begin to work my way down her body again, intending to catalogue every dip and curve with my tongue and lips, tasting all the pink hues of her before I bury my tongue in her sweet heat.

"We shouldn't. I should go home."

"It's barely eleven." My protest is a low rumble across the bud of her nipple before it disappears between my lips.

"I need to be home by midnight, at the latest. *Oh, Carson,*" she cries as I slide my hand between her legs, all agile fingers and flicking tongue.

"Time for at least three more orgasms before you turn into a pumpkin, pumpkin."

"But we should talk."

My lips come off her breast with a pop, tongue swirling over her ribcage. "Ardeo nights aren't exactly renowned for their scintillating conversations." Immediately, I want to bite off my tongue as her body stiffens against mine. "Fee, I—"

"No, it's fine." Grabbing the sheet, she yanks it between us, trying to cover herself. "We shouldn't kid ourselves. Just because we're not out there," she mutters, trying to wriggle from under me, "doesn't mean we're any different."

I press my forehead to hers, stilling her, almost wishing she could see inside my head. See how this *is* different. That it always has been. How else would I —*could I*—have recognised that she's the one for me?

She's the one for me.

Nothing has ever rung so true or ever felt so painful, the words winding themselves like barbs around my heart. *But what if I'm not the one for her?*

"You know that's not true." I fall back against the mattress, wrapping my arm around her waist, desperate for things not to end this way. How can I make her see this?

"How can I know it? How can you?"

"Fee, stop." I press my chin to her head, pulling her body tight to mine. "We'll talk, but like this. Please don't pull away." Should I start? Should I tell her I tried to do the right thing, to stay away from her? That I couldn't bear to leave the city while she was here? Before I have to decide where to begin, she begins to speak, her words so soft I almost have to strain to hear.

"What you said earlier, about me being here—"

"You don't have to tell me." Because I find I no longer care. I want her always. *All ways.* And if she wants to be fucked by two men, who the fuck am I to deny her that, provided I'm always one of them? If that's why she was here, I'll just have to man up. Then murder the other fucker afterwards.

"But I want to tell you. Make you understand. Coming here tonight, it was a mistake." Her hand covers mine, pressing it tighter, as though worried I might pull away. How little she knows. She doesn't need to explain herself because if we're counting mistakes and things that ought to be explained, my confessions should probably come first.

And the pertinent word there was if.

"I don't mean I regret it, not now. But that it *was* a mistake. I thought I was coming to a singles night which I'd only agreed to as a favour to Beth." She turns her head then. Maybe she wants me to see the truth of it on her face. I press my lips to her shoulder instead because a look can go both ways. "A friend." She laughs unhappily. "No, she's not even a friend. Just a colleague." A long silence follows, each of us lost to the chaos of our own minds. But then she begins again. "I want to apologise for that night in the den when I-I was a coward."

"You don't need to say anything."

"But I do. Because I hid—I was frightened. The way you make me feel, Carson, it terrifies me."

"I know. I feel it, too." I tighten my arms as a flare of fierce yearning burns through me. *I want her so much.*

"I can't be sorry I came here tonight. Not now," she adds in a whisper as she turns in my arms to face me one more. "But you won't ever see me here again."

I know right here and now, I won't ever be back here, either. And that feels . . . like sunshine hitting the corners of my soul. But I can't explain that right now. Not yet. Maybe not ever. Time will tell, I suppose. But for now, I'm drawn to touch her, my thumb stroking where the light crests her cheekbone.

My God, she is lovely. I'll never be able to give her up after this. Because I am the one. The one that's her forever. She just has to see it. And she will.

"You're staring," she whispers, turning her head to bite the end of my thumb.

The action sparks a wave of sensation from my spine down. Does she know how sexy that is? How hard it's made me? Again.

"How can I not stare at something so beautiful?" Her mouth is lush and ripe. The bow of her lip is highly defined and so goddamned tempting. Her bottom lip is soft and full and just begging to be kissed. I could do that. Kiss her again. Kiss away her fears and words, press my lips against hers in the promise of other things. But as weird as it sounds, I don't need that right now. The sex was stellar—fucking wonderous—and worth waiting another five years for. But just lying here next to her, watching her. Well, it's different. It's nothing, yet it's everything. And those are the moments to treasure, right?

"You don't just have to stare," she whispers.

"What do you suggest?" I reply with a tiny flex against her.

"The art of suggestion?" she teases, her eyes darken with a mixture of shock and desire. It's the kind of look that short-circuits the wiring of my brain, especially as she reaches between us, her fingers trailing over my crown.

"No, darling, I think you'll find that's my cock."

"Decidedly unsubtle." I groan as she takes me in her fist. "But very supple."

I press my lips against hers at her first tentative stroke, then rise above her as a thought enters my head.

"What are you doing?" Her voice wavers with a little laughter as I lean over her and grab a condom from the nightstand.

"I'm constructing a masterpiece." Back on my knees, I wrap my fingers around her hip, encouraging her onto her front.

"By kissing my bottom?" This time she definitely giggles as she moves onto her front, like a good little girl. She turns her head over her shoulder, her gaze dipping to where my hand is wrapped around my hard cock. "Did you just call me a good little girl?"

"Don't question the creator of your pleasure."

"Yes, you're a regular virtuoso." But her teasing tone doesn't last, not as I pull her up by the hips, bringing her up on her knees. She sighs as I draw featherlight fingertips down her spine, then gasps as I rudely spread her thighs wide. As I press my crown to her silky pussy, she keens, stretching out like a cat.

My first thrust is hard and fast, her body offering no resistance, her fingers tightening around the pillow.

"You're so big like this."

"Only like this?" I rotate my hips, then thrust back in.

"Oh, Carson. What are you doing to me?"

I might not be able to pen her a sonnet, but this I can do as I tighten my hands on her hips, pressing my lips to the elegant arch of her spine. *Another tremble, another sigh.* I withdraw almost fully, and she mourns the loss of me audibly.

"In this bed," I rasp, sinking myself to the hilt once again. "I am the poet. You, my darling, are the poetry."

22

CARSON

I wake alone, as expected, in my hotel suite that I'm sure Fee would be surprised to learn is just a short walk from my apartment. I'm okay about being alone. Well, I'm not lonely, at least. And though I would have preferred to wake to her warm body, I appreciate she has other priorities. I know one day soon I'll wake to the feel of her warm body against mine and know there will be other nights we fall asleep tangled in the other's arms. One day not too far away, moments before she slips into the darkness of sleep, I'll get to whisper a very important question to her: would she like to be woken *by* breakfast in bed the following morning or woken *as* my breakfast.

A grin creeps across my face. That moment isn't too far away. And in the interim, I have new memories of her when I take my stiff cock into my hand. Not that I do so this morning as I playback the moments before she left. It was obvious she wasn't about to invite me back to her place, *my place,* as she'd almost retreated into herself.

We'd dressed almost silently, and though she'd tried to discourage me from walking with her, I'd done so anyway.

"I don't need you to take me home," she'd almost whispered, her gaze on the floor of the private elevator car. "I mean back to the apartment." She'd frowned. "Your apartment, I mean."

I'd preferred *home.* One day soon, she'll call it that in earnest. Hopefully, with me in it.

"I'm not letting you go home by yourself." I'd clasped my hands to my back to stop from reaching out and touching her. From giving her something else she felt she needed to forbid.

"This isn't a date." Her gaze had caught mine then, her meaning clear.

Foolish Fee. I had her tonight, and I'd have her forever. A sentiment I feel this morning deep in the pit of my gut.

"You can't expect me to wave you off in a cab," I'd replied, almost offhand.

"What I expect is for you to be mindful of my wishes." I could almost feel her building back her walls high once more.

The elevator began to slow, and Fee sprang from the doors before they were fully open. Hot on her heels, I found my hands on her waist as she pushed through the front door.

"Just wait. Please." I turned her to face me, and I slid out of my jacket, placing it on her shoulders. My fingers were reluctant to relinquish the silky strands of her hair as I'd pulled it free from the collar, but I'd forced myself to take her shoulders in my hands. "Fee—"

"Please don't make this any harder than it already is." Her gaze slid away, her dark eyes beginning to glisten in the streetlight.

"You can't go home alone, and if you won't let me take you, Miller here will." Her head swung around, maybe recognising him as the security guard from a few hours before. *A few hours and a lifetime ago.* When her gaze returned, she didn't look comforted. "I'd trust him with my life." In fact, I had.

"This will be a secret, won't it?" She'd raised her eyes to me along with her question as I'd opened the rear passenger door. "What happened tonight. We can't talk about it afterwards." Her dark eyes were trusting and maybe a little frightened.

In answer, I'd grasped my lapels, pulling her closer and pressing my lips to her head. I'd murmured something disingenuous about NDAs; I can't remember exactly what, not that it matters. She might be restricted from discussing the events of the night and my obligations to our members are paramount, but that doesn't mean to say she and I won't ever speak of it again. In fact, I think I might find myself recounting every little detail. To her. At the first opportunity I get. And I'll certainly think about it. About how swollen and slippery she felt. How she'd gasped as I'd buried myself to the hilt. Her body taut under mine, she'd held me there as she adjusted to the invasion, her fingernails digging into my shoulders as though to make sure I wouldn't move. I was so hard, the blood in my veins turning to steam as I realised she was watching me, cataloguing my every reaction, my every held breath.

As if she could commit it all to memory.

As if we'd never get a repeat.

As if I'd ever let her go after this.

But she'd nodded just once, reassured, and climbed into the car. I stood on the sidewalk and watched the rear lights grow smaller and smaller. A wave of melancholy had washed over me. I'd felt bereft. Until I'd found her panties in my pocket. Tiny, frivolous things that I hadn't paid any attention to as I'd slipped them off. But I'd paid attention then, bringing them to my nose with a deep inhale.

I don't know how to describe this feeling. I just know I'll never get my fill.

And now, the following morning, I stretch out in the bed as a warm happiness spreads through my insides. I can almost feel her still in my hands and almost certainly taste her on my tongue.

Today is going to be a good day.

FEE

"Bye, sweetie! Don't forget to fasten your coat. And tighten your scarf!"

Lulu doesn't answer. Instead, she waves over her shoulder as she excitedly hurries down the hall after Sophia, who'd come back this morning after the pair made some deal about going to the café on the corner for smoothies while I was out last night. Maybe I should feel bad for shoving twenty dollars into the older girl's hand, but I would've paid ten times more just to get Lulu out of the house before she begins to wonder what the heck is going on with her basket case of a mother.

I close the door behind the pair and sag against it, then take the kind of deep breath that seems to begin at the tips of my toes. Relief. And little guilt for feeling that way? But it's been so hard to be myself this morning, hard to be Fee, the sensible. Fee, the mummy. It's like my equilibrium has been shattered. Saturday mornings are usually nice and chilled for Lu and me. We putter around in our *jammies*, eat breakfast, read or watch TV before heading out to do something. A park. A museum. A movie. Dependant on the weather and where we are, I suppose. Instead, this morning, I'd turned into some manic and overly bright version of me. I'd pranced around the kitchen like I was auditioning for a part in a kid's TV show, cracking jokes and making pancakes when all I wanted to do was take myself off to my bedroom, wash my stiff feeling face, put on clean pyjamas, and eat my body weight in chocolate.

Or maybe reminisce.

Because I'm not sad. And it's not guilt or shame I'm experiencing, strangely. But the temptation to close my eyes and let my mind drift is so bloody strong. Maybe I'm just overwhelmed, and that's why my body still feels the ghost of his touch, my heart tender with feelings I'd ignored for far too long.

Tears might be cathartic and better on the bum than chocolate, I tell myself as I push off from the door. But housework might be more useful. A little bit of ordinary. Boring. The usual life of me.

I make my way to the laundry room, pulling out a tangle of socks and T-shirts from the drier and begin to fold. My eyes are still dry, and my skin oversensitive. The task should be soothing, or mindless at least, something humdrum to take my attention elsewhere, but I just can't force myself to focus on anything. I want to think about last night and examine everything that he said. Scrutinise the possession in his kiss and his fingertips and make sense of every tiny nuance. If I close my eyes, I can still see myself in the mirror, revelling in the power he gave me. Maybe it's the knowledge that last night was a one-off that makes me feel so off-balance. Maybe I want to revel in the memories because I know I can never do it again.

Would it have happened if I hadn't stopped to watch the trio? Threesomes have never been my thing, fantasy or otherwise, and I struggle to make complete sense of it. I think it was how powerful she seemed. She wasn't a woman being used by two men; she was their queen. And she was worshipped.

As Carson worshipped me.

I do feel the first sting of tears as I bundle the still warm laundry into my arms. I bustle through the kitchen and past the maid's room to the other side of the apartment that houses the bedrooms.

If only he'd just left us in that room.

If only he hadn't turned up, upsetting the apple cart that is my life. I promised myself I wouldn't do this, that I wouldn't throw myself at a man until I could trust him with my heart. And instead, I end up having sex with a man who may or may not be responsible for some kind of sex club.

He certainly hadn't been a first-timer. Or there by accident.

"Adult lifestyles, my arse," I mutter, shoving knickers and socks into one of Lulu's drawers and pyjamas into another. "Rich people are another level of crazy."

I straighten her duvet, centre a fluffy pillow, and give Norman a quick sniff, then resolve to put him through the washing machine sometime soon when Lulu won't be home for the length of a quick wash and a fluff dry cycle. On my way out, I pause at the door, my fingers looped around the handle as I take a final look.

Carson Hayes, who the fuck are you really?

Beyond the teasing and inappropriateness and the skills of a porn star, surely lies a heart of gold. He's been so lovely to Lulu; pancakes and popcorn and princess bedrooms. But it's not just material things. It's in the way he interacts with her. He's so sweet with her, and not in that condescendingly syrupy way that childless adults often try on with kids.

I've been baffled about his intentions. But I just don't see how this room can be some kind of elaborate and, let's be honest, very strange attempt to get into my knickers again. It's more like an act of kindness. Of good. But as I pull the door closed, I wonder how good a man can truly be when he's involved in a club called Ardeo.

I make my way to the kitchen and fill the kettle, trying very hard to move my brain on from the topic of him with little success. I can't stop thinking about how I'd felt so at home in his strong arms, how he'd made the experience much less about his gratification and more about my exploration. He once said that there's a little wildness in anyone but that it takes the right person to bring it out.

I hate that he's right.

But I don't hate that he was that person for me.

I'd lain awake most of the night playing the evening back, trying to convince myself that I'm not in over my head. That it's just a case of old flames burning longer than anticipated. But if that's the case, why did it seem like he was slotting away my every word, my reaction like they were pieces of a puzzle to make sense of later.

Reaching up into the cabinet, I pull out a mug and bang it down against the countertop in frustration. I tell myself that I've made him more than he is. That the memories of last night are not the kind to be cherished.

It doesn't make me want him less.

I'll have to face him again, I know. But what will I say to him?

What I expect is for you to be mindful of my wishes.

That's what I'd told him as he'd handed me into the car. But my wishes are something I won't ever speak out loud. A wish is a desire, and a desire is a dangerous thing. So instead, I'll say:

It was a mistake. All of it. I shouldn't have been there. I shouldn't have allowed myself to follow you.

Except we both saw my reaction, watched my face. Saw the truth of it there.

Last night doesn't change things.

Even though nothing will ever be the same. Not for me and not between us.

I don't want to speak about it.

Another lie. Because I do. I want to talk about it at length and in detail. I want to know why he's involved in Ardeo and what that means. I want to ask him about the blur of faces as he led me through the room, the bodies parting like the Red Sea for Moses himself. They weren't interested in me, not exactly. Their attention was all for him. I want to know who he is and what I mean to him.

I want to know all that and more, yet I won't mention one damned thing.

I can't stay here. That much, I will say.

Beth said last night that her sister was moving out on Monday, that we'll have the keys for Friday, so I just have to hang tight until then.

The kettle begins to whistle, and I pour hot water into the mug, realising I haven't gotten as far as adding the teabag. So I take care of that, swirling the liquid with a teaspoon to hurry the process along.

Last night, after everything, after fingers and mouths, gasping breaths and wet, sucking sounds, after watching myself enjoy being devoured, we'd lain on the bed together, my back to Carson's chest. His arm had wrapped around my waist, his chin over my head, almost like a tree overhangs a sapling. I'd felt incredibly dainty next to him. Fragile, even. And so protected. But then I'd remembered where we were. Not in a hotel or a bed in his home, but a place where people meet to have sex. A place they fuck and nothing else.

It suddenly didn't feel so special after all.

I was fooling myself. He'd always be that man, wouldn't he? Drawn to the pleasures monogamy couldn't bring.

A leopard never changes his spots, after all.

I squeeze a little honey into my cup and resolve to ball up the memories of last night, stuffing them to the very back of my mind. *Into the dirty laundry cupboard, where all the secrets are kept.*

Swiping up the newspaper to scan the classifieds section, I carry it and my cuppa over to the kitchen table when my phone buzzes with a text.

ROSE: **I'll be in New York next month!** Her text is followed by a line of emojis; cocktail glasses, heart eyes, and cake and is quickly followed by another.

Will you be free?

ME: **What kind of question is that? I'm there for whatever with my bestie! And now I am so excited!!**

Time spent with Rose is always fab. Girl time is just what I need. Except . . . girl time usually involves wine, and wine is often the precursor for spilling secrets.

ROSE: **Good. We're going to party so hard after bedtime!**

ME: **So, between eight p.m. and ten?**

I'll just have to drink my wine with soda water and endure her ribbing. She's become such a wine snob since she married Remy. But if I don't drink too much, maybe I won't be tempted to spill.

ROSE: **Rock on! Sending an email your way with the details.**

ME: **Can't wait.**

I wonder if Carson will want to see her.

The thought is unbidden, rising quickly and followed by another and an accompanying wave of distaste. Does he really have a thing for her?

It didn't seem so last night.

You are mine, Fiadh, his dark voice echoes in my head. *This body and your wild heart were made for me.*

I take a mouthful of my tea, scalding my tongue. It's no more than I deserve because I really need to stop thinking about him. It's just not fair.

Flipping open the New York Post, I pull my earphones out from my pocket and jam them into my ears, hoping some loud, angry girl music will drown out my woes.

I've known obsession before. I think we all have. Humans are, after all, thinking creatures. Some of us are overthinking creatures.

I know Rose has her foundation, a healthy obsession in a lot of ways.

Charles has his hair, though for how many more years, I'm not sure. *It is a little thin.*

And Lulu, my lovely magpie, has the shiny things she likes to borrow. Something I hope she'll grow out of.

My obsessions have largely been body issues; matters I've overcome through learning and time. I'm not sure how either of these will help me overcome my latest obsession of a man with a body built for sin and the belief that he should share it.

23

CARSON

A little after noon, I find myself at my front door, my finger poised over the bell.

Ah, what the hell. I pull my keys from my pockets and, with only the slightest twinge of discomfort, let myself in.

Honey, I'm home.

I can't help but smile. I'm sure hearing that would drive her a little crazy, which I guess is the whole point. Drive her crazy to the point of giving in. Grind her down until she agrees to spend more time with me.

Because all good things come to those who wait.

And tease.

I take off my jacket, hanging it in the hall closet, my shoes echoing against the parquet floor as I seek out my target in the communal areas of the apartment first. *Kitchen, living room, den.* Maybe I'll get lucky and find her in the bath again.

But I don't. Instead, I discover her sitting at the kitchen table, poring over a copy of the *New York Post* . A mug of something hot and steamy stands on the table next to it.

Not coffee. Maybe tea? My eyes flick to the stovetop and find an unfamiliar tea kettle sitting on top.

I pause at the doorway without making my presence known. She's wearing earphones, her head bobbing along to music that sounds a little tinny from here. But earphones mean no Lulu.

Which is . . . interesting.

Her feet bare, one curls around the leg of the chair, the other taps the tiles in time with the music. She wears tight blue yoga pants and a striped sweater that appears to be several sizes too big and all the colours of the rainbow. No ponytail today, her hair falling like a golden sheet across her shoulders and down her back. And thank the good Lord, black-framed glasses. It's like being hot for two different women. The virtuous girl next door with her bare feet and sunny hair and the siren last night who left me holding her underwear.

She reaches for her mug and takes a slurp. Yes, a goddamn slurp! The kind that should be reserved for ice cream. Or my dick. I find myself smothering a chuckle as I slot away the tiny insight that seems *almost* charming as she sets down her mug. Making a bracelet of her fingers, she pushes the baggy sleeve up her arm from the wrist. She turns the page and twists in her seat, maybe suffering a little muscle twinge from last night, which I can fully appreciate given I woke this morning feeling like I'd ab crunched for days.

As Fee twists back again, the sweater slips from her left shoulder, baring a pale slice of her skin. I immediately feel myself harden. Since when has a little bared shoulder become an erotic sight? *Since it's her shoulder* would be the answer to that.

Another page turn, then she leans over the newspaper

as though to read something at the top right-hand corner. She slides her hair over her right shoulder, twisting it to hold it in place. Desire floods my veins, images filling my head. I'd come up behind her, take her hair in my fist. Hold her in place while I tease her with my tongue and teeth. Her body would stiffen at first, shock swiftly giving way to pleasure. Her lashes would flutter closed, and the noises she'd make—

Would be nothing like the sound of her taking another pirate-sized swig of her drink. I find myself shaking my head at this secret glimpse of her. Brits do appreciate all things tea. Tea as an afternoon meal with sandwiches and scones. Tea cake; a dense confection with raisins. Teatime; a period between leaving work and an evening meal. Tea is the nation's favourite drink, so they claim. The number one brew served piping hot and often the colour of red bricks. Though I believe it was Eleanor Roosevelt who said, "*A woman is like a tea bag; you can't tell how strong she is until you put her in hot water.*'

Time to boil the kettle, angel.

I pound my fist on the open door. She spins in her seat to face me, banging her elbow on the edge of the table in her haste. "Jesus, Mary, and Joseph!"

"I doubt you'd have heard even their entrance." Not over the slurping.

"You nearly scared the pants off me," she exclaims, slapping the newspaper shut.

I duck as though examining the validity, then give a shrug. *What a pity.* I wonder what she didn't want me to see in the newspaper. Not that I think there's anything of particular interest in the *Post*.

"You didn't hear me." I tap my ear, indicating her

earphones that she'd already pulled free, angry tinny music humming from them.

"How long have you been standing there? What are you doing here?" She discards the buds to the table, tinny music halting as she taps her phone.

"Do you have any idea how sexy you look." It isn't quite the answer she is anticipating. Honestly, it comes as kind of a shock to me, too. "That slice of skin right here?" I tap my own shoulder. "It's playing peekaboo through your hair like something I'm not supposed to see."

"You're titillated by my shoulder?"

"I'm hot for all of you." I lean against the door frame, allowing my eyes to roam over her once more. I almost feel like I should apologise because last night should've been what we both needed to work this thing, this overwhelming attraction between us, out of our systems. But it hadn't happened like that, going instead in the opposite direction. More attraction. More need. Heightened senses and heightened feelings.

"You didn't answer my question. What are you doing here?"

It's not irritation but skittishness she tries to conceal as she grabs her cup, almost sliding to the other side of the kitchen as though to put the maximum distance—and a marble island bench—between us.

"I came for clean shirts." Maybe I should've said I came for my jacket, but it seems like a reasonable excuse, judging by her expression. Right now, I guess either is a more welcome explanation than the admission *because I had to see you.*

"Oh. Okay." She turns and dumps her still hot drink down the sink, her next question delivered carefully. "Are you staying in the city?"

"Yes. I have business here." Unfinished business called Fee.

"In the place from last night?" She pivots back quickly, though her own expression is strangely blank. *Or maybe carefully so.*

"No." I swallow my grin, allowing it instead to spread through my ribcage. That's interest, right there. Aloof and unconcerned, she is not. She's curious and maybe even a little jealous.

"What's so funny?" She folds her arms across her chest, sending a glare my way.

You are, my sweet. Funny and a little feisty.

"I left right after you did last night. Just so you know, there was nothing that held my interest once you'd gone. Nothing and no one."

"What you do with yourself is no concern of mine."

"Isn't it?"

"No," she replies, her gaze refusing to hold mine.

"As for where I'm staying, I hear the YMCA has some pretty nice rooms." Her expression softens, her arms too. She looks as though to speak when I ruin it by opening my big mouth again. "But I don't really care to share a bathroom."

"I don't really care where you stayed or who you stayed with."

"Your mouth said 'stayed with' but your eyes said 'fucked'." I rub my hand across my chin as though in contemplation. "Do you really think I'd want anyone else after what passed between us?"

"We had sex, Carson."

"We had more than sex. What we had was a connection."

"Yes, a connection. Tab A fits into slot B. That kind of connection."

"Sure." I push from the door frame and watch her eyes widen as I reduce the space between us, though she might breathe a sigh of relief as I pause at the island. "If that's what you want to tell yourself," I say, leaning back against it.

"I'm not telling myself anything. That's how it was."

"So where in your tab equation does my sucking your pussy until you screamed exactly fit?"

"Do you have to be so crass?"

"Do you have to be such a coward?" She rears back as though I've slapped her. Something I would cut off my hand before I'd ever do in earnest. "Your words, Fee, not mine. The strength of your feelings for me frightens you."

"The strength of my attraction," she amends. "Like Alice going down the rabbit hole, I'm worried where this will end."

"You don't ever need to worry. I've got you."

"No, Carson. You don't."

Her voice holds a note of finality I'm sure she thinks she means. And yeah, these words are hurtful to hear. But if I allow myself to think she's telling the truth, then I actually don't deserve her. She's just lashing out, keeping me at arm's length. She's been looking after herself far too long, cutting herself off from the joys that life can offer. That I can offer.

She's not a coward, but she is scared.

Maybe today was too soon to talk to her.

Maybe talk isn't what she needs. Maybe it's action.

"But I'm not supposed to mention any of this. Oops," she adds deathly sweetly, drawing her thumb and forefinger across her lips as though to seal them.

We weren't talking about Ardeo, but I can go with the flow.

"That's fine. The punishment will hold. Floggings are usually meted out before the bar opens." A little teasing on my part makes her bite like a Rottweiler.

"Then I'm afraid my punishment will have to be delivered in absentia because I'm not setting foot in that place again." I begin to laugh, and she begins to fume. "I suppose you think this is funny?"

"It is a little. You have to admit." Like I'd ever allow anyone to lay a hand on her skin.

"What are you, like, twelve?"

"On a scale of one to ten, I am. You know that."

"I see now. So you've turned up to tease me. Go ahead, then. Get it over with."

"To tease you?"

"Yes. I told you last night was a one-time-only thing. I won't be goaded into it again."

"I don't remember you needing any kind of encouragement. I do remember the orgasms, though. Was it six or seven? I lost count around the time that I—"

"For the love of all that is holy." Her cry is an appeal to the ceiling. Or the heavens. "I'm not having this conversation with you. Ever! Just please get your shirts and leave."

"You're going to throw me out of my own home? You're not going to offer me my room to save me from the Y? Or I could bunk with you. I don't mind."

I swear she growls under her breath, and I catch myself in a retort. She just makes it so fucking easy for me. But this is getting us nowhere. So I start again, my expression suitably penitent.

"I'm sorry. I didn't come here to annoy you, despite

what you might think. I came to make sure you were okay. And truthfully, I just wanted to see you again." I clamp my mouth closed to prevent every thought I have, every moment I envisage for the future, every plea, from falling off my tongue.

Patience is key.

"I'm fine." Fine with a capital F as I watch her thread her hair behind her ears, her colour heightened. "So now you can leave. I'm asking you nicely. Please *go away.* And I know that sounds really horrible because this is your home, but we'll be out of it soon enough—next week, in fact." She grasps one baggy sleeve of her sweater, yanking it up her arm roughly, only to blow out a breath as it immediately slides down again. "And everything will be the same as before."

Oh, sweet girl, as if anything will ever be the same.

"Rose did say you'd found somewhere else to stay," I begin. At least, you think you have. Sorry, darling, I'm about to ruin that for you because if you move somewhere else, how will I make you see that you need me? "Is it somewhere close by? Rose said your office and Lulu's school is an easy commute from here. Where is Lulu, by the way?"

"She's gone for ice cream with Sophia. The babysitter." She reaches out, her fingertips drumming against the kitchen counter, pulling her hand back just as quick.

"And your new apartment?"

"It's not particularly close," she answers evasively, "but we'll make it work."

"Why would you want to, I wonder. When you could stay here as long as you want."

"Because of this." She holds out her hand, indicating my presence with some exasperation. "Because of you!"

Because of last night, she means.

"Fee." I fill her name with such mocking. "This is only the second time I've visited. In weeks. And the first was a complete accident." A complete and happy accident that has unequivocally changed the course of many things.

"But you're here now, after everything I said when I left last night."

"I told you. Clean shirts."

She raises one solitary brow as though to say *really? You're sticking with that?*

"And I wanted to check in. Last night must've been a lot for you to take in."

"Pardon the pun?" she snipes, suddenly all attitude and cocked hip.

I don't return the cheap shot.

"We're friends, you and me, right?"

"We are not friends, Carson. How can we be?"

"Maybe you can fool yourself, but you can't fool me. Just like you can't stop me from wanting . . . to help you," I manage to add.

Her eyes widen as I move closer, her hand rising to her collarbone. But this won't play out like last time. Because last time I cornered her in the kitchen, I'd felt compelled to close the space between us, not really knowing what I was doing or what I was asking of her. I only knew I wanted her, that she'd haunted my dreams since she crept out of the hotel room in Saint Odile. This time is different. This time, my motive is clear, and my actions a thousand times more calculated. I want her no less. In fact, I want a lifetime of more. But I'll play the long game because I want more than the gratification that one kiss, one touch, one fuck can bring.

I know I'll have to seduce her; silky words and

taunting touches, but not now. Because right now, she's overthinking. Regretting, maybe? Second-guessing, definitely. It's not that she doesn't want to talk about last night because I'm sure she has questions balanced on the tip of her tongue. About me. About my role there. About my motivations. But she won't ask because she's likely told herself she can't. The lid to Pandora's box is firmly jammed shut.

Wherever her head is right now, she needs to move on. No teasing, no real talk. Maybe I should appeal to her sense of practicality.

"Did Lulu like her room?" I ask softly, gratified as she allows me to take her hands, which is where I keep my gaze. Her hands are cool to the touch, her fingers fine-boned and elegant under the pads of my thumbs.

"She loved it. I can't even describe to you how special it was to see her excitement. Even if I can't make out why you would do that for her."

"I wanted her to feel at home," I reply simply.

"But we were never staying. It makes no sense."

I shrug but not to feign disinterest. "Maybe not to you. Maybe not even to me. But I'm glad she liked it."

"Like doesn't even cover it."

I risk a glance up from my hands at the smile in her tone. A smile she quickly hides as she tries to pull away.

"But Lu understands this is your home, not ours. And yes, she'll be upset to leave it, but she says she'll visit when she comes back to water your plants."

I find myself chuckling. Her mother doesn't exactly sound happy about that.

"I mean if you still want her to."

"What about when I am here? Will you both visit with Uncle Carson?"

"You really are a manipulative shit, do you know that?"

From a chuckle to a laugh, I let my hands fall from hers.

"Am I? What exactly is wrong with wanting to get to know you better?"

"We can't be friends. Don't you see that? How could we be when the three times I've been near you, I've jumped you?"

"I'm not complaining. I was participating. Wholeheartedly."

"Don't you see? That's not me. That's not who I am. I don't sleep around, and I don't have casual sex! It's you—it's your fault! You bring out the worst in me. We're like fire and water!"

"Oil?"

"See? My brain doesn't even work when you're around!"

"It's managing a lot of no's right now," I mutter, following her to the other side of the room.

"For once," she retorts with a manic laugh as she swings around to face me, but whatever she's about to say goes unsaid.

"Uncle Carson!" Lulu's excited voice announces her arrival before her arms wrap around my legs.

"Hey, look, it's a koala." A koala in a pink jacket and blue scarf, both already half hanging off. Her cheeks are ruddy from the outdoors, her eyes bright, and her fingers cold.

"You call me such silly things," she says, laughing . . . while trying to climb me. "You know I'm just Lulu."

"There's no such thing as *just* Lulu." I bend to ruffle her hair, finding my fingers snagging in the wildness of it. "There's Lulu, the great. Lulu, the magnificent—"

"And Lulu, the koala!" Pulling off her scarf and coat, she throws them somewhere behind her.

Is it weird that I've missed this little whirlwind?

"Lulu, get down," her mother commands with the kind of effectiveness you'd imagine when I'm helping the kid travel the opposite direction as I slide my hand under her arm, lifting her onto my back.

"You can't climb people," her mother protests. A couple of steps and she's in front of me. I suck in a deep breath of her scent as, her body almost flush with mine, she reaches over my shoulder. I twist, our bodies connecting, the kid out of reach.

"The lies we tell them, huh?" My lips ghost the delicate shell of her ear. "I bet we tell them they're not supposed to lick people, too." She probably thinks I don't notice her shiver or the way her eyes flutter closed.

"Ew! Licking people is *dig*susting!" Lulu announces, her hands tightening around my neck as her mother stumbles back, all kinds of flushed and annoyed. Maybe as much at herself as with me.

"I'm, er, gonna get going, Miss Fee."

I swing around at the voice. That's right. Lulu wasn't out alone.

"Oh, yes, thank you, Sophia," Fee answers. "But wait. Let me give you a little pocket money."

"No." She holds up her hands. "Really, there's no need. You paid for the smoothies, and we had fun hanging out, right, Lu?"

"Sophia let me catch a Pokémon, and we had cookies, too!" Lu's announcement rattles my eardrum. I wince, Fee sending me a look as though to say, *serves you right.* "Uncle Car, did you know Sophia looks after me when Mommy goes out?"

"Well, hello, Sophia." I mock a little bow in front of the girl who looks to be around eighteen. Eighteen and tongue-tied, as she hazards a little wave my way.

"Does Mommy go out very often?" I ask a little carelessly, bouncing the kid on my back, twisting her from her mother's warning glare.

Wait, that look was probably for me.

"She went out last night, and she looked like a beautiful princess," Lu replies. "Didn't she, Soph?"

"Yeah," the teenager replies a little bashfully. "You looked *so* pretty, Miss Fee."

"Mommy?" Lulu pipes up. "Will you wear the silver dress when you go out with Mr Farrow?"

She flinches, her gaze slipping from mine. "I . . . I don't think so. I'm just going to walk Sophia out."

Goodbyes are said, and the pair leaves the room.

"Who is this Mr Farrow?" I ask, swinging Lulu around to my chest so we're face-to-face.

"He's one of my teachers. I'm making them go on a date."

"You are, are you?" She nods happily, and I find myself sighing. "That's . . . that's too bad."

"Why?" Taking my cheeks in her little hands, she stares at me quite solemnly. Those eyes. They don't belong to a kid at all. "Do you love my mommy, Uncle Carson?"

I inhale a deep breath, and I don't mean to part with the words, though I do.

"Yeah. I love your mommy. So do me a favour. Don't set her up with any more Mr Farrows."

24

FEE

"Ah!" Standing in the hallway outside Lulu's room, I hear rather than see Carson smack his lips together on account. "Most enjoyable!"

Carson's manner is ordinarily very cultured, but he seems to be laying it on really thick for Lulu's amusement. I'm not hanging out in the hall for no reason. I'm hiding, though the urge to bust in on them is so tempting. Fist against my mouth, I've listened in and chuckled as Carson has played the courtly jester to Lulu's bossy queen.

"It was a delicious cup of tea, Princess Lulu."

And now they're having a tea party. How bloody precious!

"It's not tea, silly," she chastises. "It's gin."

I press my fist tighter to smother a snigger. Honestly, this isn't my influence. If I was drinking hard liquor from a teacup, my first choice wouldn't be gin.

"Gin?" he replies. "I thought I was invited to a tea party in the princess suite, not a gin joint."

"Gin is what my granny drinks."

"If it's good enough for Granny, I guess it's good enough for a tea party."

"Gin party," she corrects. "Granny says when you're in need, a real friend will take your hand. Then put a glass of gin in it."

"I think me and your granny would get along well."

"You'd probably make her all giggly." I can almost see her scrunching her nose. "She'd say 'Carson Hayes is a *fine thing*'."

My daughter does a decent impersonation of my mother. And I'd have to agree with her. Whether in a tux or running gear, or dressed for a few beers down the pub, Carson Hayes is a *fyne* thing, indeed.

And a naked Carson Hayes is a demigod. Something my mother might imagine but never see.

Anything you don't see with your own eyes there's a doubt about. Her words echo in my ear, but I banish the thought of him naked to the dirty linen closet of my brain.

"What does she call you?" I hear him ask.

"Achushla," Lulu answers simply. Pulse of my heart, it means. And that's true for both her granny and me. "And you," she adds, "call me all kinds of silly things."

Lulu has such a wealth of affection for him. And also for his possessions. For instance, last Tuesday, I'd noticed just in time that she'd pocketed his Montblanc pen to take to school. Apparently, a silver fountain pen would much improve her letters.

God loves a tryer, my mother's voice says next.

"I only call you nice things," Carson protests. "Koalas are pretty cute, right?"

"Are koalas begetarian?"

"Bege-what? Oh, vegetarian. They sure are. They eat

eucalyptus leaves but occasionally *branch* out to eat other greenery."

The chuckle he seemed to be expecting doesn't come. Tree jokes aren't really made for a four-year-old audience. But bless his cotton socks for trying and for taking tea.

It sounds like he's making her day.

"If you were a vegebale, Uncle Car, you'd be a cutecumber."

"Is that so?"

It's not very motherly of me to be thinking of exactly how cute his cutecumber is. Yet I do.

Back to the dirty laundry for you!

"And if you were a potato," he says, a smile leaking through his words, "you'd be a sweet potato."

"What do you think Mommy would be?"

"A *fine*apple. Definitely."

"I'm sorry I told Mr Farrow Mommy likes him."

"Do you think she really does?"

I find myself leaning a little closer as Carson's voice drops, and my heart gives a little pinch. But Lulu doesn't answer. Maybe she shrugged or shook her head. The truth is, I haven't an opinion of Mr Farrow, or Leo as he insisted I call him. *Neither for or against.* I also haven't agreed to go out with him. We've spoken a couple of times, and he's made it clear that he'd like to take me out on a date but that the ball is firmly in my court now. I told myself I wouldn't, not because he's her teacher (he only takes her class for a couple of technology lessons each week) but also because I wasn't interested.

It's not so strange that I failed to mention any of this earlier in the kitchen. And maybe I'm a more horrible person than I thought, considering the spark of satisfaction I'd felt once I'd realised Carson was annoyed by the possibility that I might be interested in another man. But I'm not the one who runs a club for the libertines of New York. I'm not the one with access to indiscriminate fucking.

"When are they supposed to be going out on this date?" I hear him ask.

"I don't know. I'm sorry. I didn't mean to make you sad."

"I'm not sad, honey. I'm just trying to work out what we're going to do about him."

What *we're* going to do?

"I could tell him Mommy is getting married!" she adds brightly.

"I don't think she's ready to hear me propose."

As if!

But as if he would or as if I'm not ready?

Ack! More thoughts for the linen cupboard of my brain.

"Maybe you should just tell her you like her best? That I like you best," she reasons, her voice full of reassurance. "Mr Farrow is nice, but I think you would look after Mommy better than him."

"I don't think your mom needs anyone to look after her. She's doing pretty well all by herself."

For the second time in as many minutes, my heart pinches. That was a compliment, I think. But it sounded sad.

"She should have someone to look after her, She's the one who always does the looking after, and that's not fair."

"You're a sweet girl, Lulu."

"I'm a sweet potato," she corrects. "And I don't want to live anywhere else. I like this 'partment too much."

"I know. But unfortunately, honey, we all have to do

things we don't want to. This room will still be here when you visit. Maybe we can even convince Mommy to sleep over sometimes."

Not for the kind of sleepovers he's talking about. I decide it's time for this party of mutual appreciation to end and tiptoe along the hall before more or less stomping back again.

"Lulu, you've got homework to do," I announce, pushing on the door. I try not to laugh—try and fail—as I find Carson sitting cross-legged between a huge teddy bear and a stuffed whale. But that's not the best part. He's wearing a silver-coloured princess crown on his head.

"Aww!" Lulu begins to whine. "We haven't even had pudding yet." She points at the packet of cookies she appears to have pilfered from the kitchen.

"Yeah, Mom. Don't spoil the vibe."

Trying very hard to ignore his tauntingly sexy smirk, I address my child. "Carson has to go home now."

"But he already is home."

I take a deep breath and try again. "Carson needs to go somewhere else, then." I turn my attention to the man in question. "Or we do."

It's not a threat. More like a promise. I can't have him here making my heart and my ovaries pinch as he takes imaginary tea—or gin—with my kid.

I don't want to feel like this.

I can't want this.

Can't want him.

As I turn on my heel, I hear him scramble up behind me.

"Fee, wait up." His hand catches my shoulder in the hallway, but I don't turn, shrugging him off and storming into the kitchen. My head is in bits, and I just want it all to go away. And why do I keep hiding behind this bloody island?

"Please, I don't want to upset you. But I just wanted to ask—"

I pivot to face him, preparing myself for whatever he's going to say. *If that's even possible.*

"This teacher. Do you think he could be your forever?"

I wasn't prepared for that. His tone isn't teasing or mocking, and for once, he isn't trying to goad a reaction. It seems like a genuine question. One he seems a little desperate to hear the answer to. I think I might do a fair impersonation of a guppy in response.

"You don't date." I notice he's still holding the crown in his hand as he places it on the island between us. Then he slides his hands into the pockets of his jeans, his broad shoulders pushed up around his ears. "I'm asking if you think you might be serious about him."

Words begin to tumble from my mouth, almost before my brain connects.

"Are you truly asking? Or could it be you're trying to remind me I haven't been out on a date in almost five years?" I fold my arms and glare across the island at him. The thought that he might be trying to manipulate me with this whole performance is making me feel as prickly as a hedgehog. "Because if that's the case, maybe you should cast your mind back to last night," I utter icily as I poke a finger in his direction. "Because that wasn't in my plans, either."

"You haven't—" His words halt, something like shock or maybe delight rippling across his face before his expression firms almost immediately again. "You haven't been on a date since before Lulu was born." This time his words are smokier. His dark eyes seem darker, too.

It's a good thing I was never destined to be a spy. Because I'd be a really shit one, considering I've just about admitted he's the only man I've slept with in forever. The only man I've slept with since the last time I slept with him.

"Oh, you're still here." Lulu appears next to him, her dark hair like a bird's nest as she stares up at him. "Are you staying to help me with my homework?"

"Would you like me to, Lu?" he asks with the kind of expression that says a smirk isn't far behind.

"No, she would not," I almost growl.

"Of course!" Lulu's attention swings my way, her expression mulish. She hasn't had a tantrum in weeks, and I really could do without her having one right now. "I'll get the cwayons."

Seriously, anyone who has been in my vagina or came out of it needs to leave this room right now!

As much as I hold to the sentiment, this isn't the kind of thing you should announce. Especially not in front of a four-year-old. No matter how much you're feeling it. Not feeling my vagina but feeling severe frustration, the kind that makes my head feel like it's about to explode.

"Uncle Carson is not staying to help you with your homework," I declare firmly. "However, if you start your homework, and if he calls before arriving one evening this week, he may come and visit us." Visit us in his own home. Honestly, this is like living in topsy-turvy ville. "Deal?"

"Deal," Lulu agrees sullenly.

"You'll have to give me your number." Why does it sound like he thinks he's won some kind of concession? I'm not doing it for him!

Maybe I'm not even doing it for Lulu.

"You can ring the landline," I answer with just the smallest of snipes and a wiggle of my fingertips. "Off you go."

Wednesday, in a week approximately three years long.

At work, Beth and I are scrupulously polite to each other, but the tentative friendship that was building seems to have disappeared over the weekend. The one time she tried to talk to me about it, I shut her down. I can't talk about it, and I don't want to hear about her experiences, either. She looked a little hurt. I expect she thinks I'm judging her, and I suppose I am, but not about how she chooses to live her life. If she wants to frequent sex clubs, who am I to tell her to do otherwise? She's over twenty-one. She can make her own decisions, but what she can't do is make decisions on my behalf.

I am disappointed that she would make plans for something as monumental (read: batshit crazy) as a trip to an 'adult lifestyle club'—and yes, even in my thoughts, this travesty of a title gets ironic inverted commas—without asking me if I'd like to visit first! Because if she had asked me, we could've had a sensible conversation about it. A conversation full of *hell no's,* but I deserved the choice, didn't I? It doesn't matter that I'd be as likely to accept that kind of invitation as I would a jaunt out on a boat to club a few baby seals to death.

Choice, Beth. Choice!

I'm trying to persuade myself that the invitation came from her heart. From a place of goodness. But, in which case, I have to think maybe her heart must be a pretty barren place.

Rich people. Again.

And, of course, rich people bring my mind back to Carson, almost full circle. I say full circle because he seems to be the one thing I can concentrate on without difficulty, my every thought seeming to begin and end with him.

Did I have a good weekend? Marta asked earlier. My mind slipped to Carson in all his weekend glory. The astonishment on his face as I'd blurted my big admission.

Shock that turned to delight.

Do I want a coffee? I think about Carson having a tea party with Lulu.

What did I think about the last session? Session = sex. Sex = Carson.

It never ends!

On the bright side, the strangeness between us hasn't seeped into work, and Beth has had no qualms about me sitting in on her sessions. This morning during her counselling session with a woman named Sarah, I found myself pondering orthorexia. As someone who has viewed life through that lens, I know it can be an almost silent condition. On the outside, sufferers can appear healthy, though perhaps a little rigid with their eating plans. A passion for healthy eating can be easily excused by friends, even envied, until obsession sets in. It's hard to envy extreme weight loss, as opposed to looking sexy in a pair of skinny jeans, and it becomes an obvious issue when you continually refuse to eat out with friends.

I fit the profile for sufferers. I'm somewhat of a perfectionist. A little anxious. I struggle when I'm not in control of a situation. Like Sarah, I sought help. I learned about behaviour modification and cognitive restructuring. And then decided I wanted to help others feel good about themselves. To be mindful. To see foods, not as a moral value but as fuel. To see we are not always what we eat.

Even when we eat donkey dick.

The thought makes me a little sick as I remember the creep from Ardeo.

And, zing! I'm back to thinking about Carson and his generous proportions again.

"Have you and Beth fallen out?"

I look up from the notes I'm studying and shake my head in answer to Marta's question. "No. We're fine."

"You're far from fine. You can't even look at each other. What happened over the weekend."

"Nothing. Nothing at all." I sit back in my chair, my eyebrows sitting somewhere near my hairline, and if I open my eyes any wider, they might fall out of my head. "Why? Has she said something?" She'd better not have.

"Yes. She's said fine a lot, too." Marta's expression twists unhappily. "But it's far from fine. In fact, it'd be more fun working in a morgue right now. I thought—" She pauses, possibly choosing her words. "You know she's going to end up sleeping with Ethan, right?"

"Do you reckon?"

"Hell, yes. But that's her business. You can't tell her anything else just because you recognise the man gives off Ken doll vibes."

"You mean because he's all buff and toned? Or because he's more than a little bit plastic?"

She smiles. "I was going for empty-headed and lacking balls."

We both set off chuckling but then fall quiet again.

"We had a difference of opinion, that's all. It wasn't about Ethan. Believe me, I'm not silly enough to think I could give anyone advice about their love life. I have enough on my own plate at the moment."

"Man trouble?" she asks.

"No," I reply a little too quickly. "I'm moving to Beth's sister's apartment this weekend, and I'm suddenly facing a lot more expenses than I thought."

My answer is a diversion, while also sadly true. There are so many fees I hadn't anticipated, and though I'll get most of them back once I send my expense sheet to HR, I still have to lay out the sums initially.

"Oh, yeah. City living does have its drawbacks."

"There's the application fee, a security deposit, renters' insurance, and utilities deposit. Then the apartment doesn't have a communal laundry, so I'll have to send it out or spend a couple of hours each week in the laundromat, which Lulu will be just peachy about. It's going to cost me a pretty packet each month in terms of my commute, and that's using the metro, not Uber or Lyft. Then there are the items that Lulu has needed for school and the new wardrobe I've had to splurge on because workout wear doesn't suit the tone of the office unless you're called Ethan, it seems. The list of expenses just goes on and on!"

"Can you get another job? Maybe something in the evening?"

"Not with Lulu at home. I mean, Ethan offered me a yoga class to run, but I couldn't at the time, but now I have a babysitter."

"And he's found someone else for the class now."

She nods, and I give a tight shrug. "I'd hoped I'd put all this behind me in my twenties."

"Unexpected expenses?" she asks, amused.

"No, working my bum off to keep my head above water."

"Well, if it helps, my brother runs a cocktail bar on the East side, and he's looking for someone to fill in for a week coming up soon. You'll be living over that way then."

"Oh." I begin to chew my lip as I consider the opportunity and how I'd manage it. I've been keeping an eye out for something since babysitting was no longer an issue, hoping to find an early morning yoga class or two to lead. But this might just work. Sophia lives on the other side of the city, but maybe she could stay over or something. "I have worked as a waitress and behind a bar, but that was back in France." Before Rose. Before Lulu.

"You'd be perfect. This is one of those French bistro-style places. Food and liquor. Upscale and with a friendly, regular crowd. He never has any problem with his staff. They love working there, but one of the girls is going back to North Carolina. I mean, it's only a week. Maybe ten days? I can give you his phone number if you think it might help."

"Thanks, Marta. It's definitely something to think about."

"Don't forget to tell him you speak French and have experience. Better yet, tell him you work with me."

"I will do. Oh, excuse me." My phone begins to buzz like a bee against my desk. "Hello?"

"Ms. Abernathy?"

"Yes?"

"This is Mr Farrow from the Lycée. Please don't worry, everything is fine. But we'd like you to come to school and collect Eloise, if you could."

"What's wrong? Is she ill?" I say, already pushing back my seat.

"She's fine. Please don't worry. There's just been . . . well, a little incident." There's a hint of something in his voice that might be amusement. The sudden, tight fist around my heart releases a tiny bit.

"Yes, of course. I'll be there very soon."

Goodbyes are said, and I end the call.

"Is everything okay?" Marta asks as I hurriedly grab the jacket from the back of my chair.

"I have to go to Lulu's school." I shove my phone into my purse distractedly. "I'll let Ethan know I've left."

"Is she sick?"

"No." Though I might be. "I think she might've just been expelled."

25

FEE

"I've just about had it with this vegable yuck." Lulu glowers over the kitchen table at me, pushing the remains of her dinner around her bowl.

"You like risotto," I answer evenly and without looking up as I continue to eat my own serving.

"I didn't go snooping," she mutters next. "And you shouldn't have told them I did."

Them being her teachers and snooping being something she is definitely guilty of. Snooping and borrowing. Again.

And then getting sent home from school.

And that wasn't even the worst of the experience. For me, at least.

"Are you going to tell him?" I look up at her quiet tone. She's still glowering but mainly to hide her embarrassment.

"No." I put down my fork because I'm really not hungry, either. What I need is a drink after the afternoon I've had. "I won't tell him." Mainly because I'll probably burst into flames. Not the sinful, God-smiting kind, but the kind of flames mortification brings.

While Lulu is in the doghouse, I feel like Carson should be there, too. Not that I'd ever tell him what happened this afternoon. No way.

"I said I was sorry." If it's possible, her brows lower even farther.

"I know you are."

"But why did they send me home?"

Probably so they could laugh in peace. After all, it's not every day a four-year-old wears a cock ring to school as a bracelet.

Please let it have been unused.

"Will I still be in trouble tomorrow?"

"You're not in trouble now." Not really. Though I think I might be the talk of the school staffroom. "It was nearly time to go home. Mr Farrow was probably just doing me a favour by saving me from coming back to school twice."

He also appeared to be quite happy, delighted even, because I'd agreed to go out with him this Saturday. I'm not sure how it happened or if I even meant to say yes. My head was in bits from embarrassment. All I know is, one minute I was facing the head of kindergarten and Mr. Farrow, there in the position of the teacher who'd confiscated the contraband, over the breadth of a desk, explaining how *that thing* lying on a folder between us couldn't possibly be mine. And next, I was walking out of the school after having agreed to meet him at a bar on Saturday night.

Urgh. Rose is going to give me such a hard time. She'll say lunch or a coffee or even a weeknight early dinner says: let's see if we're compatible. Saturday night first dates, according to her, send the wrong signal. That they say sex.

But there's nothing I can do about that now, so he can think what he likes. *If he's even been to the same dating rules TED talk as Rose.* Maybe I can persuade him to accompany me to the movies. Nothing about a trip to the movies screams *available for sex*, does it?

I certainly wasn't giving out sexy vibes this afternoon. *Vibe being the operative word.* I was so indignant. Outraged. Irate! Though not about his offer of a date. I protested that Lulu couldn't have known what she was wearing, obviously. It's not called a wrist ring! I said that the charges were ridiculous. When in fact, I was the one being ridiculous. There were no charges, I was reassured. This was just a little chat.

My feathers unruffled a little before I began to protest that I didn't possess the anatomy to make use of *it*. I mean, in retrospect, I'm sure the vibrating component works well enough without a penis. But gladly, I didn't say that. Instead, I just word vomited a load of denials and truths that I really should've kept to myself.

She must've gotten it from one of her little friends—someone with a father or an older brother, perhaps?

But no, Lulu had already confessed to bringing it in from home.

Well, it's not mine. I don't even have a penis!

Blank faces greeted that proclamation.

More than that, I'd added, *I currently lack the regular use of a penis in my life!*

How I came to agree to a date after that is still a bit of a blur.

What the blueberry fluff muffin have I gotten myself into?

I'm a Saturday-night-agreeing, first-date-planning, single mother of a daughter who took a cock ring to school. What kind of message does that send, if not desperate? Or desperately horny?

The one upside of this whole situation is that a date with another man is gold in the stakes to annoy Carson. Or at least, it should've been. Given today is Wednesday and we haven't seen him since Sunday, the point might be moot. He hasn't even so much as called, and I don't know how I feel about that.

Do I want to go out on this date?

Not particularly.

Would I tell Carson that?

Absolutely not. I'd probably do the opposite and lay it on a little thick just to annoy him. After all, I'm not the one with the sexy skeletons dangling in my closet. Probably hanging from silk restraints, still wearing naughty knickers, and—

I halt the thought. I shouldn't be thinking about closets and Carson in the same sentence. Why do I feel so conflicted about him? Or maybe I don't feel conflicted at all but rather jealous and resentful that he lives his life without caring for anything. But one thing I do recognise is I'm coming to delight baiting him almost as much as he seems to enjoy annoying the life out of me.

I find it hard to understand how he can be so sweet one minute and the next, all taunting and teasing and all kinds of smoky and sexy. I mean, inappropriate. I hate that I love that look on him even as it makes the blood boil in my veins. I just don't know whether I'm on my arse or my elbow when he's around.

But he's so amazing with Lulu, and when I listened in to their gin party conversation, he seemed genuinely unhappy about the teacher's interest. And not the "no one else can play with my toys" kind of upset. It's almost like he's hiding his real feelings from me. So maybe that makes cowards out of us both.

I don't want to go out on a date with anyone else, but I will.

It might be we both need punishing.

CARSON

Every morning this week, I've woken with a throbbing cock and her name on my lips. Which, I guess, is more than I'd had for a long time, but still nowhere near enough. Fee is the last thing I think of at night. The ghost of her haunts my mornings, my arms reaching out for her in the moments before I become fully awake and leaving me with a hollowness as I realise she's not with me.

She should be. She will be. Soon.

Over the years, I've gone to great pains to keep my life compartmentalised. To keep Ardeo and Hayes Industries separate; to keep my philanthropy under wraps. Philanthropy in the guise of penance, my pound of flesh more a pounding of flesh than anything. But I've paid my dues. I deserve something for me now. I see no reason to bring up the past with Fee. I'm not sure how I could explain who I was back then. How angry my grandfather made me. How I wanted to obliterate every sign of him, even the parts of him I carried within myself.

Even after he died, I sought to punish him. Punish his name and everything he stood for. Punish him through me. To confide in Fee would only bring her pain. Ardeo is a big enough obstacle for her—for us—to get over. At the moment, she thinks the club is just a New York gig, not the worldwide entity it is.

But I'll walk away from it all tomorrow just to be with her.

If she'll have me.

What the fuck am I thinking? Of course, she'll have me. The answer is in the way she'd put the island between us on Sunday because she can't trust herself. It's in the way her cheeks burned red, and her eyes turned black, their dilation almost stealing that golden edge. It was in her fingers twitching by her sides, though probably against the notion to choke me. But I'd take that reaction over indifference.

Anger is heat. It's passion. It's lips I can peel from her teeth, replacing them with my own. It's whispered chastisements as she rides me hard. It's future fucking in the laundry room while the kids are eating breakfast next door. It's a lifetime of passion. Of trials and tribulations. It's love in perpetual action.

For Fee, I know there's been no one else but me. No one inside her *since* me. That means something, and even if that something is because she'd told herself she was waiting for the right man to come along. Her one. Her forever. That's fine.

Because I was the one she chose Saturday. She shared her secrets, and she chose my hands to hold her safe as she unravelled. As she came undone.

That shit counts for something.

I'm her one. Even if she doesn't know it yet, even if I have to make her see.

Starting tonight, I'll be her shoulder to cry on, the voice of reason after she discovers her new apartment has fallen through. It didn't take much to fuck up her plans, though I'd initially considered a move might be a good one. I could've pursued her by the traditional route. Dates and dinners. Weekends in the park. Wooing her might've been a novel experience for me and a way for her to view me as a serious contender for her heart.

But Allison and Bethany Aaron are the daughters of David Aaron, and the whole family is fucking mercenary. There's no way Fee could be beholden to them. The contracts weren't yet signed, not that I would've allowed that to stand in my way. I offered Allison the equivalent of twelve months rent for the three-month initial lease Fee had agreed, though I arranged it all through an intermediary. That's all it had taken.

And of course, Bethany Aaron brought her to Ardeo. And because of Ardeo and because of Bethany and because of this fuckhead of a teacher, I don't have time to woo and court her as she deserves. This part of our relationship needs to be more of a smash and grab. I can't help but fixate on the fact that there's been no one else inside her but me. Call me a motherfucking caveman, but I'd fight the world to keep it that way.

Serious and for keeps. I know she's it for me.

As for Lulu, I love that kid. I may not have given her life, but I'll make it my life's fucking work to help her find her place in it.

Right after she's done helping me dig a big old hole for the teacher man.

26

CARSON

When I call at the apartment—my apartment—on Thursday evening, I ring the bell this time. No need to annoy Fee right off the bat during this visit.

"Uncle Carson!"

At least someone is happy to see me as Lulu opens the front door, launching herself at me.

"Oh, it's you," Fee mutters, widening the door. The sight of her might just steal my breath a little. It looks like she hasn't changed since she got home from the office, her navy dress fluttering demurely around her knees, the top half like something a ballerina would wear. She begins to thread her arms through the sleeves of a cream cardigan, concealing the jaunty capped sleeves of her dress and how they show off her toned arms to perfection. And those fucking glasses. From Fiadh, the weekend goddess, to the woman before me who is just one wooden ruler away from becoming every man's teacher fantasy.

"I really don't want to know what you're thinking," she says, pulling the sides of her cardigan closer.

"You sure?" Don't you want me to be the teacher's pet?

In lieu of an answer, she rolls her eyes.

"Such enthusiasm," I return, ducking to spring Lulu up onto my back, which was where she seemed to be climbing. When I straighten, Fee has already turned away and is walking back down the hall.

"What's up with Mommy?" As if I didn't already know.

"The 'partment fell froo," Lu whisper-hisses in my ear, almost making me chortle. "Are you tick-lish?" The kid's tone makes it sound like she's discovered some gem.

"I am *not* ticklish." But I might have sensitive ears. Kind of. Okay, so I like having my ears nibbled on in certain circumstances, but it's circumstances far removed from these. My eyes track Fee's movement up ahead, my mind wandering to her choice of hosiery. *Hose or stockings?*

She's practical-minded, but what I've seen of her lingerie choices is encouraging.

We reach the kitchen, and I settle Lu on one of the high stools. She grabs her iPad, her attention absorbed almost immediately.

"Aren't you going to ask what I'm doing here?" I drop my jacket to another stool and move around the end of the island to lean against it. Crossing one ankle over the other, I casually fold my arms. Fee doesn't take the pectoral/bicep bait. Instead, I pull the already open newspaper closer.

"I said it was okay for you to visit." Without looking up, she begins to flick through the pages, albeit a little violently.

"I'd hate to see how you treat the guests you weren't expecting."

"It was homework bribery, remember?" At this, she looks up, her eyes skimming over me briefly. "Sorry. Ignore me. I'm just a little distracted."

"I can see that."

"Well, I'd tell you to make yourself home, except you already are." She looks as though she might cry as her attention returns to the newspaper.

"Is there anything I can help you with?" She shakes her head but doesn't look up. This won't do. "Lulu said something about the apartment. Is there a problem?"

"Nothing I can't handle." Her words are as dissonant as untuned piano keys.

"Don't look at that one." I nod, gesturing at the newspaper, which is open to the classifieds, several listings circled by in blue ink.

"Which?" she asks, looking up.

"The one at the top of the page. That's not a good area to live."

"No?" She glances down and back again, apparently satisfied with my earnest expression. Which makes me feel bad. A little bad. Maybe a thimble full. In truth, I can't even see the listing she has circled from here. She might be interested in a timeshare in Acapulco or a date with destiny via the personal ads—over my dead body—but I know what she's looking at by virtue of being the one to fuck up her (as was) imminent lease.

"Maybe you should search for a realtor on the internet. I could probably recommend someone."

Her expression twists. "No thanks." No need to ask where she thought I'd know a realtor, judging by her haughty tone.

My chest huffs with a small chuckle. "I have a realtor who works on my behalf."

"I doubt we're looking in the same price brackets."

"You know you can stay here, right? Until you find something."

"And where will you go?" She glances up, un-fucking-amused. "One of the spare bedrooms? Or do you still have a room reserved at the Y?"

"A suite. Amazing bunkbeds. Seriously, though. I have places to be. You can stay here."

"And when you're not doing God knows what, God knows where?" Her lemon-sucking expression stops her from adding *with God knows who.*

Who? Why, you!

"Can I go and watch Disney?" Lulu asks suddenly.

"No. It's nearly time for bed."

"But I don't want to," she complains loudly.

"Inside voice," comes her mother's directive.

"It's not fair. Uncle Car is here!"

As Lu whines the four-year-old litany of the unjust, it seems as though Fee's resolve is weakening. Before she changes her mind, I lean closer and murmur, "You're sure you can trust me to be alone in the same room as you?"

"I think I can handle it. Handle you," she adds quickly, swiping the paper away.

"I'm a big boy. You know I take a lot of handling."

Rising to my provocation, she turns her attention to Lulu. "Off you go and brush your teeth. Now."

The phrase "brook no opposition" springs to mind. I do love a woman who can take charge.

Wonders upon wonders, Lulu slips from her seat, muttering her unhappy adieus as she reaches the kitchen door, along with the proclamation of, "I'm not happy about this."

"Your displeasure is duly noted," answers her mom.

"Julie what?" Her button nose scrunches in confusion.

"Honestly, I think I should book her a hearing test." The words fall in an exasperated rush before she adds, "If you want to take part in the school camp out, you need to go to bed without any fuss."

"Fine," she mutters, swinging on her heel.

"Er, have you forgotten something?"

"Good. Night. Uncle. Carson." The kid's leave-taking is delivered bullet-style.

"See you later, alligator."

Her brow creases with consternation the moment before she turns. "Night . . . snake."

I hope that wasn't a reflection of my personality.

Fee follows her out, and I make my way into the dining, pulling open the drink's cabinet. I pour a couple of fingers of scotch into a couple of glasses, then carry them back to the kitchen, taking a seat on one of the high stools. Pulling my phone from the back pocket of my pants, I set it facedown, turning the newspaper to face me.

West Harlem. Washington Heights. Those would be a fucking awful commute.

By the time Fee returns, I've moved the newspaper back, and I'm almost finished with my drink.

"I can keep my hands to myself," I begin, "but I couldn't resist the good scotch. Your poison, right?" Using two fingers, I push the glass towards her when she pauses at the end of the island where I'd earlier stood.

"Thank you." She studies me from under her lashes, waiting for a punchline that doesn't come.

"What was with the bribery earlier?"

"Lu, you mean? They're having a sleepover on the school premises as part of a drive to raise money for the homeless. She wants to go." She adds a tight shrug.

"And you don't want her to go?"

"I've volunteered, so I'll be there, but . . ." She stops,

maybe working through what she wants to say. "She said lots of the dads are getting involved."

"A private school in Manhattan?" I answer sceptically.

"That's what she hears from her friends."

"Probably wishful thinking."

"If I'm in town,"—which I know I will be—"I could come along if you like."

"I'm sure you have other things to do," she scoffs a little too casually to mean it completely.

Things to do other than you?

"You don't want me there?"

"It's just . . . because . . ." She begins to flounder, her gaze slipping to the door behind me as though she'd escape.

"Because I'm not her dad?"

"I don't want her to become too attached. We're not going to be here forever."

"I respect that." And I'll follow you wherever. I can ignore Hayes Industries from anywhere in the world.

"Well, the offer is there, but in the meantime, you're welcome to stay here."

With me. Forever.

"And I say again, it wouldn't be appropriate. Rose would never have asked if we could stay in the first place if she thought I'd still be here. I'm sure of it."

"Wouldn't she?" Something tells me Rose would be delighted if she were a fly on the wall right now. *Yeah, because she doesn't know about Ardeo*, my unhelpful mind chooses to supply.

"Rose doesn't know you as well as she thinks," she answers dispassionately, almost as though reading my mind.

"I'm pretty sure I could say the same for you."

"I'm not the one who owns a sex club. Sorry, an adult lifestyle club," she amends acidly.

"No, babe. You're just the one hanging out there."

"I am not your babe," she retorts. "And I told you it was all a mistake."

"We're getting off track here. So Rose doesn't know us to the depths of our souls. I think we can both agree we're entitled to our secrets."

"And I suppose this is a secret you think we should keep from her."

Oh, such vitriol. Where did that come from? Could Rose have told her about me hitting on her all those years ago? If that's the case, I like that she doesn't like it.

"You mean, what happened between us? Go ahead and tell her. Something tells me she might not be so surprised."

"Because you can't help yourself?"

"Saturday wasn't all on me," I answer calmly. "I guess what I'm saying is how do we truly know anyone?" I half turn to slide my phone from the countertop, realising it's Fee's phone I have in my hand. Swapping it for the other, I slide it open as I turn back and begin to scroll. What am I doing here? Stalling for time. "But if it's an impartial party you need extra reassurance from—"

"Will you get your mummy to vouch for you?" she taunts oh, so sweetly.

Sweet like arsenic.

"Not quite." A smile tugs at my lips. I think Mom would've liked Fee, as sentimental as that sounds.

"Oh, so you're going to phone a friend?" she continues, warming to her theme.

"I don't really have time for a séance, and the rest of

my family would be the last people I'd call for a reference, so I guess that leaves phoning a friend."

"Oh, God." The high colour fades from her cheeks, her expression a little sick. "I'm sorry." I glance down at where her slim fingers curl around my forearm. "Sometimes, my mouth just runs away with me. I do remember you'd said your mum had passed."

"It was a long time ago."

"I'm so sorry. You must think I'm a complete bitch."

"I don't think that." Rotating my arm, I catch her hand as it retracts. "Not at all." I grab my phone and place it in her hand. "Jonathan Alred."

"Who?" Her eyes dart back and forth between my face and the screen.

"I'm not phoning a friend. You are."

"What for?"

"For a reference. If Rose isn't enough."

"So he's, what? Someone who works for you? A former frat house buddy?" I laugh, which only succeeds in raising her hackles. "Or maybe another man about town who—"

"Man about town? It really has been a while since you put yourself out there, hasn't it?"

"That's none of your business," she answers primly. I also think she might whisper *prick* as she put the phone on the countertop and turns away from me.

She's right. I am being a prick. Last time, she had a reprieve. This time, I'm working it. Just a little bit.

"Go on, take a look." When it becomes clear she'd rather touch my prostate than my phone, I turn the screen back to face me. "Truthfully, he's not so much a friend as a business associate who'll vouch for me. You know, as an upstanding member of the community."

"Upstanding?"

"Well, I'm sitting just now, but you know what I mean."

"Does this community of yours know how you make your money?"

"That I'm essentially a trust fund kid, all grown now? Or that I'm the majority shareholder and CEO of Hayes Industries."

"You know that's not what I'm talking about." She throws back a little of her scotch, closing her eyes against the burn.

"Linking me to Ardeo would be a little harder. Though it's a legitimate business, it's hidden behind a shell company and a few other things to protect my partners and me. And our members, of course."

She glowers at me.

"And honestly, this whole deviant schtick is getting a little old, given you're tainted by association."

"I told you, I was there by mistake."

"So you've said. Anytime you want to ask about Ardeo, just say the word."

"I'm not interested," she grates out, throwing back the rest of her drink before rinsing her glass at the sink.

"Well, I guess we're back to the matter at hand." I glance down at my phone. "If you don't want to speak with Jonathan, you could email him. It's Jonathon at relief global dot org."

"Relief? As in the charity?" Her brow creases but not for long. "So your friend does a little charity work—"

"As do I."

"That doesn't mean he's a reliable source."

"What if he runs the charity? What if it's his life work? What if he lives and breathes Christian values?" Yada, yada, yada. Blah, blah, blah. While this is all very true, I've no idea what he'd actually say if she chose to call him. Do I do a lot of charity work? Yes. Does he know anything about my personal life? Not even a little bit. "Or I could give you the number for the head of The American Red Cross? UNICEF?" I glance up, gratified by her expression. *Close your mouth, angel, before I find something to fill it.* "Would either of these be reliable enough for you? I could offer you the number of a Senator or two, good people, though I can't help but be of the opinion that anyone who seeks public office should probably be prevented from holding it. What do you think?"

"I think you're trying to impress me."

Not sure if she'd have been impressed to find those good senators naked at the bottom of a pile of pussy, as they no doubt would've been on Saturday night.

"I can think of so many other ways to impress you. Better ways." I turn and put my phone back on the counter next to hers before my gaze rakes over her again. *Before she freezes my ass with one of those arctic fucking glances.* "What I'm trying to do is make you see the logic in staying. At least until you find somewhere suitable."

"At this rate, my twelve months will be up," she mutters.

"Would that be so bad, staying here the whole time?"

How about a whole lifetime? New York. France. In a yurt in Outer Mongolia. Wherever she wants, just the three of us. And any more that might come along. How crazy is it that I want to see her round with our child? Make a family.

"Now you're taking the p—" She halts, takes a deep breath, and begins again. "It all sounds like an awful lot of trouble to get me into bed."

Hell, who needs a bed. The thought rushes through my

head, unbidden, and I close my eyes against the accompanying images. *Or maybe to enjoy them without her censure.*

"While I'm certain we've established I would very much like to do so, I'm no Bluebeard. I think I can keep my hands to myself."

But she's already shaking her head. "It doesn't matter. I can't stay here."

"Okay." I shrug as though done. "So let's move on." My tone is reasonable, even if my words are total bullshit. Move on? How? When it feels like my world has shifted on its axis. There is no drawing a line under it, no moving on. I can barely sleep for the thought of her under my roof. Watching my TV. Sitting on my chairs. Sleeping in my bed. I have never felt like this before. I can't get her out of my fucking head, and I don't want to. The scent of her hair, the silk of her skin, the taste of her lingering on my tongue. If I'd any notion how Saturday would've amplified my craving, I might not have led her into that room.

And I'm a fucking liar.

One who won't be satisfied until she's wrapped around me again. Until she admits she feels the same way.

"Thank you." Her fingers pluck at her lip, and my God, how the sight makes my dick ache. "It's just. Well, Saturday complicates things for me."

At least she acknowledges it wasn't all one-sided.

Fuck, she was a treat for the eyes. For the soul, even. I drag my gaze the length of her frame; toned legs, a waist built for my hands, breasts that are a perfect handful. My gaze travels up the elegant column of her neck, farther to lips that might beg for a kiss if they weren't pursed with disapproval.

And even that does it for me.

"If you're *quite* finished ogling."

"Ogle?" A grin cracks my face; there really was no restraining it.

And finished? Not even close.

"Give me my phone." She holds out her hand along with the command as though fully expecting me to pass it over. "Please."

"What's it worth to you?"

"I'm not even going to dignify that with an answer."

"Then I'm not going to grace you with your phone." Grabbing both handsets, I stand from the stool and slip one into each of the front pockets of my pants. *It's kind of crowded down there.* "If you want it, you'll have to come and get it." I pat them for good measure. And just to see her eyes drop.

"Fine." She swings on her heel. "I'll just use the landline."

"Sure. Call a friend. Call a hotel. Call fucking Rose! Tell her how you can't trust yourself to be in the same room as me." Her footsteps falter, and I think she's going to carry on, that she's going to walk out of the room when instead, she whips around to face me.

"You see, this is why I can't be in the same room. I don't know which version of Carson I'm going to get!"

"Then let me tell you." I'm off the stool in an instant, stalking across the room to where she stands on the threshold. Her gaze widens as her fight or flight instincts kick in. "There is only one version," I say, taking her chin in my hand. "And that's the one who wants you in his arms again. The one who's been guarding his heart for far too long, the same as you. The one who wants you to take a chance on him."

"You're too big a risk," she whispers, tears teetering on

her lids. She jerks away, leaving my hand suspended in the air. "And you're wrong."

"Am I?" I fold my arms across my chest, unable to hold back my sneer. "Five years and you've never dated once. Never fucked someone else."

"Did they teach you to be a tactless dick at your fancy prep school?"

"No, they taught me to tell the truth."

"I can tell the truth, too. You're right. Five years is far too long. Felicitations to you," she almost spits, her gaze roaming over me contemptuously. "So you cracked the seal for me last Saturday. But guess what? I have a date soon. And it looks like I've got a lot of catching up to do."

I take a step towards her when she whirls around, almost spinning out into the hallway. "You know where the door is. I'll let you see yourself out."

27

CARSON

"Eat me!"

"What was that, honey?" I pause at the doorway to the den, a bowl of popcorn in one hand, my scotch in the other, but Lulu doesn't answer. She's too engrossed in the huge TV screen she's standing in front of, just a pyjamaed silhouette with wild, dark hair.

"Hey, Lu, are you sure your mommy is okay with you watching this?" It's animated, true, but so is a lot of other stuff not intended for kids' impressionable sensibilities. As I take my seat in the middle of the sectional, she doesn't immediately answer, engrossed in the exchange playing out in front, her tiny hands balled into fists.

"Do you know the muffin man?" she parrots, reciting the lines of the scene without an ounce of attention for me. So I guess it's a safe bet that she's seen this once or ten times before. It must have received the parental seal of approval. "The muffin man who lives on Drury—" Lulu sniffs and turns. "Ooh, popcorn!" she announces, drawn by the buttery aroma.

As she makes a dive for the cushion next to me, she

wiggles her shoulder under my arm to reach the bowl. As she smashes a tiny handful to her mouth, my elbow hovers awkwardly in the air for a moment before I slide it across the back of the sectional.

I wonder if the schoolteacher is right this minute walking down the street with his arm around her. *Knock that shit off,* I tell myself. The attitude of a caveman isn't going to help when she finds you here.

So she didn't exactly say her date was Saturday night, but it took very little effort to find out what actual day. I could've called Rose under some bullshit pretext, but as I'd already had a little chat with Ed Martinez, (who, along with his daytime counterparts, I give very generously to at the holidays) about keeping an eye on things, Fee being new to the city. So, I gave him a call and I asked him to let me know when Fee left the building. Not every time, I'm not some virtual fucking stalker, just when she went out in the evening this week. Alone. Before he agreed he would, I had to tell him the whole story, and I found myself admitting that I love her.

Yes, Ed Martinez, the doorman, is the first to hear of my love.

Great going, asshole.

But he kind of commiserated with me, and as he'd already agreed to keep an eye on things on my behalf—again, not like a stalker, but as someone who wanted dearly for her to come to no harm—he said he'd let me know the minute she left the building. Alone.

"I hope you know what you're doing," he said as I'd made my way to the elevator.

My answer? "Ed, I haven't a fucking clue, but I'm rolling with it."

And now here I am, sitting on my couch, drinking my

scotch, watching *Shrek*, of all things. But it's an improvement on the last (acid drop) movie of Lulu's choosing, so there is at least that.

"I've been to Drury Lane, you know." Lulu tips her chin and, along with the statement, sprays a little half-masticated popcorn at my chest.

"Yeah?"

She nods as she grabs another handful of popcorn, wriggling closer. *If only I could get her mother this close.* "When we went to London in the summer, Granny and Grandpa took me to the theatre, and we walked down Drury Lane."

"Did you see the muffin man?"

"No." She rests her head against my chest, and I feel her ribs expand with a long inhale. "Just coffee shops with muffins and donuts and things in the windows."

"Too bad. Maybe he moved to a new house."

"The muffin man isn't real, Uncle Car." Mouth wide, she palms another handful of popcorn, pressing it to her face. Her expression turns thoughtful as she chews. "But there was a man outside of the theatre. He was shouting and holding a Bible."

"Like a street preacher?"

She shrugs, unsure. "Grandpa said he was a God botherer, but he didn't look like he was bothering God, just the people coming out of the theatre."

"What show did you go to see?"

"*Matilda*. I put a red ribbon in my hair."

Red ribbons mean something else entirely at Ardeo. It's strange, but for the first time, I find myself wondering if our members with children find the whole ribbon thing a little creepy. I push the question to one side for examination later. I'm guessing Matilda wore a red ribbon in the show, though I can't be sure. I'm also not sure why someone would be drawn to preach fire and brimstone, old testament-style, decrying the sins of PG-rated musicals and plays.

Maybe his issue was with the casinos nearby?

"Did he scare you?"

"No, but my granny scared him." She chuckles at the recollection. "She was very, very angry."

"Did she tell him God isn't real?"

"What?"

"Nothing."

"God is like Santa Claus," she sermonises quite suddenly. "If you don't believe, you don't receive."

"And what does God give you?"

"Blessings."

I guess hedging your bets is as good a reason as any. "What happened with the street preacher? The guy with the Bible?" I qualify.

"We were eating an ice cream, and he shouted *gluten!*"

"Gluten?" I tug on my earlobe, surprised I can still hear. Lulu's quest for retelling a tale is certainly a faithful one because that wasn't what her mom refers to an inside voice. "Sounds like he was intolerant to a lot of things." When she says nothing, it becomes clear my four-year-old audience is a little young to get the reference. "Do you think it might have been glutton he yelled?"

She shrugs."My granny said he should *come here to her and call her fat*," she intones, mimicking a loud, angry Irish accent. A pretty good one, too. "That just means come here," she advises, breaking character. "And then I yelled *my granny isn't fat* because she isn't. She's just fluffy. And I was going to kick him, but before I could, Granny threatened to shove his Bible up his hole." She cackles as she throws herself back against the cushions laughing loud and long. "And then do you know what he did?" she asks, pushing up on her elbows as she attempts to blow a chunk of hair from her face. "The man with the Bible?"

"I have a feeling you're about to tell me," I answer, pushing the strands away for her.

"He ran away before she could show him what hole. Because she meant his bum hole!" She begins to cackle again, her hand slapping the cushions in mirth before she stops abruptly. "Don't tell Mommy I told you what his hole is. She says it's not for little girls to say."

"Your secret is safe with me. Your granny sounds pretty fearsome. I think I would've run, too."

"She wouldn't say that to you." She eyes me consideringly. "She'd say *that man is a fine thing*." According to her impersonation, Lulu's granny has a deep voice and fluttery hands. "Then she'd tell Mommy that she could do lots worst. And to take you on a date."

"Does your mommy go out on many dates?" Fishing, fishing, fishing.

"Just sometimes with Uncle Charles," she answers, pronouncing his name the French way. *Sharles.*

"Uncle Charles, huh?" My gut tightens unpleasantly. Who the fuck is Charles? I'd put money on him not being Lulu's uncle. "Does she go out with Charles often?"

She answers with a shrug. "Sometimes he sleeps over, and when he wakes up, we watch cartoons together, and he makes crepes."

Motherfucker.

Out of the mouths of babes comes the truth. So much for five years. I wonder if Rose knows about this asshole Charles. Maybe she can give me his address so I can beat his ass.

"Are his crepes as good as my pancakes?" Petty? Absolutely. But not as petty as asking her mother who has the bigger dick. Which I might. Just to hear her tell me something I already know.

"I like them both," she answers, the little diplomat. "I like crepes with chocolate sauce and your pancakes with maple syrup."

"Don't forget the bacon. Can't have pancakes without bacon."

"Yucky!" She giggles, not yet a sweet and salty converts.

"So, what does your Mommy say about Charles." I know, quizzing the kid isn't cool. It's not exactly healthy either, but here I am with a dozen other questions for her.

And a dozen more for her mother when she gets home.

Does it change how I feel about her? I guess that depends on her answers, though I already know it won't make me want her less.

She shrugs. "Uncle Charles says Mommy is his friend wif benefits."

"I'm not sure that's the kind of thing Uncle Charles should be talking to you about."

The little girl opens her mouth to speak, but another voice answers.

"Isn't it?"

We both turn to where Fee stands in the doorway, wearing an enigmatic expression. Otherwise known as a shit-eating grin. One I suddenly want to make her pay for by putting her over my knee.

"Mommy!" Lulu shouts before beginning to climb over the back of the couch.

"Lu, please!" But her mother's voice lacks the tone of

chastisement as she lifts her over the back of the sectional. "How come you're not in bed?" she asks as her daughter's feet find the floor.

"Uncle Car said I could wait up."

"Strange. I could've sworn I left Sophia in charge."

I'll say this: she looks neither annoyed nor disappointed to find me here. She kind of looks like the cat that got the cream.

"How was your date?" Lulu asks, throwing her arms around Fee's waist. "Did you go anywhere nice? Did he bring you flowers? Did you kiss like this?" She begins to make smacking noises in the air as she pivots and begins running her hands up and down her forearms.

"Yeah, *Mommy*. Tell us how your date went." Bringing my knee up onto the couch, I hook my elbow over the back of the sectional to face her.

"Hello, Carson." Her gaze lowers, her greeting suddenly cool. She drops her purse to the console before untying the belt of her coat. "What are you doing here?"

In the apartment I own, you mean? Oh, just hanging out. Making sure you're not bringing anyone home.

"Watching *Shrek*. How about you? What have *you* been up to?" My gaze roams over her, almost as though looking for evidence. A tight, fine knit woollen dress that falls to her calves, black boots that disappear under the hem, and a pale blue scarf wrapped neatly around her neck. Her makeup is light but perfect, and she hasn't a hair out of place in her usual (and as hot as fuck) high ponytail. I fucking love her hair. I love how she gasps when I twist the length of it in my fist. Love how it ripples like silk between my fingers.

What I don't love is that she's not wearing her glasses, inexplicably.

Ignoring the twist in my gut and the twitch of my cock, my eyes roam over her once more. It's not as though I'm expecting to find evidence of sexual congress in her appearance, not exactly, but the level of my relief not finding any is pretty ridiculous. And this Charles? Something tells me all is not how it seems.

Just a date. No outward evidence of kissing, touching, fucking.

Breathe . . .

"Where did Sophia go?" Ignoring my question, Fee instead directs her attention to Lulu once more.

"She left when Uncle Car got here. We've been watching a movie. Come and watch it with us. *Pleeease!*"

"You sent her home?" Fee glances my way, though she doesn't look at me for nearly long enough.

"The kid looked kind of uncomfortable being here with me, so I paid her"—plus an extra fifty that she was very excited about—"and she left."

"I'm not surprised, seeing as how you made her blush last time you were here. Oh, don't worry about it," she adds airily. "I doubt you even notice the effect you have on women."

"I notice the effect I have on you," I kind of purr.

"Yes, on account of the hives, I suppose you would."

"Blush, not hives."

"Sophia was supposed to wait for her cousin to pick her up," she says, moving swiftly on, though I doubt even she thinks turning her head is going to hide her sudden colour in her cheeks. I love it when I'm proved right.

"Her dad is working tonight, right? So I guess she'll be sitting in the back office right now losing brain cells to her social media accounts."

"I suppose."

"What's the problem? She got paid premium for a couple of hours of work, and now she's hanging out, virtually, with her friends. And we watched a movie. Everyone wins." Especially me, now that Fee's home looking so pristine.

Read: untouched by teacher-boy's hands.

"Well, thank you." Her thanks seem uncomfortable, but I'm happy she's not about to fight me over the babysitter's money.

"Been anywhere nice?" I ask, my tone mild.

"To the cinema," she returns similarly.

Fuck the cinema. What kind of man would want to share her attention on a date? A fucking idiot because this is the kind of woman who deserves all of your attention. She should be draped with diamonds and showered in champagne and caviar. She deserves the very best, not carpets sticky with soda and a hundred other people on the same fucking date.

"Was the movie a good one?" Lulu continues with her barrage of questions.

"Did he buy you candy?" I kind of taunt.

"Uncle Car?" Lulu lays her hand on my arm. "Did you know Mommy loves Reeces's penis?"

She fucking what? Charles and the teacher and now Reece? My eyes skate to Fee, her shoulders shaking with a bout of laughter she's struggling to contain.

"It's true." She nods. "I really do."

"This Reece . . ." Fuck. *Fuck!* "Do you think this is maybe something you shouldn't be telling your kid?"

"Did a bit of popcorn go the wrong way down, Uncle Car?" Lu leans over the back of the couch and begins slapping my back.

"Maybe Uncle Carson would like some Reese's *Pieces* to help the popcorn go down."

"Ha." Blow out a breath. "Real funny. You almost gave me a heart attack."

"Oh?" So much meaning in that one airily delivered little sound.

And that's another smack to her ass as punishment.

"You thought I'd been out with someone called Reece?" she asks. Heckles. Whatever.

Dating Reece would be bad enough. Becoming acquainted with Reece's penis would be fucking unacceptable.

"Actually, my date was called Leo." A superior little smile plays about her lips. She's not high on her date. She's high on fucking with me. Torturing me.

As Lulu takes the opportunity to run around the sectional to sit next to me, I find myself leaning over the back of the sofa a little more.

"And how was Leo's p—" Penis? No. "Performance?"

"As a movie companion? A little poor." She slides her scarf from her neck, looping it over the back of the couch and pressing her hand atop. "He talked all the way through. Apparently, he doesn't understand French, despite working at a French-speaking school. And he slurps, too." Something they have in common. "What are you smiling at?"

"Me? Nothing. Nothing at all."

"Mommy, come and watch the movie with us." Lulu tugs on Fee's hand, and she allows herself to be led to the front of the couch. "You sit here," she says, directing her mother to sit on my right. "And I'll sit here," she announces, happily climbing between us. "There, we're a Lulu sandwich now!"

"I think that Uncle Carson is more used to being the centre of attention," Fee murmurs pointedly as she folds her arms.

I slide my arm across the back of the seating, leaning in to whisper in her ear. "Am I at the centre of your attention, Fiadh?"

"Annoyance, more like."

"Attention is attention."

"You would see it that way." Her words might be cool, but her cheeks are not. I know she's as affected as I am sitting close to the person you want but tell yourself you can't have. I'm just a little ahead of the curve. "But you do you," she adds airily.

"I'd rather do you." I pull on her ponytail a little, my cock twitching at her quick intake of breath and the sharp rise of her breasts. "Anytime you want me to be the meat, I'm there for it."

"What if I want to be the meat?" Her words are as sultry as the heavy-lidded glance she sends my way.

My thoughts shoot off in a hundred different directions, my insides fiery and molten as a prickle of heat spreads over my skin. At Ardeo, she had been entranced by a three-way scene; not my preferred three-way, but it wouldn't be the first time I'd shared a woman in this way. *MFM.* I'd always choose two women over being one of a pair of dicks, but I'm not sure I'd like to share Fee in any combination.

Given the way I feel about her, could I put her needs before my desire?

"Oh, God. You're seriously considering it, aren't you?" The corner of her mouth tilts. It isn't a smile; more like a mockery of one. Or maybe a mockery of me.

"I'm more than considering it. I'm making plans." Even

if I don't understand the tumult she raises in me, the tormenting mixture of emotions and need. How can I want to protect her at the very same time as I want to defile her?

"Hush!" Lu's reprimand breaks the moment, making us both jump and her mother's expression stern. "Can't you see Donkey is talking?"

"Sorry, sweetheart. I was listening. It's just a pity the donkey has nothing new to say." The latter, she adds in an undertone.

"You're not 'opposed to talk, for goodness' sake!"

"Sorry, princess Lu," I intone seriously. Though, right now, maybe dictator Lu might be more appropriate. I turn back to the elder of my two companions. "Did he take you anywhere else, this Leo?"

"Why?"

"Maybe I want to know what I missed out on."

"You would *not* have taken me to the movies," she says with a little huff.

I twist until I'm facing her, place the popcorn down, then lift the kid from the seat between us, relocating her to the left of me.

"Hey! I'm the meat!"

"Mommy keeps talking. You'll be able to hear better from there." I plant the bowl of popcorn on her lap, hoping the whole manoeuvre will shield her little ears from this conversation.

"You're right. I would've taken you somewhere much better." I would've taken her to heaven via a hastily booked suite in the nearest hotel.

"Why? Because you have an aversion to pleasant dinners and darkly atmospheric theatre spaces?"

"Dark and atmospheric is my jam. I thought you knew

that. But I do have an aversion to you going on dates when you won't give me a chance."

"Is that all?" she asks innocently, despite being fully aware she's driving me crazy.

"No, as it happens, it isn't. Because I also have an aversion to finding out you have a long-standing friends-with-benefits arrangement back in France." Even if I don't truly believe it.

"I have what?" she asks, her tone far too delighted for this type of topic. She also doesn't modulate her volume, meaning the little dictator beside me begins to mutter.

"You heard me." My brows pull in. Why do I feel like I'm being laughed at?

"Oh, I know who you mean! Hey, Lu?" She leans around me to catch her daughter's attention. "What does Grandpa say about Uncle Charles?"

The kid mutters something that sounds like *for fluff's sake*, but I don't rat her out.

"Lu?" Fee pushes my shoulder, pressing me back to better see, and my mind immediately returns to the time she did the same, on this very couch, right before straddling me. "I asked you a question."

Lulu picks up the remote and pauses the TV. She then turns to face her mother with attitude. This kid has an expression for everything. "Grandpa says Charles's crepes are crap 'cause they're just flat pancakes."

"And I know I'm not 'opposed to say that, but I didn't. Grandpa did. So it doesn't count." She turns her palm up in a kind of appeal. *Be reasonable*. "That's the deal."

"She's going to make a good lawyer one day," I interject.

"Grandpa says I'll be in the trades moonion."

"Trade union? He's a union man, huh?"

"No, he's a grandpa, silly. I'm going to be a racing car driver. Or get a taxi," she announces with a little shimmy. "A pink one."

I try not to laugh. I really do.

"We'll talk about this later, but for now, tell Carson what Grandpa says about Charles. Please," she adds, though it sounds more like a last warning.

"That he's as camp as a row of pink tents?"

"No, the other thing."

"Oh." Lulu frowns, appearing to indulge in a little thinking. "Do you mean when he says he was a friend of Dorothy? Because that's not true. I asked Charles, and he said he doesn't have any friends called Dorothy. Now can I *please* watch the end of *Shrek* in peace?"

28

FEE

We spend the next twenty minutes sitting side by side, thighs flush, our breathing seemingly synchronised. *Yes, I noticed.* At one point, Lu complains of being cold, and instead of putting her to bed because it's way past her bedtime anyway, Carson pulls out a huge, fluffy throw hidden away in the ottoman part of the sectional.

"Spend many nights curled up on the sofa, do you?"

"It's the first time it's been used." He sends me a quizzical look. "The interior decorator seemed to think it went with the sofa. Something about the authentic vibe and, if I remember correctly, heterogeneous elements."

"I'm sure she did," I answer, a little miffed. I can't seem to help myself.

The past few days have felt like a month of trials and tribulations. On top of Lulu's school drama, I've lost my apartment before even getting to move in, stared down from up on my high horse at Carson's offer to stay, only to have viewed two more flea pit spaces during lunch today, plus one very clean and modern but totally unsuitable communal apartment after work. *I can't take Lulu to live with a group of strangers.*

Then to top it all off, I endured a date with a man I have no interest in because I'd weaved my web of idiocy so tight, I'd tripped over myself.

Given the things I'd said to Carson last night, I shouldn't have expected him to be here right now. Is it weird that I did? Weirder still to find that I'm relieved?

"He, actually. The interior guy," he says, moving from quizzical to just plain amused.

I should've known he'd take my displeasure as encouragement as his hand slips under the throw, his fingers entwining with mine.

Something else that shouldn't warm the pit of my stomach, though it does.

"I'm so happy your date was a bust," he announces happily.

"I didn't say that." I vow silently to keep my eyes on Princess Fiona, currently in her ogre form.

"You didn't need to." Surprisingly, his answers don't contain even a hint of smugness.

It's a mistake, allowing myself to sit here. A mistake I'm pretty sure I am asking for. Or at least, my nipples seemed to be asking. Or maybe that's just now. He smells *so good*. Too good to be sitting next to, that's for sure. His cologne is clean and sort of citrusy-smelling, and the heat his body is throwing out is immense. I've never known a body to run as hot as his does. It makes me want to lie across him like a cat on a hearth rug.

My date was pleasant, and Leo was perfectly nice. And I might've even thought that's what I wanted, once upon a time. Because nice is good. Safe. Nice is good father material. Nice won't ever abandon you when you're pregnant. But it seems I now crave the touch of a different man altogether. A man who annoys me as much as he makes me smile.

My eyes still glued to the TV, I don't take in a thing as Carson's thumb swipes over my knuckles back and forth, back then forth again. It's pleasantly soothing and nothing I'd ever associate with this man. But then he turns my palm and does something to the inside of my wrist that, I swear, feels like the flick of a tongue.

The flick of a tongue between my legs.

"I'll . . ." I twist quite suddenly to face him, finding my hand on his chest. His heart beats slow and steady under my fingertips, and his eyes seem so dark and smoky and full of forbidden things. "Just be a minute," I finish, almost springing from the sofa and getting tangled in the throw.

"Careful," he murmurs, pulling on the opposite end, which might unravel the throw from my legs, but it also twists my dress from the waist. As I manoeuvre the knitted fabric back into position, my ovaries give a little pinch. Lulu has nodded off, her arms thrown around Carson, her little face is squashed against his ribs. As he repositions her against a cushion, he smiles down at her with such a look of fondness that it takes my breath away. As he looks up, he shares that smile with me, and I panic.

"N-nature calls!" I stutter, stumbling away. I make it to my bedroom, mainly to prevent myself from saying or doing anything stupid. *Anything else stupid.*

Nature calls? What, like, caw-caw!

Unzipping my boots, I throw them into the corner before pacing across the rug once or four times. How long does it take a person to pee, hypothetically? And wash their hands? *Maybe I'll do just that.* Hands can never be too clean, right? Deciding I've been gone sufficiently long enough, I make my way back into the den, resolved to put an end to this evening. To rest my scrambled brain.

"Well, it's been a long day," I announce, walking back into the empty room.

Hmm. The throw lies haphazardly over the back of the sofa, the cushions askew.

Maybe he carried Lulu to bed?

Noticing the light spilling out into the other hallway, I cross the room. *It's coming from the dining room.* As I stick my head through the open door, Carson looks up.

"Want one?" Standing at the open drink's cabinet, he reaches into an old-fashioned silver ice bucket, depositing a cube of ice into his glass.

"You put ice in there?"

"There's a machine." He taps the bottom of the cabinet with his shoe, and I find myself frowning. It's a beautiful piece of furniture, Art Deco. Maybe burr walnut. "It's supposed to be used." He twists his glass. "Can I tempt you?"

He already knows the answer to that. As for the drink, I shake my head.

"Is there a reason you're hovering in the doorway?" He rests his elbow on the top of the cabinet, the picture of ease.

"You put Lulu to bed," I assert.

"Was that not okay?"

"No. It was just a surprise. She didn't give you any trouble?" Lulu can be super crabby when she's woken from a snooze.

He shakes his head. "I was sleepily instructed to wish her good night in the vein of, *bonne nuit, mon petit chou.*"

"It's just a little thing we do." I struggle to hold in my smile along with the admission.

"Night light was duly switched on, Norman tucked in beside her, but brushing either her teeth or her hair was beyond my capabilities."

"Those are beyond a Norland nanny's capabilities. It's a posh school for nannies," I add as his brow quirks. "Caregivers to royalty and the like. They wear uniforms and look very serious." I'm babbling . . . and apparently walking deeper into the room, much to Carson's obvious pleasure.

"Are you going to tell me about your date?" He motions to a couple of imposing chairs placed on either side of the black marble fireplace, another Art Deco original. The ebony-coloured dining suite is a grand affair to seat a dozen, at least. A hooped base, one side houses a bench with some kind of furry rug, the other chairs with backs shaped like clouds. Around the room, several sconces are lit, making the large room seem snug. I find myself perched on the end of my seat by the fireplace as Carson settles back in his, bringing his right ankle over his knee, his glass dangling carelessly from his fingertips.

"I told you, it was good."

"That's not exactly what you said. He talked too much, and he was a sloppy drinker."

"You were paying attention." I duck my head, hoping to hide not my smile but how delighted I sound.

"I always pay attention when it comes to you. You know that. Just like you know those aren't the details I'm interested in."

"Do I?" My retort wavers with mirth.

"Was he a sloppy kisser, too?"

"I don't think that's any of your business."

He tried. I swerved.

"I want it to be."

"What are you smiling at?" I ask, a little exasperated. This man and his million smiles drive me slightly loopy. *Or maybe that's just his mouth. Because even just looking at it makes me lose brain cells.*

"Because I want it to be my business and my business alone. And because he didn't kiss you."

"I didn't say that."

"No, you didn't have to. I can just tell."

"Okay, Houdini," I mutter in return. Well, he did make my new knickers disappear. I consider them as collateral damage, and I'm disinclined to ask for them back. "And actually, speaking of tricks, I have something to thank you for. Sorry, I got that wrong. I meant I've got something to punch you for."

"Really?" He chuckles.

"Yes, because my darling daughter borrowed something quite particular from you and wore it to school on her wrist."

"You're gonna punch me because she wore one of my watches to school? Please don't tell me it was the Patek Phillipe Chronograph," he says, pressing his hand to his face.

"Is that the silver one?" It's a decent guess because a good number of the watches in that drawer are.

"With the black strap," he almost groans.

"No, it wasn't that one. In fact, what she borrowed is worn a little south of the wrist. Maybe even sometimes adjacent to it." I give a little shrug. "And speaking of wearing, I do hope it was brand new."

He looks back at me, his expression completely blank. "You're gonna have to spell it out for me because I have no idea what you're talking about."

I'm not going to say it. How can I without turning the

colour of a beetroot? Instead, I change tack. "You know how you have a watch drawer in your closet?" Carson nods. "It's a bit unusual. Not everyone has a watch drawer."

"No," he agrees. "Some people prefer to keep their watches in a safe. Some in a bank."

Rich people, he means. Most people have two arms and one watch. Sometimes they might have two—one for every day and one for special—but few people have a drawer full.

"Just take it from me. It's a bit unusual. But you also have a drawer full of other *unusual* things," I say very, very carefully. Or tellingly. Or with a great big hint.

"Oh." And that right there is the light dawning in his eyes. "That drawer."

"Yes, *that* drawer." I take a quick breath. "Maybe something fell out of it because, quite frankly, I hate to think of Lulu managing to somehow climb up high enough to see *in* to it."

"Like you have, you mean." A tiny smirk plays against his lips.

"That's beside the point. Because the point is, on Friday afternoon, Lulu was sent home from school early for wearing a . . . a . . . sex toy around her wrist."

"I'm having all kinds of trouble picturing it," he says quite seriously, leaning his cheek against his fist. "You're gonna have to spell this one out for me."

"For God's sake, Carson. My child wore a cock ring on her wrist to school!" He bursts into peals of raucous laughter, the kind that would shake the walls of a lesser address. In fact, I almost expect the neighbours to begin banging on the wall. But then I remember where we are and that Carson owns the whole top floor. "And it's not something she got from me," I mutter mulishly, not willing to join in. I didn't mention it for shits and giggles. I'm annoyed. Or at least, I want to be.

"I didn't give it to her."

"No, but it's your drawer. And, yes, it's your business, and I probably shouldn't have been looking in there, but what the hell? The things in there are . . . well, they're . . ."

"Gross?"

"Yes!"

"Cheap?"

"Very."

"And all kinds of disgusting?"

"The worst!" I agree.

"They're also my friend's idea of a joke."

"It must be a very long-standing joke, judging by the number of monstrosities in—in there." Oops. No need to mention I've also had a peek in the chest in his bedroom. The stylishly chic chest that is also big enough to stuff your sexual submissive in, should that be your (and his or her) thing.

"It's been going on a while. The joke started around the same time as Ardeo was founded."

I feel myself stiffen. The urge to stand, to move away from this change in our discussion is overwhelming. But there's something about his expression that keeps my bum glued to the seat.

"I know you tell yourself there are other reasons you can't be with me, but Ardeo is the number one. What you saw there frightened you."

"I don't know. Not exactly. I just know I can't be with a man who views sex so casually. And before you try to make me feel guilty by association, I truly was there by accident."

"Maybe there are no accidents. Maybe there's only synchronicity and the universe conspiring to bring us together."

"That makes no sense," I almost whisper, my gaze unable to hold his.

"Doesn't it?" He brings his glass to his mouth, and I suddenly long to be that receptacle. I might not have harboured any desire or expectations for going out with Leo tonight, but I didn't expect one date to push me so strongly in the opposite direction.

"Who knows the way these things work," he says, resting the base of the glass against his strong thigh. "Two people meet five years ago in France. They have the most amazing night, but despite being tied together by a friend, they never once meet. Until now. Does that not strike you as strange?"

"Yes. It's odd."

"What would've brought you into my arms again? Nothing. Not here and not in France. It took a night where you could give yourself over without fear of being judged, even when the only person judging you is yourself."

"And that night has passed. It's gone." I almost add *I can't be with you again*. But I'm suddenly tired of that broken record. Who am I seeking to punish here?

"Maybe not as part of Ardeo." He angles his gaze my way, his eyes running over me possessively. "But that's not what I'm asking."

"You shouldn't say those things." Not unless you're sure. Not unless you mean them.

"Do you want to know about Ardeo?" he asks as he runs his forefinger around the rim of his drink.

I shake my head, hoping to dislodge the urge to yell *yes. Tell me ALL the things!*

"I know what Rose told you, that I don't date. But we both know I'm neither celibate nor gay."

"You don't need to spell it out," I snap. "I know you don't have relationships. You just have sex." *You just have sex there. Indiscriminately. Often. With multiple partners at one time, I expect.*

"It's been easier that way. Sex. Fucking. At first, it was the novelty of it, and then everything changed. It became a way of life. A way of not letting anyone in. I guess we're the same in that respect."

"I don't . . ." He's right, despite my protests. We just took our lives to different extremes.

"We're both closed off." There's a note of something wretched in his tone as he stares unseeingly at the grate in the fireplace. "I never told anyone about you. About that night five years ago. Maybe some of the best moments in life are the ones you can't admit to out loud." He looks up then, seeming to come back to himself. "I'm giving it up, Fee. Ardeo. Giving up my stake in the business, and I'm not going back."

"You can't do that," I protest, even as my heart lifts in my chest cavity like it has tiny wings. I don't want that, do I? "Not because of me."

"Why not? I want you to give me a chance to show you I can make you happy."

"But we hardly get along like a house on fire!" I find myself on my feet, pacing away and then back again. Raising a finger as though I've something to add when I don't because even my brain is screaming, *give the man a chance!*

I like him. I like him so bloody much. And Lulu likes him, too.

"Don't we?" He springs up quite suddenly, like a lion

after a gazelle. "Don't you ever find yourself wondering when I'll turn up next? Wonder what I'm doing? Where I am? Because I wonder about you. I want to know where you are and what you're thinking. I find myself staring at my watch when I know you'll be on your way to school, you and Lu. I think about you living here, under my roof, wishing with every fibre of me that I was here with you, too. And let me tell you," he adds, his voice a low rasp, "the thought of you being with another man tonight made me fucking burn. So I'd say we get along just fine. As fiery as all fuck, but that's the opposite to apathy."

"Relationships aren't built on fire," I mumble, stumbling backwards.

"Aren't they?" His eyes fall to my lips as he moves with me.

"What if I make you miserable?"

"I'd rather be miserable because of you than be miserable without you. And if nothing else," he utters, all silky mouthed, "there's always the sex."

My bottom hits something solid, my fingers revealing the dining table as his eyes roam over me covetously, his hands holding me, adding to the sense he'd make me his.

"I'm not interested in being your toy." Somehow, this comes out much weaker than I'd thought it would, even as my hand presses to the centre of his chest.

"What happens if I'm asking to be yours? Just for the next fifty years or so. I see the way you look at me, Fee."

I hate that he's right.

I hate that the whole time he's been sitting there, I've been trying desperately not to watch how his hands hold his glass. Watch the shapes his mouth makes as he speaks. He's just so comfortable in his own skin. Something I would love to be. I want to bury my nose in that little triangle of skin his shirt collar exposes, inhaling lungsful of his warmth and his scent. I'd slide my hands under his shirt, already knowing how smooth his skin feels. Knowing how his muscles would ripple with pleasure and how that would feel under my fingertips. The sounds he'd make at the scrape of my nails.

I know I'm wrong. So wrong, as I watch, almost out of myself, as my hand balls in the soft fabric of his shirt to pull him closer. His face is a mixture of light and shadow, hope and maybe dread as I hold my fist there. But then I tug, and my last thought before our mouths meet is his mouth is not the most expressive part of him. Because his love radiates.

Our kiss is . . . unravelling. Carson's lips are tender and unhurried yet so masterful, his arms resting against my waist as he dictates the pace, forcing me to slow as he attempts to temper my need. But there's no slowing this train as my fingers tighten against his biceps. Tight. Tighter. Willing him on, dragging him with me towards a derail. Yet he just groans against my mouth, the sound one of masculine approval, the pace of his kiss never altering.

"I need you."

It takes me a moment to compute the words are mine. I screw my eyes tight, sensing the triumphant smile pressed against my lips. But it doesn't last long, not as he begins to devour me. Frantic fingers and desperate lips, tongues tangle and teeth clash as the glass I'd forgotten he was holding clashes against the wooden surface of the table. Two hands now. Two hands that hold and squeeze me. Own me. Make me wholly his.

"*You are . . .*" Edible? I think that's what he says as kisses rain down against my neck. The rough evening stubble on his cheeks and chin is a delicious layer of sensation. His questing hands pull up my dress, and as the wool reaches mid-thigh, his groan is one of quiet agony. It is the sexiest of sounds.

"Please tell me you thought about me when you put these on." His fingers spread wide against the smooth skin bared at the top of my lacy hold-up stockings, slipping around to the backs of my thighs, pulling me against his hard cock.

"I didn't think about you putting them on." Turning my head, I bite the top of his ear, making him curse and convulse against me. "I thought about you taking them off. With your teeth."

"You sweet thing."

My head falls back at his words, giving him access to more of my skin, more of me, as he fluidly drops to his heels in front of me. Pushing the hem of my dress higher, he coaxes my fingers around the fabric to hold it.

His soft curse tells me how much he appreciates the sight. *Lacy stocking tops, my underwear almost sheer.* But he doesn't touch me, not at first, though it's almost as though I can feel his tongue already, my gossamer knickers already wet as he spans his hands over my hips, framing the very centre of me.

"Look at how you want me." There is both truth and awe in his words, and the desire in his expression is intoxicating. As he blows a soft breath against my centre, my entire body trembles and yearns for him. The swipe of his thumb is exchanged for the warmth of his breath, his caresses working me until the sheer fabric clings wetly.

"I do. So, so much." My words are no longer a wish in the dark, a thought in my head I've tried to push away. "Please, Carson, don't make me wait. Put your mouth on me."

"*Fuck.*" His head drops to my waist, the word a groan that vibrates to the very centre of me. His forefinger hooks my underwear to the side, and I jerk as the pad of his forefinger brushes my clit before his tongue becomes an immediate and very welcome slick invasion between my legs.

I cry out, the knot of my orgasm pulling tight almost instantaneously. His tongue begins to lap and slide, his thumb petting my clit in the sweetest of percussions, my legs almost buckling.

"Yes! *Oh, God, yes!*" My breath is tight, my words hoarse, and my brain is blind to all thoughts but how I want this so badly, this pinnacle. I need it, my fingers grasping the edge of the table as I arch into him.

"That's it, sweet girl. Take your pleasure."

"Stop. Talking." But despite my instructions, his words elevate the experience and drive me wild.

"Make me lick you fucking dry."

"Oh, God!"

Engulfing my clit, he spears two fingers deep inside me. Sucking and licking, he twists his fingers and fucks me until I'm thrashing and wild. White heat rushes through my veins like pure liquid heat, the sensation between my legs building and twisting before bursting at its peak. I begin to jerk under him, coming so hard and so fast, his tongue meeting my climax, my body rising on my toes as I welcome them both.

When I finally come back to myself, the only thing holding me up against the table is his hand.

"I . . ." I groan, a ragged, needy sound, as his tongue swipes me once more, my flesh throbbing and overstimulated.

He stands then, pulling my dress up and over my head

before spinning me almost roughly to face the table. My palms hit the table at the same moment his own smacks the cheeks of my arse—once, twice—in quick succession, his voice a low rumble in my ear.

"That's for liking Reece's penis and going to the movies with someone other than me. And that one," he says, slapping me again, "is because you liked it a little too much."

I did. Hell, yes, I did, a heady mixture of shock and delight washing through me.

He squeezes my cheeks, handling me like I'm entirely his before his body meets mine, chest to back. A kiss pressed to the nape of my neck. My ponytail held in his fist as his free hand wraps around my ribs, holding me tight as he whispers a sweet litany of filth.

How beautiful my pussy is. How I'm the juiciest thing ever served on this table. How he's going to spread me wide and fuck me so very hard. I convulse against him, my breaths shallow as he kisses and licks from behind, his fingers twisting and teasing at my front, my breasts spilling free from their cups.

He's being . . . delightfully rough. And then I realise what this is. This is Ardeo. This is his version of the table and two men. This is him seeing me, fulfilling my fantasy as his fingers fill and maul, the low rumble of his commands driving me wild.

I don't need four hands. I just need his. Excitement washes through me as he draws my underwear down my legs. He unhooks my bra faster than a man can say—

"Open for me, angel." His voice is somewhere between a breath and a groan as I widen my thighs. I can feel him behind me, sense his eyes on me.

And I want this. Want him watching. Because he's

mine. All mine. He isn't at some fucking club, being touched by anonymous hands. He's here with me, looking at me, *wanting me*.

As much as I want him.

"Like that?" I whisper, sliding my legs a little wider still.

"Yeah, just like that. You are some fucking delectable sight."

As he turns me this time, it's to seat me against the edge.

"One of us is wearing far too many clothes," I whisper, beginning to unfasten the buttons of his shirt as his hand lifts to his mouth in an attempt to hide a smile. A mouth that, just moments ago, was coated in my arousal. Arousal that coats his thumbs as his large hands move to press my thighs wider, shirt forgotten.

"You look like a wet fucking dream." His gaze is hooded. He stares down, his smile no more as he presses me wide. "Like you were made for me."

'Yes," I agree a little breathlessly, grounding myself by gripping the smooth edge of the table. "I want you so badly I almost can't take it."

His eyes track up from their focus between my legs. His voice is dark as he asserts, "But you will. You'll take it all."

He pulls his half-unfastened shirt over his head before he makes quick work of his belt, his cock bouncing between us, rude and ruddy. I sigh as he presses hard to soft, swiping his silky crown against me.

I pull his mouth down to mine, shuddering at the brush of him, sucking hard on his bottom lip.

"You'd tempt the devil." His assertion betrays a tremulous smile, contradicted by the dark look in his eyes.

"He does seem to be at the doorbell again. He's just not using his fingers to ring . . *it*."

Carson chuckles, yet his movements are so practised, his wide crown gliding past my entrance to caress my clit before sliding back again.

"I can't hear the noise for my pulse," he groans.

"Open wide," he whispers.

"I've heard about men like you before," I answer with a sly smile, right before he kisses me.

"Don't you trust me?"

"Not a bit."

"Clever girl," he whispers, pressing the glass he holds in his hand to my lips. I groan as the fiery liquid rolls across my tongue, and as I swallow, Carson follows the motion with his tongue.

"I want to feel myself here." A kiss. A lick. "Feel you spasm around me." His dark and velvety words set off a series of empty ripples between my legs. As his tongue swipes my lips, I taste myself very briefly, gasping at the splash of liquid between my breasts.

"Oh, it's cold!" And then it's hot as his tongue follows the trail, sucking, licking, his hum of appreciation making me ache with need as he takes my nipple into his mouth. But then I'm crying out as something cold and smooth begins to circle my other nipple. The ice—his fingertips—circling my nipple in a divine kind of torture.

His hot mouth engulfs the hard nipple, his tongue an exquisite contrast against the sting of cold. My moan is so loud as I realise where he intends to place his chilled fingers next, a smile so wicked pressed against my breast.

My body surges against the chill of his fingers as he presses against my clit, then pinches it. Tortures me just a little until I'm a squirming, pleading thing.

"It's almost as though you don't like it."

"You're mean." I don't have the wherewithal to pout, though my response seems to take care of that anyway.

"However will I make it better?" he purrs as the subtle shift of our bodies brings us closer. And without any real thought for my actions or the consequences, I move against the press of him with a libidinous exhale.

Another growl, another undulation, and he glides, part perfection, part tease, through my wetness once again.

"Cold," I moan, canting my hips.

"So fucking hot." His answer is rough, his gaze fixed to where we almost join. "I've never. Not like this." His words are halting and strained, their significance rocking through me and rattling my brain.

Maybe I shouldn't trust him. Many women wouldn't. *A man with his past*. But if I can trust him with my heart, my daughter's heart, I can trust him with my body.

I'm so wet that, with the smallest change in angle, I know he'd slip inside.

"I want you. Need to feel you," I whisper as I move instinctively against him, my insides yearning to be stretched by him.

"Are you on the pill?" My scent lingers on his fingers, and as he tips my chin, bringing my gaze up to his, I shake my head. "This is madness." His jaw tightens, but he doesn't move.

"Welcome to my world because this is how you make me feel." My words are soft and a little taunting as I slide my heels and my hands around him. "Unhinged."

"Angel, there's no going back after this."

"So fuck me, Carson. Make me yours right now."

His hips rock forward. The look on his face is one I'll

remember forever, and I could listen to the sound he makes on a loop.

"Oh, yes!" I hold him there, the beginning of my orgasm fluttering around him as he breathes heavily into my neck. A moment later, he pulls back and thrusts slowly back in.

"Look at how we fit," he rasps. "You were made for me, sweet girl." His hands anchored to my hips, he begins to punctuate his thrusts with words of desire and words of love as he builds a rhythm with each snap of his hips.

I'm lost to the feel of him, the possession in his hold, and the words falling almost incoherently from his lips. *You're mine. I'm never letting go. This is forever.* I swallow the words down, storing them in my heart as my insides spiral and pulse harder than ever before.

"That's . . . that's it," he rasps.

I cry out. I plead. I come apart. And when the world returns, I know only Carson's arms, his hands on my face, and his lips whispering the promises of lifetimes. A moment later, his movements turn erratic, and then I feel the loss of him as he pulls back. I look down to where he holds himself in his hand the second before he begins to lash my lacy stocking tops with the ropes of his climax.

29

CARSON

I wake bathed in sunshine and the possibilities of the day . . . and with a small, dark-headed child staring at me from the end of Fee's bed.

"Good morning, princess." I push myself up against the pillows, brushing away the hair that's fallen into my eyes.

"Why are you sleeping in Mummy's bed?" She suddenly sounds very English and has the kind of intonation that sounds very much like, "Off with his head!" which is a worry. I'm very fond of both of my heads, and I wouldn't like to part with either.

"Why am I sleeping in Mommy's bed?" I repeat, wondering what the G-rating answer for this question would be. My gaze slides to her mother lying on her back, her arms spread wide because the woman is a fucking bed hog. Her blonde hair covers her face like a golden veil, and it seems that at some point during the night, she's slipped on a tank top. As I covertly lift the corner of the cover, I realise that's all she's wearing. Which is one more item of clothing than me.

This could be problematic.

"Yes, that's what I asked. There are lots of bedrooms in this 'partment, so why are you in this bed?" She pokes her forefinger into the mattress. "You have your own bed, and it's not this one."

"Well, it's like I told you. I love your mommy." The words seem to spring from my mouth without any thought. Yeah, I'd told Lulu, but I'd yet to say it to her mother. Well, that's not strictly true. I'd said it last night multiple times. Pressed the words against multiple parts of her body. Various declarations of love and numerous orgasms. It was quite honestly the best night of my life, even if Fee maintained "declarations of love don't count when you're inside me".

Shows what she knows.

"You love her!" Lulu repeats with enough volume to wake Fee, whose body jerks against the pillow before falling straight back.

"Morning, sleepyhead." I smile over at her. Was waking a shock, or was it my words of love?

"Lu?" she croaks sleepily.

"Yep, we have a little company." A little company with a big personality.

Fee sits up with the speed of a jack-in-the-box. "But I set my alarm."

"Apparently, not early enough."

"I turned it off," Lu announces, exceedingly pleased with her bad little self. "When my eyes seed Uncle Carson in your bed. He said he loves you."

"Yep, what she said." I point a finger gun Lulu's way, who giggles loudly and begins to bounce on the bed.

"Does that mean I get a puppy?"

"If you want one," I answer.

At the same time, her mother yells, "No!"

"But does it mean you'll be my daddy now?"

Was the puppy/dad combo some kind of kiddie-level reverse psychology?

"Lu, that's not how—"

"No, that's a fair question," I say, patting Fee's thigh over the covers. She's discomfited. And a little disconcerted. I get it. But I also kind of feel like this has been a long time in coming.

I decide to keep my hand there on her thigh. Because I can. Because life is good.

"You don't want just any old man to be your daddy, Lu."

"You're not that old," she says, her words delivered like a pat to my hand. "You only have very tiny wrinkles." I'm not sure how her squinting is supposed to make me feel better. "And I like you anyway. You make good pancakes."

"At least until the arthritis sets in." Fee snickers, earning her a tickling squeeze. "Stop that!"

"But a daddy needs to have more skills than pancakes."

"Yes, he should also be good at tickles and bouncing on the bed with Mommy."

"Er, sure."

"It's best not to ask," Fee says, leaning in.

"What else should he be good at?"

Fucked if I know. My dad was kind of aloof, loving from an arm's length distance. On the other hand, my grandfather was fucking effusive and so much fun, and look at what a bastard he turned out to be. But I digress.

"I think we should find that out together. Sort of like an interview or an internship for the position."

"So, I'd be, like your boss?" She cocks her head to one side like a terrier.

"No. That's not what he means at all." Fee's accompanying laughter almost seems like a warning.

I turn to her with a smirk. "I thought my days of being a freelancer were over."

"Seriously though, I really don't think you should jump the gun," she replies, a little more serious now.

"You're not getting rid of me. And you and me, princess, are going on a range of potential daddy-daughter dates."

"Dates," she repeats, a little delighted. "Like when Mr Farrow took Mommy to the movies yesterday?"

"No, nothing like that." Her little face falls at my words. "Our dates will be so much better."

"What will we do on our dates?"

"Whatever you like. Name it. We'll spend some time together to see if you like the fit."

"Do you and Mommy fit?"

As Fee smothers her giggle in her pillow, I manage to nod solemnly.

"Very, very well."

"Can daddies make *pain perdu* for breakfast?" she ponders next. French toast by any other name is just as diabetes-inducing, especially if I'm making it.

"For you, I would love to. But do you think I could put some clothes on first?"

"Carson!" Fee's hand swipes out, almost smacking me in my balls.

"*Oof!*"

"Why have you got no clothes on?" the little girl asks, aghast.

"Because he forgot to pack his jammies."

"Carson, you need to bring jammies to a sleepover." Lu holds out her hands, palms up as she speaks as though to say, 'be reasonable'.

Or maybe responsible.

This parenting business is going to be a steep learning curve.

And I can't fucking wait.

"Fuck that, man. No way! You don't get to ring out." Tucker throws the letter down on this desk, ringing the imaginary BUD/S bell three times before leaning back in his chair.

"I'm not ringing out," I answer carefully, crossing over to the window of Tucker's office. The head office of Ardeo is housed in one of the newer buildings off Madison Avenue. Monochrome with Lego-coloured accents and furniture that, other than the sizing, looks like it belongs in a kindergarten. The aesthetic is open and modern and the antithesis of my own mausoleum-like space over at Hayes Industries. "I'm just done."

"But this is your gig—your baby. You're the baller, man!"

"Not anymore."

"You've known this chick for what? Five goddamned minutes?"

"I don't have to explain myself to you. We're not shutting down. Your position—everyone's position is safe."

"But you're the key here, Car. You're the glue that keeps this group of fucking misfits together. And the members, don't forget the members. They're here because of who you are."

"They'll still come."

"Less pussy will, that's for sure."

I ponder the double entendre before deciding I don't care for his meaning either way. "That's your one cheap shot," I say evenly, looking down at the ant-like folks below. "The next one knocks you on your ass."

"Okay," he scoffs.

"And loses you a friend."

"Jeez, okay!" He holds up his hands in a placating gesture. "You're fuckin' serious?"

"As a heart attack." I turn to face him to be sure we're clear.

"You're in love."

I begin to chuckle at his tone and the look on his face. "I think the general convention is to be happy for me, not disgusted."

"Why?" Like a toddler throwing a tantrum, he throws himself back in his chair. "Love is like undergoing a frontal lobotomy," he says, addressing the ceiling.

"If Ardeo ever fails, you can take your words to Hallmark."

"I speak the truth," he says, jack-knifing straight in his seat. "Love, same as having your cranium fucked, robs a man of his ability to function on his own."

"Isn't that the point of love? A bond. Of the chance to be selfless rather than selfish?"

"Now who's interviewing for Hallmark? Love, Car, is nature's way of avoiding extinction. It's a trick. A con. A fucking swizz!"

His words make me think of Lulu. He's not right where she's concerned. If her biological father wanted nothing to do with either her or her mother, then that wasn't love. *His fucking loss*, I think. That kid has enough love in her life without him. And maybe I'll never fill his shoes, but I'll give it my all to fill her heart. In fact, we have a date this afternoon at The Russian Tea Room, just the two of us. That's why I'm wearing a suit and why Lulu is going to wear a pretty dress. It's what afternoon tea dictates. At least, in her book.

I'm just happy she hasn't requested I wear the crown. Because I probably would.

"Question." Tucker's voice brings my attention back to him. "If you're really doing this, how are you splitting your shares? Between the team?"

"Fiduciary concerns overcoming fraternal?"

"We'll always be brothers. That's why, as your second in command, I think you'll be giving them to me." A grin cracks his features, and it echoes on my own face, though for completely different reasons.

"I didn't say I was giving up the money, Tucker. Just my position and, of course, the salary that goes along with it. My share of the profits will still come to me. It's all in my letter of resignation."

"Like you need the money," he grumbles, picking up a pen from his desk.

"You've done okay out of this."

"I've done fucking amazing. But in the words of someone very smart, greed is fucking good. And if I know you, and I do," he says, waving the pen admonishingly. "You'll donate your share of the profits to some lame-ass charity." He knows me so well. "Well, I guess I'd better ask around to see if anyone wants to take over for you."

"As director?"

"No, in the bedroom. You bring in the fancy crowd, sure. But maybe one or two of the other guys wants in on the same action. Give the ladies what they want," he says with all the finesse of a snake oil seller. "Or maybe one of the girls wants in on that action."

"No girls," I find myself growling immediately. "Ardeo isn't that kind of operation."

"That's kind of sexist, Car. What's good for the goose has got to be good for the gander."

"No. Fucking. Girls." A wash of heat crashes over me, my fist balling by my sides, my skin seared by a million hot pins. Anger rarely gets the better of me these days, but it's like a black veil when it does. And right now, I don't feel right. I feel amped, itchy, and uncontrolled. But I can't step outside of myself. Not now. I can't let it get the better of me. Judging by his thoughtful expression, Tucker knows that, too. He's one of the few people who has seen what my temper can do.

"Okay, no girls. No problem," he answers with a shrug as though he doesn't really care either way. He might know about my temper, but he doesn't know about my grandfather. He doesn't know about me. About what my temper did.

I blink heavily, forcing the images, the anger away, and nod decisively, just once. "Good."

"Does she know about you, this woman? About what you do at Ardeo?"

A dozen things run through my head all at once as faces and questions from the past are suddenly staring at me. My parents. My siblings. The last day I spent with my grandfather. Clouds of debris over Manhattan morphing into primitive villages in Afghanistan. People I know, and people I don't. A sea of dusty faces tracked with tears.

"Car? You okay?"

I look up, coming back to the moment, shaking off the clinging thoughts as though they're droplets of water.

"Yeah, I'm fine." Fine, fierce, and hiding things. "She doesn't know. Not everything. She's—the woman I love." I can't bring myself to say her name in his presence, just as I can't bring myself to tell her any of this. The worst of this.

"That's the way, brother. Admit nothing. Deny everything."

Defend the indefensible. Some secrets will stay with me until the day I die.

30

FEE

"I wonder what parents did before the advent of TV." I step out from the laundry room a little drunkenly, tightening my ponytail with both hands, freeing up my boobs from Carson's wandering hands. "Stop that!"

"Come back into the laundry room, little girl. I want to show you something."

"I think I've seen it already," I sing-song back, trying to step away without giggling. Failing on both counts as he pulls my back against his hard chest.

"You haven't seen it enough."

"Really? Didn't my attentions just leave it looking like a deflated pink sock?" I'd only gone in there to get clean socks out of the drier for Lulu when Carson had followed me in. Not that I'm complaining. Not at all.

"Well, now it's hard again. And aching to show you a good time. To make up for lost time."

"Carson . . ." His name is a sigh as I tilt my head, exposing more of my neck to his lips. I really don't have time for this.

Maybe just a few more minutes . . .

"You know dropping pants and panties to the laundry room floor is totally acceptable."

"Yes, but I'm not sure you're supposed to be still in them the moment before they hit the floor."

"My laundry room, my rules. We just have to thank God and Goofy for creating cartoons," his low voice rumbles even as he pushes me against the sink. His body follows, coating mine like a second skin.

"Will that be her excuse to her teacher when she's late for school?"

"She can tell her the dog ate her mother."

"That's supposed to be homework."

"Well, this dog is going to eat you."

"Then he'd better do it quickly," I rasp, pushing my bottom back against him. "Because we have about five minutes before Lulu comes to look for us." I begin pulling at my T-shirt, freeing space for his hands. "Wait. Over here." Shuffling towards the island, I practically drag Carson with me. "I'll be able to see Lulu come in from here."

"We could always go back into the laundry room," he purrs. "I'll keep my foot against the door and switch the drier on."

"Yes, because that worked out so well yesterday. *Oh, yes!*" I spread my legs as his hand slips down my stomach and into my knickers. I think my eyes might roll back in my head just a little. "Not that I was the noisy one."

"Only because it's hard to be loud when your mouth is full."

"Twice in two days. I think you're developing a laundry room fetish, Mr Hayes."

"My fetish is for any room you're in. More specifically, getting you naked in any room you're in."

"You're a wicked, wicked man."

"But I'm your wicked man."

And this is a situation I'm perfectly okay with.

In the past two weeks, I've come to know the many facets of Carson. First and foremost, he seems to live to tease me. He also seems to live his life without much drive for work. I guess that's what comes from being born into the kind of money I know nothing about. I'll admit, it's been hard to get my mind around our differences in this respect. I've worried about introducing him to my family and haven't involved him in our weekly family FaceTime call. My dad is a foreman who works in construction, and my mum is a nurse, so we don't exactly move in the same circles. Of course, I reason that he's good to me and good for and to Lulu. My heart just melts watching the pair interact. Lulu has yet to call him anything other than Uncle Carson or Uncle Car, and I'm fine with that. It's way too soon, even if it does feel sort of right. The pair are like a mutual appreciation society, and in the apartment, where one can be found, so can the other.

But then I've found myself watching Carson when we're out and about—when we're at a coffee shop or in the park with Lulu—and I see the very real way he interacts with people. He's just a regular guy. No airs, no graces, and no interest in throwing around his status or wallet. He's just extra smart and charming and a little more annoying than the regular kind of man. As well as being built like a Greek god with a dirty mind and oodles and oodles of stamina.

He's a good man.

The best of men, even.

I can say that now, now that I know about the reasons behind Ardeo. It started as a way for him to help his men.

I mean, I didn't even know he was in the military. Of course, now I know where his military bearing comes from and those broad, broad swimmer's shoulders. I kind of wish he still had his uniform. I'd totally be into that kind of role-play. Because, yes, we've dabbled with a little of that. He's insatiable. And *so* creative. And seems to have a sixth sense about what I want when it comes to the bedroom. *Want, need, even just think about!*

As for how he's conducted his life, never engaging in a relationship, and confining his sex life to Ardeo nights? Maybe he's right to draw comparisons between us. We'd just been guarding our hearts by different methods.

We've talked about so much, and I know we've still got a lot to learn, but he's promised me a lifetime. Perhaps it'll happen, or maybe it won't, but I can't ever see a time when I'll regret taking a chance on him. A chance on us.

"What are you doing . . ." Elbows on the marble countertop, I glance behind me. Then down. "Oh."

"Oh," he repeats, though not in the same tone. His eyes are alight with wickedness as he hooks his thumbs into the sides of my yoga pants, pulling them down along with my underwear. "I think we'll leave them here," he murmurs as they reach my knees.

"We haven't got time to mess aro—*uund!*"

My insides flame as his hand connects with my flesh. Not my bum, though there has been a good deal of spanking going on the last few weeks. I've found I'm really quite into being spanked and stroked and manhandled by his big hands. He even once pulled me over his knee. But this. This is something different as his slap lands squarely between my legs. The sensation radiates from my clit to my stomach and my breasts, exploding from the top of my head.

"I knew you'd like that."

"I didn't—" Denials are quick to my tongue and pointless as he slides two fingers deep inside me. I'm on my toes immediately, rolling my lips together to mute my pleasure as he twists his wrist, then pulls them out.

"You didn't what?" he asks smugly, causing me to turn my head over my shoulder. "Just look at the mess you've made of my fingers. You didn't like it, not even one little bit?"

"You are evil."

"Not yet I'm not." He watches me with the kind of intensity that makes my vision go a little hazy. "Just wait until I try the spatula."

"You really shouldn't say those sorts of things." I'm aware of the almost wanton drop in my tone.

"Why is that?" he asks oh, so reasonably.

"Because I might drag you into the laundry room and tie you go to the washing machine . . . with my stockings."

"That sounds kinky. Count me in."

His hands move over the roundness of my bottom, the light of something devilish lurking there. My breath halts in my throat as I anticipate what he's about to do, the sensation, the sensation unravelling, my body tilting of its own accord to help him. As I drop my head to my arms, a groan expands my ribs against the edge of the island as he presses his mouth to my centre, causing heat, white-hot and sudden, to pulse through me.

The sounds I make are raw and plaintive, though I try to muffle them against my arm as his tongue begins to swirl magically.

Manically?

Wonderfully.

"Oh, my God. Yes, like that!" I moan, pushing back

into his face, my arms reaching out, my fingertips pressing against the cool marble.

"Sweet girl, you are so lush and so ripe—"

"What's lush tripe?"

Carson's tongue stills, and my head whips up, finding myself looking into the face of my daughter. We're pretty much eye level as she sits on a high stool on the other side of the island, peering at me like a sparrow perched on a branch.

"T-tripe means rubbish. That's what Grandpa says." Where the words come from, I have no idea as my heart begins to bounce around my ribcage like a skinhead on speed.

"What are you doing?" Elbow pressed to the marble, she cups her cheek to her hand.

"What are *you* doing?"

"Asking for milk and cookies." She smiles cheekily, almost like she knows she's got me over a barrel. Or rather that Carson has me over a kitchen island while my yoga pants are around my knees.

But she can't know that. *The world is not that cruel.*

"For breakfast?"

She nods.

"Well, I'll think about it," I answer, acting as though the fact Carson is on his knees while my daughter barters with me is no big deal.

"Stop!" His tongue flicks over my butt cheek, and I squeak.

"I didn't do noffin'," she complains. "Why are you wiggling? Have you got worms? When Poppy had worms, she got all wriggly. And she kept licking her bum. Remember?"

"I am not licking my bum." Someone else happens to

be doing it for me, his breathless chuckle tickling my skin. I lash out with my foot and try not to fall as Carson's fingers wrap my ankle. "I'm also not a golden retriever."

"Can I have cookies?"

"Go and sit down. I'll bring them in."

"Yay!" Lulu scrambles down from the stool and skips off in the direction of the door, pivoting as she reaches it. "Oh, Uncle Carson? Could you pass Mommy my pink cup? It's in the cupboard you're looking in. I hope there's no lush tripe rubbish in it!"

"Well, fuck." Like a meerkat peeking from its burrow, Carson's head pops over the countertop. "Do you think she saw anything?"

I shake my head as I try not to laugh at his expression.

"If she had, she'd be asking some very awkward questions about your chores!"

After an unhealthy and hurried breakfast (contrary to Carson's assertion, oatmeal cookies are not the same as a bowl of oatmeal), we leave the apartment together, Lulu and me parting from Carson at the entrance. He's off for a run in the park while Lulu and I are dressed for school and work, respectively. Two of us are dressed for the weather, and one is dressed to be thoroughly objectified. And not just by me, as his thin T-shirt clings to him like a second skin.

"I hope you run fast."

"Why?" he asks with a quizzical smile.

"I don't like the idea of you being caught. You know, I could hang my coat from these nipples," I whisper as he pulls me in for a kiss, unable to resist tweaking one as I slide my already chilled hands between us.

"Don't start something you can't finish," he says, wagging an admonishing finger.

"Spoilsport." His smile turns wolfish.

"How do I look?" I turn my head over my shoulder, making sure Lulu is still chatting to the morning doorman, whose name I don't know. I'm not fishing for compliments but asking about my lipstick after Carson had kissed me more than was appropriate for a morning goodbye.

"Well, your eyes are glistening, and your cheeks are a pretty pink."

"Ah, but which cheeks?"

"Naughty girl." He towers over me, making me feel all kinds of dainty and girly and giggly as I find myself blinking up into his mock-admonishing expression.

"That's a very serious face, Mr Hayes," I purr.

"I just can't believe my good fortune, Ms Fee." This man kills me with sweetness and orgasms in quick succession. "I was just thinking you look beautiful this morning. Much too attractive." His eyes flick over me hungrily. "The sum of these parts too well put together."

"Too attractive?" I can feel my eyebrows creeping up my face as I struggle to hold in my amusement. "You'd prefer me to look like something the cat dragged in?"

"Yes. That's what I'm thinking." He grasps the lapels of my jacket, pulling me in for one last press of his lips. "A little tousled and well ridden might keep the competition away. You know what that means?" I shake my head even though my body seems to get it. "I'll just have to try a little harder tomorrow."

A tiny explosion of delight spreads from my chest to my face.

"Practise tonight?"

"I'll bring dinner."

This man only gets better and better.

"Do you think we should tell Rose?" I ask suddenly. "Maybe call her tonight? Tell her over the phone?"

"Your call." He shrugs as if the question doesn't matter to him at all. And just like that, the last tiny threads of anxiety snap. I wasn't really worried that he fancied her still, was I? At any rate, I'm not now.

"No. I think we should tell her together when she's here next month."

"Sounds good to me. I should bring earplugs because there will be screaming."

"At you or at me?" I ask sweetly.

"She'll go full girly mode. Glue our names together. You know, like a portmanteau."

"You're so full of it." I narrow my eyes playfully. "Feeon. The cool kids call that a ship."

"Whatever, it has a terrible ring to it." He bops his finger against my nose before turning and holding out his arms. "Hey, Lu."

Lulu's eyes light up, then she fist bumps the doorman before launching herself into Carson's arms. "Be good for your mommy?"

"Yep!"

"And learn all the things today at school." She gives an affirmative nod before pressing a kiss to his cheek. "That's my princess," he says, setting her feet to the ground.

My happy little Lulu turns before swinging back to face him again.

"Uncle Car? If I'm a princess, what does that make Mommy?"

His smile spreads slowly, rich and sweet and reminding me of spilled honey.

"Why, that's easy. She's the queen of my heart."

I'm first into the office this morning, which makes a change. Who would've thought the positive effect Carson has on my life would extend to my timekeeping? Not that the issue was wholly mine to begin with, but he certainly incentivises waking earlier in the morning. Waking before a certain little girl. Also, an extra pair of hands is very welcome in our morning quest to get to school on time. And Lulu really is a much nicer child to be around when she's not plonked in front of a bowl of cereal or a slice of toast, it turns out. But it's more than that, because Carson just seems to have a way with Lulu. The man could charm birds from the trees. The female ones, at least. His appeal probably transcends the barrier of species.

"You're far too happy for a Wednesday morning."

I'm sorting out my desk drawer when Beth walks into the office, her smile taking any sting, perceived or otherwise, from her words. I won't say we're getting along any better, but we do make an effort. We're professionals, after all. We also just happen to be different people with a different sense of what's acceptable. Live and let live, I guess. And people who throws stones should avoid living in glass houses.

"It's halfway to the weekend," I reply cheerfully.

"And that's why you were humming a Taylor Swift song when I came in?"

"Was I?" I run a few bars through my head. Story checks out, Fluffing hell! "It seems I was." I can't hold onto my smile, the goofy thing feeling like it's taking over half of my face.

"It must be love. Or at least, amazing sex."

"I'm sorry?" I feel the smile almost freeze to my face.

"I've been back to Ardeo since that night, did you know?"

"How would I know?" I answer carefully. Why is she bringing this up? This is a topic we've purposely danced around with since then but never discussed. I thought it was by some kind of silent agreement that, after that night, she'd realised we hadn't spoken about it, not because of a lack of opportunity but because I wasn't comfortable discussing it. Because I didn't want to be reminded that she'd deceived me, because I didn't want to hear the details of her night, but most of all because I didn't want to share my own night.

"It wasn't here in the city. As well as exclusive, the events tend to be a little elusive. Announced last minute and in all kinds of places all over the world." That isn't something Carson mentioned to me, but why would he? Neither of us would have drawn any comfort from that discussion.

"I'm pleased you had a good time." Opening my laptop, I press the power button, hoping to hide behind the pretext of work.

"Well, it was in Aruba last weekend. Who doesn't like a little getaway?" Beth continues, all chatty Cathy as she hooks her coat over the back of her chair before pulling off her woollen beret. *Raspberry-coloured.* "I didn't like the idea of a five-hour flight for just the weekend, but I'm so glad I went." Her gaze seems to turn inward, her tiny smile almost suggestive as she forgets to put away her hat. "What about you?" she suddenly asks.

"What about me? I'm fine. Well."

"Did you find somewhere else to live?"

"Ah. No. At least, not yet." Though I will have to. Or, at least, I suppose I should. You can't really start a relationship off with this kind of dependence. But I'm not going to think about it right now because then I just start thinking about other stuff, like how Rose will react (Amazingly, according to Carson, complete with congratulations and possible confetti cannons) and what we'll do when it's time for me to go back to France, which is something we haven't discussed. "I'm still looking," I add when it becomes clear she's staring at me.

"Listen, Fee." She slides a glance over her shoulder before moving across the office to carefully lower herself into the seat on the opposite side of my small desk. "I never asked you what happened that night. I just assumed you got tired of the guy who was hitting on you and left."

"I did get tired of him. Sick and tired. Did you hear his lines? Vomit inducing." Yes, I'm babbling. I'm also pretty certain she's as aware of my sidestepping as well as I am.

"It's just, well, on Friday, you went to the bagel joint down the street for lunch. You didn't see me, but I was there with my aunt. We were seated at a table in the back," she adds as though to prevent any offence. I might feel the need to express given she didn't make her presence known. *As if.*

"I've become a bit obsessed with their lox bagel." I don't know why I'm telling her this except that I'd like to direct the conversation somewhere else as my stomach begins to ache forebodingly.

"Sure." Beth smiles tightly. "My aunt asked about you.

She said you seemed familiar." I return her smile with a blank look. "And then we kind of worked out between us that she'd seen you at Ardeo."

"Your aunt was there?"

"It's less weird than it sounds. Tessie is my father's younger sister, but she's more like a contemporary. She's how I got my membership. You have to be nominated and seconded."

"Like a country club? No way," I find myself squeaking.

"Kind of, I suppose." She barks out a laugh. "I guess I never realised the similarities. Anyway, Tessie said that night, the night you were there, she saw you go off with someone. I thought you left, but she said otherwise." At this, Beth crosses one knee over the other, straightening her skirt quite primly.

"I did. I'm sorry I didn't say. Believe it or not, I saw someone I knew, and I . . . I left with him."

"Yeah, she saw who you left with. I've got to hand it to you, Fee. Out of all the women who were there that night, I thought you'd be the last to snag Carson Hayes."

I physically flinch. "We shouldn't be talking about this." Because I don't want to. Because it has nothing to do with anyone but him and me. I'm well aware I'm not supermodel material—

"No, sorry, I didn't mean it like that. Why not you? I mean, you're gorgeous. And so is he," she adds hastily.

"Still, that stuff you signed." On my behalf. The words hang awkwardly in the air between us.

"I know, I shouldn't have. But I guess that just means it's not legally binding as far as you're concerned."

"What?"

"The need for secrecy." She waves her hand as though that line of questioning doesn't matter. "The point is, I thought, after the things you said, you'd be the last person to leave on his arm. I said that to Tessie, too."

With a scrap of information, her words become faster in delivery, the knot in my stomach tightening. It's almost as though I know where she's going with this, but how can I? But what my body seems to discern is that this conversation will come to no good. Yet I don't move from my seat, and I don't tell her to shut up.

"I told her I'd invited you without telling you exactly what Ardeo is. I also told her you probably wouldn't have the cash to bid."

"Bid?"

"Yeah. For him. I mean, no offence."

No offence? More like no idea. What is she talking about?

"But then she said he'd cancelled the auction that night, so we were wondering—"

I hold up my hand like a stop sign, and she immediately halts. Bringing it back to my lap, I try to ignore the tremble in my bloodless fingers and how the knot in my stomach is making me feel nauseous. But the hardest thing to ignore is the sense of foreboding that suggest what I'm about to say next will change everything.

"Say that again, please Beth. The bit about money."

"Carson Hayes." Again, she looks over her shoulder as though afraid she'll be overheard. "You mean you didn't know?"

31

CARSON

What is it? What's happened?

I burst in through the front door, the words balanced on the tip of my tongue. I don't know what I'd expected. Maybe noise. Mayhem. God forbid, Lulu crying after some accident.

I need you to come to the apartment. Urgently.

That's what her text had read. So here I am, dashing through an apartment that's as quiet as a mausoleum.

"Fee? Fee, where are you?"

As I stride past the kitchen, the sounds of something shattering overlays the sound of my harsh breathing. I find her in her bedroom with a suitcase open on the bed, a duffel bag next to it, and Fee in the middle of the floor wrapping her hand in a scarf.

I'm on my knees next to her in an instant, her hand cradled in mine. "That's a lot of blood," I say, unravelling the scarf. A framed picture of her parents lies on the rug, shards of glass sticking out from it. "What's wrong?" I'm not talking about the smashed glass. I'm asking about the bags. Is someone ill? Does she need to get home? "Angel, tell me what happened."

"You ruined everything."

My gaze drifts to the smashed frame even though I know that's not what she's talking about. But maybe I'm still fooling myself as I bring my fingers to her chin, tilting her gaze to mine. What I see there makes my stomach twist with anxiety. With guilt. I should say something, deny whatever it is she thinks she knows, but my thoughts scatter like marbles rolling around the floor because I know what that look means. I've seen betrayal. Suffered it. The clarity of the situation is suddenly blinding. I'm a fucking idiot for thinking I could hide this from her.

Did I refuse to tell her to save her the pain or me?

My second thought? *Whoever fucked me over, I'll fucking murder them.*

"You ruined it," she repeats, tears tipping over her eyelids. Her hands push at my shoulders as she scrambles to stand, her body heaving with silent sobs as she leaves me on the floor. She turns her back to me as she begins shoving T-shirts and underwear into the ruck, the duffel bag. A wave of nausea washes over me as I drag myself up and follow her. What the fuck do I say? I have no defence. My body works on pure need and instinct as I press myself against her, my lips at her temple as I bring my hands over hers, stilling them.

"Don't," she whispers, snatching them back, stumbling away from me. "I don't want you to touch me."

A fist squeezes around my heart, turning it to dust. She knows. She knows, and there isn't a damned thing I can do about it. Except maybe tell her the truth. All of it.

"I need you to listen to me, Fee. I know you're angry—"

"I'm not angry!" she yells, whipping around to sear me with a glare that would make Medusa proud. "I'm hurting. You hurt, hurt—" Her words falter, draining away. Her neck moves as she swallows, her expression hardening in the blink of an eye. "I just don't know which hurts more. That you lied to me or that you could think so little of yourself."

"It's not like that," I answer flatly, my next words rising in force and volume. "If you would just give me a minute, a moment of your fucking attention to explain!"

"A minute of my attention? There has been nothing but you for weeks! You have consumed my every thought—you saw to that! You could've had any minute," she says, flinging out her arm, her voice brittle and brimming with pain. "Any minute out of so many to tell me the truth. To explain. Instead, you decided for me. You chose ignorance, but instead, someone else sought to enlighten me to the fact that the man I love screws women for money." Her voice cracks, her expression fucking wretched. "Tell me it's not true."

I wish I could. I would lie to her in a heartbeat to unsee the way she's looking at me. To hear that most glorious of admissions under different circumstances.

She loves me. I'd felt it in my heart, but I'd yet to hear the words. And now this. Now fucking this.

"Who told you?"

"That's the question you ask?" Her sadness crushes me.

I pivot away from her, pacing across the room because if I don't, I think my need to hold her might only serve to hurt her. Not that I would ever . . . but I need to explain, and she needs to hear me, but I can't trust myself to touch her.

I roll my neck and stretch my shoulders, everything feeling too tight. I could crawl out of my own fucking skin as I slip the jacket from my back, hurling it across the room to a chair.

"You're not leaving." My words are low and filled with fury. Not at her but that she would leave, my shoes scuff against the floor in my haste. In my panic. But she doesn't acknowledge me. Not even as I prop my hands on my hips to stop myself from touching her. To stop myself from crowding her in. "Not until we talk."

"The time to talk has passed." She swipes up a hairbrush, tossing it to the open case, picking up a small box next. "There's nothing left to say."

"The fuck there isn't," I snarl, snatching the box out of her hand. "You don't understand—"

"How could I?" She snatches the box back. "How could I understand how you could do this—hide this? I've spent most of the morning wondering what this means. Hours of constant thinking until my head ached, and I still can't make any sense of it—not one fucking bit!"

"So listen to me!" I pluck the box once more from her hand and throw it across the room.

"Go on then. Tell me it's not true. Tell me you haven't fucked women for money."

"I can't."

She lifts trembling fingers to her lips to stifle a tiny sob. Her pain is like a punch to my solar plexus.

"Nothing you can say will make this better. Will make this go away. You screwed women for money. You, who could already buy half of Manhattan. I know you don't have a self-esteem issue. Is it an addiction? How many times—"

"No. No," I add stronger, my hands cupping her face,

my heart screaming out for her to see the only thing I'm addicted to is her. Is making her happy. Loving her and Lulu. "It wasn't like that. And I haven't . . . not once. Not since you."

"Yes, I hear it's making the Manhattan elite very unhappy," she says with a watery laugh. "The women, at least. Was it just for kicks? Do you get off on it?"

"In the beginning. A long time ago." *But that's not why*, my mind screams as I swipe my thumbs under her eyes, wiping away her tears.

"Poor impulse control?" Her eyes flick between mine as though trying to discern the truth, her next words so very cold. "But that's not you, is it? You're all about control."

"Fee . . ."

"I mean, just look at me, still living here. Because you manipulated me. Because you planned for me to be here. Tell me that's not true."

"I wanted you here, yes."

She jerks away, snatching up a shirt as she begins to fold it carelessly. "And you made sure it happened because Carson Hayes always gets what he wants. Doesn't he?" Her head swings around, her expression arctic. "What kind of a man professes to love a woman yet treats her like this?"

"If you just listen to me, I'll tell you," I roar. But she doesn't waver, doesn't shake, continuing calmly on with her folding.

"Would you? Would you really?" Her tone is almost conversational, but I hear the tremor in it. See how her hands shake. "How could you possibly explain your manipulation? How you've shown me just enough care and attention to keep me here? Just enough truth to make me think I was getting to know you. The man I met five years ago."

"What the hell are you talking about?" I'm not that man anymore. I wasn't allowed to be. But with her, I hoped I could be.

"I listened as you told me how Ardeo began. I tried to put myself in your place, watching your friends suffer, no longer fighting for their country but fighting for their place in the world. Some of them fighting for their lives still, and some their sanity. I told myself you did an admirable thing, that you gave them an income and a purpose, or even just giving them one more day where they wouldn't crash their cars or blow out their brains.

"But this. This I can't understand. There is no way to make this anything other than sordid and wrong. You, Carson." Her gaze sweeps me up then down. "How . . ."

The answers I have, the things I could tell her, turn to dust on my tongue.

"How could you possibly explain how you cheated me out of the lease on my apartment?" She swipes angrily at her tears, her voice suddenly stronger despite them. "How could you justify lying to my face while manipulating the situation to suit you?"

"That's not what that was. You don't know the Aarons. They're fucking ruthless."

"You're right. I don't know them. And I don't know you."

"You do. You know I love you. You know I'd do anything for you."

"Except tell me the truth. Maybe you only love the idea of love. And while we're on the subject of the Aarons, they certainly seem to know you. One of them in particular."

Dread suddenly clings to me like a wet towel.

Tess Aaron.

I fucked her last fall. The fuck of her life, as she later described it. The bidding reached fever pitch, and after a month of bids and counterbids, she won. The deed was done over the course of a couple of hours, and as a consequence, Rose's foundation got a substantial donation. Anonymously, obviously.

"Please. Just sit down and let me explain."

"I thought you didn't kiss and tell. It's against the rules, isn't it? Did you really think those rules would protect you? That they'd hide your shame?"

"Fuck you."

"No, I don't think I will anymore. I can't afford you."

32

FEE

I come slowly to consciousness, wrapped in warmth, the backs of my eyelids coloured pink and gold as stained by the sun, almost like I'm waking from a nap in the garden in France.

I stretch my feet to the end of the bed, the cold sheets a shock to my bare legs and toes. Then a car horn honks somewhere in the distance, another louder and more angry following. A garbage truck trundles under the window, tyres wet against the road. Plastic scrapes, tin and glass clattering, pulling me from my pleasant dreams. Sand, sunshine, and Carson.

"*Oof!*" I take a sock to the gut and, when I reach for the cause, find Lulu's heel embed in my abdomen. It's the last straw, the thing that jerks me awake, pulling me from sleep, pushing away my dreams and replacing them with a not so pleasant reality.

I groan as I roll over, peeling my swollen eyelids from eyeballs that feel the size and texture of tennis balls. It wasn't sunshine that coloured my lids but the pendant light hanging above the bed I forgot to switch off. And the warmth cosseting me was the heat of my daughter.

But today is different because at least I haven't jerked awake with panic, my heart beating out of my chest and the sheets slicked in a cold sweat. Does that mean things are getting better? What stage of grief am I at now? Past denial, I think. Still swimming in anger, sadness. Fighting futility.

My feet touch the floorboards, the air around my bare legs frigid as I make my way to the bathroom, grabbing a sweater on the way and resolving to avoid my reflection in the mirror. I made the mistake of looking yesterday. It wasn't pretty, and it just made me want to cry more. And without meaning to sound clichéd, this last week I have cried a river. Mostly in the privacy of this cold bathroom so as not to make Lulu worry any more than she has. I've never felt more foolish or more wretched.

Or more alone.

I pee. Wash my hands. Go back to the bedroom to shove some clothes on, remembering to switch off the light this time. I fill a cup with water in the tiny kitchen and shove it into the microwave because my kettle is still at Carson's.

I almost can't believe I thought I'd be happy here in Beth's sister's apartment. Not that I can muster any cheerful thoughts as far as this move is concerned. The thermostat is on the blink, and November in New York is no bloody joke. But it's not even that. I'd accused Carson of manipulating me, of being the worst kind of human, yet I'd still taken the keys for this place from his hand when he'd proffered them. It had felt like the final nail in the coffin of our relationship as I'd curled my hand around them.

I'd railed and yelled when he'd asked where I'd go. Told him I'd rather live under a bridge than stay one more minute in any place that was his. Dramatic, right? But what else is there to conceal a heart and eyes that were bleeding infinite sadness.

I'd probably have booked us into some cheap hotel, but even through my rage, through my haze of grief, I knew the solution was only temporary.

So I swallowed my high-handed ideals and put my daughter first.

But we're not staying here. We can't. Even if I don't know where the hell to turn. Next week, I have four shifts in Marta's brother's bar. I'd forgotten all about it until he'd called. Sophia will come home with Lu and me to help out, and I've agreed to pay her Uber fare home with her cousin. The money will help, and it'll give me something else to concentrate on in the evenings when Lulu is asleep.

It'll stop me from fixating. Imagining. Seeing him. Seeing him with women. His hands and lips and smiles no longer for me. How many women were there? Did he enjoy it? Did they? *Of course they did.* How fucking could he? How could he taint himself like that? How could he think that he could keep it from me? How could I—

I force my mind in another direction. These are the things I contemplate in the darkness, a madness I can only allow to reign while Lulu sleeps.

I'm worth more than this, I remind myself.

I have an example to set.

I made a mistake in opening my heart to the wrong man.

It doesn't define me.

It only crushes me.

"Mommy, this 'partment is so cold."

"I know, sweets." I turn to find Lulu at the doorway. Wild hair and pink pyjamas, fluffy socks that have wriggled their way down her ankles, making her look like she's wearing long clown shoes. I snatch her up and carry her into the living room, covering her with a throw. Apparently, Ally has someone coming to look at the thermostat "soon", whatever that means. "Want milk and cookies for breakfast?"

"It's Saturday," she says, her voice brimming with recrimination because she knows the cupboards are practically bare. I haven't had the bandwidth for a full grocery shop and left our small pantry of staples with my kettle.

"We'll go out for pancakes. And hot chocolate. How about that?"

"Can Uncle Car come with us?"

"He's still away on business."

"And his 'partment is still broken?"

"Yes, his apartment is still broken." I'd told her there was a flood, and that's the smallest of the lies I've fed her. But I'll tell her the truth this weekend. Or some semblance of it. I guess I was just giving myself enough time for it to sink into my own head.

"You promise my bedroom will be okay?"

"Yes, I promise." If okay means empty.

I'm pleased I'd saved the news that Rose will be here in less than a week, along with Remy and Rocco and the rest of their entourage. I'm not sure how I'll handle it myself. I can't see how I can tell Rose what happened between Carson and me, not without telling her I'd kept that night secret all these years. How could I tell her that the man she regards almost as highly as her husband has screwed women for money? Would she believe me? She'd certainly be as confused as me. As hurt. As disgusted. Maybe that makes me a hypocrite as someone who has always championed choice because not only do I not understand his choices but I also don't get his motivation.

Why? With all the blessings the world has bestowed on him, why would he do this?

The only thing I can come up with is he did it for kicks. And maybe that's why he couldn't tell me.

I'll think of what to tell Rose another day and just concentrate on how good their visit will be for Lulu. It'll be something else for her to concentrate on when I break the news that Carson is no longer going to be a part of our lives.

That there will be no more Lulu-Carson dates.

That there will be no puppy.

No potential daddy.

She'll learn that men are a disappointment earlier than most of us. That they do indeed 'suck big hairy ones'. I blame myself for that.

33

CARSON

I can't bear to look at you.

It's the last thing I hear before I drift off to a liquor-aided sleep and the first that whispers to me in the morning.

God, I miss her. I fucking miss them both.

And I've no idea what to do about it. What can I do? Send flowers? A bunch? A hundred? A field full? How many bouquets say, *please forgive me. I can't be without you*?

What about diamonds? Fucking poetry. Do I prostrate myself at her feet?

I'd do it all. Give her anything. But what good would it do when she won't even look at me?

I've tried. I've begged. I've called. I've turned up at her door.

"*Don't do this, Carson,*" she'd whispered. "*Don't do this to Lulu. Don't confuse her more.*"

And she was right. I'd turned into that fucking man. The weak one who operates from a place of selfishness, not selflessness. *And that's not supposed to be how love works.*

What good would it do because I was fucking wrong. I

should've told her the truth long before now. Explained the unexplainable.

Days pass, turning into night and back again. I don't go to work. I barely function. I stay in my hotel suite, not my apartment. And think I eat, but mostly, I run. Nowhere to be and no one waiting for me, I run. And, as has become my habit, I always find myself in the same place.

Outside that fucking apartment.

The apartment I paid for, a hateful part of my brain whispers. But what choice did she have after I left her with so little? She wasn't going to stay with me, not at that point, according to her, not anymore. She could barely fucking look at me and was running away. Just like before. Just like always. But she didn't have to run to some flea pit hotel, and I know she wouldn't have turned to Rose.

I stand across the street, neither dressed for the chill nor feeling it, like some sad sack just waiting for the light to come on. Just to see the silhouette of her against the window.

The way she looked at me.

The hurt and regret.

The way she shrank from my touch.

It's nothing more than I deserve.

When the drapes draw closed, signalling she's in for the night, that she's safe, I run again. Through the streets of Manhattan, dodging pedestrians, cars, and cabs on my way back to the hotel. Tonight, with each pound of my feet against the pavement, my rage grows and builds, the image of what my life could've been running through my head on a loop.

Kisses with a hundred meanings. A thousand reasons to hold hands. And only one motive to tell her I love her, over and over again.

Because I do. Because I always will.

I see her expression, the hurt I caused. The pain.

A lifetime of moments stolen.

And this, this is what I grieve for. This is what roils my stomach, powering my legs faster and faster until the muscles burn, until the frigid air turns my throat raw and I want to scream at the injustice of it. Because yes, this is my fault, but the cause is *him.*

He's not even here, yet I hate him still.

Penance. Punishment. Penance. Punishment.

My feet pound against the pavement, my skull thudding until it's fit to burst, on and on until I'm panting and sweating and shaking like a fucking idiot, crouched outside my hotel.

That she can't bear to look at me is little wonder.

I can't stand it myself.

"Where the fuck have you been?"

"I thought I said I wasn't to be disturbed." My voice is void of inflection and I don't bother to look up from my laptop as the door bursts open with such force, it almost collides with the wall.

Immediately, Tucker begins to laugh like I've just repeated the funniest joke ever heard.

"Did you not hear him out there, cussing up a storm because I told him you didn't want to see anyone?" Aimee follows him in, her tone aggrieved.

"Yet here he is," I murmur, trying to absorb the information in front of me, because this morning I'd decided I was done with letting Fee dictate the terms of this breakup. I'd decided I respect her opinion but not her pussy-assed way of doing things. She can be disgusted, ashamed for and because of me, but she will listen to what I have to say before she decides she wants nothing more to do with me.

Which is obviously not the outcome I'm counting on.

She found out. I should have told her. But now there are no more lies between us. And sure, love is supposed to be selfless, but I've decided if I allow her to walk away, then I'm doing her a disservice because no man will ever love her the way that I can.

Conceited? She'd better fucking believe it.

"I'm your assistant, not your guard dog," Aimee snaps the minute before the door slams again. This time, closed.

"Why, Carson. Could it be your winning streak with women is over?" Tucker retorts with an amused glance behind him. "They normally come running into the rooms you're in, not the other way around."

I scan the remains of the email from Ed Martinez, which finishes with the pronouncement that he's uncomfortable spying for me. What a joke. If anyone is spying on my behalf, it would technically be Sophia, as it would be inappropriate for me to contact the girl directly. Therefore, Ed is our intermediary. But fuck it, if spying is a wish to keep the people you love safe, then I'm the guilty one. Not them.

I jot down the name of the bar his daughter says Fee will be working in next week and close my laptop before sitting back in my seat.

Pretty bartenders attract all kinds of assholes.

Maybe I'll add myself to that list.

"What do you want?" I settle a little deeper into my chair, steepling my fingers under my chin.

"Well first, I guess I want you to stop with that cold superior fucking look. That shit doesn't wash with me."

"Tucker, I don't have time for this."

"Brother, the way I see it, you've got nothing but time."

"And you discern that how?" Screw superior looks. How about a superior tone, asshole?

"You're not answering your phone or your emails, and your personal assistant out there has been giving me the runaround for days."

"Not nearly well enough," I retort, gesturing to his presence with a flick of my hand.

"You look like shit, Hayes."

"Thanks for your concern," I reply deadpan.

"Actually, if shit took a shit, it would look like you." Ignoring me, he drops into the chair on the other side of my desk. "I'm guessing by your sorry assed expression that the thing with the girl fell through."

I don't answer. I'm pretty sure I don't move.

"You know, if you tap that finger any harder, the fucker will snap off," he asserts with a smirk.

I curl my hand into a fist.

"If there's a point to you being here, I'd love to hear it. You know, right before you leave."

"I've been worried about you," he says baldly.

"I don't know why. We can go weeks without talking."

"Days, asshole. And only when you're travelling. Which you're clearly not," he adds, suddenly pissy.

"Spit it the fuck out, whatever it is you feel you need to say."

"That look you're wearing? I know it. And I know the feeling behind it. She's gone, right? The love of your life, whoever she is, because you didn't think to introduce her to me. The person who isn't supposed to forsake you, forsook."

"Did someone buy you a dictionary?"

"Let me put it to you like that Hallmark verse you think I should write." He holds out his hands as though envisaging his words up in neon lights. "This. Too. Will. Pass." Lowering his arms again, the asshole adds nothing else. Not a smile of encouragement. Not a look of sympathy. Nothing.

I fold my arms across my chest. "I thank you for your concern, but I'd thank you more sincerely if you'd leave."

"I forgot to mention that the reason you look like you do is because it passes like a motherfucking kidney stone."

If you've been deployed to a desert theatre, you know first-hand that kidney stones are no joke. But that's not why I don't feel like laughing.

"Car, you've seen what love can do when it goes wrong. I thought that's why you stuck to the auctions and shit. Because you'd seen what love did to me and the others."

"I've never explained my reasons to you. Don't ask me to do so now."

"I'm not asking. I just figured you were the smartest out of all of us. But I guess even the smart ones make mistakes."

I couldn't even begin to explain the mistakes I've made. I'm not sure I could explain them to myself.

"Can you get her back?" he asks.

I would walk over hot coals, tear down the fucking world to make it so.

I need to find a way to explain the unexplainable. To rationalise my actions to a woman who looked at me like I hung the stars and the moon just for her entertainment a few days ago. Now all I see when she looks at me is pity and shame.

"I guess that was a no."

I raise my head at Tucker's assumption. For a moment, I'd forgotten he was in the room. A blessed moment as it happens, as the asshole carries on.

"Sometimes, it's for the best. If you're already seeing cracks in a relationship that's only a few weeks old, it doesn't exactly—"

"Okay, Dr Phil. Say what you need to, then fuck off." Leave me to sort out my own problems. Because there has to be a solution. Some way out of this.

"At least Dr Phil's patients acknowledge their problems."

"Dr Phil's patients also invite his assistance," I retort meaningfully, my patience wearing paper-thin.

"Fuck it. I just wanted to say that what you're feeling right now seems like it's never going to go away. That it'll never get better. Like it's the biggest thing in the world and that you'll never feel joy again."

"Tucker—"

"I'm just here to tell you that you'll get through it." His shoulders rise and fall with a deep breath. "And if you try to tell me you don't know what I'm talking about, then I'm gonna take you outside and administer the ass-kicking of your life. Because friendship goes both ways."

I pause and acknowledge that, in his own unique way, he's trying to help.

"Okay, so how do I make this go away? How does anyone get over feeling like this?"

"There is no making," he says with a sad-looking smile. ""You gotta fake it. Fake it each and every day."

"Pretend I feel okay? That's your big piece of advice?"

"Fake it 'till you make it. And in the meantime, get back on the horse, so to speak."

I huff a half chuckle.

"Think of it as ripping off a Band-Aid. The longer you wait, the more painful it'll be. Casual fucking is where it's at, my friend. All of the pleasure and none of the pain."

"What if I can't move on? What if she's the one for me?"

"We all think that at one time or another. You can't resist her. Can't think of anyone *but* her, like she was made only for you. But then later, you find out she was no siren. She was just a false alarm. Come back to Ardeo. You'll see."

"Those days are over for me. No more auctions. No more money exchanging hands, no matter how altruistic."

"Noble exploits? Is that what you've been telling yourself?"

"What would you call it?" I ask, my voice dark, my hands tightening against the chair arms.

"Car, it was never about donating money to starving kids. It was just a way for you to torture yourself."

34

FEE

Life returns to some semblance of normal, outwardly at least. On the inside, I feel brittle, almost like if someone were to lean on me, I'd shatter into a million pieces. But I don't have to worry about that because I won't let anyone get too close. Not again.

We're settling into a new way of life that's less than perfect, and Lulu makes no bones about her displeasure at the changes. Though I can't blame her, her crabbiness is wearing.

The apartment isn't warm enough.

Agreed.

She hates waking early, and she detests the commute.

So much this!

Her teacher is a poo-poo head.

Mainly because he's not Carson.

She hates sleeping with me.

So I relegated myself to the couch.

New York is stinky, and she wants to go back to France.

That makes two of us, not that I'll admit this out loud to anyone. Mostly, I just want to retreat somewhere I don't have to pretend to be okay. Where I can just hole up until my aching heart heals. Where I can reflect on Carson's expression as he'd stood at the door and come to some conclusion about what it all means.

Why? How?

I want so much to hear him recount all the sordid details until his words make my ears bleed and I can't stand to even think of him anymore.

But I won't ask him. I won't belittle myself. And I won't allow his honeyed barbs to flay my skin. Ardeo is Latin for blaze, according to the internet. I certainly feel like I've been burned. Head down. Plough on. That's the tone of my life going forward.

I remember when I didn't want to move out of the maid's quarters. I'd almost experienced a sense of not belonging on the fancy side of the apartment. That I'd be left with a bill I couldn't pay. That feeling seems almost prophetic now.

There are small signs of improvement in Lulu's mood in the coming days, though they mostly occur when Sophia collects Lu from school. Her help has meant I've been able to go straight to Marta's brother's bar for my five-hour long shifts. I'd agreed to work Tuesday through to Thursday, and he'd offered me the same for the following week. Which is great, except when the first Friday comes along, I find myself on the roster again.

So here I am; day five of a thirteen-hour day.

I remember vividly now what I hated about working in bars. The sticky floors, the drunk customers, the requirement to be nice to people who really don't deserve it.

"What do you mean you're not serving food now?"

I sigh and fix the man on the other side of the bar with

the kind of look I ordinarily reserve for Lulu when she's on the brink of a meltdown.

"Just what I said. As of ten minutes ago,"—I glance behind me to encourage him to see the time for himself —"the kitchen closed."

"This is not fuckin' acceptable," he snarls, pointing a menacing finger my way. Or maybe he thinks it's menacing. Personally, I think it makes him look like a colossal prick. "I want to see the manager."

"Hmm. Me too."

"What?"

"I'd like to see her, too." Mostly to help me load the huge mountain of dirty glasses into the machine, but unfortunately, she seems to be a little work shy and has gone home. I'm not at all sure she's living up to her job title of supervisor unless she's doing it remotely somehow. "I'm afraid you'll have to come back tomorrow. She's what you might call indisposed."

She was also indisposed yesterday when her boyfriend turned up halfway through her shift. She skulked off early then, too. Either the security cameras are just bits of plastic or she's counting on no one ever looking at the footage. But I'm not going to be here long enough to let any of this concern me. Just like I'm not going to let this cockhead spoil my cast iron cultivated zen, either.

Think of the tips, I tell myself. Obviously, not from him.

"I am a fucking regular!"

"And I'm Meghan Markle."

"Meghan?" For a minute, he looks almost to be considering the truth in this. But really, would she be working in some crummy bar on the Upper East Side? In a blonde wig, faking an English accent?

No, I don't think so either.

"Listen, mate, you are a grown man who doesn't even have the excuse of being drunk to blame for his rudeness." Because the rock star has been drinking soda all night. "And you're throwing a tantrum over a Reuben. Sort your flippin' life out." And with that, I walk to the opposite end of the bar.

Zen. Zen. I am so motherfluffin' Zen.

"Has anyone ever told you you have beautiful eyes?"

And . . . there goes my Zen.

I stifle a sigh, not bothering to look up. Instead, I choose to tidy the tray of cocktail shakers, citrus juicers, and muddlers sitting beneath the two feet of mahogany separating me and my smooth-talking compliment-*er*.

Maybe if I ignore him, he'll realise this compliment-*ee* wants no part of his bullshizzery.

"Are they, like, gold or something?"

"Or something," I mutter. It was probably a lucky guess. I doubt he can tell the colour of my eyes in the dim lighting. I'm also far from flattered, given he's the third man to say something similar tonight. Also, it's strange how they all seem to think my *beautiful eyes* are glued to the front of my T-shirt. Anyway, I'm pleased the crowd has thinned out, maybe thanks to an earlier deluge of rain of almost biblical proportions.

I wonder if there's something in the Manhattan water supply that makes beer goggles super effective?

"They're definitely gold. Are you modest or shy? Well, why don't I break the ice by telling you about me."

Oh, go on then. If you must. I mean, it's not like the more you talk, the more you irritate me, is it?

I feel like I should stick my head out of the window to check if there's a full moon tonight because the dogs are out in full force, preening and howling at the bitches. And boy, do I feel like a bitch.

"My name is Kristoff," he says, obviously not picking up on my crumbling Zen. "I'm a single thirty-five Taurus. I enjoy cooking and I love to snuggle, which makes me either perfect or gay. Do you wanna find out which?"

"Absolutely," I say as I straighten, not missing the flicker of surprised satisfaction in his gaze. "My best friend is gay. I could set you up with him."

"What?" Bewilderment ripples across his face. "I'm not . . . gay."

"Really?" My expression twists. "How do you know? You sound pretty confused to me."

"No, you misunderstand. I want *you* to come home with me."

I wipe my beer sticky fingers on the front of my stupid apron as I consider the man in front of me. He's objectively handsome. Well dressed and leanly built, and he has such soulful brown eyes . . . which just goes to show how deceptive appearances can be given the crap he's spouting. But the icing on the cake that is Kristoff might as well be cat-food flavoured as far as I'm concerned.

Don't worry, Kris. It's not you; it's me. I've been ruined for other men by a man out of my price range.

"What do you say?" He cocks one perfectly slim eyebrow in the kind of action that seems to say "I'm perfect rebound material".

Sure you are. At least until I wake up in a bed in a strange hotel suite with not even your phone number for company. Or worse still, discover you sell sex for shits and giggles.

Urgh, men!

"Come on," he says with an amused huff. "I'm into you, I'm handsome and solvent—"

"And your Porsche is the same colour as my eyes?"

"What?"

"Nothing." This time, I don't muffle my sigh. "Look, I don't sleep with men I meet in bars. No matter what side of it I'm standing on. Not even the rich ones." Or the ones pretending to be rich ones.

"I cook a mean breakfast." He adds an eyebrow wiggle that is, quite frankly, baffling. *Go on, love. Let me give you one tonight and I'll chuck in bacon and eggs in the morning!* "You'll need it, because I can go all night long."

I bet he'd eat himself if he could.

"And I have something else that might interest you." He glances down meaningfully. "I'm packing, if you know what I mean."

"Hmm. Let me think about that for a minute." I tap my bottom lip with my forefinger, appearing to contemplate this temptation when the only thing I actually contemplate is how much I suddenly want to jump over the bar and smack him over the head with a stool. "Tell me, exactly *how* well-endowed are we talking about here?"

"Beautiful, I have nine rock-hard inches just for you."

And I have a little vomit in my mouth.

"Is it pretty?" I find myself purring, which is weird, because:

1. Only one person has ever made me feel cat-like.
2. Penises usually have that lump of feckless flesh attached to them called *man*.
3. I've only ever met one pretty penis in my life

(see: point 1) and that was enough heartache for me.

"Pretty?" he repeats. "I've been told so, on occasion."

"Well, Kris. It was Kris, wasn't it?"

"Kristoff." He smiles as I mirror his stance, leaning my elbows against the bar as I find one of the long cocktail spoons in my hand. Just look at him. He totally thinks this is in the bag, and by *this,* I mean me, and by *bag*, I mean his bed.

"Well, Kris, it's like this . . ." I tap the spoon against the bar top, then stroke it a little suggestively for good measure. His eyes avidly follow the motion, rising to mine as I pause. "I'm afraid I find myself in the position of having to decline."

"I like a girl who plays hard to get."

"I'm serious." My shoulders slump, my lips already pursed because I am seriously uninterested and seriously unimpressed.

"Just tell me how you like your eggs in the morning."

"I like them un-flipping-fertilised!" My answer explodes from gritted teeth. "Are your ears painted on because I would rather be poked in the eye with a syphilitic penis than go home with you!" As I get to the end of my outburst, I realise I'm holding the long spoon in what might be considered a threatening way. A *scoop-out-your-eyeball* sort of way.

"Okay, I get it!" Kristoff holds up his hands as though I'm holding a gun to his face, not a bloody spoon. "You're not interested."

"Finally!" Metal clanks against metal as I drop the spoon to the sink. "Now, just . . . go away!"

He scrambles from the chair and I turn to a waiting

customer when my stomach lurches. An acid queasiness washes through me, because that's not a customer sitting at the end of the bar.

It's the devil himself.

Or, at least, the man who recently broke my heart.

I stick my hands into the back pockets of my pants because the urge to grab the paring knife next to the chopping board full of lemons and limes is so tempting.

"Did you not see me almost de-eyeball that creep," I say almost conversationally, coming to a stop in front of the gorgeousness that is Carson Hayes. He's dressed in jeans, an open-necked shirt and a sports jacket. His arm rests casually on the bar top yet his spine is quite straight. An understated though super expensive watch wraps his masculine wrist, his thumb and forefinger bracketing a lowball glass. He looks like he's on a photo shoot for GQ magazine. All he's missing is the backdrop. Maybe an English country house with a vintage Jaguar parked on the drive.

Wait, that's a Taylor Swift music video, right?

Who served him? I'm going to add their name to my murder by spoon list.

How come I didn't sense his presence? Is that not weird? Does it mean I'm getting over him?

My mind is awash with questions, questions I can barely concentrate on for the thundering of my heart.

"I saw." His mouth plays at a smile, not quite giving in.

Oh, man, I played what went on at the other end of the bar all wrong. If I'd realised Carson was here, I might've used Kristoff as a ploy. A *look-at-me-so-happy-and-moving-on-without-you* kind of ploy.

Dammit.

"And that was just for hitting on me. The mood I'm in, imagine what I'd do to someone I really don't like."

"I am imagining." His gaze sweeps over me, and I swear it feels like the brush of fingertips. My nipples stand to attention under my pale T-shirt, poking the sides of my apron. I pull my hands from my back pockets and fold my arms over my chest as I take a deep breath as I remind myself that if there's anyone who needs de-eyeballing in this bar, it's him.

"Well . . . well, just you stop that."

"Stop imagining?" His forefinger and thumb grasp his glass, his voice all silky and smirky and amused—all the things he has no right to be. Not the way we left things. Not the way he turned up at my doorstep days afterwards, looking as desperate and as crushed as I'd felt. As I still feel some moments.

"What are you doing here?" I demand.

"What does it look like?" He lifts his glass in a careless gesture, though the glint in his eyes is anything but casual. "I'm happy to see you can take care of yourself."

"Yes. That's right. I can."

"I'm not sure your boss will see it as a reasonable defence. Isn't the customer always right?"

"Not when he's offering you his dick."

A muscle in his jaw tightens, his answer almost grated from between clenched teeth. "He did what?"

"Didn't you hear? And that wasn't my first offer of the night. Bar tending certainly has its perks when you're trying to get over someone." Number one perk being the large lump of wood between me and him as I continue needling him. "Apparently, he had nine inches just for me."

"I promise you, the only way he'd be able to deliver on that promise would be in instalments."

I burst out laughing, covering my mouth with my hand and hating myself just a little for letting him make me feel any sort of joy.

"I can't believe you'd be impressed by that kind of lame ass pickup line."

"I didn't say I was impressed." And just like that, my mirth stops like a capped tap.

"Were you interested?" he asks. His tone is casual but his expression is tense.

"That's got nothing to do with you. Not anymore." I grab a cloth and begin to wipe the bar top vigorously. Confused doesn't even touch how I feel seeing him here looking all kinds of gorgeous and attentive and possessive. I know I should walk away but I'm also conscious of the attention he's drawing. I'll be gutted, torn apart, if as a result of my goading and feigned indifference he ends up in the arms of the gorgeous brunette sitting a little way down from him. I've been ignoring the dirty looks she's been throwing my way. She's probably praying for a stampede of customers to fall in through the doors. Not that it would matter because we're overstaffed as it is.

But it's not just her. I don't want to surrender his attention to anyone, including the cluster of blondes who've just moved from a coveted table spot to stools at the bar. I guess I could go on, recount the looks he's drawing, as conflict churns inside me, my wrath and indignation swirling and softening like butter. He hurt me and that stings. But he was mine. This man who is as magnificent as the moon, he once shone for me. And now I stand before him, tired and grotty after a very long week. I'm wearing my hair in a messy bun that isn't at all chic and my apron makes me look like a medieval blacksmith. Meanwhile, women who glitter and glow in their Friday night finery await their chance to orbit him.

Once he relinquishes my attention.

Or I his?

"I'm sure you have much better pickup lines." I lift my gaze though not my head, not quite realising what I've said until I notice his eyes widening almost infinitesimally.

He picks up his drink and leans back in his seat, the sudden image of content manliness. *Or maybe smug.* I prepare myself to hear his retort, for words of supreme confidence to fall from his lips. Yet, what he offers tugs at my heart.

"None as good as yours, angel. I do love a girl with a pun."

Love. It's such a tiny word yet it creates such complications.

A girl. One of many. One of the crowd who paid for his attentions in ways more dangerous than money passing hands.

The glass poised at his mouth doesn't hide how his smile falls at whatever he reads in my expression.

"Hey, Fee?" Chad or Brad, or whatever his name is, touches my shoulder. "We're so overstaffed. I'm happy to take one for the team, but Shellie says you've been here every night this week, so do you wanna go?"

"Leave early?" And avoid making more mistakes? Maybe even bigger ones? "Can I?"

"Sure."

"Thank you."

"Wait, Fee." I hear Carson's voice, but I don't stop, and I don't look back.

"Doing the same things and expecting different results is the definition of madness," I find myself muttering as I pull off my apron and shove it onto the top shelf of my temporary locker. As I pull out my purse, my gaze snags on my reflection in the tiny mirror stuck to the inside of the door. "Face it. You have terrible taste in men." I slam my locker door shut on my reflection and head out of the staffroom, and out through the darkened kitchen. No way I'm leaving by the front door, sinister dark alleyway be damned.

I step out into the cold night, slamming the metal security door behind me.

"We should talk."

"Jesus Christ on a bike!" I yell, my body almost jumping out from my skin. "You scared the living daylights out of me," I yell, whipping around angrily.

"Yeah, well. Skulking around back alleyways isn't going to provide the best of experiences." Carson's voice is a low rumble in the darkness.

"The point of skulking," I say, pressing my hand over my hammering heart, "was to avoid you."

"Noted."

"Because I've got nothing to say to you." The remains of my adrenaline spike make my hands shake. At least, that's what I tell myself as I hook my purse higher over my shoulder.

"But I have things I want to say to you." He stands in the centre of the alleyway, his hands in his pockets and his feet planted wide, half of him still in darkness, half in the glow of a nearby streetlight. "Things you need to hear."

"There is nothing you could possibly say to change how I feel." Tightening my hand on the strap of my purse, I bustle my way past, giving him the widest of berths. Yet I find his fingers on my arm anyway. *His fingers on my arm, his heart in his eyes.*

"Maybe not. But would you listen to me anyway? Please?"

I lift my chin in defiance of his words and then, against my better judgment, I nod.

35

FEE

I allow him to lead me to a bar on the opposite side of the street that happens to be a sports bar; the New York version of a spit and sawdust joint. I duck under his arm as he pushes the door open, and slide into a booth by the window. Carson heads to the bar. I glance around at the huge TV screens and the sporting paraphernalia hanging from the walls. It's after ten now, and like the bar I've just escaped, the crowd is sparse.

My eyes are drawn to Carson, my gaze tracing the breadth of his shoulders with the kind of fascination I'm pleased he can't see. A broad back, strong thighs and long legs. The sum of these parts well put together, other parts making no sense at all.

Why, Carson? Why could you let women use you like that?

Is it some kind of kink? Because this isn't any ordinary kind of prostitution, if there is such a thing.

"The wine selection isn't great," he says as he slides a glass of something that appears to be whisky onto the table next to me. He takes the seat across from me, rather than next to me, and for that, I'm grateful. I can't have him invading my space with his cologne and pheromones. It's hard enough just to look at him.

"Is it okay?" he asks as I take a sip from my drink.

I nod, ignoring the clink of the singular cube of ice and the memories it brings. *Cold fingers and warm mouths. The kind of sex you only read about. The kind of connection that speaks of lifetimes.*

I still at Carson's intake of breath. Though I'd prefer not to look at him, I feel like I owe him my attention.

"I want to apologise," he begins. "I know it isn't enough. One tiny word isn't going to take away what I've put you through, but I want you to know that I could only see my own pain when you left. Like the magnitude of what I've done, who I've been, didn't hit me until you were already gone."

I don't know how to answer that, and though I'm normally the type of person who'd rather say something, anything, than leave an awkward, unfilled space, there is nothing I can add here.

Nothing that would make either of us feel better.

"I told you how Ardeo started, how the parties grew into their own entity." I shrug. This isn't something I'm likely to forget, though he bulldozes on. "How it gave the guys something tangible to look forward to. An outlet. A business. Money in the bank. But what I did wasn't part of Ardeo. Not really." Something like regret ripples across his countenance, his attention falling to the glass he's nursing. "I never explained to you about my grandfather."

"Please don't tell me this is a family concern," I find myself muttering, almost as though to myself.

His gaze lifts, but not his head. "It concerns my family. But no, not like you're thinking."

"Are you an addict?" I find myself blurting out. Had I even considered this as possibility? Not consciously, at least.

"No." His jaw tightens, his gaze sad but sincere. "I didn't do . . . what I did with great regularity. I wasn't addicted to the act or to the thrill, if that's what you're asking."

"You don't have to mince words to protect me."

"Fucking then," he adds baldly. I flinch. "No, it wasn't a compulsion. It was always calculated and controlled."

"Why does that not surprise me?" I snatch up my glass as my stomach cramps.

"You know that when we met in France, my grandfather had passed the day before. He was the biggest influence in my life. Up until a few months before he died, his influence was positive. I knew he wasn't well regarded by a lot of people. That he was seen as brash and offensive, but I put that down to jealousy mostly. He was a very wealthy man and quite ruthless." He swallows then, his eyes sliding away for a beat before coming to meet mine again. "I just didn't realise quite how ruthless he was. I idolised him. I thought he was old-fashioned, and yeah, a little sexist. A man of his time, I guess. What I didn't know was that he was an abuser, and that label covers a lot of sins, but what I mean to say is he abused women. Used his power against them. The man was a rapist."

I bring my hand to my mouth, not sure what to say. He looks so angry, almost as though the admission was his. But he would never—

"It's not common knowledge and nothing I'd like to hear anyone say. It's enough that finding out changed everything. He destroyed what I thought I knew about love. He destroyed what was left of my family. And if you ask my siblings how he died, they'll tell you I killed him."

"I don't believe that."

"There's a lot about me you don't know."

"You said we had a lifetime to find out," I almost whisper, my eyes sliding to the big screen behind him. Whatever game is playing, I can't say I'm watching as I wish with all my heart I'd kept those words to myself.

"And I meant it."

His use of the past tense makes my eyes sting, though I force the tears back.

"But you're right. I didn't kill him. It was an aneurysm. It happened after I confronted him. After I told him I would no longer work for him. I was supposed to head up the family business. I was being fucking groomed. I have his name, right? But I told him to shove it. That I'd tell everyone why, even if that last threat was a lie." He raises his glass as though toasting the sentiment. Light glints from his watch like a warning as he throws it back. He leans back in his chair and gestures to the waitress for another. "And then he died, and everything came to me. Carson Hayes the fucking third."

"It wasn't your fault." His eyes dip when I cover his hand with my own.

"Tell that to my family. Tell that to the people who lost their livelihoods when I set out to destroy Hayes Industries almost immediately. I was going to have revenge. If not for those women, then for me."

"You were angry. Suffering from shock and grief."

"I think the word you're looking for is betrayal. And I was going to make him pay, alive or dead. I'd raze Hayes Industries to the fucking ground."

"But you didn't." I surmise, at least.

"No. I pulled my head out of my ass because it wasn't his business anymore. It was mine. My responsibility. I was suddenly accountable to and for a worldwide workforce."

For the first time, I think I realise this is who he is. Carson Hayes is a man of principal, as odd as it feels to say, given what's passed between us. But if I put aside my own anger and grief, I see he is a man who assumes responsibility for those around him, not for prestige, appearances, or accolades, but because he was born to be this man. His friends, his men, and his employees. How he'd taken Lulu and me under his wing long before he'd taken us into his heart.

This time it isn't so easy to hold back the prickle of tears, though I manage to stem the flow, gathering them against my fingertips.

"Given your shock and your grief," I say, stifling a tiny sniff, "I'd imagine most people would understand. Forgive you for what you think you did to the company."

"I couldn't tell my family the truth. I didn't want them to suffer through it, and there was always the possibility they'd say I was making it up. Jealousy there, too, I guess. I was his favourite. He left everything to me, and they see this as a great injustice. Like some medieval fucked up patricide."

"I don't know what to say." It sounds quite pathetic, but it's also very true. I am lost for words.

"Maybe not yet you don't." My stomach twists again as I watch his shoulders move with the kind of sigh that seems to have been dragged from the depths of his soul. "Punishment," he says, the word hanging in the air between us.

"What about it?" I answer eventually.

"You know the expression, the punishment should fit the crime? It seemed almost too perfect the first time."

I don't know which hurts more, my stomach or my head. But as the waitress puts down his drink, I say nothing. What can I say? There's no comfort for either of us.

"Ardeo was meant to be an outlet for the guys, but I hung out there, too. You might not see or admit the symmetry in our cowardice," he says, using a finger to gesture between us, "but it's there. You withdrew from relationships after St Odile. I threw myself into sex to drown it."

"I had nothing to do with this. You can't—"

"Blame you?" he asks fiercely. "How could I blame you? You were the one good thing to come out of that time. I think that, on some level, my brain registered I was never going to get better than you. Better than that night. So then in—"

"I don't need to hear the rest." I begin an undignified slide from the booth until Carson's hand reaches out lightning-quick, clamping around my wrist.

"Yes, you do. You need to hear it all."

"Find a priest if you want absolution," I hiss, "because I can't give it to you."

"Your body can, Fee. Your touch. But don't worry, I don't expect that. I just need you to hear what I have to say. Please."

I lower myself back into the chair. Why is it humans feel the need to torture themselves so?

"It started as a joke. I wasn't in the mood that night, and a woman, a daughter of some big fashion house, jokingly offered me money to fuck her. In jest. She knew I didn't need the money, but somehow the thought grew and twisted until it seemed like the most fucked up justice in the world. My grandfather built his empire on the backs of women—that's true. The shit I could tell you would make you ill. But what a way to redress the imbalance by flipping those tables."

"I don't want to hear this," I whisper. It hurts too much to hear it. To see the harsh reality on his face.

"It gets worse. I didn't sell myself for gain. I made those women donate to Rose's foundation. Let them fight to fuck me using the power of the almighty dollar."

I gasp, my mouth wide open in shock. "You . . . You weren't atoning for his sins," I whisper, feeling ill.

"I thought it was justice. Giving women back the power. Giving them what they wanted, making them pay for it, yes, but then ensuring other women benefited from it. I thought I was guarding my heart. But it turns out, I was just ruining it."

"Do you remember saying that a man knows his actions say more about him than his words?"

His eyes reflect his confusion. His hurt. And maybe a better person wouldn't take this route, but I have to. I can't do this. I can feel sorry for him, pity him, but this is bigger than the two of us. Bigger than him and me.

"The day on the mountain, the night at the inn. I've remembered so much of it. How you touched me. Held me. You made me feel like a goddess. Like I was worth something."

"You're worth the earth to me. I would rip it apart just to be with you."

"But don't you see? Your actions say more about you than your words. Not about your grandfather, which I can't say I'll ever be able to comprehend, but at least I can try to understand better than I did. What I'm talking about is how you lied to me." My words are plaintive, my voice breaking at last. "Yes, you did what you did, but then you chose not to tell me. You kept me in the dark. You locked me out."

"I thought I was protecting you."

"It's hard enough to understand how you could value yourself so little . . ." I wipe the back of my hand under my nose before pressing the meat of my palms to my watering eyes. My tears will no longer be controlled. "I don't know which hurts most."

"I didn't mean to hurt you."

"Lies always hurt," I murmur.

"Put yourself in my position—"

"I would *never!*" I'm not a violent person, cocktail spoons aside, but I feel so angry as I savagely push back my chair. "I've been in some horrible predicaments in my life. Times where I've been poor and hungry, living in a billionaire's bloody paradise. I've been propositioned and touched while working in fancy cocktail bars, and it would've been so easy to give in. To allow someone to keep me. But I'd rather be hungry than sell myself." My eyes sweep over him, his posture stiffening under my gaze.

"You've obviously already made up your mind," he utters icily.

"What do your actions say about you, Carson? What do they say about me?"

"My actions say I love you!" he roars. The bar falls silent. Or maybe I'm just not hearing anything but him. "From the very first day. From finding you in my bathtub. From the day I found you broken down at the side of the road, I have put you first. Above all things. My actions say I would do anything for you."

My mind floods with all the joy Carson has brought

into my life, big and small. From apartments and bedrooms to popcorn and movies and the cups of tea he's learned to make me. But if he can't love himself, how can he ever truly love me?

"Yes, I believe you would do anything for me. Anything but tell me the truth."

36

FEE

"Next time I'm back, we're going to Bermuda," Rose mutters, throwing herself into a chair.

"Who? You and Remy?"

"No, me and you," she says as she untangles a dozen or so gift bags from her fingertips. *Hershey's Chocolate World, M & M's, the Disney Store, and more.* "Now I see why Remy said he had meetings. I bet he's really gone for a massage," she says, her eyes narrowing.

"You were the one that thought Ellen's might be a good idea for lunch," Everett mutters, his tone not so much betraying his disgust as vomiting it all over. He drops his share of the booty onto the coffee table between Rose and me before asking, "Where do you want this?"

This being my daughter, asleep in Rhett's arms, her dark head resting against his shoulder.

"Put her on the sofa, would you?" I wiggle very carefully to the other end of the cream sofa, cautious not to disturb a sleeping Rocco. The pair had gone to sleep in the car—the hotel's chauffeur driven Bentley, thank you very much—on the way back from a fun-filled, kid centric day.

"I thought it would be nice for Lulu," Rose retorts, sending Rhett the briefest of glances. "She loves a sing along, especially if it's a Disney one."

"That was before she became a New York diva," I say with a quiet chuckle, marvelling at the weight of Rocco and his sleeping, snuffling, musky smelling boy charms. "Thanks, Rhett." The cushions dip as he lays my daughter down. I know he likes to pretend to be the big hard soldier man, but not even he can resist smiling down at a sleeping child.

"It's like a creche in here," he says, almost coming back to himself. *Reputations to protect and appearances to uphold, I suppose.* "Where's Helga, anyway?"

"Her name is Arianne," Rose replies snarkily. "Rocco loves her, so you're not allowed to upset the nanny, you big lug."

"Manny, more like," he says replies. "The woman's chin is hairier than mine. I notice you didn't make her traipse around Times Square."

"Yeah, because it's a touristy nightmare and she's a little mature."

"Old as f—flock, you mean."

"Stop that," she protests. "She's an excellent nanny."

"Flock," I snicker quietly entertained. Ah, the joys of being around children.

Rhett harrumphs. "I'm going to see if Remy has finished with his meetings."

"Rhett, you and I both know he's hiding out at the gym," Rose teases.

"Not true. We worked out this morning while you lot were still sleeping."

"I didn't say he was working out. I said he was *hiding* out."

"I don't blame him." He throws the retort over his shoulder as he leaves the room. "The butler's here," he calls once out of sight. "Want me to ask him to get you two ladies of leisure a coffee?"

"Wine," Rose shouts back before turning back. "Was it just me, or did he use the word "ladies" kind of ironically?"

God, I've missed her face. "As if he'd even dare."

She and Remy are only in New York for a few days, but she certainly seems to be hell-bent on making them memorable for us. I wasn't surprised to learn they'd rented out several suites at the St. Regis, but I'd been moved to find there was also one reserved for Lulu and me.

We're not here long enough to waste time travelling backward and forward from the hotel to your place, so you'll stay at the hotel with us, okay?

A suite. A motherfluffin' suite. Maybe not as fancy as this one with its Art Deco furnishings, chandeliers, crown mouldings, and original parquet flooring, but it's still pretty ritzy. Or St Regis-y, as the case may be. Lulu, who was clearly born for better things, had run straight to the windows overlooking Central Park, proclaiming it to be "just like Uncle Carson's 'partment", while also leaving the glass sticky with fingerprints.

But that's my friend. So generous. And I've missed her so much, and the heating is still on the blink in our place, so for once, I wasn't about to argue with her about the cost of keeping us here with her.

"I can't believe how much Rocco has changed," I say, nestling my lips against his hair. *Dark like Rose's but wavy like Remy's.* My heart gives a little pinch. There's just something about little ones that does this to me. It's a reminder, I suppose. Probably biological.

"I know he's mine, and I'm not supposed to say it, but he's such a sweet boy." Rose's smile is almost radiant before she comes back to herself. "Seriously though, I'm coming back, and you and me are flying to Bermuda for a few days. It's just a ninety-minute flight away. We'll pack light—"

"What? With kids?" I scoff.

"Oh, they aren't coming. Remy and Rocco can do a little bonding, and you know your mom and dad will jump at the chance to have a Lulu all to themselves. So packing light, sunscreen and bikinis light. No kids, no Times Square, no show tunes, or carousels, or noise, or M & M's. Just cocktails, the beach, you, me, and a little bliss."

"I am so down for that."

Rose looks behind her, almost as though to make sure Rhett has truly left.

"I thought Lulu would've loved Ellen's."

"She did have fun," I protest.

"She's gotten a little sophisticated in her time away. And she would, too, going on dates with Uncle Carson to the Russian Tea Rooms."

My heart gives a little flutter at the mention of his name though I quickly school my expression. "Yeah, he took her for afternoon tea." I'm no great teller of untruths, but I'd prepared for Carson's name coming up and decided it would be best to stick to some version of the truth.

The version that says we'd struck up a friendship. *True.*

The version that says Lulu really likes him. *Also true.*

The version that says I haven't seen him for a couple of weeks. *Again, true. Fourteen days to be exact, but who's counting.*

"He was really good with her while we stayed with him. Well, you know, we didn't stay with him, but there were a few occasions when our paths crossed." Sometimes bodily. Like bumper cars. Banging and crashing, though not really trying to get past. More like . . . in.

Carson Hayes is really good at *getting in*.

Into my knickers. Into my body. Into my heart.

"It's not like you to allow Lu to go anywhere with a stranger."

"He's not really a stranger, though, is he? He's your friend, and your endorsement of him was good enough for me."

Rose peers at me as though she's not really sure what to say. "He is really good with Rocco," she seems to ponder, her eyes slipping to her son. "Let me take him. He'll probably sleep a couple of hours now."

"And then poor Arianne gets all the cranky fun later?"

"Hopefully not too cranky. I've booked us a table at the restaurant. I thought we could dine *en famille*. An early dinner?"

"That works for me. Lulu is mostly restaurant trained these days. Do you remember when she was Rocco's age? I would've rather spent the evening sticking a fork into the toaster repeatedly than take her anywhere near a restaurant. Do you remember how rotten she was?"

"She wasn't rotten. Just high spirited."

"If high spirited means bad tempered and loud, then yes. God, how she would scream if there wasn't *sketti* on the menu!"

"Yeah." Rose smiles fondly. "I'd forgotten about that.

And how she used to be covered from eyebrow to chin with sauce by the time she'd finished."

"Us too, sometimes. Remember when she tipped her bowl of spaghetti into Charles's lap?"

"Oh, his face. I thought he was going to faint!"

"I thought he was going to send me the bill for a new Dolce and Gabbana suit. You kind of forget how hard it is. And the horror stories, even the ones you can laugh about afterwards."

"Lulu is a one-off," she says with a slow shake of her head.

"It's probably just as well."

"She's a great kid, Fee."

"Of course she is. She takes after me." Even as I say it, I know it's not true. I tend to think of Lulu as her own person, as we all are, I suppose. It's just, she has so many personality traits that I don't recognise as either one of mine or as having come from my family. But none of that matters because she's the apple of my eye. My treasure. My gorgeous girl.

"You know, Remy's mom blames me for every flaw in Rocco's temperament."

"Flaws shmaws," I assert snort. "He's perfect."

"But it's always the mother's fault, right?"

I nod and smile but, in my case, who else could be blamed?

"I'm sure Remy was *such* a darling child," I say, rolling my eyes just a touch.

"Exactly! He swears like a sailor, yet I get blamed for Rocco's slip up!"

"Oh-oh. Rocco said his first swear, did he?"

"That sleeping sweetheart is like his father. And by that, I mean he does nothing by halves. I literally cannot say a thing in front of him without expecting it to be repeated."

"I bet that makes for some interesting conversations."

"Oh, yes. Last week we had the dragon over for dinner."

I think I'd have gone with ice queen if I'd been asked to describe her. Remy's mother is almost ageless and very beautiful, but so cold you could keep your drink chilled by placing it next to her bum.

"I don't think she was too impressed that Rocco ate with us."

"Children are to be seen and not heard?"

"Yeah, like that. Anyway, my little man was sitting in his chair, and behaving so well, when all of a sudden, he yells, *"ah, sit!"* And he didn't mean please be seated—repose yourself," she says, adding a flourish of her hand. "That boy had the intonation down."

"Oh, dear," I answer with a giggle. "What happened next?"

"Remy coughed behind his napkin, and I could see he was close to losing it, his damn shoulders shaking and stuff. Not cool. If Rocco had realised, it probably would've resulted in him running around yelling *shit! shit!* at the top of his voice for a month. Before *grand-mère* could imply his American side must be to blame for his vulgarity, I told him off. You know, we don't say words like that, Rocco, no matter how cross we are."

"No, we say much worse things."

"But out of the earshot of our impressionable offspring."

"At least we try."

"But then I made the mistake of asking him what made him feel so angry that he had said such a bad word, and the fruit of my loins muttered something that sounded suspiciously like, '*Rocco drop him fuckin' fork*'."

"I thought boys were supposed to be late talkers," I say, snickering.

"Well, the one I got is pretty erudite. *Il est exactement comme son père,"* she says. He's just like his father.

"Your French really has improved, and your accent is excellent." The language didn't come easy to Rose.

"I try," she replies with a sly smile. "I had to really try because all Remy wanted to do for the longest time was teach me the kinds of words that can't be said in polite company."

"Or any company?"

"Well, just company."

Rocco begins to stir and, as I pass him into Rose's arms, we make plans to reconvene at six for an early diner with the kids in Astor Court, the St Regis's fabulous dining room. *With its muted atmosphere and pristine table linens. God help their cream carpets and soft furnishings.*

"I thought Arianne could bring the kids back to the suite after, and we could go to the bar for some fun adult time." Rose's eyes flare a little comically over the top of his head. "That sounded a little kinkier than I meant it to."

Oh, how little she knows . . .

"Nope, it sounds fab. Lulu will love some Rocco time as much as I would love some non-sexual fun adult time, too."

"Don't get me started." She waggles a finger in my direction. "You know my opinion on that topic."

"Yes, yes. Use it before you lose it."

"No, do it because it's fun!"

"I do recall," I murmur mostly to myself as I slide one

hand under Lulu's thighs and the other under her back. I'm just preparing to lift her when Rose adds,

"And speaking of fun, I hope you don't mind, but Carson's promised to come along."

And this is the reason, as I lift my child, I don't see her sleepy hand shoot out and sock me in the eye.

"Here you go, slugger." Rhett places the water bottle back on the table after topping up Lulu's glass.

"Thank you," she replies with a glower. "And I told you, Uncle Rhett, it was an accident."

"Pay him no mind, sweets. He's just teasing. Aren't you, Everett?" Rose matches Lulu's glower with one of her own.

"What I am is jealous. Not because I want to smack your mum one. Much," he adds in an undertone, "but because of the power in that hit."

"It was an accident," Lu repeats, this time with a growl. "I'm trying very hard not to call you a weenie head, but you're making it very hard!"

"Lulu!" I cover my giggle with my napkin—a giggle that's a little too manic for the topic.

"Weenie head is Uncle Rhett's middle name," Remy asserts with authority.

I add an unattractive snort to my giggles, my entire being probably thirty percent wine right now. I was plied with it after Lulu socked me one this afternoon when Rose assumed I was mute with shock because of the pain. Little did she know the pain wasn't physical but emotional.

And it made me curse quite loudly all the same.

I suppose I really should be thanking my daughter for

giving me something to swear about. Though, right now, my eye socket is a little tender, and the initial shock of both the announcement and the impact of Lulu's fist has worn off. But what hasn't alleviated is the anxious kind of flutter the experience has left me with.

I've missed Carson so, so much, though I've tried really hard to banish him from my brain. I've refused to consider where he is or where he might've been, what he might be doing and who he might be doing it with. It has undoubtably been the hardest two weeks of my life, even harder than when my parents flew back to London two weeks after I'd given birth. No one can prepare you for being solely responsible for a brand-new human and the anxiety that brings. But it's because of that tiny human, who isn't really so tiny anymore, yet just as precious, that I know I can't be with him.

I have to be worth more than being lied to.

Because if I'm not, how will I teach Lulu what she is worth?

And now I have to sit through a dinner. Well, not a dinner, thankfully. Six o'clock is a very unfashionable hour to dine in New York. Lulu and Rocco have already eaten, and the adults have picked at entrees with the logic that we might order food in the cocktail bar later. But me? I'm too wired to eat. I've stuck purely to wine because I'm not sure I'll be able to sit across from Carson otherwise.

"You haven't got your glasses on."

I turn to Everett's assertion. "Ten points for observation." Realising that sounded a little snarky, I add, "The frame aggravated the bruise, but I can still see you, so no pulling faces."

"Yeah, Uncle Rhett, nobody likes a *juice bag*."

I give a tiny shake of my head. "Lulu has brought some delightful gems home from school lately."

"Took some delightful gems to school too, so I hear." Remy's gaze dances over the rim of his wine glass. "Gems like . . . rings?"

"I can't believe you told him that." I mutter press my head to my hands.

"I'm so sorry," Rose splutters, her hands actually clutching her stomach as she begins to laugh. "How could I keep that to myself?"

"What are they laughing at, Mommy?" Lulu tugs unhappily on my sleeve, her displeasure clear. No one enjoys the sense they're being laughed at.

"Just grown-up things," I reassure her. Which is very true. Any conversation that includes the words "cock ring" or euphemistic variants thereof, aren't meant for little ears.

"I have some questions about that." Rose holds up her hand like a kid eager in class. "But maybe I'm asking the wrong person." Her eyes slide behind me and, just like that, I know Carson is here.

37

CARSON

At first, I'd considered Rose was calling to rip me a new one. I hadn't spoken to her for a while, and at the back of my mind was the consideration that Fee might need someone to talk to. A shoulder to cry on that wasn't mine. It quickly became clear that wasn't the purpose of her call, and I found myself oddly offended. I didn't want her to hurt, yet I would have welcomed some sign that I wasn't alone in my misery. So I thought about not coming tonight. About making some bullshit excuse when Rose invited me. But I was kidding myself, considering my evening run still brings me past her building most evenings. Considering that I'm also still making Ed Martinez uncomfortable in my quest to keep her safe.

So, no. I wasn't about to pass up the opportunity to spend some time in her company, no matter how painful it might turn out to be. Maybe what I have is a sickness, but it's a sickness I can do nothing but endure. A suffering I'll undertake to see her again.

Tension tightens my shoulders as I enter the restaurant, pausing before being directed to the Durrand table. I'm no more than a few steps in before I find I have a limpet called Lulu clinging to my leg.

"Uncle Carson!"

"Hey, princess." I boost her up into my arms and just stare a little at her effusive delight. "You've grown," I accuse, narrowing my eyes before pressing a smacking kiss to her cheek. God, I've missed this kid. I've missed her so fucking much. Maybe because she's an extension of the woman I love, or perhaps the love I have for Lulu is the kind that's grown independent of her mother. I don't pretend to understand how or why. I just know what I know.

"Of course I've growed. Your business trip has been very, very long."

"Business trip?" *So that's what Fee told her*, I think wearily. Seems like a cop-out, but I guess it's not my choice to make.

Not anymore. Not ever.

But a business trip isn't a permanent thing. Maybe—

Fuck it. I take a fortifying breath, preparing myself to look at Fee, preparing myself to see her again. Tonight *will* be tough. I've already resigned myself to that. Pretending to be on politely and friendly terms with the woman I love. *A woman who wants no part of me.* But then I find that might not be strictly true as I deposit Lulu to the chair next to Fee, our eyes meeting over the top of her dark head.

The connection is . . . fuck. Like a jolt. An indescribable jolt of longing.

My throat closes over all the things I want to say as I press my hand to the back of her chair, brushing my lips against her cheek. Once, twice, as French custom dictates, regardless of the fact we're neither French nor in France. I thought I could do cool, affect friendly, but I'm suddenly swallowed by the need to touch her. My thumb sweep across her back, touching the skin available to me, finding comfort in her reaction. The sharp rise of her breast. Her held breath, a half gasp. Midnight in her eyes as I pull back.

"Fiadh." Her name is like silk on my tongue. *You look beautiful,* I don't say though I want to.

Come back to me.

I straighten, sensing the silence around the table, and when I turn, quizzical faces stare back at me.

"Rose." I struggle to master my smile, partly because I'm happy to see her, partly because I'm just so fucking relieved. Clasping my hands to her shoulders, I press my cheek to hers in the more appropriate rendition of a French greeting. *Air kisses, once, twice. Pull back.*

"You went all South of France on Fee." Rose's tone sounds playfully suspicious.

I went *south*? I pull my mind out of the gutter as I release her. She just meant the extra kiss I gave Fee, even if my mind took her words someplace much dirtier.

Like, under the table linens, my face pressed to my darling's sweet pussy.

"Don't be greedy." I shoot Rose a brazen wink before greeting her son. "Hey, Rocco."

"*Oncle Car!*" The kid's sticky fingers pat my neck affectionately, though he's more interested in his dish of ice cream.

I give a bemused but unruffled Remy the same treatment. After all, air kisses aren't considered an unmanly way to greet a friend in France, though I find myself barking out a loud laugh as Rhett shoves out his hand.

"Not a fan of *faire la bise*?" To give a kiss.

"Depends who's offering," he grunts in return. "I generally like them when they come from someone better looking than you."

"Uncle Car." Lulu tugs on the sleeve of my jacket. "Come and be the meat in the sandwich."

Cue another round of puzzled looks at the Durrand table.

"What?" Lulu asks, her gaze touching them each in turn. You know you're causing a stir when a four-year-old picks up on it. "I want Uncle Carson to sit between me and Mommy."

I take the proffered seat, silently inhaling Fee's scent as we sit so close I can feel the press of her shoulder. I find my arm lifting almost by itself as though I'd wrap it around the back of her chair. Instead, I awkwardly reach over my chest, pulling on Lulu's pigtail instead.

"Who tamed your hair, wild thing?"

"Arianne did it. She doesn't pull like Mommy." She slides Fee a superior look, though her mother is currently too fascinated by the contents of her glass to notice. "We're going to watch The Lion King after dinner with her. Want to come?" Opening my mouth is as far as I get to an answer. "Has the flood been fixed yet? Can we move back in? I miss my bedroom."

"You had a flood?" Rose's voice sounds across the table. "Don't you live in the penthouse?"

"It was more like a leak," I answer. "We had a lot of rain." My gaze slides to Fee's. Or it would, if she'd only look at me, instead of wishing she could disappear behind, or into, her wine glass.

"You didn't tell me that." Maybe it's the suspicion in Rose's tone that causes Fee to eventually lift her head to reveal something that makes blood begin to boil in my veins.

I find my fingers at her chin as I coax her gaze upwards, my voice a low growl.

"Who did this to you?"

38

FEE

"You're sure you don't have something to tell me?" Rose tilts her head back, resting it against my shoulder. "Not even a teenie weenie bit of news?"

"No, I told you already. You're reading into the situation too much."

"But the way he looked at you when he thought you'd been hurt. That was like, *badum-badum-badum!*" Hands clasped together, she makes as though to pound them over her heart.

The way he looked at me? What about how I'd returned that look? Had my heart bled from my eyes? It certainly felt like it. The war of heart and head is hard fought, but no more so than when your chin in balanced in the hand of the cause of your confusion.

He'd stared at me with such fierce intensity.

"I think he wants you," she whispers urgently in my ear.

"You're a goofball." Jerking my shoulder dislodges her head, but not her words.

Her eyes narrow teasingly, her lips curving into a

knowing sort of smile. "I'm also right. And that man can seduce with just a smile."

"Do you think that's what's going on over there?" I ask carefully. I suppose I know that smile better than anyone else in this room. But damn his gorgeous mouth for even thinking of smiling at anyone else. *Especially the woman he's sitting next to.* And damn his inscrutable gaze for sliding my way.

He can't win, can he? Want me, don't want me.

Just please. Want me.

Rose sits forward, reaching for her wine glass before she tilts her head, seeming to consider the pair.

"No. He's not hitting on her. Women just gravitate to him. It doesn't matter where he sits, or who he sits with, they just seem to appear. Why do you ask?" Her attention swings my way, her eyes mischievous. "Do you *lurve* him?" she whispers playfully.

"You're drunk."

"He's looking *o-ver,*" my best friend sing-songs.

"Stop it," I hiss, silently warning myself not to build up my hopes. What for, I'm not sure.

A night? A lifetime? A little peace?

Why the heck did I drink so much wine?

But I'm getting ahead of myself. It wasn't necessarily longing I heard in his sigh when he pressed his cheek to mine. And when he saw my shiner of an eye, of course he was upset. He's a good person. He looks after those he loves.

Loves. Really? Maybe he's just a better actor than me.

Of course he's a good actor, my mind so helpfully supplies. There wouldn't be bidding wars to spend a night in his bed otherwise. Because his attraction has to be more than just about sex, right? No woman would pay huge numbers for just a quick screw. Even with someone who can make knickers disintegrate with just a teasing smile.

I wonder if he's interested in what's in *her* knickers? The brunette next to him, chatting animatedly. T*he brunette with a spectacularly large bottom*, I think to myself uncharitably.

"Remy, come dance with me." Rose stands suddenly, pulling on his hand.

"Ma, Rose. There isn't really a dance floor," he answers in that laconic way of his. Yet as she tugs, his body follows hers.

"When have you ever needed a designated space to put your hands on me?" Rose answers, firing me a wink over her shoulder as the pair leave.

Rhett then drops to the seat Rose has just vacated. "That was a big sigh."

"Was it?" I shoot him a quizzical glance. "I was just thinking I should go. I promised to tuck Lulu in."

The kids have gone off to watch a movie. It's probably a good idea for me to leave because watching Carson flirt (or watching her flirt with him, as the case may be) is making me feel more stabby than I have a right to be.

But my God, Kim K has nothing on that arse. I can't see her face so I'm able to console myself with the thought that she might look like a bucket full of bumholes.

"Arianne might have a chin like a Viking but she's great with the ankle biters."

"She should be. It's her job." And one she'll be paid for very well, if I know Rose.

"I'm just saying you should stay. Relax. Enjoy yourself for a bit."

"Do you think it's my turn to get a round of drinks in or something?"

"There's no being nice to you," Everett grumbles, folding his arms over his chest.

My attention slides back to the bar at the same moment as the woman flicks the shimmering sheet of her dark hair over her shoulder. I get a glimpse of her almost feline beauty and my heart sinks to my strappy heels. She's gorgeous, and not one bit like a bucket full of you know whats. Not only that, she's also perfectly pulled together. I bet she never gets a black eye from being thumped by one of her kids. *Current or future offspring.* She looks like the kind of woman who always has a perfect manicure, unlike me. I've already torn a fingernail after Rose treated us to a mani-pedi this afternoon. I just bet she's one of those women who never has a hair out of place when she wears a high ponytail. And her level of pristine probably emerges from mad, passionate sexy times with nary a smudged lip line.

Knowing I find him irresistible is one thing.

Seeing that reflected in other women is . . . discomforting.

Bollocks. It's fucking horrible! My sweary brain yells.

I watch as she presses her hand to Carson's shoulder and, whatever she says makes him grin like a schoolboy. I can imagine him as a kid. Floppy-haired and boisterous. But it's been a while since he was innocent.

And whose fault is that?

Probably not his. Not wholly his, at least.

Try as I might to stand up, to walk away, to turn my thoughts from him, I just can't seem to manage it. *Because I don't want to.* But I sense rather than feel Rhett following my line of sight, almost as though he can devine my thoughts.

"Lulu seems to like him," he says evenly.

"What's that supposed to mean?"

"You tell me. You're the one with the eyes falling out of her head."

"It's not like that," I murmur in a tone more dignified than I feel.

"You could do worse."

"You don't even like him," I scoff. He's never had a good thing to say about Carson, as I recall.

"I don't like many people," he notes, his tone dry. "But he's all right. For a yank, I mean. And I suppose for someone who has been through the shit he has."

"What do you mean?" I feel myself stiffen. Does *he* know?

"Just his life. Losing his mum during 9/11 and the reason he signed up. That shit messes with you." Everett slides brief glance, but I don't ask him to explain. It would only invite more pain. There's so much I don't know about him.

We were supposed to have a lifetime to learn.

"And then there is his family." Rhett scratches his cheek as he considers the man he's trying to interest me in. *Like I need the encouragement.* "They're more fucked up than the Borgias, though without the incest. He's bound to have his boundaries skewed."

"You're making him sound like a real catch."

"Yeah," he agrees. "But I saw the way you were watching him, and the way he was watching you. And something occurred to me. If he was a no hoper, a complete twat, Lulu would've figured him out in five minutes flat."

"She's a child, not an oracle."

"She's a one off," he asserts, his tone not exactly complimentary.

If only things were as simple as children see them. Or Everett. Of course I'm watching him. Thinking about him. Thinking about what he did. And it's sort of heart crushing when I try to wrap my thoughts around why he could think he was worth so little. The reasons he sold himself. I don't mean for charity. How he could twist his grandfather's sins into something so hurtful and sordid, and why did he seek to punish himself? How could he possibly think he could atone for sins committed against women he never knew?

It's all so vile for someone so very beautiful.

But maybe he'd say the same for me, because he offered me his heart on a platter only for me to stick my heel through it.

"You could do a lot worse than him, you know."

"That's hardly a ringing endorsement." As well as a strange turn of events. Everett saying something borderline complimentary? Maybe he's not well.

"Coming from me, I think you'll find it is."

"Hmph."

"Jesus, I'm trying to make it easy for you here, Fee. You're staring at the man as though you dropped your heart in his pocket and you're waiting for him to notice."

"Make it easy?" I retort. "I don't—"

"Know your arse from your elbow. I give up," he mutters metaphorically throwing up his hands.

"You're in a shitty mood." Talk about deflecting. I slide my clutch from the table and stand. "If Rose comes back, tell her I've gone to check on the kids."

"I'm gonna get another drink."

And then he's gone, his flounce way more effective than mine.

I slap down my clutch and key card, then pull off these tortures called shoes.

"Why can't life be easy?" I mutter, my footsteps muffled against the plush carpet.

I'm not hiding. Well, I guess I am. But I wasn't lying when I said I was going to check on the kids. The pair were sleeping so sweetly, and Arianne was reading a book, and while I was going to carry Lulu back to our suite, my phone had buzzed with Rose's text and a demand that I "get my ass back" because Carson was at the bar and getting shots.

No thank you! I don't have a nanny to wake with my child in the morning. Besides, I need to keep a clear head. But I will go back down. Soon. Once I've had a little think about what I'm going to say to Carson. Because I need to.

No, I *want* to.

Urgh! Why does this have to be so complicated?

Our suite is two bedrooms on either side of a small lounge. It's very French looking with original crown mouldings and red damask walls. The tables have cabriole legs, the lamps are ornate, and all three rooms feature sumptuous soft furnishings. The double doors that lead to the larger of the two bedrooms are open, the bed linens already turned down for the night. I drop onto the padded bench at the end of the bed, taking a moment to contemplate my pink painted toenails.

Our mani-pedi appointment this afternoon was fun. Champagne, magazines, silly conversations, and a little gossiping was a good way to spend an hour or so. My toes do look super pretty, and though the idea was Rose's, and nothing to do with the possibility of seeing Carson this evening, I can't say the same for the rest of my preparations.

I draw my fingertips up my smooth, bare legs as I consider the buffing, shaving, and slathering session I'd undertook before getting ready this evening. Did I think he might appreciate the sight? Did I plan for him to?

I certainly didn't expect him to be sitting with some other woman while I gawked at him. What would I do if I could start the evening over again?

Maybe I'd drop my clutch to the bar and slide onto the seat next to him.

Maybe I'd say, *You look like one hell of a fun night followed by a week of stalking.* It'd be completely unsubtle, but that would be the point. I'd force myself to smile brightly so he'd know I was playing. I can almost imagine his expression, see him choking a little on his drink before setting it down.

That's my pickup line, I'd announce as though it was the most normal thing in the world. *I've shown you mine. Now you have to show me yours.*

Impertinent, yes. But wouldn't that be the point?

I have to show you mine? His voice would be deep and smooth with just an edge of confusion, the kind that'd quirk in the corners of those sensuous lips.

Oh, God, the thought of those lips, that mouth, has me arching almost sinuously against the bench as I rock forward on my pelvis.

"Yes, show me yours, Carson," I announce to the empty room before turning back to my little imaginary funfest with all the finesse of a kid in the quest for a cookie.

What are you doing, Fee? I imagine him saying. *How many of those have you had?* He'd glance down at my glass.

No. No. That doesn't work for me. I haven't had enough to drink, because if I had, I wouldn't be sliding up the hem of my dress in my empty bedroom. Because he'd be here doing it for me.

Don't you look dapper, I begin again, imagining sliding my hand down his lapel, drawn not by the feel of it, but by the solid frame of him beneath.

And you, as always, look incredible, Fiadh. I love it when he says my name in that smoky way of his.

"Yes, yes, I do," I whisper. "and I'm all silky smooth and just waiting for you." And hot, I find, as I cup my hand between my legs, holding myself.

We could get into a lot of trouble, he'd say with a soft chuckle as he'd twist his glass, acting a little reticent as he pretends to examine the contents. Then he'd lift it to his mouth, and I'd get a little hot and bothered watching the way his neck moves as he swallows.

I imagine placing my lips against his neck. My tongue. Follow the motion of the muscle, licking the hollow of his throat.

Maybe I'm looking for trouble, I'd say.

And you think I'm it?

I haven't quite made up my mind. And that would be a lie, the kind of lie I tell myself as I press a finger over the thin fabric of my underwear, teasing myself just a little harder.

But you haven't laid it on me yet, and you know you want to. So, hit me with your best pickup line.

And then I'd wait. I'd watch. Resist the urge to squirm,

probably feeling equal amounts hot and reckless. He'd crook a finger, oh, so deliberately, beckoning me forward, and I'd lean in, bringing my ear almost to his mouth as something hot and sweet would bloom inside me.

"Yes, that that." Like the feeling blooms now."

Music would continue to play, voices around us would be loud, their words indistinct. I'd try not to tremble as his breath would blow against my neck. Try and fail miserably.

See how I made you come with one finger, his low voice would say. *Imagine how proficient the rest of me is.*

"Oh, God."

I close my eyes and lean back on my palm, my right hand pressed hard between my legs. I haven't orgasmed since him. I haven't wanted to. I've been too sad, but Christ, do I need to now as I rotate my palm. A ragged sigh seems to come from the very depths of me as I hold and squeeze, imagining my hand as his. The air-conditioning turns over, the press of cool air making the loose strands of my hair dance against my shoulders. It reminds me of his thumb's caress at the dinner table, the ache of having him so near.

"I want . . . " So much that I can barely breathe as I rock against my own hand, recalling the heft and heat of him, imagining how, if he were here, he'd separate me from my clothes like a hot knife through butter.

I trail my fingers upwards, sliding them under the elastic of my underwear. *I'm so wet already,* I think as I paint the aching knot of my clit in my own arousal. The first brush makes me twitch, the second I imagine as his hand sliding into deep inside me.

I splay my legs, my body an impossible arch as my fingers dip and swirl. My eyes screwed tight, I see Carson before me, on his knees, his tongue taking, his lips sucking, his voice thick. How he'd watch me, his eyes dark, his mouth delivering dirty rasping compliments between kisses and licks. His hair would be so silky in my fingertips, the dark thatch of it stark against my skin.

"Oh, Jesus!" My thighs jolt, my abs drawing tight as I reach that point where there's no going back. There's only me, my hand, my memories, and the phantom of the man driving me towards climax.

Sweet, sweet girl. Fuck my fingers. Fuck them hard.

I rock into my hand, the images his words invoke pushing me over that blinding edge as I cry out his name.

The room is silent but for the sound of my heavy breath and the soft snap of elastic as I remove my hand. I collapse forward, my eyes fluttering open to the view of my prettily painted toenails. It takes my brain a moment to compute the pair of dark brogues between them, but it catches up pretty darned quick as an angry deep voice rasps,

"Did you arrange this between the two of you?"

39

CARSON

"Did you arrange this between the two of you?"

Sliding the hotel key card from between two fingers, I tap it rapidly against my thigh. The key card Rose just handed me with the pouting directive of "*please go and see what she's doing, Car*."

And now I've seen.

Fuck, have I seen.

And while I'm rock hard and throbbing, I'm also pissed, though I can't quite arrange my thoughts to the point where I understand why I feel like this. Watching Fee was the hottest thing I've seen since, well, since the last time I was between her legs. But, Jesus, I feel twisted up inside.

"Well?" I growl like an asshole and nudge her foot with my shoe, feet that, moments ago were throwing gang signs as she'd climaxed. *Maybe I shouldn't be standing here. Maybe I should be on my knees between her feet instead.* "Is this some fucked up punishment? A way to torture me?"

"Carson . . . I . . ." Fee's chest rises and falls, the flush across her skin even deeper than it was a few moments before. She blinks heavily, her hands fluttering by her sides almost as though she's wondering if she should rub her eyes. Maybe shake her head? Pinch herself to see if she's dreaming. Or maybe more appropriately, suffering from some kind of nightmare. Because if she and Rose did concoct this peep show, I'm guessing my reaction isn't the one they were counting on.

"I've missed you," she says, her voice sounding small. Bringing her knees together, she begins to primly pull her dress down her thighs.

Is that what I want to hear her say? I would've fallen to my knees to hear that very thing on any day between today and when she left. But right now, I'm not so sure. I feel like a fucking fool. I don't know what it is she wants from me, and I'm almost too scared to ask. *Because I know what I want from her, and that's everything.*

I hurt her and I can't take that back. I've castigated myself, railed against my own stupidity. Wondered how I could've been such a conceited fucking idiot. She left me and she had every right to, every reason. Because when I took a good look at myself, I saw what she saw. My way of life wasn't about settling old scores or punishing his name. It wasn't righteous in its depravity in any way. What I saw when I took a good look at me was something sordid. What I saw was shame, wrapped up in a pretty frame.

How could she ever want me again?

But sitting next to her in the restaurant earlier, hearing, seeing, that she hadn't told a soul the truth of us. Of me. It gave me hope. Hope she'd let me make it up to her over the course of a lifetime.

But the thing I'm just coming to understand about hope is that it might be a thing with feathers, just like the poem says. Hope can be light and airy and without consequence. Have I hoped in vain?

"Tell me what the fuck this is, Fee. What does it mean? Can you explain it to me because—" I blow out a breath and run a hand through my hair. I want her so fucking much and I can almost taste her. My fingers ache to tug her up from the bench, to pull her to my chest and press my lips to her head. Or press her back against the mattress to fucking defile her. It would be so easy and maybe I could even kid myself that I'm okay with just sex. Fall into those intense rhythms we make, lose myself in her and the moment. But the truth is, I don't think I'll ever be able to settle for being anything but her forever.

These weeks have been hell and a taste of what I've missed isn't enough. I'm not a performing fucking seal, driven only by lust. Except—

You reap what you fucking sow, right?

"I didn't mean for you to see. This wasn't . . . isn't what you think it is." The words hang between us and I try to let their meaning sink in. "I think I was just hoping to take the edge off."

"The edge?" I repeat. Or maybe sneer.

"Yes." Her eyes search mine and she swallows. "I came up to check on the kids. It's true," she adds fervently as my eyes flick over her, denying her words. "I was going to put my pyjamas on and go to bed but then I decided I wouldn't—that I'd go back down to the bar and force myself to speak with you."

"Force yourself into a conversation with me?" I fold my arms across my chest and stare down at her, making my expression one of anger, not pain.

"You were pretty preoccupied." There's more than a hint of rebuke in her tone. Because I lingered too long at the bar? Does she not realise it was because sitting next to her without touching her made me feel like I was bursting out of my fucking skin?

"Me? Well, we sat side by side the whole time in the restaurant and you barely lifted your gaze from your glass. Yet you sat happily talking to Everett like you hadn't a care in the world." While I'd forced myself not to stalk over to him, to tear him limb from limb.

"Everett? There's nothing between us."

"But I think he'd like there to be. Maybe Rose should've slipped him the hotel key card."

"He looks out for me, he's not—"

"He wants in your fucking panties," I roar. "Admit it!"

"Okay, maybe I will!" she yells back, her eyes flinty and her hands balled into fists. I'm sure she'd like to jump up, plant those fists in my face, but she can't get up from the bench, not the way I'm crowding her in. And I'm not gonna move. "Maybe I'll admit it. When you admit you wanted to fuck Kim Kardashian's older sister!"

"Kim who?"

"Her, the girl with the big arse sitting next to you at the bar."

"Are you jealous?"

"No! Yes. That's not the point!"

"You sat and talked to Everett, yet you couldn't even look at me."

"Because I can't look at you without wanting you." Now *that* was definitely a rebuke. "And I've tried so hard not to want you."

"Don't play games with me," I growl, finding her chin in my hand. "You can't cast me aside like an unwanted toy and get jealous when someone else wants to play with me."

"You're not a toy," she grates out, twisting her head away. "Don't call yourself that."

"Isn't that what I am to you?" I ask, throwing my arms wide. "Is that the reason you can't look at me."

Her head suddenly dips as she feed her hands between her clasped knees. "I miss you and I'm sorry."

I'm not sure if it's her words or her position that makes it look like she's praying.

"You're sorry you miss me?"

Her head comes up fast, the gold rim around her eyes an angry flare. "It would be so easy to say yes, that I hate myself for missing you, but that's not it. What I'm sorry for is that you couldn't tell me the truth. But at least I now understand why you didn't. Why you couldn't. I'm not making excuses for your lies because that would be foolish of me, and I promised myself a long time ago that I was worth more than being lied to. And I am, Carson. I'm worth so much more." Tears brim against her eyelids though she refuses to let them overflow. I want to drop to my knees because I know I was wrong. Would it help? I'd do anything for her forgiveness, but the words are a ball of thorns, choking my throat.

"I thought that if you lied to me once, what was there to stop you doing it again?"

"Fee." I make a plea of her name, desperate for her to hear that I would tear out my heart if it would help her understand.

"Just listen to me, please." Something flares in my chest as she reaches out to take my hand. When she stands, she presses her other hand over my heart. "I need you to hear what I have to say."

Jaw tight, I nod and tighten my fingers around hers.

"That night, five years ago, it changed the course of my

life. I know I was already pregnant, but by the time I realised, I was already on the road to fixing the broken things in my life. And that was because you made me feel worth something. And I know that sounds silly because it was only one night, and it was only sex, but you did. You helped me see that I was worthy of love, including my own.

"And then I found you again. Or you found me. And I tried so hard not to give you my heart. But I did. And you weren't kind to it. I don't agree with what you did, how you lived your life, but I understand that was before I was a part of it. But when you hid from me, when you lied, I didn't know how I could rationalise that to myself. And what about Lulu? She needs to learn her worth, too. If I allowed you to treat me badly, how could I ever teach her what she is worth? And she's worth everything to me."

"I know that, angel. Lulu deserves the world." Please let me give it to her.

She squeezes my hand and I go back to listening.

"But tonight, I realised something. And that is no one ever taught you what you are worth."

She moves closer, her hands smooth and soft as she cups my face. A million emotions tumble and turn inside me. Exhilaration, dread, fear. And hope, fucking hope, feather-like and floating. As she swallows tightly, I find my hands tight on her hips as I ground myself to her.

"You made me see before. I'd like to help you this time. Show you your worth in this world. I think it's about time." She tips up on her toes, her eyes soft and watery, her breath a sweet wisp across my face.

"Don't do this, Fee. Not unless you mean it." My hands manacle her wrists, my need for this to be true as grasping and rough as I feel.

"You mean, don't kiss you?" Her words ghost my lips, my chin. Press where my pulse is hammering. Make me groan and convulse as she sucks over the vein.

"Not if you don't mean it." My whisper is harsh, her wrists still in my hands. "I'd do anything for you, but I don't think I could take watching you leave again."

Her head pulls back, her gaze reflecting the truth in my words, and in her lips is the want in my fingertips.

"Kiss me, Carson. Kiss me back."

Our hands are caught between us as she flattens herself against me, her parted lips more a prelude than a real kiss. I tilt my head, closing the tiny space between us but it's her lips that close the deal as she sucks my lower lip between hers.

"Touch me." Breath tight, she brings my hand to her breast. "I need you so badly, Carson. I ache for you."

I half groan at the lush press of her against my hand, and she joins me in the sound as my thumb swipes her hardened nipple. Our kiss becomes deeper, wetter, our tongues tangling as our fingers grasp.

"Make me your sweet girl."

"I've dreamed of you saying that." My voice is hoarse and full of the unsaid as I clasp and knead, my free hand sliding around to her ass, pulling her tight against me.

"*Oh!*"

"Every damned night you were there, with me. In my bed, giving yourself to me."

"I want that." Her hand plucks my shirt from my pants, her fingers searing my skin.

"No hesitation, all heart."

"Yes. Oh, Carson, I love you."

The tenuous hold I had on myself snaps like a bow string, a surge of something so enormous washing over me like a tidal wave. With a groan or a growl, or whatever the fuck that sound was, I grab the hem of her tight dress, pulling it up and over her thighs. Then she's in my arms, her legs clasped around me, her intimate heat burning through the cotton of my shirt.

"Say that again," I demand, raining kisses against her cheeks, her lips, her neck.

"No hesitation. All heart. Carson Hayes, I love you."

"Thank the Lord. *Fucking yes.*"

I've changed my mind. Hope is a thing with wings. Wings like an angel, and blonde hair, and legs that I'd be happy to die between. I swallow her tight little moans and slide my tongue into her mouth. She tastes so sweet and warm, and the heat of her pussy pressed against me is fucking unreal. I want to lift her up onto my shoulders to fuck her with my tongue.

"So much for taking the edge off." Her words are a shaky breath in my ear, the sensation rippling down my spine. I carry her over to the side of the bed, pressing her to the mattress, my body following hers.

"I need you naked," I rasp, running my hands down her sides, making her gasp a little when I get side-tracked. "Jesus, angel, your panties are soaked through." I cup her, squeeze, and she rocks against me a little wildly.

"Because I've missed you."

"Yeah?" I drag the word out as I press my thumb against the tight knot of her clit. "So you were thinking about me when you touched yourself."

Maybe something in my tone makes her push up onto her elbows. But she's not watching my face. "I was thinking about coming down to the bar, sliding onto the stool next to you."

"And that made you come?"

"Thinking about seducing you did."

"I would've swallowed my tongue."

Her head drops back as I slide my finger under the fabric, the slick feel of her heat almost overwhelming. "*Yes, like that,*" she whispers, grasping my wrist as though to keep me there.

"Or maybe I would've persuaded you to take a little walk," I say, pressing my knee to the mattress. "Because the whole time I was at the bar, I was thinking about you. Watching you. Hoping you were a little jealous."

"Wicked man. Oh, God. You're really good at that." She undulates against me and I swallow her tight breaths as I work my fingers in and out of her, just loving the way she feels. The way she moves. The way she just fucking is.

"You're so wet, Fee." The kind of wet I can't resist painting across her lips, tracing the line with my tongue.

She tastes just like I remember. *Like today, tomorrow. Like forever.*

I drag my hands to her sides, suddenly desperate to see her naked, to feel her under me. "Where the fuck is the zipper."

"Don't you dare tear it," she says, rolling to her side a little.

"I'll buy you another."

"But I won't have this one to wear tonight."

"We're not going back to the bar, sweet girl. Not when we have time to make up for."

"We'll see." As her fingers pull on the concealed zipper, my smile widens.

"Come here." I begin to pull the loosened dress from her shoulder down. "You're not going to do me out of my dreams."

"Of getting me naked?"

"Of making you mine."

Fee laughs and as I knead and squeeze, sucking my mark into her skin, her hands making short work of my shirt and belt as, between us, we work my pants and boxers to my hips. My hard cock bounces free between us.

"Think we're naked enough now?" Her fingers stroke over the silky tip, making me hiss out a curse as she takes me in her fist.

I swallow hard, watching where she holds me. I think I might forget what words actually are, but that's okay as she wraps her hands around my neck, bringing my mouth down to meet hers.

My mouth pressed to hers. My pulse in her hand. My heart hers.

"Angel." I brush the hair from her face, pulling back so our eyes meet, so she can see the truth in me "It has never been like this. This intense. This wonderful."

"Maybe that's why they call it making love."

"Making love, yeah." I find myself nodding. That's what this is. It's overpowering and immense, consuming, and wonderful, and so fucking scary. But it's the best. "I love you, Fee. And there's nothing else more I want in this world than to be beside you."

"Sounds great. But can you be *inside* me? Like, right now?"

Oh, yes, I can.

We both groan as I slide my crown past her opening, higher over the soft rise of her clit. A prelude to sinking into her bliss. Her hands curl in the bed linens, gripping the snowy fabric, tightening as I press myself to her entrance and thrust.

"Oh, Carson!" My grunt is a counterpoint to her cry,

heat rushes through my veins, my whole body crying out for this.

"Jesus, I'm not going to last long, angel." Screwing my eyes tight, I pull back and drive into her slow and deep.

"You feel so hot," she whispers, the sting of her fingernails making me stretch and purr like a cat.

"And you feel like heaven." I thrust again, gripping the back of her thigh, spreading her open. She's perfect. Every part of her built for me. Built to take me. Built to make a better man of me. And fuck, I'll do it. I'll be it for her, or I'll die fucking trying.

"Oh, God!" She tightens around me, thank fuck, because I'm not going to last as a bolt of panic, or pleasure, shoots through me, beginning at my fucking heels. My body jerks against her, and I pick up the pace, touching and kneading, tasting and feeling, doing everything in my power to possess her.

"I'm too close," I rasp, beginning to pull away only to feel the bite of her nails at my back.

"No, stay." Her body clenches around me, her warmth and wetness a testament to how much she wants this. So I stay. All in. Now and forever.

My arms tremble as I drive into her again and again as beneath me, she cries out her love and her pleasure. As she hits her peak, I drop down onto my arms and press my mouth to hers and with one last undulating thrust, I fall the fuck apart.

Minutes, hours, decades later . . .

"Oh, God. That was . . ."

"Embarrassingly quick." My words sound weird and I wonder how long it'll be before my limbs feel like mine again. "Just give me a few minutes."

"Where are you going?"

"I plan on spending those few minutes enjoying myself." I press my lips to her stomach, my eyes on her face. She looks so gorgeous, her hair a mess, her skin carrying the marks of our love. Wrapping my arms around her waist I just inhale the fuck out of her.

"What are you—Oh, my God! My eyes!" cries a voice that sounds much like Rose's.

Both of our heads jerk upwards to find her spinning away from the bedroom door.

"Rose," I growl. "What the hell are you doing here?"

"What am I doing? What are you—actually don't answer that!"

40

CARSON

"Hurry back."

"You're sure you want me to come back?"

Fee's mouth opens with a retort, hands rising to her hips, hips I can't help but hug, pulling her reticent yet luscious form against me.

"Now, I didn't mean it like that," I murmur, pressing my lips against her neck. "I just meant maybe you'd like to spend the day with Remy and Rose. You know, given they're flying back to France this evening."

"Oh, you're not getting out of breakfast with the French inquisition so easily. You'd better get this butt back here—" her hands give the globes of my ass a tight squeeze "*—back here* pretty bloody quick."

"Yes, ma'am." I mirror her actions, my cock growing hard between us.

"Which means we don't have time for this," she replies, despite rubbing her body against mine. Squeezing *and* rubbing.

"You want to know what I'm thinking?"

"No!" The word is at least fifty percent giggle, and my

body follows hers as she tries to twist from my grasp. "It's already written on your face. And we don't have time."

"I can be quick."

"That's not something any woman wants to hear. Oh!" Her gaze darkens, the tenor of that little noise very different as I press my teeth over her T-shirt covered nipple.

"That's what I mean by quick. You won't even have to take off your clothes."

"Speaking of clothes, do you really want to sit across the table from Everett in last night's crumpled shirt? Listening to him tease you about being a dirty stop out, asking if you want a lift so you don't have to endure the walk of shame."

"Fuck that. I'm doing a victory lap, and Rose will back me up."

"Did you see how excited she was. Well, once we'd put our clothes back on." Rose had said later she was sure she'd catch us making out. She got a little more than she was bargaining for. "She looked like she was auditioning for Riverdance."

"I think I need to meet your dad," I find myself saying, though Fee doesn't reply. Not immediately.

"Mum and dad are still coming to visit." She regards me kind of steadily.

"Yeah, but I don't think I want to wait that long."

"He's a very entertaining man, my dad. But not so funny that you'd—"

"Quit stalling. You know exactly why I want to meet him."

"Hmm." She turns from me all luscious and sassy, a smile hiding in those pursed lips. "I don't think—"

Catching her arm, I turn her to face me. "I want to

marry you," I say, pulling her to my chest. "And I want to do it right, get your family's blessing. And then maybe someday, if you're a good little girl, I might just ask you."

"I might ask you first." Her eyes sparkle as she presses her hands to my chest.

"That is an idea I can get behind." And so I do, spinning her to face the couch, pressing my body over hers. My body. My hands. My mark. I just can't get enough of her.

"Carson—"

"Just let me love you a little right now."

"Your little always makes my knees feel like jelly." Her words are tremulous even as she hooks her thumbs into the waistband of her pants. Her eyes are bright as she twists her head over her shoulder, and I pause in the act of loosening my fly in fucking awe of the love shining there.

Love, desire, and delight.

"Sweet girl, I forget I have knees at all every time I look at you."

"What are you two doing?" A sudden and suspicious little voice intones.

I drop my head to Fee's back as I stuff a very hard dick back into my pants.

"This hotel suite is not my happy place," I mutter, pulling Fee's pants back over her ass.

"I thought you sounded very happy last night," Fee whispers. When she turns to face me, she's the picture of wide-eyed goodness. "In fact, some would say you were positively exuberant."

"You, angel," I murmur, bringing my lips to her ear. "Only you get to hear my exuberance."

"Somebody is 'apossed to answer my question," the

little dictator in pink pyjamas declares, her tiny hands in the air like pink starfishes.

"Well, and I guess princess Lu here." Pressing my lips to Fee's temple, I round the couch. "Morning, princess." When I hold out my arms, she launches herself into them. "Did you sleep well?"

"'Sept for the giggling," she mutters.

"Norman kept you awake, huh?"

"No, Mommy did. Did you eat cheese before bed?" she accuses, turning her attention to Fee.

"Yes. Cheese. That must've been it. It gave me such funny dreams."

"I'm not even gonna ask." These Frenglish types are a little weird but a lot loveable. "But I should go." I bend to set Lulu down when her hands tighten on my neck.

"No! I don't want you to go!"

"I'll be back in time for breakfast, sweetheart."

"Really?" The mixture of concern and distrust on her face makes my heart pinch.

"And then we can all go back home?" Her voice is so small, and there's a tiny wobble of vulnerability that gets me right in the feels. *I have houses. Apartments. Places to live. But it's been a long time since I had a home.*

"I . . . would like nothing better than that." I know it's wrong to have this conversation in front of Lulu but, "My girls back under my roof? Any roof. I'd even take that yurt in Outer Mongolia."

"What yurt?" Fee asks, her expression scrunched.

"Any yurt. Any place you want to live, as long as it's together."

"You wouldn't like to live in the new 'partment," Lulu intones seriously as, hand on my cheek, she steers my attention her way. "The heating is fucked."

"Lulu!"

Even I know you're not supposed to laugh, but I do. *Hell, do I.*

"Well, that's what the man said who came to fix it. It's true, Mommy, remember? The man with the fat bum hanging out of his pants."

"Okay, so that's true," Fee agrees.

"The man with the big bum said—"

"Lulu, enough. I need to speak to Uncle Carson." The little girl quietens in my arms. "It's true that the heat isn't working, but that doesn't mean we should rush into things."

"Who's rushing?"

"This really has been a whirlwind, but it's only been a few weeks."

"Months," I argue.

"Okay, a couple of months. Which is technically also just a few weeks."

I don't give a fuck how long, but if she wants to play it this way, okay.

"Fine. Then you and Lulu will move back in. I'll go live under some other roof. Maybe a canvas one. Or maybe under a bridge, if I have to."

"Right." She folds her arms across her chest. "Maybe you'll get a room at the Y again?"

"Or maybe I'll just sleep in a doorway somewhere."

"Like the people with no homes we learned about at school?" Lulu's expression is the very picture of concern.

"You play dirty, Mr Hayes." Fee's gaze sweeps over me before she schools her expression again.

"And that's why you love me." And why you look at me as though you want to ride my face.

"Look, we'll all go back to your fancy apartment

together and figure this out. But only," she says, brandishing a finger my way, "because it would not do for Lulu to announce at her very exclusive and private school that her Uncle Carson lives under a bridge. Even if he's more troll-like than unfortunate."

"I can assume the demeanour of unfortunate, if it helps." When I do, I can see she's trying very hard not to laugh.

"Innocence!" she cries. "He tried it on, but it just didn't fit." I try another expression only to hear her say, "Now you just look more troll-like than ever."

"And like a troll, I'm gonna let this billy goat gruff go over the bridge because I have a bigger billy goat in my sights!" Lulu giggles as I drop her playfully to the couch, quickly rounding it to grab Fee. "You know what trolls do to billy goats, right?"

"I believe they eat them," she whispers, biting back a grin.

"When the littlest billy goat isn't around," I whisper into her neck, relishing her shiver. "Come live in sin with me, Fee. I don't think I can wait long to make an honest woman out of you."

"Uncle Car," says a little voice from behind. "I think you can be the daddy now. And then we'll get a puppy and a maybe a baby brother."

Fee's body shakes against my own as she begins to giggle. "See what you've gotten yourself into now?"

"Just one baby brother, huh?" Glancing over my shoulder, I shoot Lulu a wink. "You don't think Norman would like a brother, too?"

"But he's a wabbit. I think Mommy would need a daddy wabbit to make a wabbit baby."

"This conversation is far too surreal for Sunday

morning," Fee decrees, pressing her hands to my cheeks. "You should go and get changed. Your presence is requested at breakfast, remember?"

"Yes, I remember." The French inquisition. "No one ever expects the French inquisition."

She snorts this cute little noise, bringing her hand to her mouth to giggle behind. "You are not twisting Monty Python quotes."

"With ruthless efficiency," I reply, doing so again.

With promises of a swift return, I press a kiss to Lulu's dark head and then another, with a very different kind of tone, to the lips of her mother. I slide my jacket on, which Remy had so helpfully delivered to the door of the suite last night, along with a warning glower and some unrepeatable rapid French. I get as far as the door when Lulu comes bursting from the other bedroom.

"Wait for me!"

"Lu, Uncle Carson will be back soon."

"Daddy," she corrects with a scowl. "And I just want to walk him to the door to say goodbye."

"Honey, this is the door." Then I notice she has her slippers on.

"Not this door, silly. The one to the outside."

And that's how I find myself in the elevator on the way down to the lobby, accompanied by the loveliest but most insistent escort in the world.

"*Psst.*" Lulu tugs on the elevator attendant's liveried sleeve. "I have my dressing gown on," she whispers, *sotto voce*.

"So I see," he whispers back. "Looks comfortable."

"This is my new daddy. We're making sure he leaves," she whispers next. I feel more than hear Fee's snuffling laugh. "He didn't bring his toothbrush or clean underwear because he didn't know this was a sleepover."

"That poor man," Fee says, as she stumbles from the elevator. "He didn't know where to look!"

"He works in a hotel." I take her hand and watch as Lulu skips through the very elegant yet staid hotel lobby, swinging Norm by his ear while drawing indulgent looks from hotel residents and staff. "I'm sure he's seen and heard all kinds of things."

"But she made it sound as though we were ushering a one-night stand from the building, like I was just trying you out for the position of daddy."

Sliding my hand across her shoulder, I press my lips to her ear. "I love it when you call me daddy."

"Stop that," she sort of giggles.

"Tell me more about positions"

"Pervert," her mouth says. Her eyes say *and I love it.*

We're so wrapped up in each other for that moment, we don't realise Lulu has tripped until a man is helping her up. Dusting her off. Handing her Norman before straightening. He turns his head, those cold blue eyes immediately finding mine. The resulting sensation is like ice water through my veins.

"Carson, what is it?"

I'm aware of Fee's fingers on my arm, feel them tightening, hear her tiny cry as I sense her following the line of my vision. Like a machine, I disconnect my gaze from the acknowledgment in his and, inclining my head, I look down at the woman who owns my heart.

I remember reading something once that a Greek philosopher wrote. He said that anger is so easy, it's anyone's business. But being angry with the right person, to the right degree and at the right time, for the right purpose and in the right way, is not in everyone's power. I find this so true today as I say,

"Fiadh, I believe you've already met my brother."

41

FEE

"I . . . I. . . " I am going to be sick. Right here, on the marble floor of the St Regis. "I didn't know you had a brother," I eventually whisper, suddenly very relieved for the solid feel of his arm under my fingers. Except, that I can feel him, experience his breath on my cheek, watch the laughter leave his eyes like a blown out match, makes this moment real.

Not the nightmare it seems.

"According to him, I don't." Carson's lips twist ironically. "This is like some fucked up joke the universe is playing."

Then why aren't we laughing? Why are we frozen to the spot while my daughter meets the man whose only contribution to her existence was some kind of prophylactic failure?

"Carson, I don't know how to say this." *Oh, my God, they're brothers. This is so, so wrong.* His fingers cover my own, pre-empting my explanation, somehow deepening his distress before I can even say the words.

"Don't," he says softly.

And so I don't. If only banishing the realisation were so easy.

Lulu glances our way, curiosity melting into anxiety before her attention is recalled. There's a woman standing next to him. *The sperm donor. The liar.* She crouches down, bringing her gaze level with Lulu's.

"Please." I try to propel Carson forward, my first instinct for my daughter over anything else.

"So fucking pathetic." The proclamation is muttered, maybe not meant for my ears, yet it feels like a knife digging into my ribcage anyway. "It's like I'd almost convinced myself she was . . ." He huffs an unhappy laugh. "Now I see why. She's not like me. She's like him."

"She's not like anyone," I retort the moment before we reach them. "She's like Lulu." And if you can't see that, can't deal with that then— "Lulu." I paste on a smile. "Come to me, please, sweets."

She's not like him. She's not. That little girl has more concern for her stuffed rabbit than he'd ever shown me. More love in her little finger than he'll ever possess.

"Car." The man I'd known once as Brett cants his head in an almost mocking greeting.

"Carson? As in the elusive brother?" The woman standing beside him is as effusive in her delight as he is cold. "Oh, my goodness! You said he couldn't make it, Simon."

"And he didn't," Simon, Brett, or whatever his name is returns. He stares back at Carson, but then his expression softens as he places his hand over the woman's fingers where they rest on his upper arm. His gaze flicks to my hand next, curled in almost the same place. *Just a different brother.* "In case you've forgotten, our engagement dinner was last night, darling."

"Oh, hush. That was just one of them. For my friends, mostly," she explains, her accent cultured with just a soft hint of something Southern. She's very pretty in that sleekly sophisticated kind of way. Caramel highlights and nude pumps, her wardrobe colour choices are muted, though very unlike her personality, I'd guess. "Not everyone can make it to Plano," she says, waving away her explanation as though we're already privy to her wedding preparation details. "But that doesn't matter now. I'm just so happy to meet you!" She steps forward, and for a frightening minute, I think she's going to throw her arms around us. Instead, she demurely holds out her hand. "Melissa. Melissa Dupriest. Soon to be Hayes. My friends call me Melly, and as you're practically family, you must call me the same." The woman brims with a nervous kind of excitement, though her genuine pleasure is clear.

"My congratulations, Melly." My hand slips from Carson's as, ever the gentleman, he reaches out to take her hand. Simon steps forward and, likewise, I find my trembling hand in his.

"Simon," he murmurs smoothly, blue gaze intent on mine. "I don't believe I've had the pleasure." It's a barb veiled in satin. A warning as he brings his other hand over our joined hands, increasing the pressure in his hold.

"It's so lovely to meet you." Melly steps forward almost impulsively, exchanging her slim hands for his masculine ones.

"I'm Fee, Carson's . . ." I'm not his girlfriend or his date; those descriptions are too asinine to describe what we have. I'm not his boo, babe, or his partner. "I'm—"

"She's mine."

In any other situation, I might've laughed, albeit delightedly, even if Carson's tone does lack any sort of inflection. I'm just grateful he's still standing beside me. That my hand is in his again.

I couldn't have known they were brothers. They're both tall, dark, and handsome, but maybe that's just my type. Isn't that almost every woman's type? Panic slithers down my spine because I haven't been one hundred percent truthful to Carson. Not about *him*. Lulu's father. Carson's brother, as it turns out.

"Well, how lovely. Isn't that lovely, Simon?" Melly practically glues herself to his side, her gaze ducking to Lulu standing silently between us, her arm wrapped around Carson's leg, quietly trying to make sense of the strange atmosphere, if I know my child. "Your little girl is such a darling."

When no one answers, Melly's beautiful manners seem to move her conversation along. "Oh, the car is here." Her attention slides to the Maybach idling at the curb, its driver already at the rear passenger door. "I don't want to leave, not when we've just met. Maybe you'd like to come to church with us this morning?"

"That's very kind of you Melly but, as you can see, we're not quite dressed for church," Carson answers, his tone smooth and unaffected. I really don't know how he's managing it, because this has got to be some kind of mind fuck for him, too. Personally, my insides feel like a bag of nerves on a spin cycle wash.

"Don't say you'll disappear before we get back," she almost pouts.

"I'm sure Simon knows exactly where to find me."

Melly's eyes widen a touch at the French pronunciation of her fiancé's name. *Cee-mon.*

"It's how our mother said it," the shit explains with a small grin.

"I like it." She all but flutters her lashes as she strokes her shoulder.

Brett. Simon. No wonder I couldn't find him.

This is such a mess.

"Darling." He begins to gently peel her fingers away. "Why don't you get into the car? I have something I'd like to speak to Carson about."

"Is it about the wedding?" she asks, her eyes suddenly bright. She looks like the kind of woman who delights in surprises. She's probably on the receiving end of them often. Flowers and diamonds. and being whisked away for romantic weekends at a moment's notice.

My eyes slide to my daughter. I wonder how she'd feel about this kind of surprise.

"You'll just have to wait and see."

I come back to the moment at the smooth sound of Simon's voice, my heart aching just a little to watch them. She's so smitten, and he seems so . . . Brett. The man I thought I knew. At least, until that last night. The night he'd accused me of being a cock tease and suggested if I knew what was good for me, I'd get on my back and let him fuck me. The years have probably made it worse than it really was. It's not like he forced me or anything.

There follows a flurry of goodbyes and whispered purrs of "don't be long". The glass doors barely have time to swish closed before Simon crouches down in front of Lulu.

"How old are you, sweetheart?"

Lulu presses her cheek to Carson's thigh as though seeking the reassurance of his solidness, much as I have.

"Cat got your tongue?"

Evidently not, as she sticks it out. He chuckles, and she scowls, probably unhappy he'd confused the point of her protruding tongue. If I know my daughter, it wasn't proof that she possesses a tongue. She was making a point, perhaps an impolite point, but a valid one.

"Do you not know how old you are?"

Lulu narrows her gaze as she pushes Norman under her arm. Without loosening her grip on the bunny or Carson, she holds out four fingers.

"How many is that?" He must not know many children, or else he wouldn't seek to patronise.

"Did you get the dumb?" her little voice says. "I showed you four."

"That many, huh?"

"Why are you looking at my mommy. Do you know her?"

"Add another nine months to that, and this all makes sense," the asshole says happily as he stands. "Sweetheart, your mommy and I know each other in a biblical sense."

CARSON

This is my brother. Hateful. Envious. A waste of fucking skin and hair. The kind of man my grandfather would've been proud of, if only he'd been able to see past me, the grandson who held his name. The Hayes business interests and fortune may be largely mine, but Simon carries on the family name. Not that he has the same sick interests as our grandfather, but he has the same capacity for hate, spite, and sadly, revenge.

I turn to Fee, knowing I'd seen all the explanation I'd ever need as we'd stepped from the elevator. There couldn't be any other reason for the alarmed hitch in her breath and the way she'd clung to me as though I were her life raft. And if that wasn't enough, the way Simon's gaze had fallen to Lulu filled in all the gaps.

It does not at all surprise me that he turned his back on Fee when she was pregnant.

But Lulu is a Hayes through and through. I see it now. See how easy it was to fool myself. Her dark hair, those piercing blue eyes so like his. She even has the family *give no fucks* attitude. I wonder if she'll learn to play pretend as well as we have because, right now, she's not so adept at hiding her feelings.

Good for you, kid.

"Sweetheart, your mommy and I know each other in a biblical sense." I step forward, ready to knock this fucker right out, stalling at Fee's low tone.

"You are a complete shit," she whispers suddenly, her words shaky and her face deathly pale. "You made sure I couldn't find you."

"Well, yeah." He answers as though she'd just offered him a beer. She couldn't find him? Then I guess . . . I thought Lulu's father was an old boyfriend?

"You fucker," I growl, yet going nowhere as Fee's fingers tighten around mine.

"Don't. Please. Not here." Her gaze dips to Lulu. A reminder. I force back this wave of resentment and wrath, seeing the concern in her little face.

Am I aiming this at the right person?

Hell yes. I'm angry with my brother.

And yes, I'm angry with Fee because something isn't ringing true, here.

For the right reasons and to the right degree?

I guess that all depends. My brother is a prick, no more so than right now. That he would use this moment to crow, to make the mother of his child feel like this? It's lower than low. It's fucking despicable. As for Fee, I'm angry she didn't wait for me, which I know makes no sense. It's unfair. But that's the strange thing about feelings. They don't always make sense.

As for timing, I know there's no place for my anger right now. Not where Lulu is.

Purpose? I guess only time will tell what his plans are because I can read him like a book.

"Don't worry, babe. We're not going to cause a scene. I know he's the big bad Navy SEAL and all, but he's not going to hit me." His gaze flicks to Lulu, intuiting perfectly why.

I've been on the receiving end of some of Fee's icy looks, and the one she sends him is nothing short of perfect. "I am not your babe. I never have been, and I never will be."

"Is this your way of saying we're not going to be one big happy family? Haven't you missed me?"

"You can't miss someone who never existed in the first place."

I find myself speculating on her response. Most people never have a real understanding of Simon. My father used to say, "still waters run deep with that boy". But I think he missed the point completely. With Simon, still rivers are just still. Like an empty void. How long did Fee date him to come to the same realisation?

"You should get your ass to church, Simon. It might be a good idea for you to start praying."

"Good one, Car!" he says, laughing off my warning. "You know, it's not like I planned it." His eyes skim over his child once more. His own flesh and blood and he'd refer to that treasure as an *it?* "But I can't say I'm not enjoying the way things are playing out."

Like we live to be his entertainment.

"Why is the man making Uncle Car angry?"

"Well, you got that right. What's your name, honey?" His tone almost avuncular;. The irony of this isn't lost on me, the injustice of it all burning in the pit of my gut.

"Ermintrude," Lu answers without missing a beat.

"That's an . . . unusual name."

"It's a stupid one. And it's not my name 'cause I don't talk to strangers. 'Specially ones who make my mommy look like she wants to cry." Then for good measure, she kicks out at him, aiming for his shin with her pink fluffy slipper. "Bullies aren't nice!" she yells, as Fee pulls her back.

This kid has him pegged, even if we are beginning to draw attention.

"I see she got the infamous Hayes temper." His gaze glides to the car idling outside, my own attention drawn by a tug to my jacket.

"I don't like this man."

"I know, princess. Why don't you and Mommy go back to the room? I'll be up soon," I add when it appears that she might protest. I cut off Fee's response with a sharp hug. "Whatever you need to say can wait. Trust me. I'll be up soon."

Aristotle was right. Righteousness in anger isn't in every man's power. But it's in mine as I watch my whole heart make their way back to the elevator.

"The rear view is just as good as I remember."

I don't turn at his insinuation, forcing myself to stay calm as I lift my hand in response to Lulu's despondent little wave. I can't look at her mother though God knows I want to. *If I look at her, I might kill him.*

The pair step into the elevator, and I turn to face him.

"You will stay away from her," I say, surprised at how my voice sounds even. "You will stay away from them both."

"Why, Car? Are you taking your position as *daddy* seriously?"

"You know what they say. It takes a bigger man to step up to the plate some other asshole left on the table."

"Kind of a tasty table, though, right?" Anger turns to ash in my veins. He wants me to hurt him. While his fiancée sits in a car idling outside, he wants me to cause a scene. "Come to think of it, that might've been where the kid was conceived," he adds, rubbing his jaw in a considering fashion. "But please tell me her name isn't Ermintrude. I mean, what the fuck?" He starts to chuckle.

I cut to the matter at heart before I lose fucking control.

"What are your plans?"

"My plans? Why, I'm going to church. I'll sing a few hymns, praise the word of the Lord, then I'm going to take my fiancée back to our suite and maybe fuck her in the ass. What about you?"

I blink. I'm not sure I breathe. Grind my molars so hard I wouldn't be surprised to find they'd turned to dust.

"Any and all contact will be facilitated through my lawyers."

"You don't think I want anything to do with that, do you? Come the fuck on!" He chortles as though this is all one big joke, but he forgets I know him. That pretty surface hides a whole lot of unpleasant.

And the woman I love dated him. One big fucked-up

coincidence, and that's a hard pill to swallow. But better than the alternative, which is letting him ruin us.

"You're going to leave now, if you know what's good for you. Turn around and get into your fucking car."

"Yeah, sure." He shrugs as though heeding my words reluctantly. "I'd say it was nice to see you, but . . ."

"You've given up lying?"

His responding smile is a little sad, though it's also one hundred percent artifice. I'm a Hayes, it seems to say.

I turn and stride away, keen to put distance between us and get back to my girls. But he isn't finished yet.

"Hey, Car?" he calls across the lobby. "What does it feel like to fuck my old pussy?"

"After the first three inches," I call back without turning, "like brand new."

"How is Lulu?" She's my immediate concern as I close the door behind me. *The one true innocent*. I don't have the stomach for breakfast, and after being near my brother, I suddenly feel like I need a shower.

"She's fine." Fee jumps up from the couch. For a moment, I think she might run to me. But she doesn't, even if she looks like she wants to as she stands by the window, twisting her fingers together. "She didn't really understand what was being said, thankfully."

"I don't know. That kid is a pretty astute judge of character," I reply unhappily.

"But she had questions. Lots of them."

In that, she's not alone. Fee said the father was an old boyfriend yet . . .

"Where is she?" I ask, shaking away the crowding thoughts.

Fee smiles weakly, wrapping her arms around herself as though trying to keep it together. Or maybe hold it all back. "She's with Rose. I thought it might be better to keep her occupied."

I nod and stride towards her, pulling her against me and wrapping her in my arms. Because fuck it all, I love her. "That was quite a shock."

"For you or for me?" she asks, risking a look up into my face.

"How are you doing?" If she notices how I don't answer, she's gracious enough not to say. Out of all the men in the world who might've been candidates for fathering Lulu, Simon would be the last man on a list of my choosing. For so many reasons, not the least that Fee and Lulu deserve so much better than a man like him.

"Apart from shaking like a leaf, you mean? I'm having difficulty understanding why he had to turn up now."

My chest moves with an agreeing huff. "I've got you." I've got you both. "It's going to be okay."

"I don't see how. My life has suddenly turned into an episode of *The Jerry Springer Show*."

"Because you had the misfortune to sleep with two brothers?" *With two Hayes brothers.* I press my lips to her hair and squeeze her tighter. "Or is this one of those *I didn't tell the father* episodes." I try to keep my words light, like it means nothing to me, but what she told me before isn't making sense. But I'm not going to fuck up again. No matter what she tells me, we'll be okay. We have to be.

"When I found out I was pregnant, I'd hoped so badly that she'd be yours." Her fervent whisper cuts me to the core. It's a longing I've come to understand, a complex tangle of emotions of what might've been. But there can be no regrets. There can only be going forward. "This was before I went to the doctors, before they worked out the dates, because if she was yours, it meant she wouldn't be his. The man who disappeared from my life before I'd even swiped my underwear up from the floor."

"It was just a one-night thing?" Does that make it better or worse? Does it make me a hypocrite for asking?

"No. I told you he was my boyfriend, and at the time, I really thought he was. But then he turned out to be a manipulative, using arsehole who fed me nothing but a pack of lies. I couldn't tell you that when you asked about him. I couldn't tell anyone. We only had sex once, and that was the last time I ever saw him. Until today."

"I'm sorry." I'm so sorry she ever met him. "He's a fucking asshole."

"I have lots of much worse titles for him." Over the years, I've had them, too. "He told me he was an IT consultant, you know? That he was working for an Italian company. That he'd be flying in and out of the country for the next few months. I liked him. He was fun. We hung out, and talked and he told me all about his family—" She halts to stifle a sob. "He said he was sharing a room in Remy's hotel with a colleague, so I never met him there. But he just fed me lie after lie, and then disappeared. Gone! His phone cut off. No trace of him. I couldn't believe that he'd hung around just to have sex with me. Not for the longest time! I still find it hard to believe. It wasn't even that good!" Her words end on a watery bubble of laughter, and I want so much to protect her from the truth, but she's probably right. Simon would've seen her as a challenge and pursued her to the end. To the bedroom. And why? Because he's fucked in the head.

"I wished so hard that she was yours because, when the time came, I'd be able to tell her that her father was a good man. Tell her how you'd been my good Samaritan, that you'd stopped to help me. I would've been able to tell her how you made me feel, how you changed things for me. I wanted her to belong to someone decent, and though we only had a few hours, I knew that was you."

"I wish it had been me." So fucking much.

"I'm not sure you would've felt the same if I'd turned up on your doorstep looking like a beached whale." Again with the brave, waterlogged laugh.

"I wouldn't have turned you away."

"I know that now. But I most likely would never have found you anyway. I didn't even have your name." She pulls away and begins to use her sleeve wipe away her tears, when I take over the task with my thumbs. "I wasn't looking for him for money or support. I wasn't stupid enough to expect any kind of fairy-tale ending. I knew he was no good, but I just wanted to be able to say, at some point, *child, this is your father*. And I so wanted that man to be you."

"Me, too, angel." My words come rough and hard. "I'd give anything for Lulu to belong to me."

"Because you're a good man. And who could resist my light-fingered little Lu?"

"I won't say I wouldn't have been scared shitless, but it might've changed the course of my life. The course of both of our lives." For the better.

"I know," she whispers.

"But at least we've found each other now."

"I couldn't tell the truth to anyone, though I was so desperate to find him that I told Charles. He helped me sneak a look at the hotel booking system, but no one by the name he gave me was staying."

"He gave you a false name?" I find myself growling. The fucker knows no limits. Has no decency. Deserves no part of my girls.

"Brett Anders, of which there was no trace and the only Americans who were registered were sharing rooms with women. I thought maybe he was cheating on someone with me, so I stopped looking. But maybe he wasn't even staying there. Who knows? But I vowed then and there that I'd be the best role model I could be. I didn't want my child to look at her mother and say that I allowed myself to be manipulated and used by men."

And that's why she never dated. Or at least why she told herself she couldn't.

"By the time I was six months pregnant, it didn't matter who her father was. Because she was mine. All mine. And I'd be enough for her."

"And you both have me now, body, heart, and soul."

And I'll be enough for them both.

42

FEE

We'd said early goodbyes to Rose and Remy, but not before I took my friend to one side to explain why Carson and I couldn't stay. I didn't go into the whole horror story, sticking to what I'd already told them with the amendment that Lulu's father had turned out to be Carson's estranged brother.

Rose had looked so sad on my behalf and had asked, "What will you do now?"

I didn't answer because I truly didn't know. I also hadn't realised Carson was standing at my back until his arms had enveloped me and he'd said, "We'll face whatever comes together."

Her expression had melted, and I'll admit I might've choked back a few tears of my own. But now we're back in the apartment, and following a day of fake cheeriness, we're tucked up in bed. The same bed, actually, with Lulu sleeping soundly between us, beneath the crisp white sheets. I guess we didn't fake enough for her. She'd practically shadowed Carson all day, clinging to him like the koala they once joked she was.

The streets below are a low distant hum that might be another world for all our thoughts. And though the room is dark, the haze of the city through the open drapes allows me to see the man I love. *And him me.*

"What happens if he wants to get to spend time with her?" My words are a sudden frightened whisper, as though speaking my fears any louder might make them true. I might know his name now, but it doesn't change how I remember him. I've always known, though maybe refused to fully admit, that something was worrying about him. What kind of person goes to the lengths he did to get me into bed? "What happens if he wants custody?" A spike of panic pierces my chest, my thoughts scattering in a dozen directions, each more frightening than the last.

"Whoever said family is a haven never sat down to dinner with my brother."

"That doesn't help."

"Fee, you're spiralling." His large hand grasps my shoulder, his concern etched in those lines that bracket his beautiful mouth. Not just beautiful because of how it looks on that gorgeous face of his, but also because of the love it shows me. The love it speaks. "All you need to know is that I won't let anything bad happen to either of you. And honestly? I don't see how Simon will be interested in being Lulu's father. He doesn't have the capacity to care for anyone but himself."

"He seemed pretty interested in Melly."

"You can bet there will be a reason behind his playacting. You know, when he asked you if you'd missed him, and I tried very hard not to redirect his teeth down the back of his throat, your reply made me think you'd guessed about him." His hand lifts from my shoulder, his fingers featherlight along the side of my face.

"Guessed what? What did I say?" I only remember the exchange in fragments interspersed with an overwhelming sense of distress.

"When you said that it was hard to miss someone who didn't exist. I thought you'd guessed. My brother is a sociopath."

My heart begins to hammer, the explanation calling out to me. It's almost as though part of me had known all along.

"I don't suppose he's ever been diagnosed," Carson continues, his large hand cupping my cheek reassuringly. "Though if he had, I doubt he'd tell anyone. His whole life, he's shown very little remorse for the things he's done, right from being a kid. No regret or contrition unless the appearance of it might aid his aims. If you knew him, if you'd seen the real him, you'd be forgiven for saying he has no moral compunction, and I know that sounds like a joke coming from me."

"No, stop," I reach out, covering his hand with mine before bringing it over my heart. "Don't compare yourself with him. You are a good person. You look after those around you. *You care*."

"I'm not sure Simon has the capacity for compassion. He'll only do what's right for him, and that includes lying and hurting those around him. He says he's not interested in pursuing any connection with Lu." I find myself bending to kiss her sleep-fluffed hair, though I'm sure I'm seeking to reassure myself more than anything else. "I do think that's probably the only true thing he said today, but I wouldn't trust that he's not going to make it look like something else. Probably just as a way to hurt me."

"I won't let him hurt you," I vow.

"I think that's my line," he replies with a wry quirk of his lips.

"Nope, families look after each other." At least, this little one will.

The quirk turns to a small smile as he adjusts his head on the pillow, the warmth in his gaze everything. "But I'm going to ask you to do one thing for me."

I raise my eyebrows as though to say *"oh, yeah?"* half expecting that one thing to be a little salacious when his expression hardens, his gaze almost shuttering.

"I want you to promise to stay away from him."

My brows move in the other direction now.

"You can't think I'd go looking for him?"

"No, but it might happen the other way around. He might come looking for you, and I can't be with you all of the time. If he comes near you, you walk the other way. You don't speak to him. Don't let him engage you in conversation, don't be drawn. He's poison."

"I don't want to have anything to do with him," I answer truthfully. If I could wipe this morning from my brain, I would do so happily.

"Promise me," he adds fiercely, not satisfied with my response.

So I do. I promise him.

"We're going to make it impossible for him to hurt us. See that he has nothing to do with Lulu. He doesn't have the capacity for love or empathy. He'll only ever see things his way. He'll use her to hurt us and rationalise it to himself as his right. We're going to make sure he can never do that."

Monday morning rolls around, and though I'm tempted to call in sick and stay home to hang out with my little girl, sense gets the better of me. I can't dwell on the thought of Simon turning up, demanding his parental rights, even if I'd spent the night swimming in and out of dreams featuring those kinds of scenarios. I know I disturbed Carson, or maybe he wasn't sleeping well either, because at one point, I'd woken to the comforting press of his body behind me. As I'd clung to Lulu, he'd wrapped himself around me, kissed my head, and whispered such reassurances to me that I must've fallen into the darkness. I'd found myself wakening as dawn became an inky smudge on the horizon, and I'd rolled into him, seeking the reassurance of his presence. Wordlessly, he'd slid me under him, my body reacting to his like a flower seeking the sun. We kissed slowly, silently, eyes burning with love, and saying all the things we couldn't voice.

And morning came, and there was no skipping school or work, despite Carson's encouragement.

"Come on, just do it. We can all hang out. Have a popcorn and pyjama day."

"You're going to be a terrible father," I'd chastised playfully.

"Yeah, but our kids will love me." He'd folded me into his arms, almost as though he was afraid to see my expression. *Or maybe me his.* "Look at how I've already charmed Lulu," he'd whispered.

"That's exactly what I'm talking about. Our children will be hellions, just like Lu."

"All five of them?" His hands drifted down to grab my bottom. "We're definitely going to have our hands full."

"Five," I'd spluttered. "Dream on!"

"Angel, when I'm not with you, dream is all I do."

But Monday was going to be like any other Monday, despite his honeyed words and his filthy promises, which included "letting me play teacher because I already owned the outfit". I'd chosen to wear a white shirt with cute puffed sleeves and a black pencil skirt for work that morning, which seemed to be the inspiration for his fantasy. All I needed, according to him, was to loosen a couple of buttons, keep my glasses on, and take hold of the ruler he'd acquired for me. And he wasn't talking in euphemisms as he'd brandished an old-fashioned wooden ruler between us.

As tempting as the ridiculous offer was, complete with waggling eyebrows and promises that he'd be very, very naughty, we'd stuck to our usual Monday plans with the concession that Carson would escort Lulu to school so I could get into the office early.

We'd left the elevator, all three of us holding hands, drawing the approving smiles of Ed the doorman. Out on the street, Carson had kissed me quite chastely, then bent to fasten the toggles on Lulu's new duffel coat when a quote I must've read somewhere sprang from the back of my mind.

"No man stands taller than when he stoops to help a child."

God, how true.

He'd straightened and swung the end of Lulu's woollen scarf around her neck, though it had covered her face up to her nose. The pair went off into a fit of laughter and I'd been struck how Carson is loveable for his own sake because of the man he is. But watching him with my child just makes him . . . gah! Irresistible. I wouldn't be at all surprised if we end up with a dozen kids.

And so the week progresses, a week when we don't

discuss our long-term living arrangements, beyond the number of bedrooms we'll need to house our future offspring, numbers which should be frightening but aren't. It's a week full of love and laughter and kisses stolen in strange places to avoid snooping four-year-olds and their pesky questions of

"What are you two doing?"

We refuse to allow the spectre of Simon to touch us and, by Wednesday, I've begun to relax. By Thursday, I've almost convinced myself that I've been overthinking things. He's not going to want to get to know Lulu. Not him.

The things Carson said about his brother ring true the more I think about my time with him. He may well be a sociopath, or at least have sociopathic tendencies. But it had started to bother me when I thought about the exchange in the hotel foyer. The way his fiancée had been clearly besotted and the way he'd played his part so well. It struck me how he pursued me back in France, how he'd wooed me with the same kind of tender affection. At least, until he got bored or his time in Monaco was coming to an end, or whatever the hell prompted him to decide he'd wasted enough time or money on his pursuit.

Six dates and a couple of fancy dinners, and I owed him.

So now not only am I concerned for my child, but I'm also concerned for Melly, who seemed like a sweetheart. But I'm stuck, because what can I do? Even if I could find her, what would I say? Remember me? Remember the sweet child in the pink pyjamas? Well, she's actually the child of your fiancé. Yes, he and I made a baby, though I'm actually in love with his brother. Do you know Simon gave me a false name? Lied to me? That he might have a mental disorder?

Who would she be more likely to believe? Me, the potential home wrecker, or the man she loves? The man who is a flawless liar? Telling her doesn't seem like much of a plan. Or a plan worth the pay off. Yet, I'm still pondering it. Pondering it between moments with Carson.

My God, I love that man.

Friday arrives and the air is cold, crisp and full of promise, especially as we're heading off for a weekend away. after work. Carson assures me the little lakeside cottage he owns, just ninety minutes from the city, does possess electricity, run-ing water, and even soft furnishings. While I'm the first to admit I'm not built to survive (or even enjoy) the wilderness, I will own that I'm looking forward to seeing him chop wood for the fire. He even promises there might be a flannel shirt involved. For Lulu's part, she's keen to shove sticks into a campfire and get her little hands on the magical morsels Carson has been telling her about called s'mores.

"Hey, Fee." I turn at the sound of Ethan's voice ringing out across the quiet office. "I'm glad you could come in a little earlier this morning."

"No problem. You do remember that I'm also leaving earlier this afternoon, right?"

He shrugs, not concerned with the details. "Anyway, this morning, there's a client who's looking for an introduction to yoga. Private classes, twice a week. It's a ten-week booking. You think you might be interested in that?"

"Absolutely!" What's better than running a yoga class? A one-on-one private session, that's what. It's a better learning environment, for sure. And yoga is just a great way to start the morning. Maybe not quite as good to starting the day with some very Carson-specific stretches, but still good. "Only, I didn't bring my stuff." I glance down at my office wear wondering why I'm only just hearing of the opportunity now.

"It's just a casual meet this morning. Fill out the paperwork, go through the health questionnaire with him. Take payment. That kind of stuff."

"Oh." Him. Most of the clinic's clients are women, though not exclusively.

"Well, I'm gonna hit the gym. Let me know if you need anything." And with that, he's gone.

I make my way into the reception area to grab an electronic tablet to register the client's details. I bend to reach the drawer behind the counter when a large hand covers mine.

"Hello, Fee. Have you got a little time for the other brother?"

43

FEE

"I was hoping you'd be in your workout clothes." Simon's words are delivered in the kind of soft whisper meant for promises. Not threats.

I jerk out from under him, plastering my body against the wall behind the reception counter, my heart beating out of my chest from sheer shock. "You shouldn't be here." My gaze flicks to the security camera on the other side of the room. I'm alone, yes, but whatever goes on in here will be recorded.

Am I seriously worried he'll attack me? He was never violent.

Calm down. Don't confuse your sociopaths with your psychopaths.

Simon turns his head slowly, his gaze following the path of mine.

"You were having trouble with the key in the drawer," he murmurs, his tone almost persuasive. "I was just helping. With a little brute force."

"I don't mean here, behind the reception desk. I mean in this building."

"Oh. I thought I'd booked a yoga session with Fee Abernathy?"

My trill of laughter sounds sort of manic, my heart tripping like the wings of a hummingbird still. *Not physical shock this time. Anxiety.* "You know that's not happening," I answer eventually.

"Pity." He leans his forearm against the high reception counter, his eyes moving over me in a thoroughly unsubtle fashion. "It was the workout wear that did it for me, you know."

"What?"

"Back then. One look at your ass in those tight pants and I just knew I had to get you out of them."

"Well, congratulations. You got what you wanted." And made a fool out of me.

"No. I got more than I wanted." His hand lifts, briefly touching his chin. "What is the kid's name again?"

Does he deserve that much from me? To hear his child's own name might be the very most I owe him.

"Her name is Eloise," I say softly. "Eloise Rose."

"Much better than Ermintrude." He smiles back at me, and for a moment, I'm reminded how charming he was. How attentive. And then I remember our last night and later, how it felt to learn of his lies.

"Well, I can see you're not interested in tripping down memory lane with me," he says, his expression much harder suddenly.

"You've got to be kidding." I sound much braver that I feel, my voice carrying across the room, because I'll be damned if I'm going to let him know his presence frightens me. I get that he probably won't physically hurt me but there are other ways to feel pain.

"You were quite taken with me, as I remember."

"Because you made it that way."

"I did, didn't I?" he answer proudly. "You were quite a challenge." This man. This mistake. How many women has he duped for kicks? "I enjoyed our time together."

"I wish I could say the same."

"Oh? I remember otherwise. But now you're fucking my brother, so that must be awkward for you. Kind of squalid, wouldn't you say?" I don't gratify him with an answer or a reaction. What Carson and I have won't be sullied by him. "I was in Monaco because of him, you know? Car. My grandfather asked me to try to talk some sense into him. He was making such crazy accusations."

Again, I say nothing. I don't so much as twitch an eyebrow.

"I wasn't staying in the hotel. I know I told you I was," he adds as though the information is of little consequence and not a lie as part of a larger deception. A larger cheat. "The first time I saw you, the sun was shining, and your hair gleamed like a sheet of silk, rippling in the scant sea breeze."

"Spare me the pretty picture and tell me what you want."

"I saw you in the street and followed you into a coffee shop." The hairs on my arms suddenly stand straight like pins. "You sat with a friend and you both talked about your love lives. I think your friend was dating a rich man and I distinctly remember overhearing you say you weren't interested in dating a man with money."

"That should've ruled you out."

"Except I followed your tight little ass back to the hotel. I saw where you worked, then contrived to be the kind of man you would be interested in."

"Why?" I find myself asking. "Monaco is full of women

who want nothing more than to hang from the arm of a rich man. I'm nothing special."

"I was bored. I needed a challenge." He shrugs, an almost gallic expression of indifference as he begins to examine his fingernails.

"You bastard." My retort is more incredulous than furious. If I had doubts about his mental state before, those doubts have disappeared. He really can't be right in the head. "So you lied, you made up a whole person, just to have sex with me?"

"No, not only. More like to see how long it took. Longer than I thought," he sort of mutters. "But the results are better than I could ever have imagined."

"No. No they're not. Lulu isn't up for discussion."

"But she's half mine." The way his lips quirk almost teasingly is like almost an echo of this brother. And disconcerting.

"Your contribution to her life was made in one night. Actually, in under a few minutes, as I recall." I could almost bite my tongue. Baiting the bear isn't the quickest way to get him out of here. "What I'm trying to say is that we don't need anything from you." Nothing in my life has ever been truer than this. To involve him would only bring Lulu heartache. How could I ever explain to her that his love could only be a thin veneer on the surface? A reflection of something he might find in her face. His love would be a pretence.

"I'd forgotten how satisfyingly pink your cheeks turn."

"There's no point in trying to flatter me."

"I wasn't. Anger isn't a good look on anyone, but believe me, it does nothing kind to your complexion."

"I'm not going to trade insults with you."

"No, because you're so much better than that," he

taunts. "You've won the good brother. The righteous one. Though I'm not sure exactly how righteous a common whore can be."

"If you're trying to frighten me off, you're wasting your time. I know exactly who he is and what's done."

"Oh. Okay. So I can shake a few more skeletons out of the family closet without fear of upsetting your delicate sensibilities?"

"Have at it."

"I suppose we are family now." His eyes move over me suggestively again. "So I'll add murder to the mix."

"Your brother fought for his country."

"I wasn't referring to government sanctioned slaughter but to the murder of his own grandfather."

"That's not true."

"Isn't it? I'm sure if you ask him, he'll tell you himself. In a fit of black rage, he held up our grandfather, an elderly and infirm man, by his throat. He shook him like a baby he was frustrated with. Maybe he didn't mean to kill him. I mean, that's what the parents of babies shaken to death say, don't they? That they snapped. That they're sorry. But he still died."

"Then why isn't he in prison?" Because this is bull, that's why.

"Because we Hayes like to keep our dirty laundry behind closed doors. And because his death certificate says abdominal aortic aneurysm. But there's no denying it was brought on by the trauma. Carson was the apple of his eye."

"I don't know why you're telling me all this, or what you think it might change."

Simon straightens from the counter, sauntering over to the receptionist's chair. He drops into it, swivelling the seat back and forth as though contemplating his next words.

"I thought it might worry you. Living under the same roof as a murderer. Allowing a murderer to raise your child. But I can see he's already told you his version of events. So I suppose I'll just have to tell you where this brings us to next."

"Can't wait," I mutter, glancing at the clock on the wall. Any minute now, Beth or Marta will turn up for work and I don't know if that will make the situation better or worse.

"I have an ultimatum. You have a child that is my flesh and blood. A child I'm entitled to be with. To bond with."

"You have no rights. None at all. I've checked." And I'm bluffing just a little. The temptation to google diagnose our legal situation was cut short when Carson had leaned over the back of the sofa where I sat, iPad in hand. He promised I had nothing to worry about. That he had the best legal representation money could buy.

So I'd stopped looking. Does that make me a fool or afraid?

"That's true at the moment. I'm not interested in being her father, but I've already started the process of petitioning for paternity."

"Why? What did I ever do to you?"

"This isn't about you, Fee. You're not important." Oh boy. He is just a twirling moustache and a swirling cape away from a cartoon villain. So why are my knees beginning to quake. "You'll be ordered to deliver Eloise for a paternity test. Once paternity is determined, and we both know the outcome of that, I'll start the process into obtaining visitation rights."

"You want to sit in a state sanctioned access centre

with a child you don't know? A child who doesn't even like you? While fractured families cry and fight and sully your Armani shoes?"

"These were actually custom made in London," he answers with a brief glance at his feet. "But you do paint a persuasive picture."

"How could you ever get to know her like that? One weekend in three is the best you can hope for." Even as I say this, my mind is racing ahead. What happens when my year is up? Will we be forced to stay here? "You think forcing her to see you will make her like you more? Love Carson less?" Because that has to be the point of this morning's intervention. If it's not about me and it's not about Lulu and it's about the hatred between two brothers.

"I don't give a fuck who she loves. But you know in your heart of hearts I can win any woman over, no matter the age. And I have all the time in the world. It might be an access centre to begin with. Then it'll be an hour at the park. Before you know it, she'll be bouncing between us, owning two of everything and never really knowing a full-time home."

"That's not going to happen." My heart begins to pound once more, my fingernails making half-moons against the meat of my palms.

"Well, that depends on you. Because this is an ultimatum, Fee. I want to hurt Carson. I want him to understand what it feels like to be cast aside."

"By bargaining with a child's love?"

"No, by you leaving him."

"You can't make me do that." The logical part of my brain seems to think this is true, yet the instinctive part, the place responsible for so much of my parenting seems to intuit what's coming. I find myself folding my arms across my chest almost as though to shield my heart against what he says next.

"That's true. I can't force you. You have to decide."

"You don't even know if Lulu is truly yours," I begin to hedge, prompting him to sigh as though pitying my naïveté.

"*Mater certissima, pater semper incertus*," he intones as though teaching a class. "Do you know what that means?"

I shake my head, wishing I had some kind of come back. Wishing it was Carson I was leaning against, instead of a white painted wall.

"Motherhood is certain, the father is always uncertain. That was what the Roman's said. It was written into their laws. Thankfully, these days, we have the benefit of paternity testing. You know she's mine, so you have to decide what's more important to you. Is it your child or is it Carson? Because if you choose to cross me, I won't be turning back. First, it'll be an access centre, then short visitations, then weekends, then school vacations. Next it will be schools of my choosing. And then, before you know it, she'll be opting to live with me full time."

"You really are delusional." Along with my retort, I manage a slow, pitying shake of my head. But I'm panicked. So panicked. He doesn't know Lulu, and this distant, older Lulu he speaks of is a stranger to me, too. But teenagers can be so contrary, full of rebellion and hormones. What if he's right? What if he can do this?

"I don't think I'm overreaching. And neither do you. She'll be a little older, and I'll spoil her. In all the ways teenage girls shouldn't be indulged."

A fist clamps around my intestines as something he once said comes back to me like a slap. He said I had the body of a teenager, and I'd laughed it off as a weirdly phrased compliment. I was skinny, yes. Because I was suffering from body issues and stress.

"I'll buy her affections," he continues, "Teenagers are so cheap. I'll buy her a car, pay for her nose job and breast implants. Indulge the little habits rich girls seem to acquire." He begins to dab his nose tellingly, in the way I've seen girls in the bathrooms of clubs do a hundred times. "And of course, you'll have to stay here. Well, at least, until she decides to come live with me permanently."

"No court is going to make us stay here. She doesn't even know you."

"No, but she will. Don't underestimate me, Fee. I can make it happen. Do you know what a good lawyer does? He digs for dirt. For muck. He'll discover all your secrets and hang them out for all and sundry to see. He'll prevent you from taking her anywhere. Maybe I'll even send her to boarding school to take her away from you. But it won't come to that, will it? Because you'll do as I ask."

"You're nuts if you think I'll do anything for you."

"Not even a blowjob for old times?"

"Get out," I growl, pushing off from the wall, my fists clenched and my brain about to burst.

"But I haven't even told you the best bit yet. End this with Carson. Because if you don't, I'll turn up to family court with proof my brother, your partner, the man raising my daughter, which, on its own already sounds so tawdry, has a history of male prostitution. How long do you think you'll hold on to Eloise then?"

44

FEE

How long do you think you'll hold on to Eloise?

I can't risk it. I can't ruin her life like that.

My mind is a mess as I shove underwear into Lulu's Hello Kitty suitcase, swiping at the constant fall of tears.

I have to leave. Today. Now. Before he has a chance to do anything.

My stomach twists as I glance toward the nightstand next to the bed I share with Carson. On it lies my iPad and my phone, both with a dozen pages of searches already open. I've looked into the validity of Simon's threats, and the reality is truly terrifying. I've searched how the legal system would stand up to protecting us here, and in London, and what it would mean if we moved back to France. I can barely think straight for his threats as I press one of Lulu's pink slippers into the corner of her case.

Where's the other?

I begin to push my hands through the piles of our clothes, searching for the other one. My mum bought them for her. If she can't find them when we get there, wherever *there* is, she'll be so sad. But not nearly as sad as when she finds out Carson won't be her daddy.

"Where the fuck is the other slipper?" I begin to yank and tear through our belongings as a painful sobs wracks my chest. If I can barely think, "I can barely fucking pack!"

The floor looks so tempting right now. I want to drop to it and curl myself into a tight ball to sob and sob. Maybe kick and scream and rage against the world. But how would that help? There's nothing that will make this better. And of one thing I'm deadly certain.

If I stay here, I risk losing my child to a man who can only hurt her.

During my internet legal fest, I read that the New York family court will consider themselves to have authority to decide on visitation and custody matters if a child has lived within the state for six months. We haven't been here six months yet, but I'm not comforted by this. Further reading reveals pretty much anyone can bring a visitation or custody case. Mothers, fathers, stepparents and cohabitants, siblings and half siblings, grandparents, relatives and friends! The list seems endless, and yes, I'm sure it's not as simple as all that, but Simon has money and connections and the kind of ammunition that could only serve to cripple. And while I know Carson has money and is sure to have his own kind of influence, he also happens to be the weapon from which the ammunition will be launched.

"Slippers," I mutter, pushing the lank hair from my face as I dash from one room to another, almost collapsing on the bed in Lulu's princess suite. All I can think of is Carson so patient sitting on the floor, wearing his silver crown as he'd attended to Lulu at her afternoon gin party, the pair conspiring to make us a family.

"It's so fucking unfair!" I grab Norman from Lu's pillow and hug him tight to my chest. *This will crush him,* I silently sob. *This will crush me.* And devastate Lulu.

How will she ever trust me again?

But my choices are few and her heart will heal, even if I'm not sure mine ever will.

If I stay, I risk losing my child. Risk ruining her life, bringing a man into it who will only hurt her. If I go, I will destroy Carson's love. I can't ask him to leave with me because his past is his past no matter where we live. No matter which jurisdiction or court of law we abide by, I risk losing her.

My choices are not few. My choices are not at all.

No matter where I go, I know my heart will always be his. And I know, once he gets over this, once he moves on from what I'm about to do, I know a man like him won't be alone very long. Maybe he'll go back to Ardeo and drown himself in women. And though the thought is crushing and makes me want to throw down against any woman who would look at him, let alone use him, could I ever really blame him for going back?

I should take solace in the fact that love will find him at some point, because a man as good as him deserves to love and be loved. He might fall in love a dozen times, he might marry, he might have children of his own. *Maybe even a bushel of them.* God knows he deserves to be on the receiving end of a child's unconditional love. And he has such a capacity to give. I should find solace, but I don't.

Forcing myself to rise from Lulu's bed, I shove Norman under my arm and cross over to the dresser to pull out more of her clothes. My face in the mirror is . . . wretched. Mascara-streaked cheeks and a red nose, but my expression? It's tortured. Desolate. And no more than I deserve.

I swallow back the rising tide of emotion before it threatens to drown me. *If the punishment fits the crime, maybe I'll drown in my own tears of self-pity.*

I swing away from the mirror, despairing how I'll ever manage to tell him.

A man like Carson Hayes will find love again, though he might grow to hate me. Or he might never ever think of me again. Meanwhile, I know my heart is truly breaking. But I have to leave. Today. Now. Get on a flight somewhere, anywhere, because I can't risk staying.

But my heart will stay here.

It will always be a part of him.

CARSON

The front door slams closed behind me and I slip off my jacket, awkwardly swapping a box of donuts between my hands as I do. The donuts are for Lulu. They're a reward for protecting my virtue this morning.

Who hits on someone in a schoolyard?

Single moms, apparently. At least, I hope she was single. Not that it matters either way to me because there's only one woman I want hitting on me. And biting on me. Scratching me a little . . .

I love it all. And I love my little family.

I've had a good day. A fruitful day. A day digging for dirt. And it turns out my brother's fiancée is the daughter of a preacher man. Not any old humble preacher, but the owner of a mega church in Texas, the kind that might make a list on Forbes if it wasn't for the fact their dealings are shrouded in secrecy. *The mystique of religion.* A church with multiple campuses and its own dedicated TV channel and with tens of thousands of members, each more faithful than the last, and each more generous.

Owning a mega church must be like winning the lottery every Sunday, watching those coffers roll in. While Melly was certainly attractive and seemed very personable, I now see where my brother's devotion truly lies.

And right there is a bargaining chip.

He's not going to risk losing that.

Dropping the donuts to the countertop, I'm whistling a happy tune to myself, because that's how I feel, when I hear something drop to the floor from somewhere deeper in the apartment. I'm pretty sure it's not the cleaning crew's day and Annie, the old housekeeper, is visiting her sister in Long Island. *I know because I sent a car to take her.*

"Fee?" I call, my footsteps echoing though the hallway.

"I'm just in the bathroom." As I walk into our bedroom, her answer comes from the adjoining bathroom. Our bedroom was *her* bedroom, the master bedroom lying abandoned in favour of one situated next to Lulu's room. *The princess suite.* That's not to say Fee and I haven't had use for the master bathroom with its bath big enough for two.

A hot bath and a couple of fingers is just the thing to wind down with.

That's what I'd said to her the night I found her floating like an ethereal Goldilocks in my tub. But when there are two in a tub, a couple of fingers are only the start of things.

"You okay in there?" Pulling off my sweater, I abandon it to the chair.

"I . . . I'll just be a minute."

The poor woman sounds fucking awful.

"Was it the squid?" I call out, thinking about the Vietnamese we had for dinner last night. I wasn't touching the squid and remember distinctly warning her against it.

"No?" comes an unsure sounding response.

"I bought Lulu donuts," I call back, not exactly shouting but pitching my voice to be heard as I drop to the bed. "I hope that's okay but they're kind of a thank you to her for protecting my virtue in the schoolyard." I begin to describe the encounter, stretched out against the mattress, my feet crossed at the ankles, my hands behind my head. ". . . I can't believe the woman was so brazen. Who hits on someone in the fucking schoolyard, while he's standing there holding a little girl's hand?" She just sidled up to me, and started asking me all kinds of unsubtle questions, flicking her goddamn hair. "Lulu was hilarious and totally had my back when the woman had said something I didn't quite catch she piped up with, "I'm sorry my Daddy didn't hear you" —I pitching my voice higher as though someone has a hold of my ball—"but he's too busy not listening. Maybe you should please not repeat it again." It's was the most polite version of fuck off I've ever heard!

I begin to cackle seeing her sassy little expression again. The kids is an original, all right. A one off. Her own fucking person and I can't wait to see her take on the world.

I turn my head towards the bathroom door when it *clicks* open.

"Hey! Oh, fuck. You look awful." Swinging my legs off the bed, I stride across the room when I notice she has her makeup bag in her hand. "You can't think you're going back to work, angel."

"No. I . . . I'm not." Her ribs expand with a sharp inhale. "I'm not going back to work because—"

I catch sight of Lulu's pink suitcase, Fee's larger silver one standing next to it. My brain immediately rejects the suggestion that she's overpacked for our weekend away. My jaw tightens. I only know what their bags look like because I'd recently sat on this very bed and watched them unpack.

"What's going on?" I ask dumbly. Feeling fucking dumb at any rate, pushing away the realisation that something here is very fucking wrong because that's not a makeup bag in her hand. It's a wash bag. And those are tears running down her face. No one cries like that because of bad squid.

"No." Fear zips down my spine as my brain acknowledges what's going on. The logical part of it, anyway. The emotional part is too fucking distraught to deal as I step closer to take her in my hands. My arms. To hold her and never let her the fuck go.

"No! Fucking no!" I swing away suddenly, not able to see this. Not ready to go through this again. "You can't take this back. Not again." I can't take it. I sling my arm over my face, elbow bent over my brow like a fucking kid refusing to allow he can be seen. If I can't be seen, I can't be here, and this can't be happening. *A-fucking-gain!* I rely on instinct rather than intellect as I pivot on the heel of my boots, storming toward her.

If she won't speak, if she won't deny this, by God, she'll feel my love as I take her head in my hands, my gaze fiercely demanding of hers. I stare at her, just stare at her as I try to make her feel the weight of my love, not my fear. My jaw is clenched so tight because I can't trust myself to speak. Not until I've mastered what I want to say, not without demanding she tell me what the fuck he's said to her. Because this has Simon all over it.

She promised she wouldn't listen to him. That she'd stay the fuck away.

But I don't say any of that as I tilt my head and slant my mouth over hers. At first, she doesn't respond beyond her halting gasp. Next come the words I force her to swallow back as I coax her mouth to open against my own. She's pliant for a moment before rousing herself, her lips responding against mine, chasing their touch.

I don't know what I'd expected to achieve. A reprieve? A stay of execution? A way to torture myself one last time? I only know I need to hold her in my arms as snapshots of our time together flood my brain, the images feeding from one to the next like pearls on a necklace.

Each one rare. Each one priceless.

Anger, pain, hurt, the fucking injustice balls in my throat, but I swallow it back as I make her feel my love.

"Talk to me, Fee. Please." My pleas are bare whispers pressed to her face.

"I was going to write you a letter." She bites her bottom lip as it begins to tremble again. A groan rises between us from somewhere deep in hell. *I feel like I'm there, at least.* "I've been so afraid. He promised to take Lulu away—"

"That's not happening. That's never happening. I would kill him with my bare hands first." Kill my own brother. Burn eternally in hell for her. "Fee. I promise you."

"I don't want you to kill. Please, just listen to me."

"I won't listen to you say you're leaving me. I won't let you go, not this time."

I bring my lips hard over hers, my kiss punishing, my fingers cradling her face as I bleed my love into her.

"Please Carson," she pants as I attack her neck. Bite over her pulse, feel her knees weaken from under her. "*No!*"

Her hands at my chest, she pushes hard, and I stagger backwards like a drunk, swiping the taste of her betrayal from my lips.

"You need to listen to me," she begs, her hands a supplication between us. "I was going to write you a letter—he gave me no choice. It was you or her!"

"You never even gave me a chance," I growl. I press my hand to the dresser behind me, curling my fingers hard against the edge.

She steps into me, balling her fists in my shirt, the dresser edge digging into my back. "Listen, just listen!"

"Why? So you can slice my heart into a million pieces?"

"So I can tell you I love you, you idiot!" She rages, succeeding in pulling my shirt loose. "I was going to write you a letter," she says again, her voice wretched as she suddenly presses her forehead to my chest. "But all I could find to say was that I couldn't leave you. Not now. Not ever."

My heart lifts, but I force myself not to move, my insides a complex tangle of love and fear and rage.

"You are worth so much more than this. Worth more than a letter. You're worth the risk."

Then she's leaning forward, pressing her hands to my cheeks and her soft lips brushing mine. Her kiss is everything. It's a relief. A succour. It's sheer fucking bliss.

"I fucking love you." It's a chastisement, not a declaration, that echoes against her neck.

"I know. I'm sorry." Her fingers begin to scrabble against my belt. "Please let me love you," she chants, as she rips my shirt over my head. "Please let me finish what I want to say."

But her eyes don't say *conversation* as my belt comes loose, and her warm hand slides into my pants.

Jesus . . . her touch. The sound that leaves my mouth is ripped and disjointed.

"Speak. If you can." Because I can't, my need to be inside her is so great as she pulls my hard cock free from the confines of my clothing. I need to own her. Keep her. Protect her from everyone but me as we tumble to the floor in an undignified heap. Fingers clutch and mouths whisper promises and love as we're swept away by relief and desire.

"Oh, God. I could never give this up," she whispers fervently, tightening her hold and making me gasp. Making me bark out a laugh, fucking painfully. Fucking ironically.

And then I realise where her other hand is.

Where she's pressing her lips.

"This heart is mine and I'm going to take the very best care of it."

I wrap my hand around the back of her neck, pulling her down to meet my lips. My mind goes a little misty around the edges as she climbs astride me. My heart still thunders under her fingers as she pushes up on her knees, allowing me to lift the hem of her skirt. She sighs as my fingers play across the fabric of her underwear, her moan meltingly hot and sweet as I slide the scrap of lace to the side, and push my fingers deep inside. She melts against me, her eyes like fire.

But I want more than this. I want her hard and fast and fucking restrained as I wrap her in my arms, pulling her down and under me.

She cries out as I thrust into her, her body offering no resistance. She throws her head back, an invitation to bite, and her fingers claws at my shoulder, causing me to hiss and buck. She's wild and unrestrained when I need the opposite. So I take her hands, pulling them above her head. I ride her then, our fingers entwined, my body rippling and undulating above her, pouring out my love until we're both sick with the need of it, until the abject pleasure drags us both under.

"Is it always going to be like this, do you think?"

We're both on our backs, lying against the rug. Sated and sore, and I'm not just talking about our carpet burns.

I move a heavy arm from my face and turn my head to look at her. "I fucking hope not. Not unless you want to see me in an early grave."

"You do know how to make a girl shut up."

"I thought you were pretty noisy." Though it sounds like I'm ready to joke, I'm not. My head is a fucking mess as I tuck my cock away. I pull myself to sit, my back pressed against the dresser. My chest still heaves, and my legs feel like fucking jelly. "I can't stand." *Up* and I can't stand *it* as I drape my arms over my bent legs, dropping my head between my shoulders.

"A captive audience," Fee murmurs with an unhappy chuckle.

"I'm all ears."

"It's about time." But there's no sting in her reprimand. "I love you, Carson. I'm sorry you came home when you did, because I was actually in the bathroom putting my toiletries back under the vanity. And the cases over there?" She points vaguely over her head, her own limbs still not quite cooperating. "They're also empty. Ready to be put away again. But I can't lose her Carson. And if I stay, he's going to try to take her away from me. He'll tell the courts about Ardeo and about the auctions."

I grit my jaw against the instinct to tell her she's not going anywhere, that she doesn't need to, but a sick part of me wants to hear her rebuke. Her denial.

Fuck her empty luggage.

"So, what are you going to do?" At least my voice sounds a little more like my own as I lift my head.

"I'm not going to do anything," she replies simply. "Because we are. We're going to fight him tooth and nail and if I have to, I'll make Lulu so fucking feral he'll be glad to get her off his hands every other weekend."

"*Make* her feral?" I dip my head again, hiding the tears shining in my eyes, though Fee's sigh draws my attention to her again. *Let's face it, my attention is never away from her long*. Her eyes reflect the glow in mine. The love and the longing that I know will last a lifetime.

"I know," she says with a wobbly smile. "Who am I kidding, eh?"

EPILOGUE

FEE

"No, princess," I hear Carson whisper. "This isn't my baby. He's yours."

"Really?" Lulu answers. "He's not an early birthday present, is he?" Her tone betrays just a tint of concern.

"You did ask for a baby brother."

"That was a long time ago, when we lived in 'merica. I changed my mind now. I want a bike," she replies, her voice rising a little plaintively on the last word.

"Well, I guess we have a problem."

"No. You can just take him back where he came from. Get a refund," she suggests quite happily.

Still feigning sleep, I snuggle deeper into my pillows, mainly to muffle my chuckle. But I can't resist sneaking a peek at the pair, wanting to laugh even harder as Lulu pats Carson on the shoulder.

You'll sort it out. You always do, the motion seems to say.

Because in Lulu's eyes, Carson is the man in her life who can and will take care of everything. He's the person she'll allow to brush her wild hair in the morning, the person she'll insist should accompany her to school. *I am sometimes allowed to tag along*. He (apparently) makes better pancakes than me, has better taste in music, and in our kitchen dance offs, he has all the moves, while I dance like a chicken.

In her eyes, he can do no wrong. And that's just so delightful to see because I know he won't ever let her down. He's setting the bar very high for any man who may come into her life later. I don't think that's an accident and more by design.

"Honey, the place we got him from doesn't do refunds," Carson says carefully.

"Why? Did you get him cheap?"

"No, I don't think so," he says with a chuckle. "At least, the cost didn't come cheap to your mother." Our eyes meet as he glances my way, his expression brimming with love. Our new baby boy was born five short days ago by emergency C-section. His appearance was utterly unplanned, but he is utterly loved.

We hadn't exactly practised safe sex for most of our relationship, leaving it to fate, I suppose. But when your heart is so full and you've promised your husband you'll consider a houseful of kids, and you really are no match for the sweet-talking beast, you can't ever regret anything.

We married in the garden of Remy and Rose's beautiful chateau nestled between the mountains, the Mediterranean, and Monaco. My dad gave me away and though Lulu was ecstatic in her role of flower girl, she held my hand as we'd walked down a verdant green and flower-draped aisle. Mum had cried. Rose, too. And Rocco had dashed around after the first new addition to our family; Mimi, Lulu's new puppy. Although, I think at that point she was calling him Trevor. *I've no idea why.*

Family and friends, new and old, our small party

included Melissa Dupriest, also now know as Tante Melly. As it turns out, I didn't need to find a way to tell her about Simon. She seemed to figure it out for herself. But that's another story.

"You're sure you didn't get him cheap?" Lulu asks again. "He's very wrinkly."

"You know we didn't buy him. Your mommy and I made him with love."

"You mean *S-E-X.*"

I'm definitely not interrupting this little *tête-à-tête* now. But I am still laughing. Ow!

"Lulu Hayes, where are you getting your information from?"

"Well, I didn't ask Siri, if that's what you mean. I saw lions doing the *S-E-X* on Animal Planet. Babies come from rubbing butts! Oh, look, Daddy, he's opening his eyes."

"What? Oh, so he is. And he's looking at you."

"Hello, little baby. I'm your big sister," she whispers with a touch of awe. "His eyes are blue, like mine and yours." Her little head swings around as she lays her little hand on Carson's cheek.

"They're blue for now. But Mommy says they might change."

"I don't think so. He's going to be just like me and you."

I watch as a range of conflicting thoughts flicker into existence in Carson's expression before fading away. What's left there is love. Just love. Carson is Lulu's father in every way that counts, including legally, thanks to the French courts. He's not yet her adopted father, but her guardian. But it's only a short matter of time until we can rectify that. The paperwork is already in place.

I suppose there will always be a chance that Simon

might decide to fight us for access to Lulu, but Carson assures me that won't ever be a problem. It might seem wrong to many that we'd choose to fight lies with lies, but I don't feel one bit of guilt about it.

It seems Simon had been trying to join Ardeo for years, though his application had never been approved. But that didn't matter because the guys there made it look like he had, all of them offering to swear they'd seen him attend. In lurid detail, if it ever came to that.

If he was going to blacken Carson, then we'd do the same. In public. In court. Whatever it takes. It might not be right in the eyes of some, but the ammunition helps me sleep better at night.

We didn't run away from New York. At least, I don't think so. I'd moved there to learn about business and ended up learning a lot more about myself. Mine and Rose's plans for a clinic are still going ahead, though it will no longer be exclusively for women, but for families instead.

We'll help them all find peace within themselves, and within their family units, whatever those family units may look like.

"Look! He's holding my hand," Lulu whispers delightedly. "You know, Daddy? I don't want to send him back."

"Are you're sure?"

"I think we should keep him. He's my baby, you said."

"Absolutely," he says, enveloping her in a hug. "I've got all the baby I need right here."

The pair tiptoe out of the door, though it isn't long before Carson is back holding a bottle of water and a couple of painkillers.

"Did I say thank you for giving me the perfect family?" he whispers, crossing from the door to the bed.

"Only about ten times today."

"Well, thank you again." His lips brush my forehead, allowing me to inhale his scent before he seats himself on the edge of the bed.

"Open wide." He waggles his eyebrows comically.

"Ha. Good try. Don't you know I'm indisposed?" I answer, pushing myself up on my elbows. His expression creases in concern until I'm settled when I get the saucy answer I'd anticipated.

"But not at this end." He pops two tiny white tablets on my tongue as I poke it out to receive them. "No rubbing butts for at least six weeks. Those were the doctor's orders. He didn't say anything about rubbing mouths." His eyes are dark and smoky as he angles his head, brushing his lips over mine.

"Funny man." Not so funny is the effect he has on my body. "So we're keeping him, I hear?" I incline my head in the direction of the bassinet and our sleeping bundle.

"It's a lady's prerogative to change her mind," he intones, as he reaches to scratch the back of his neck. "Though I might've also promised she could help choose his name."

"We are not calling him Trevor, Carson." I don't even know where she got that name from.

"I might let you tell her that."

"Oh, God. I feel so grotty," I say, stretching and then wincing as I experience a round of stabbing pains.

"Angel, you look so beautiful, it makes my heart ache."

I narrow my gaze in his direction. "You are so full of it. I'm going to need plastic surgery after this, I just know it."

"Ha! As if I'd ever let you mess with this face. Or this

body," he adds with a wicked gleam. I purse my lips and refrain from mentioning that when he looks at me like that, it's not good for my blood pressure. Or other things.

"I'll at least need a facial before I run the gauntlet of the dreaded yummy mummies at the school gate.

"A facial? Now that's an idea I can get behind. Or, I should say, in front of."

"You're such a pervert."

"Where you're concerned," he murmurs, laying his head on the pillow next to mine. "I'm happy to be guilty as charged. As long as I'm your pervert, and I get to lie next to you in our yurt for the next fifty years, I really don't give a damn about anything else."

ACKNOWLEDGMENTS

A HUGE thanks to Elizabeth, Lisa, and Michelle.

As always, this would be a sows ear of a book without your help.

To Michelle C & Annette (good cop and also good cop) for trying to get my bum in some kind of order. I am a work in progress!

Thank you to the Lambs for hanging out in my corner of Romancelandia. You rock my socks! Also, thank you to you lovely people who pick up this book, the girlies who read my stuff religiously and those giving a Donna Alam book their first whirl. You both amaze and humble me. I just don't possess the words to say exactly how much.

ABOUT THE AUTHOR

USA Today bestseller Donna is a writer of love stories with heart, humour, and heat. When not bashing away at her keyboard, she can often be found hiding from her responsibilities with a book in her hand and a mop of a dog at her feet.

Get to hear all the news by joining her newsletter or come say hello in her private reader group, Donna's Lambs.

Keep in contact

Donna's Lambs
Donna's VIP Newsletter
mail@donnaalam.com
www.DonnaAlam.com

Printed in Great Britain
by Amazon

26214677R00324